Madeleine Férat

Madeleine Férat

A Realistic Novel

Émile Zola

MINT EDITIONS

Madeleine Férat: A Realistic Novel was first published in 1889.

This edition published by Mint Editions 2021.

ISBN 9781513282169 | E-ISBN 9781513287188

Published by Mint Editions®

 MINT
EDITIONS

minteditionbooks.com

Publishing Director: Jennifer Newens
Design & Production: Rachel Lopez Metzger
Project Manager: Micaela Clark
Typesetting: Westchester Publishing Services

To Edouard Manet

The day when, with an indignant voice, I undertook the defence of your talent, I did not know you. There were fools who then dared to say that we were two friends in search of scandal. Since these fools placed our hands one in the other, may our hands remain for ever united. The crowd willed that you should have my friendship; this friendship is now complete and durable, and as a public proof of it, I dedicate to you this book.

—Émile Zola

CONTENTS

I

William and Madeleine got off at Fontenay station. It was a Monday, and the train was almost empty. Five or six fellow-passengers, inhabitants of the district, who were returning home, presented themselves at the platform-exit with the two young people, and dispersed each in his own direction, without bestowing a glance on the surroundings, like folks in a hurry to get home.

When they were outside the station, the young man offered his arm to the young woman, as though they had not left the streets of Paris. They turned to the left, and went at a leisurely pace up the magnificent avenue of trees which extends from Sceaux to Fontenay. As they ascended, they watched the train at the bottom of the slope start again on its journey with laboured and deep-drawn puffs.

When it was lost to sight among the trees, William turned towards his companion, and said to her with a smile:

"I told you I am not acquainted with the neighbourhood, and I hardly know for certain where we are going to."

"Let us take this path," answered Madeleine, simply, "and then we shall not have to go through the streets of Sceaux."

They took the lane to Champs-Girard. Here, there is a sudden gap in the line of trees bordering the wide avenue which enables one to get a view of the rising ground of Fontenay; down in the bottom, there are gardens and square meadows where huge clumps of poplars rise up straight and full of vigour; then, up the slope, there are cultivated fields, dividing the surface of the country into brown and green tracts, and, right at the top, on the very edge of the horizon, you can catch a glimpse through the trees of the low white houses of the village. Towards the end of September, the sun, as it dips down between four and five o'clock, makes this bit of nature lovely. The young couple, who were alone in the path, stopped instinctively before this nook of landscape, whose dark green—almost black—verdure was hardly yet tinged with the first golden hues of autumn.

They were still arm in arm. There was between them that indefinable constraint—the result of a newly-formed intimacy—which has made too rapid progress. When they came to think that they had only known each other for eight days at the most, they experienced a sort of uneasy feeling at finding themselves thus alone in presence of each other, in the open fields, like happy lovers. Feeling themselves still strangers and compelled to treat one another as comrades, they hardly dared to look at one another; they conversed only in hesitating sentences, as if from fear of giving mutual offence unwittingly. Each was for the other the unknown—the unknown which terrifies and yet attracts. In the lagging walk like that of lovers, in their pleasant and light words, even in the smiles which they exchanged the moment their eyes met, one could read the uneasiness and embarrassment of two beings whom hazard has unceremoniously brought together. Never had William thought he would suffer so much from his first adventure, and he waited its end with real anguish.

They had begun to walk on again, casting glances on the hill-side, their fits of silence only broken by intermittent conversation, in which they gave vent to none of their real thoughts, but simply to pass remarks about the trees, the sky, or the landscape which was spread out before them.

Madeleine was approaching her twentieth year. She had on a very simple dress of grey material set off with a trimming of blue ribbons; and on her head of gorgeous bright red hair, which seemed to emit a golden gleam and was twisted and done up behind in an enormous chignon, she wore a little round straw hat. She was a tall, handsome girl, and her strong, supple limbs gave promise of rare energy. Her face was characteristic. The upper part was firm, almost masculine in its sternness; there were no soft lines in the forehead: the temples, the nose, and cheekbones were angular, and gave to the face the cold, hard appearance of marble; in this severe setting were large eyes, of a dull grey green colour, yet at times a smile would impart to them an intelligent brightness. The lower part of the face, on the contrary, was of exquisite delicacy: there was a voluptuous softness in the cheeks, and in the corners of the mouth, where nestled two light dimples; the chin was double, the upper one small and nervous, the lower one soft and round; the features were here no longer hard and stiff, they were plump, lively, and covered with a silky down; they had an infinite variety of expression and a charming delicacy where the down was wanting: in the centre the lips bright and rosy, though somewhat thick, seemed too red for this fair face, at once stern and childish.

This strange physiognomy was in fact a combination of sternness and childishness. When the upper part was at rest, when the lips were contracted in moments of thought or anger, one could see nothing but the harsh forehead, the nervous outline of the nose, the dull eyes, the firm, strong features. Then, the moment a smile relaxed the mouth, the upper part seemed to soften, leaving nothing visible, but the soft lines of the cheeks and the chin. It might be called the smile of a little girl on the face of a grown woman. The complexion was of soft, transparent whiteness, with just a touch or two of red about the angles of the temples, while the veins gave a soft blue tinge to this satin-like skin.

Often would Madeleine's ordinary expression, an expression of stern pride, melt suddenly into a look of unspeakable tenderness, the tenderness of a weak and conquered woman. One phase of her being had never developed beyond childhood. As she followed the narrow path leaning on William's arm, she had serious moods which made the young fellow feel peculiarly dejected, while at times she would be subject to sudden fits of unconstraint and involuntary submissiveness which restored him to hope. By her firm and somewhat measured tread one saw at once that she had ceased to be a young girl.

William was five years older than Madeleine. He was tall and thin and of aristocratic bearing. His long face, with its sharp features, would have been ugly, but for the purity of his complexion and the loftiness of his brow. His whole aspect betokened the intelligent and yet enfeebled descendant of a strong race. At times, he would be seized with a sudden nervous shudder and seem as timid as a child. Slightly bent, he spoke with hesitating gestures, scanning Madeleine with his eyes before opening his lips. He was afraid of displeasing her and trembled lest his person, his attitude, or his voice should be disagreeable to her.

Always distrustful of himself, he appeared humble and fawning. Yet, when he thought himself slighted, he would draw himself up in a burst of pride. It was in this pride that his strength lay. He would perhaps have been guilty of acts of cowardice, had there not been in him an innate proudness, a nervous susceptibility which made him resist everything which hurt his finer feelings. He was one of those beings with tender and deep emotions who feel a poignant need of love and tranquillity, who willingly allow themselves to be lulled into an eternal peacefulness; these beings, with the sensitiveness of a woman, easily forget the world for the retreat of their own heart, in the certitude of their own nobleness, the moment the world entangles them in its shame and misery. If William forgot himself in Madeleine's smiles, if he felt an exquisite delight in surveying her pearly complexion, there would come at times, unconsciously, a curl of disdain on his lips, when his young companion cast on him a cold, almost deriding glance.

The young couple had turned the bend in the road to Champs-Girard, and were now in a lane which extends with hopeless monotony between two grey walls. They hastened on in order to get out of this narrow passage. Then they continued their walk across fields where the footpath was hardly defined. They passed by the foot of the hill where the enormous Robinson chestnut-trees grow, and arrived at Aulnay. This quick walk had heated their blood. The genial warmth of the sun dispelled their restraint, in the free air which blew on their faces from the fresh warm wind. The tacit state of warfare in which they alighted from the train had gradually given place to the familiarity of comrades. They were forgetting their previous stiffness: the country was filling them with such a feeling of comfort, that they no longer thought of eyeing one another or standing on their guard.

At Aulnay they stopped for a moment in the shade of the big trees, under which it is always delightfully cool. They had been warm in the sun; they now felt the delicious coolness of the leaves as they fell on their shoulders.

"Hang it, if I know where we are," exclaimed William after they had recovered their breath. "Do people eat, I wonder, in this country?"

"Yes, no fear," replied Madeleine gaily, "we shall be at table in half-an-hour. Come this way."

She led him quickly towards the lane bordered with palings which leads on to the open country. Here, she withdrew her arm from William's, and began to run like a young dog filled with a sudden feeling of friskiness. All her girlishness awoke in her, and she again became a little child in the cool shade, in the chilly silence under the trees. Her smiles lit up her whole face and imparted a luminous transparency to her grey eyes: the girlish graces of her cheeks and lips softened the hard lines of her forehead. She would run forward, then come back, shouting joyously, holding her skirts in her hand, filling the lane with the rustling of her dress and leaving behind her a vague perfume of violet. William kept looking at her with supreme delight: he had forgotten the cold, proud woman, he felt happy, he indulged his feelings of tenderness for this big child who would run away from him with a wave of the hand to follow her, and then, suddenly turning round, run up and lean half-wearily, half-caressingly on his shoulder.

In one place, the road has been cut through a sand hill, and the surface of the ground is covered with a fine dust into which the feet sink. Madeleine took a delight in picking the softest places. She would raise little shrill cries as she felt her boots disappearing. She would try to take long strides, and laugh, when held back by the moving sand, at not being able to get on, just as a twelve-year-old girl would have done.

Then the road ascends with sudden turns between wooded knolls. This end of the valley has a lonely and wild aspect which takes one by surprise on emerging from the cool shades of Aulnay: a few rocks peep out of the ground, the grass on the slopes is browned by the sun, and big briars struggle in the ditches. Madeleine took William's arm in silence: she was tired, and was touched with an indefinable feeling on this stony, deserted road, where there was no house to be seen, and which wound about in a sort of ominous hollow. Still trembling from the effects of her gambols and laughter she put no check on herself. William felt her warm arm press against his own. At this moment, he knew that this woman was his, that there was in her, beneath the implacable energy of her mind, a feeble heart which stood in need of caresses. When she raised her eyes towards him, she looked at him with tender humility, and with tearful smiles. She was becoming docile and coquettish; she appeared to be seeking for the young man's love like a poor shy woman. Fatigue, the deliciousness of the shade, the awakening of the youthful feeling, the wild place she was passing through, all imparted to her being an emotion of love—one of those languors of the senses which make the proudest woman fall into the arms of a man.

William and Madeleine were slowly ascending. At times the young woman's foot slipped on a stone and she checked herself by clinging to her companion's arm. This clinging was a caress; neither of them attempted to disguise it. They had ceased to talk, they were satisfied with exchanging smiles. This language was sufficient to give expression to the only feeling which was filling their hearts. Madeleine's face was charming under the sunshade; it had a tender paleness with shadows of silvery grey; round the mouth played rosy gleams, and at the corner of the lips, on William's side, there was a little network of bluish veins of such delicacy, that he felt one of those wild longings to imprint a kiss on this very spot. He was shy, and hesitated till they were at the top of the steep. Here, as they came suddenly on the plain extended before them, it seemed to the young couple that they were no longer concealed. Although the country was deserted, they were afraid of this broad expanse. They separated, uncomfortable, embarrassed again.

The road follows the edge of the high ground. To the left are strawberry-patches, and immense open fields of corn planted with a few scattered trees and losing themselves at the horizon. In the distance the Verrières wood traces a black line, which seems to border the sky with a mourning band. To the right are slopes, displaying to view several miles of country; first come dark and brown tracts of land, and enormous masses of foliage; then the tints and lines become more indistinct, the landscape is lost to view in a bluish atmosphere, terminated by low hills whose pale violet hue mingles with the soft yellow of the sky.

It is an immensity, a veritable sea of hills and valleys, relieved here and there by the white reflection of a house and the sombre ray of a cluster of poplars.

Madeleine stopped, serious and thoughtful, before this immensity. Warm gusts of air were blowing, a storm was slowly rising from the bottom of the valley. The sun had just disappeared behind a thick mass of vapour, and heavy clouds of coppery grey were gathering from every point of the horizon. She had again assumed her stern, taciturn expression: she seemed to have forgotten her companion, and was looking at the country with curious attention, as though it was an old acquaintance. Then she fixed her eyes on the dark clouds and seemed to indulge in painful recollections.

William, who stood a few paces off, watched her uneasily. He felt that a gulf was increasing every moment between them. What could she be thinking of like that? he could not bear the idea of not being all-in-all to this woman. He kept saying to himself, with secret terror, that she had lived twenty years without him. These twenty years seemed to him a terrible blank.

Certainly, she knew the country, perhaps she had been here before with a lover. William was dying with the wish to question her, but he did not dare to do so openly he dreaded getting an answer which might blight his love. He could not, however, resist saying hesitatingly:

"You used to come here sometimes then, Madeleine?"

"Yes," she replied shortly, "often—Let us hurry on, it might rain."

They started again, at a short distance from one another, both absorbed in their own thoughts. In this way they came to the open road. Here, on the edge of the wood, is the inn to which Madeleine led her companion. It is an ugly square building, all cracked and blackened by the rain; at the back, on the side of the wood, a kind of yard planted with stunted trees is enclosed by a quick-set hedge. Against this hedge lean five or six arbours covered with hop-plants. They are the private rooms belonging to the inn: tables and benches of rough wood are placed along them fixed in the ground: the bottoms of the glasses have left red rings on the table tops.

The landlady, a big, coarse woman, uttered a cry of surprise as she saw Madeleine.

"Well! really!" she exclaimed, "I thought you were dead: I've not seen you for more than three months—And how are you—"

Just then she perceived William and refrained from putting another question which she had on her lips. She even seemed taken aback by the presence of this young man whom she did not know. The latter saw her astonishment and said to himself that she was doubtless expecting to see another face.

"Well, well," she went on, adopting a less familiar tone, "you want some dinner, don't you? You shall have a table laid in one of the arbours."

Madeleine-had received the landlady's marks of friendship very calmly. She took off her shawl and bonnet and went to put them in a room on the ground floor, which was let at night to belated Parisians. She seemed quite at home.

William had gone into the yard. He walked up and down, not knowing quite what to do with himself. Nobody paid any attention to him, while the scullery-maid and the dog even were giving a warm welcome to Madeleine.

When she came back, she was smiling again. She stopped for a second on the threshold; her hair, free and uncovered, shone in the last rays of sunlight, giving a marble whiteness to her skin: her chest and shoulders, no longer covered with her shawl, had a powerful breadth and exquisite suppleness. The young man cast a look, full of uneasy admiration, on this lovely creature vibrating with life. Another had doubtless seen her thus, smiling on the threshold of this door. In the distress which this thought caused him, he felt a violent wish to take Madeleine in his arms, to press her to his bosom that she might forget this house, this yard, and these arbours, and think only of him.

"Let us have dinner, quick!" she exclaimed joyously. Now then, Marie, gather a big dish of strawberries—I'm hungry."

She was forgetting William. She looked into every arbour, trying to find the one where the cloth was laid. At last she found it.

"I declare, I won't sit on that seat," she said, "I remember it is full of big nails which tore my dress. Set the table here, Marie."

She placed herself in front of the white cloth, on which the servant had not yet had time to put the plates. Then she bethought herself of William, and saw him standing a few paces off.

"Well," said she to him, "are you not coming to sit down? You stand there like a taper."

Then she burst out laughing. The storm which was coming on made her feel nervously gay. Her gestures were without animation, her words short. The gloomy weather, on the contrary, filled William with dejection; he dropped on to his chair with listless limbs and answered only in monosyllables. The dinner lasted for more than an hour. The young couple were alone in the yard: for, during the week, the country inns are generally empty. Madeleine talked the whole time: she talked about her younger days, about her stay in a Ternes boarding-school, relating with a thousand details the silly tricks of the governesses and the pranks of the scholars: on this subject she was inexhaustible, continually finding among her recollections some good story which made her laugh before she began. She told all this with childish smiles, and in a young girl's tone of voice. Several times, William tried to bring her to a less remote subject; like those wretches who are suffering and who are always itching to put their hands to their wound, he would have liked to hear her speak of her immediate past, of her grown-up life: he skilfully changed the conversation so as to get her to tell how she had come to tear her dress in one of these arbours. But Madeleine eluded his questions, and rushed off, with a sort of infatuation, into the naive stories of her early days. This seemed to soothe her, to relieve her high-strung feelings, and to make her accept more naturally her tête-á-tête with a young fellow whom she had scarcely known a week. When William looked at her with a gaze full of longing desire, when he put out his hand to stroke hers, she would take a strange pleasure in keeping her eyes raised and beginning a tale with: "I was five years old then—"

Towards the end of dinner, as they were at dessert, big drops of rain wet the cloth. The day had suddenly come to a close. The thunder was rumbling in the distance and coming near with the dull sustained roar of an army on the march. A bright flash of lightning ran across the white table-cloth.

"Here comes the storm," said Madeleine. "Oh! I love the lightning."

She got up and went into the middle of the yard to get a better view. William remained seated in the arbour. He was in pain. A storm gave him a strange feeling of dread. His mind remained firm, and he had

ÉMILE ZOLA

no fear of being struck by lightning, but his whole body revolted at the noise of thunder, especially at the blinding flashes of the electric fluid. When a flash dazzled his eyes he seemed to receive a violent blow in the chest, and felt a pang of pain in his breast which left him trembling and aghast.

This was purely a nervous phenomenon. But it was very like fear, very like cowardice, and William was grieved at appearing a poltroon in presence of Madeleine. He had shaded his eyes with his hand. At last, unable to fight against the rebellion of all his nerves, he shouted to his young companion; he asked her in a voice which he tried to render calm, if it would not be more prudent to go and finish their dessert inside the restaurant.

"Why it hardly rains at all," replied Madeleine. "We can stay a bit longer."

"I should prefer to go in," he answered haltingly, "the sight of the lightning makes me feel bad."

She looked at him with an air of astonishment.

"Very well," she said simply. "Let us go in, then."

A maid carried the dinner things into the public room of the inn, a large bare apartment, with blackened walls and no furniture but chairs and benches. William sat down, with his back to the windows, before a plate of strawberries which he left untouched. Madeleine soon finished hers; then she got up and went and opened a window which looked out on the yard. Leaning on the sill, she surveyed the sky now all ablaze.

The storm was bursting with terrible violence. It had settled over the wood, weighing down the air beneath the blazing canopy of clouds. The rain had ceased, a few sudden gusts of wind were twisting and bending the trees. The flashes of lightning followed each other with such rapidity that it was quite light outside—a bluish kind of light which made the country look like a scene in a melodrama. The peals of thunder were not repeated in the echoes of the valley: they were as clear and sharp as detonations of artillery. The lightning looked as if it must strike the trees round the inn. Between each peal, the silence was appalling.

William felt extremely uncomfortable at the thought of a window being open behind his back. In spite of himself, a sort of nervous impulse made him turn his head and he saw Madeleine quite pale in the violet light of the flashes. Her golden hair, which had been wetted by the rain in the yard, fell over her shoulders, and now seemed lit up by every sudden blaze.

"Oh! how fine it is," she exclaimed. "Just come and look, William. There is a tree over there which looks all a-blaze. You might fancy that the flashes of lightning were rushing about in the wood like wild-beasts let loose. And the sky!—Well! it's a wonderful display of fireworks."

The young fellow could no longer resist the mad desire he felt of going and closing the shutters. He rose.

"Come now," he said impatiently, "shut the window. It is quite dangerous for you to stand there like that."

He stepped forward and touched Madeleine on the arm. She turned half round.

"You are afraid then?" she said to him.

And she burst into a loud laugh, one of those derisive laughs a woman gives when she wishes to scoff at you.

William hung his head. He hesitated for a moment before going to sit down again at the table; then, overcome by his distress, he murmured: "I implore you."

Just then, the clouds burst and torrents of water came down. A hurricane got up and drove the rain in a stream right into the room. Madeleine was fain to close the window. She came and sat down in front of William.

After a short silence she said:

"When I was a little girl, my father used to take me in his arms, when there was a thunderstorm, and carry me to the window. I recollect how, for the first few times, I used to hide my face against his shoulder; afterwards I used to be amused at watching the lightning—But you are afraid, are you not?"

William raised his head.

"I am not afraid," he replied gently, "I am in pain."

There was another period of silence. The storm continued with terrible flashes. For nearly three hours the thunder never ceased to rumble.

William sat the whole of this time on his chair, crushed and motionless, his face pale and weary. Seeing his nervous shudders, Madeleine was convinced at last that he really did suffer; she watched him with interest and surprise, quite astonished that a man should have more delicate nerves than a woman.

These three hours were desperately long for the young couple. They hardly spoke. Their lovers' dinner had a strange termination. At last the

ÉMILE ZOLA

thunder passed away, and the rain became less heavy. Madeleine went and opened the window.

"It is all over," she said. "Come, William, the lightning has stopped."

The young man feeling relieved and breathing freely once more, came and leaned on the window sill by the side of her. They stood there a minute. Then she put her hand out.

"It hardly rains at all now," she remarked. "We must be off, if we don't want to miss the last train."

The landlady came into the room.

"You are going to spend the night here, are you not?" she asked. "I will go and get your room ready."

"No, no," quietly replied Madeleine, "we are not going to stay here, I don't want to. We only came for dinner, did we not, William? We will start now."

"Why it's impossible! The roads are quite impassable. You will never get to your destination."

The young woman seemed very concerned. She fidgeted uneasily and repeated:

"No, I want to be off; we ought not to stay the night."

"Just as you like," replied the landlady, "only, if you venture out, you will sleep in the fields, instead of under shelter, that's all."

William said nothing: he simply looked at Madeleine in an imploring way. The latter avoided his glances; she was walking up and down with an agitated step, a prey to a violent struggle. In spite of her firm determination not to look at her companion, she at last bestowed a glance on him; she saw him so humble, so submissive before her, that her will relented. One mutual look and she gave way. She took a few more steps with stern brow and cold face. Then, in a clear decisive tone, she said to the landlady:

"All right, we will stay here."

"Then I will go and get the blue room ready."

Madeleine started suddenly.

"No, not that, another one," she replied in a strange tone.

"But all the others are taken."

The young woman hesitated again. There was a fresh struggle in her mind. She murmured:

"We had better leave."

But she met William's beseeching look a second time. She yielded. While the bed was being got ready, the young couple went outside the inn. They walked on and sat down on the trunk of a fallen tree, lying in a meadow at the entrance to the wood.

In the freshness after the rain, the smell of the fields could be felt afar. The air, still warm, was balmy with cool breezes, the verdure and wet soil exhaled a pungent perfume. Strange sounds proceeded from the wood, sounds of dripping leaves and herbage drinking in the fallen rain.

All nature was pervaded with a thrill, that delicious thrill which the fields have when a storm has beaten the dust down. And this thrill, so universal on this gloomy night, robbed the darkness of its mysterious pervading charm.

One half of the sky, exquisitely clear, was studded with stars; the other half was still veiled with a dark curtain of clouds which were slowly moving away. The young couple, sitting side by side on the tree-trunk, could not distinguish each other's face; they saw each other indistinctly in the thick shadow cast over them by a clump of tall trees. They sat there for a few minutes without speaking. They were listening to their thoughts. There was no need to tell them aloud.

"You don't love me, Madeleine," murmured William at last.

"You are mistaken, my dear," slowly answered the young woman, "I think I love you. Only I have not had time to ask and answer myself—I should have liked to wait a little longer."

There was another spell of silence. The young man's pride was passing through an ordeal: he would have wished to see his loved one fall into his arms of her own accord, not to be induced to do so by a sort of fatality.

"What distresses me," he replied in a low tone, "is the thought that it is to chance that I owe your presence here—You would not have consented to stay, would you, if the roads had been passable?"

"Oh! you don't know me," exclaimed Madeleine: "if I stay, it is because I want to. I would have gone away when the thunderstorm was at its height, rather than have stayed here against my wish."

She began to look thoughtful; then, in a half-distinct tone, as if she were talking to herself, she added:

"I don't know what will happen to me later on. I consider myself quite capable of asserting my wishes, but it is so difficult to regulate one's life."

She stopped: she was on the point of confessing to William that it was a strange feeling of compassion only which had induced her to stay.

Women yield oftener than is thought, out of pity, out of a need which they feel to be kind. She had seen the young man shudder so during the thunderstorm, he had looked at her with such tearful eyes, that she had not felt able to refuse to put herself in his hands.

William saw that this surrender of herself was almost like a gift of charity. All his susceptibilities were aroused, for he felt that an offer of love of this kind was a blow to his pride.

"You are right," he answered, "we ought to wait a bit longer. Would you like us to start? Now, it is I who am asking you to go back to Paris."

He spoke in a proud tone. Madeleine noticed the change in his voice.

"Why, what is the matter with you, my dear?" she asked in surprise.

"Let us go," he repeated, "let us go, I implore you."

She gave a despondent shrug.

"What is the good now?" she said. "We shall have to come to it sooner or later. Since the day we first met, I have felt myself yours. I had dreamed of burying myself in a convent, I had sworn not to commit a second fault. So long as I only bad one lover, I kept my pride. Today, I feel that I am prostrate in shame. Don't be angry with me for speaking so frankly."

She pronounced these words with such sadness that the young man's pride softened. He became meek and cringing.

"You don't know who I am," he said. "Trust yourself to me. I am not like other men. I will love you as my wife, and I will make you happy, I swear to you."

Madeleine did not answer. She thought she had some experience of life: she said to herself that William would leave her some day, and that shame would come. Still she was strong, and she knew that she could resist; but she felt no inclination for resistance, in spite of the reasonings of her own mind. All her resolutions were giving way in a fatal hour. She was astonished herself at accepting, so easily, what, the day before even, she would have resented with cold energy.

William was thinking. For the first time, the young woman had just spoken to him of her past, had confessed to him that she had a lover; this lover, the remembrance of whom, living and indelible, he could trace in each gesture, in each word that his companion uttered, this lover seemed to him to set himself between them, now that his spirit had been evoked.

The two remained silent for a long time, resolved to be united and waiting the hour for retiring to rest with singular mistrust. They felt weighed down with oppressive and uneasy thoughts; not a word of love, not a term of endearment rose to their lips; if they had spoken, they would have told one another of their disquietude. William was holding Madeleine's hand; but it lay cold and motionless in his. He could never have thought that his first love-prattle would have been so full of anxiety. Night was encircling him and his loved one with its shade and its mystery; they were alone, separated from the world, buried in the weird charm of a night of storm, and nothing touched their heart-strings but the fear and uncertainty of the morrow.

And around them, nature, steeped in rain, was tardily going to rest, trembling still with a last thrill of delight. The cool air was pervading everything; the pungent odour of wet mould and leaves was wafted along laden with overpowering intoxicating strength, like the vinous smell from a vat. Every cloud had now disappeared from the sky; the expanse of sombre blue was peopled with a living swarm of stars.

Madeleine gave a sudden shudder.

"I am cold," she said, "let us go in."

They entered the inn without exchanging a word. The landlady showed them up to their room, and left them, leaving on the corner of the table a candle which cast a flickering light on the walls. It was a small room, hung with a vile paper with big blue flowers, faded in big patches by the damp. A large deal bedstead, painted a dull red, took up nearly the whole floor. A chilly air fell from the ceiling, there was a lurking odour of mustiness in the corners.

The young couple shivered as they entered. They felt as if wet sheets were being put on their shoulders. They remained silent walking about the room. William wanted to close the shutters and fumbled a long time without succeeding; there was something in the way somewhere.

"There is a catch at the top," said Madeleine in spite of herself.

William looked her in the face, with an instinctive movement. They both turned quite pale. Both suffered from this involuntary confession; the young woman knew of the catch, she had slept in this room.

Next morning Madeleine woke first. She got quietly out of bed and dressed herself watching William who was still sleeping. There was a touch almost of anger in her gaze. An indefinable expression of regret passed over her hard serious brow, which the smile of her lips was powerless to soften. At times she raised her eyes; from her lover's face she would pass to the inspection of the walls of the room, of certain

ÉMILE ZOLA

stains on the ceiling which she knew again. She felt alone, she did not fear to indulge in her memories of the past. At one moment, as she cast her eyes on the pillow where William's head was reposing, she shuddered as if she had expected to find another head there.

When she was dressed, she went and opened the window and leaned with her elbows on the sill, gazing on the fields now yellow in the sunlight. She had mused there nearly half an hour, her brow refreshed, her face relaxed by calmer thoughts, by distant hopes, when a slight noise made her turn round.

The sleeper had just awoke. His eyes still heavy with slumber, with a vague smile of awakening on his lips, that sweet smile of recognition on the morrow of a night of love, he held out his arms to Madeleine as she approached.

"Do you love me?" he asked her in a low deep tone.

She smiled in her turn, one of her fond loving girlish smiles. The room passed from her vision, she felt pervaded with tenderness at the young fellow's endearing question.

She returned William's kiss.

II

Madeleine Férat was the daughter of a machine-maker. Her father, who was born in a little village in the mountains of Auvergne, came bare-footed and with empty pockets, to seek his fortune in Paris. He was one of those thick-set broad-shouldered Auvergnians, with a dogged obstinacy for work. He put himself apprentice to a machine-maker, and there, for nearly ten years, he filed and hammered with all the might his hard hands were capable of. Sou by sou he amassed a few thousand francs. From the first stroke he had made with his hammer, he had said to himself that he would only stop when he had saved enough money to commence business on his own account.

When he thought himself well enough off, he rented a sort of shed in the neighbourhood of Montrouge, and set up as a boiler-maker. It was the first step on the road to fortune; the first stone in those vast workshops which he dreamed of being at the head of later on. For ten more years, he lived in his shed, filing and hammering with renewed ardour, never indulging in a single amusement, never taking a day's holiday. Little by little, he enlarged the shed, one by one he increased the number of his workmen; at last he was able to buy the ground and build immense workshops, on the very spot where his little wood erection had formerly stood. The goods that he made had increased in size too; kitchen-boilers had become factory-boilers. The railways with which France was then being covered, furnished him with abundance of work, and put enormous profits into his hands. His dream was being realised; he was rich.

Up to this time, he had stuck to his anvil, resolved to make as much money as possible, without ever asking himself what he would do with this money. Forty sous a-day were more than enough for him to live on. His industrious habits, his ignorance of the pleasures, and of even the commodities of life, made a fortune useless to him. He had made himself rich more out of blind obstinacy than from any wish to derive any comfort from his wealth.

He had vowed to become a master in his turn, and his whole existence had been spent in making his vow good. When he had amassed nearly a million francs, he asked himself what he could possibly do with it. He was moreover by no means a miser.

First he built, close to his workshops, a little plain house which he decorated and furnished with a certain amount of comfort. But he could not feel at ease on the carpets of his rooms, he preferred to pass his days with his workmen, among his grimy furnaces. He might perhaps have decided to let his house and go back to the apartments he occupied before above his office, had not an important event transpired which modified his whole existence and changed his whole being.

Beneath the gruffness of his voice and the austerity of his manners, Férat was as gentle as a child. He would not have crushed a fly. All the tenderness of his nature was lying dormant, stifled by his life of toil, when he met an orphan, a poor girl who was living with an aged relative. Marguerite was so pale, so delicate that she would not have been taken for a girl of more than sixteen; she had one of those sweet submissive faces which move strong men. Férat was attracted and touched by this child who smiled with a timid air, with the humility of a devoted servant. He had always lived among coarse workmen, he knew nothing of the charms of weakness, and immediately fell in love with Marguerite's delicate hands and childish face. He married her almost at once, and carried her off to his house like a little girl, in his arms. Once his wife, he loved her with a devotion bordering on worship. He doted on her paleness, her unhealthy appearance, all her frailties as a suffering woman whom he did not dare touch with his horny hands. He had never been in love before; on going over his past life, the only tender feeling that he could remember was one of a sacred nature, which his mother had inspired him with for a white image of the Holy Virgin, who seemed to smile mysteriously under her veil, in one of the shrines of his native village. In Marguerite he seemed to find again this Holy Virgin; there was the same maidenly smile, the same saintly serenity, the same affectionate kindness. From the very first, he had made his wife an idol and a queen; she was supreme in the house, filling it with a perfume of elegance and comfort; she transformed the cold home, which the former workman had built, into a fragrant retreat, all warm with love. For nearly a year, Férat hardly gave a thought to his workshops; he was absorbed in that exquisite and, to him, new delight of having a frail being to love. What charmed him and at times moved him to tears, was the gratitude which Marguerite showed him. Each look of hers would thank him for the happiness and wealth he had given her. She remained humble in her sovereignty; she adored her husband as a master, as a benefactor, like a woman who can find no affection deep enough to pay her debt of felicity. She had married Férat without looking at his swarthy face, without thinking of his forty years, moved simply by an almost filial affection. She had divined that he was kind. "I love you," she would often say to her husband, "because you are strong and do not disdain my weakness; I love you because I was nothing and you have made me your wife." And Férat, as he heard these words murmured in a meek endearing voice, would press her to his bosom, his heart full of unutterable love.

After they had been married a year, Marguerite became enceinte. Her pregnancy was a painful one. A few days before the crisis, the doctor took Férat aside and told him that he was not without apprehensions. The young wife's constitution seemed to him so delicate, that the sharp pangs of child-birth made him feel afraid for her. Férat was almost out of his senses for a week; he would smile on his wife, as she lay on a long chair, and then go and sob in the street; he would pass whole nights in his deserted workshops, and come every hour to ask for news; at times, when his anguish seemed to choke him, he would take a hammer and then strike furiously at the anvils, as if to soothe his anger. The terrible moment came at last, the fears of the doctor were realised. Marguerite died in giving birth to a daughter.

Férat's grief was fearful. His tears were dried up. When the poor woman was buried, he shut himself up in the house, and stayed there in a fit of gloomy dejection. At times, he would be seized with crises of blind frenzy. He invariably spent the night in his dark silent workshops; till morning came, he would walk up and down among the motionless machinery, the tools, the bits of iron-ore that lay about. Gradually, the sight of these instruments of his fortune would send him into a paroxysm of rage. He had conquered misery and had not been able to conquer death. For twenty years, his powerful hands had made the bending of iron a plaything, and yet they had been powerless to save the object of his love. And he would exclaim:

"I am a coward then, and as weak as a child; had I been strong I should not have been robbed."

For a month, no one dared to disturb this man's grief. Then, one day, the nurse, who was suckling little Madéleine put the child into his arms. Férat had forgotten that he had a daughter. The tears came at last as he saw this poor little creature, hot scalding tears which eased both his head and his heart. He looked at Madeleine for a long time.

"She is feeble and delicate like her mother," he muttered, "she will die just as she did."

From that time, his despair melted away. He got into the way of thinking that Marguerite was not altogether dead. He had loved his wife like a father; he was able, by loving his daughter, to deceive himself, to persuade himself that his heart had lost nothing. The child was very frail; she seemed to get her little pale face from her poor dead mother. Férat was delighted at first not to find his own strong nature reproduced in Madeleine; he could thus picture to himself that it was to her solely that she owed her birth. When he danced her on his knees, the strange fancy would come over him that his wife had died in order to become a child again, and that he might love her with fresh affection. Up to two years of age, Madeleine was a puny child. She was always hovering between life and death. The offspring of a dying mother, she had in her eyes a shadowy vagueness which her smile was seldom able to dispel. Her father loved her the more for her sufferings. It was her very weakness which saved her; illness could get no hold on this poor little body. The doctors gave her up, and she went on living; she was like the flame of one of those pale night-lamps which flickers yet never goes out. Then, at two years old, health suddenly burst on her; in a few months the shadow of death was dispelled from her eyes, the blood mounted to her lips and cheeks. It was a resurrection.

Hitherto she had resembled a pale speechless corpse; she could neither laugh nor play. When her legs became strong and she could stand, she filled the house with her prattle and the patter of her toddling limbs. Her father would call her, with his arms stretched out towards her, and then she would rush to him with that hesitating step which is one of the charms of children. Férat would play with his daughter for hours; he would carry her into the workshops among the frightful din of the machinery, saying that he wanted to make her as courageous as a boy. And to make her laugh, he found out little childish tricks that a mother would not have invented.

One curious circumstance redoubled the good fellow's worship of his child. As Madeleine grew, she became more and more like him. During her earlier days, when she lay in her cradle, trembling all over with fever, she had her mother's gentle mournful face. Now, vibrating with life, broad-set and full of vigour, she looked like a boy; she had Férat's grey eyes and stern brow, and, like him, she was violent and obstinate. But, as the effect of the drama of her birth, there always remained with her a sort of nervous shudder, an innate weakness which would subdue her in the height of her violent childish anger. Then she would weep bitterly, and become submissive. If the upper part of her features had borrowed the sternness of the old workman's face, she always bore a strong likeness to her mother in the weakness of her mouth and the loving meekness of her smiles.

She grew, and Férat dreamed of a prince for her husband. He had assumed again the superintendence of his workshops, for he knew now what he would do with his millions. He would have liked to heap up treasures at the feet of his dear little idol. He launched out into important speculations, no longer content with the profits of his trade, and risking his fortune in order to double it. All of a sudden came a fall in the price of iron which ruined him.

Madeleine was then six years old. Férat displayed incredible energy. He hardly staggered under the mortal blow which had struck him. With the accurate and rapid perception of men of action, he calculated that his daughter was young and that he had still time to earn her a dowry; but he could not start his giant's task in France: he must have, as his field of operation, a country where fortunes are made rapidly. His resolution was formed in a few hours. He decided on going to America. Madeleine should await his return in a Paris boarding-school.

He disputed, sou by sou, the remains of his fortune, and succeeded in saving an income of two thousand francs, which he placed in Madeleine's name. He thought that the child would then always have bread if any misfortune happened to him. As for himself, he set out with a hundred francs in his pocket. The day before he went away, he carried Madeleine to the house of a fellow-countryman of his and asked him to look after her. Lobrichon, who had come to Paris about the same time as himself, had started as a dealer in old clothes and rags; later on, he had become a cloth merchant, and in this trade had made a nice round fortune. Férat had every confidence in this old comrade.

He told Madeleine that he would come back in the evening; he nearly fainted as he received the caresses of her little arms, and went out reeling like a drunken man. He bade farewell to Lobrichon in the next room.

"If I die out yonder," he said to him in a choking voice, "you will be a father to her."

He never reached America. The vessel which carried him, caught in a sudden gale, was driven back and wrecked on the coast of France. Madeleine only heard of the death of her father a long time after.

The day after Férat had started, Lobrichon took the child to a boarding-school at Les Ternes, which an old lady with whom he was acquainted had recommended to him as an excellent establishment. The two thousand frances were amply sufficient to pay for her board and tuition, and the former dealer in second-hand clothes was not sorry to get rid at once of a little brat whose noisy games disturbed the selfish upstart's quiet.

The school, surrounded by big gardens, was a very comfortable retreat. The ladies who kept it, took only a few pupils; they had put their terms high so as to have none but rich men's daughters. They taught their scholars excellent manners; the tuition was more in bows and fashionable simpers than in the catechism and orthography. When a young lady left their school, she was perfectly ignorant, but she could enter a drawing-room, a perfect mistress of coquetry, equipped with every Parisian grace. The ladies knew their trade, and had succeeded in earning for their establishment a reputation for stylish elegance. They conferred an honour on a family by taking charge of a child and undertaking to turn her out a wonderful charming doll.

Madeleine was never at home amongst such surroundings. She was wanting in pliancy, she was noisy and impulsive. During play-hours, she romped like a boy, with joyous transports that disturbed the elegant retreat. Had her father brought her up by his side, she would have become fearless, frank, straightforward, and proudly strong.

It was her little school-mates who taught her to be a woman. At first, by her actions and shouts, she displeased these young ten year old dolls who were already learned in the art of not disarranging the folds of their skirts. The pupils played very little: they used to walk up and down the paths like important personages, and there were little brats no higher than one's stick who could already throw a kiss with their gloved fingers. Madeleine learnt from these charming dolls a host of things which she was completely ignorant of. In secluded corners, behind the foliage of some hedge, she came on knots of them who were talking about men: she joined in these conversations, with the eager curiosity of the woman awakening in the child, and thus received the precocious education of her life. The worst thing was that these little imps, knowing as they thought themselves to be, chattered aloud; they openly declared their wishes for a lover: they confided to one another their little fondnesses for the young fellows they had met the last time they walked out; they read to one another the long love letters they used to write during the English class, and never concealed their hope of being carried off some night or other. There was no danger to sly compliant beings in such talk as this. In the case of Madeleine, on the contrary, it exerted a life-long influence.

She inherited from her father his clear head, his rapid and logical workman's decision. Directly the child thought that she was beginning to know something of life, she tried to form a definite idea of the world, from what she saw and heard in the school. She concluded, from the childish chatter of her school-companions, that there was no harm in falling in love with a man, and that she might take the first that came. The word marriage was hardly ever pronounced by these young misses. Madeleine, whose ideas were always simple ideas, ideas of action, imagined that a woman picked up a lover in the street and walked away quietly on his arm. These thoughts never made her uneasy in the slightest, she was of a cold temperament and talked about love with her friends as she would have talked of her toilet. She used to say to herself only: "If I am ever in love with a man, I will do as Blanche does: I will write long letters to him, and try to make him run away with me." And there was, in her reverie, a thought of opposition which filled her with delight: it was the only thing that she looked forward to with pleasure.

In later life, when she knew from experience something of the infamy of the world, she would smile sadly as she remembered her girlish thoughts. But there always remained deep down in her heart, unknown even to herself, the idea that it is quite logical and straightforward for a woman, when she is in love with a man, to tell him so and to go off with him.

Such a character would have been fit to become the seat of the strongest will. Unfortunately, there was nothing to develop its frankness and strength. Madeleine wanted simply to follow a broad smooth road: her desire was for peace, for everything that is powerful and serene. It would have been enough to arm her against her hours of weakness, to cure her of that trembling feeling of servile love which she had inherited from her mother. She received, on the contrary, an education which redoubled this feeling. She had the look of a good-natured noisy boy: her mistresses simply wished to turn her into a little hypocritical girl. If they had not succeeded, it was because her nature refused to school itself in little graceful bows, in languishing drooping looks, in false smiles which the heart and face belied. But, all the same, she grew up surrounded by young coquettes, in an atmosphere laden with the enervating perfumes of the drawing-room. The honeyed words of her governesses, who had instructions to make themselves the servants of their pupils, the chamber-maids of this little colony of heiresses, all this softened her will. Every day she would hear around her the words: "Don't think, don't look strong: learn to be weak; it is for that that you are here." She lost, as the result of all these instructions in coquetry, a few of her headstrong ways, without succeeding in marking out for herself a course of conduct, but her character was less complete and further astray from its true path. The notion of what was required of her as a woman almost escaped her: she replaced it by a deep love for frankness and independence. She was to walk straight before her, like a man, with strange moments of weakness, but never false, and strong enough to do penance the day she was guilty of infamous conduct.

The secluded life which she led implanted still more deeply in her mind the false notions which she had formed of the world. Lobrichon, under whose guardianship she had been placed, came to see her at rare intervals, and thought he did his duty by giving her a little pat on the cheek and enjoining on her to be very good. A mother would have enlightened her on the errors of her mind. She grew up with no companionship but her thoughts, and only listening to the advice of others with a sort of distrust. The most childish ideas assumed for her a serious nature, because she accepted them as the only possible rule of conduct. Her companions when they came back from their Sunday visit to their relations, would tell her each time something of the outer world. During this time, she remained in the school more and more persuaded of the correctness of her errors. She even spent her holidays shut up alone with her thoughts. Lobrichon, who was afraid of her noisiness, kept her at a distance. In this way nine years passed. Madeleine was then fifteen, already a woman and destined henceforth to preserve the indelible traces of the dreams in which she had grown up.

She had been taught dancing and music. She could paint very nicely in water-colour and do every imaginable kind of embroidery. Yet she would have been incapable of hemming dusters or making her own bed. As for her knowledge, it was composed of a little grammar, a little arithmetic, and a good deal of sacred history. Her hand-writing had been carefully looked after, and yet, to the despair of her teachers, it had remained thick and cramped. Here her learning stopped. She was charged with bowing too stiffly and spoiling the effect of her smile by the cold expression of her grey eyes.

When she was fifteen, Lobrichon, who for some time had been coming to see her nearly every day, asked her if she would like to leave the school. She was in no hurry to enter on the unknown, but as she grew up she began to feel a disdain for the honeyed voice of her teachers and the acquired graces of her companions. She answered Lobrichon that she was ready to follow him. Next day, she was sleeping in a little house which her father's friend had just bought at Passy.

The former second-hand clothes dealer was nursing a project. He had retired from trade at the age of sixty. For more than thirty years he had led the life of a miser, eating very little, depriving himself of a wife, entirely absorbed in the one object of increasing his fortune. Like Férat, he was a tremendous worker, but he worked for future enjoyment. He intended, when he was rich, to indulge his appetites to the full. When the fortune came, he hired a good cook, bought a quiet country house with a garden in front and a yard behind, and resolved to marry the daughter of his old friend.

Madeleine did not possess a sou, but she was tall and strong, and had already an amplitude of bosom which answered to Lobrichon's ideal. Besides, he had only made up his mind after careful deliberation. The child was still young; he said that he could bring her up for his own sole delight, and let her develop slowly under his eyes, enjoying thus a foretaste of pleasure in the sight of her ripening beauty; then, he would have her a perfect virgin, he would fashion her to suit his own desires, like a seraglio slave. Thus there entered into his project of preparing a young girl to be his wife, the monstrous refinement of a man whose appetites have been weaned for many a year.

For four years, Madeleine lived peacefully in the little house at Passy. She had only changed her prison, but she did not complain of the active surveillance of her guardian; she felt no desire to go out, spending whole days in embroidery work, without experiencing any of those feelings of discomfort which are so oppressive to girls of her age. Her senses lay dormant till an unusually late period. Besides, Lobrichon was very attentive to his dear child; he would often take her delicate hands in his, or kiss her on the forehead with his warm lips. She received his caresses with a calm smile, and never noticed the strange looks of the old fellow, when she took her neckerchief off in his presence just as she would have done before her father.

She had just completed her eighteenth year, when one night the old rag-dealer so far forgot himself as to kiss her on the lips. She thrust him away with an instinctive movement of revolt, and looked him in the face, still unable to understand anything. The old man fell on his knees, and stammered out words unfit for her to hear. The wretch, who for months and months had been tormented by his burning passion, had been unable to act his part of disinterested protector to the end. Perhaps Madeleine would have married him, had he not been guilty of this outrage. She withdrew quietly, declaring in a distinct voice that she would leave the house next day.

Lobrichon, when left by himself, saw what an irreparable fault he had just committed. He knew Madeleine and was sure she would keep her word. He lost his head, and thought of nothing now but satisfying his passion. He said to himself that a forcible attempt might perhaps subdue the young girl, and make her cast herself vanquished into his arms. Towards midnight he went up to his ward's bed-chamber; he had a key for this room, and often, on warm nights, he had slipped in, in order to look at the half-naked child as she lay in the disorder of sleep.

Madeleine was suddenly awakened by a strange feverish sensation. The night lamp had not been quite turned out, and she saw Lobrichon who had crept up to her side and was trying to press her to his breast. With incredible force she took him with both hands by the throat, jumped hastily on to the floor, and held the wretch on the bed till the death-rattle came through his teeth. The sight of this old fellow, pale and livid, in his shirt, the thought that his limbs had touched hers, filled her with horrible disgust. It seemed to her that she was no longer a virgin. She held on to Lobrichon for a second without moving an inch, looking at him fixedly with her grey eyes and asking herself if she was not going to strangle him; then she thrust him away with such violence that he knocked his head against the wall of the recess and fell back in a swoon.

The young girl dressed herself hastily and left the house. She walked down towards the Seine. As she went along the embankments, she heard the clock strike one. She walked straight on, saying to herself that she would do so till morning and then look for a room. She had become calm, and merely felt profoundly sad. There was one idea only in her head; passion was infamous, and she would never love. There was always before her eyes the sight of the white legs of the old man in his shirt.

When she got to the Pont-Neuf, she turned off into the Rue Dauphine, to avoid a band of students who were hammering away at the walls. She continued to go straight on, no longer knowing where the road would take her to. Soon she noticed that a man was following her; she wanted to escape, but the man began to run and overtook her. Then, with the decision and frankness of her nature, she turned towards the stranger and, in a few words, told him her history. He politely offered her his arm, and advised her to accept his hospitality. He was a tall young fellow with a bright and sympathetic face. Madeleine examined him in silence, then, calmly and confidingly, she took his arm.

The young man had a room in an hotel in the Rue Soufflot. He told his companion to lie down on the bed; as for himself, he would sleep very well on the sofa. Madeleine pondered; she looked round the room which was littered with swords and pipes; she surveyed her protector, who treated her as a comrade with cordial familiarity. She noticed a pair of lady's gloves on the table. Her companion smilingly reassured her; he told her that no lady would come to disturb them, and that, besides, if he had been married, he would not have run after her in the street. Madeleine blushed.

Next morning, she woke up in the young man's arms. She had thrown herself into them of her own accord, impelled by a sudden surrender of herself for which she could not account. What she had refused to Lobrichon with savage revolt, she had actually granted two hours later to a stranger. She felt no regret. She was simply astonished.

When her lover learned that the story she had given the night before was no idle tale, he seemed very much surprised. He thought he had met a wily woman who was inventing falsehoods to make him run after her all the more. All the little scene she had acted before getting into the bed had seemed to him got up beforehand. Otherwise, he would have acted more discreetly, he would above all have reflected on the serious consequences of such an intimacy. He was a decent fellow who did not object to amuse himself, but he had a wholesome dread of serious love affairs. He had calculated that he was simply showing hospitality to Madeleine for a night and that he would see her go off next morning. He was very much cast down at his mistake.

"My poor child," he said to Madeleine in a voice of emotion, "we have been guilty of a serious error. Forgive me and forget—me. I have to leave France in a few weeks and I don't know if I shall ever come back."

The young girl listened to this confession pretty calmly. In short, she was not at all in love with this young fellow. For him their intimacy was an adventure, for her an accident from which her ignorance had not been able to protect her. The thought of the coming departure of her lover could not yet break her heart, but the idea of an immediate separation was peculiarly distressing. In an indistinct way she said to herself that this man was her husband and that she could not leave him like that. She took one turn round the room, lost in thought, looking for her clothes; then she came back, sat down on the edge of the bed, and said hesitatingly:

"Listen, keep me with you as long as you stay in Paris. It will be more seemly."

This last phrase, so touchingly naive, deeply affected the young fellow. He became aware of the life-long misery he had just given to the life of this big child who had confided herself to him with the calmness of a little girl. He drew her to his breast, and answered that his home was hers.

During the day, Madeleine went to fetch her belongings. She had an interview with her guardian, and made him submit to everything she wished. The old man, fearing a scandal, and still all shaken with the struggle of the night, stood trembling before her. She made him promise never to try to see her again. She carried off the title-deeds of her income of two thousand francs. This money was a great source of pride to her; it enabled her to stay with her lover without selling herself.

That very night, she was peacefully embroidering in the room in the Rue Soufflot as she had been the night before at her guardian's. Her life did not seem to her too much changed. She did not think she had anything to blush for. None of her feelings of independence and frankness had been wounded in the fault she had committed. She had surrendered herself freely, and she could not yet understand the terrible consequences of this surrender. The future did not concern her.

The esteem which her lover had for women was only that which young men feel who have to do with creatures of an inferior class; but he had the boisterous good-nature of a strong man who lives a happy life. To tell the truth, he speedily forgot his remorse and ceased to pity Madeleine's fate. He was soon in love with her after his fashion; he thought her very handsome and took a pleasure in showing her to his friends. He treated her as his mistress, taking her on Sundays to Verrières or somewhere else, and to supper with his comrades' mistresses during the week. These people now simply called her Madeleine.

She would perhaps have rebelled if she had not been charmed with her lover; he had a happy disposition, and made her laugh like a child even at the things that hurt her. She gradually accepted her position. Unknown to herself, her mind was becoming sullied, and she was growing accustomed to shame.

The student, who had just been appointed army-surgeon the day before they met, expected his orders to start every day. But they did not come, and Madeleine saw the months pass by, saying to herself that she would perhaps be a widow next day. She had only expected to stay a few weeks in the Rue Soufflot. She stayed there a year. At first she simply felt a kind of affection for the man she was living with. When at the end of two months she began to live in anxious expectation of his departure, her existence was a series of shocks which gradually bound her to him. Had he set off at once, she would perhaps have seen him go away without too much despair. But to be always fearing to lose him and yet have him always with her, this succeeded finally in uniting her to him in a close bond. She never loved him passionately; she rather received his impression, she felt herself becoming a part of him, and she saw that he was taking entire possession of her body and mind. Now she found that she could not forget him.

One day, she went with one of her new lady friends on a little journey. This friend, a law-student's mistress, was called Louise, and she was going to see a child that she had put to nurse some sixty miles from Paris. The young women were not to return till the third day, but bad weather came on and they hastened back a day sooner than they had arranged. In a corner of the compartment of the train in which they were returning, Madeleine pondered with a feeling of sadness on the scene which she had just witnessed; the caresses of the mother and the prattle of the child had revealed to her a world of unknown emotions. She was seized with a sudden feeling of anguish at the idea that she too might have become a mother. Then the thought of the near departure of the man she was living with filled her with dismay, like an irreparable calamity of which she had never dreamed. She saw her fall, she saw her false and painful position; she was eager to get home to put her arms round her lover, to beseech him earnestly to marry her and never leave her.

She arrived in the Rue Soufflot in a state of feverish excitement. She had forgotten the slender tie, ready to be snapped at any moment, which she had accepted; she wished in her turn to take entire possession of the man whose memory would possess her for life. When she opened the door of the room in the hotel, she suddenly stopped stupefied on the threshold.

ÉMILE ZOLA

Her lover was bending down in front of the window, fastening the buckles of his trunk; by his side lay a travelling bag and another trunk already fastened up. Madeleine's clothes and belongings were spread out in disorder on the bed. The young fellow had received his orders to set off that very morning, and he had hastened to make his preparations, emptying the drawers, separating his own things from Madeleine's. He wanted to get away before his mistress came back, really believing himself to be acting under an impulse of kindness. He thought a letter of explanation would have been quite sufficient.

When he turned round and saw Madeleine on the threshold, he could not suppress a movement of vexation. He got up and went towards her with a somewhat forced smile.

"My dear girl," he said as he kissed her, "the time for good-bye has come. I wanted to go away without seeing you again. That would have avoided a painful scene for both of us. You see, I was leaving your things on the bed."

Madeleine felt as if she would faint. She sat down on a chair, without thinking of taking off her hat. She was very pale and could not find what to say. Her tearless burning eyes kept looking first at the trunks and then at the heap of her clothes; it was this unfeeling division of property which put the separation in such a harsh and odious light. Their linen no longer lay side by side in the same drawer; she was henceforth nothing to her lover.

The young fellow was just finishing the fastening up of his last trunk.

"They are sending me to the devil," he went on, trying to laugh. "I am going to Cochin China."

Madeleine was able to speak at last.

"Very well," she said in a hollow voice. "I will go with you to the station."

She could not think that she had any right to utter a single reproach to this man. He had warned her beforehand, and it was she who had wished to stay. But her feelings revolted, and she felt a strange longing to clasp him round the neck and beg him not to go. Her pride nailed her to her chair. She wished to appear calm, and not to show the young man, who was whistling coolly, how his departure was tugging at her heart-strings.

Towards evening, a few friends came. They all went in a body to the station, Madeleine smiling, and her lover gaily joking, comforted by her apparent good spirits. He had never felt towards her anything but a good-natured affection, and he went away happy at seeing her so calm. Just as he was going into the waiting-room, he was cruel without meaning to be.

"I don't ask you to wait for me, dear girl," he said. "Console yourself and forget me."

He went off. Madeleine, who had, up to this, preserved a strange pained smile, went mechanically out of the station, without feeling the ground under her feet. She did not even notice that one of the young doctor's friends was taking her by the arm and going with her. She had been walking in this way nearly a quarter of an hour, stunned, hearing and seeing nothing, when the noise of a voice falling on the chilly silence of her brain, gradually compelled her to listen in spite of herself. The student was proposing to her unceremoniously to share his room with him, now that she was free. When she understood his meaning, she looked at the young fellow with an air of terror; then she let go his arm with a movement of supreme disgust, and ran and shut herself up in the room in the Rue Soufflot. There, all alone at last, she could sob to her heart's desire.

Her sobs were sobs of shame and despair. She was a widow, and her grief at her desertion had just been sullied by a proposal which, to her, seemed monstrous. Never yet had she so cruelly comprehended the misery of her position. The right to weep was being denied her. The world seemed to think that she had already been able to obliterate the kisses of her first lover. And yet she felt that these kisses were in her soul: she said to herself that they would always be burning there. Then, in the midst of her tears she swore to remain a widow. She felt the eternity of the bonds of the flesh; any fresh love would degrade her and fill her with avenging memories.

She did not sleep in the Rue Soufflot. She went the same night, and took up her quarters in another hotel in the Rue de l'Est. There she lived for two months, unsociable and solitary. One time, she had thought of shutting herself up in a convent. But she did not feel that she had faith enough. While she was at school, God had been represented to her as a nice young man. She did not believe in a God like that.

It was at this period that she met William.

III

Véteuil is a little town of ten thousand inhabitants, situated on the borders of Normandy. The streets are clean and deserted. It is a place that has had its day. People who want to travel by rail have to go fifteen miles by coach, and wait for the trains that pass through Mantes. Round the town, the open country is very fertile; it spreads out in rich grazing-land intersected by rows of poplars: a brook, on its way to the Seine, cuts a course through these broad flat tracts and traverses them with a long line of trees and reeds.

It was in this forsaken hole that William was born. His father, Monsieur de Viargue, was one of the last representatives of the old nobility of the district. Born in Germany, during the "emigration," he came to France with the Bourbons, as into a foreign and hostile country. His mother had been cruelly banished, and was now lying in a cemetery at Berlin: his father had died on the scaffold. He could not pardon the soil which had drunk the blood of his guillotined father, and did not cover the corpse of his poor mother. The restoration gave him back his family possessions, he recovered the title and the position attached to his name, but he preserved a no less bitter hatred against that accursed France which he did not recognise as his country. He went and buried himself at Véteuil, refusing preferment, turning a deaf ear to the offers of Louis XVIII and Charles X, and disdaining to live amongst a people who had assassinated his kindred. He would often repeat that he was no Frenchman; he called the Germans his fellow countrymen, and spoke of himself as though he were a veritable exile.

He was still young when he came to France. Tall, strong, and of fiery activity, he soon grew mortally bored in the inaction which he was imposing on himself. He wished to live alone, far from all public events. But his intelligence was of too high an order, the restlessness of his mind was too great, to be satisfied with the boorish pleasures of field sports. The dull unoccupied life which he was setting himself dismayed him. He looked round for something to do. By a singular inconsistency, he was fond of science, that new spirit of method the breath of which had turned upside down the old world that he regretted. He devoted himself to the study of chemistry, he who would dream of the splendour of the nobility under Louis XIV.

He was a strange scholar, a solitary scholar who studied and made researches for himself only. He turned into a huge laboratory a room in La Noiraude, the name given in the country to the château which he lived in, at five minutes' walk from Véteuil. In it he would spend whole days, bending over his crucibles, always eager, and yet never succeeding in satisfying his curiosity. He was a member of no learned society, and would shut the door in the face of people who came to talk with him about his researches. He wanted to be considered a gentleman. His servants were never, under pain of dismissal, to make any allusion to him, or to the employment of his time. He looked upon his taste for chemistry as a passion whose secret follies no one had a right to penetrate.

For nearly forty years, he shut himself up every morning in his laboratory. There, his disregard for the bustle of the world became more pronounced. Though he never owned it, he buried his loves and his hatreds in his retorts and alembics. When he had weighed the substance in his powerful hands, he forgot all about France, and his father's death on the scaffold, and his mother's in a foreign land: nothing of the gentleman remained but his cold and haughty sceptical nature. The scholar had killed the man.

No one, moreover, could get to the bottom of this strange organization. His own friends were ignorant of the sudden void that had been made in his heart. He kept to himself the secret of the blank, that blank which he thought he had touched with his finger. If he still lived far from the world in exile, as he never ceased to say, it was because he despised his fellow-men both rich and poor, and compared himself to a worm. But he remained solemn and disdainful, icy even in his coldness. He never lowered his mask of pride.

There was, however, one shock in the calm existence of this man. A foolish young woman, the wife of a notary in Véteuil, threw herself into his arms. He was then forty, and still treated his neighbours like serfs. He kept the young woman as his mistress, publicly acknowledged her ten miles round, and even had the audacity to keep her at La Noiraude. This was an unprecedented scandal in the little town. The brusque ways of Monsieur de Viargue had already caused the finger of dislike to be pointed at him. When he lived openly with the wife of the notary, people were for tearing him to pieces. The husband, a poor fellow who had a mortal dread of losing his place, kept quiet for the two years that the intimacy lasted. He shut his eyes and ears, and seemed to

ÉMILE ZOLA

believe that his wife was merely spending a little holiday at Monsieur de Viargue's. The woman became enciente and was delivered of her child in the château. A few months later, she grew tired of her lover, who was again passing his days in the laboratory. One fine morning, she went back to her husband, taking care to forget her child. The count was not fool enough to run after her. The notary quietly took her back, as if she had returned from a journey. Next day, he went for a walk with her on his arm, through the streets of the town, and from that day she became a model wife. Twenty years after, this scandal had not died out at Véteuil.

William, the child of this singular intimacy, was brought up at La Noiraude. His father, who had had for his mistress only a passing affection, mingled with a little disdain, accepted this child of fortune with perfect indifference. He let him live with him, that he might not be accused of wishing to hide the living testimony of his folly: but, as the memory of the notary's wife was disagreeable to him, he never troubled his head about him. The poor creature grew up in almost complete solitude. His mother, who had not even felt any reason for getting her husband to leave Véteuil, never tried to see him. This woman saw now how foolish she had been: she trembled as she thought of the consequences her fault might have: age was creeping on her, and she followed the dictates of her plebeian blood and became religious and prudish.

The woman who proved a real mother to William, was an old servant who had been in the family when Monsieur de Viargue was born. Geneviève and the count's mother had been foster-sisters. The latter, who belonged to the nobility of central France, had taken Geneviève with her to Germany, at the time of the emigration, and Monsieur de Viargue, on his return to France, after the death of his mother, had brought her to Véteuil. She was a country-woman from the Cévennes, belonging to the reformed religion, with a narrow zealous mind, filled with all the fanaticism of the early Calvinists, whose blood she felt flowing in her veins. Tall and lank, with sunken eyes, and a big pointed nose, she reminded one of those old witches who used to be burnt at the stake. She carried everywhere an enormous sombre-looking Bible with its binding strengthened with iron clasps; morning and night, she read a few verses from it in a high shrill voice. Sometimes she would come across some of those awful words of anger which the terrible God of the Jews heaped on his dismayed people. The count put up with what he called her madness: he knew the strict uprightness, the sovereign justice of this over-excited nature. Besides, he looked upon Geneviève as a sacred legacy from his mother. She was more a supreme mistress than a servant in the house.

At seventy she was still doing heavy work. She had several servants under her, but she took great pride in setting herself hard tasks. She was humble and yet incredibly vain. She managed everything at La Noiraude, getting up at day-break, setting each the example of indefatigable activity, and fulfilling her duty with the toughness of a woman who has never felt ill.

One of the greatest troubles of her life was the passion of her master for science. As she saw him shut himself up during long days in a room littered with strange apparatus, she firmly believed that he had become a wizard. When she passed the door of this room and heard the noise of his bellows, she would clasp her hands in terror, convinced that he was hastening on the fire of hell with his breath. One day, she had the courage to go in and solemnly adjure the count, by the name of his mother, to save his soul by renouncing an accursed work. Monsieur de Viargue gently put her to the door, smiling and promising to reconcile himself to God later on when he died. From that time, she prayed for him morning and night. She would often repeat in a sort of prophetic ecstasy, that she heard the devil prowling about every night, and that great calamities were threatening La Noiraude.

Geneviève looked upon the scandalous intimacy of the count with the notary's wife as a first warning of God's anger. The day this woman came to live in the château, she was seized with righteous indignation. She declared to her master that she could not live in the same house with this creature, and that she gave up her place to her. And she did as she said: she went and took up her quarters in a sort of summer-house that Monsieur de Viargue possessed at the further end of the park. The country people who went along by the side of the park wall used to catch the sound of her shrill voice chanting the verses of her big Bible at all hours of the day. The count did not disturb her, he visited her several times, receiving with an impassive air the fervent sermons which she made him listen to. Once only did he nearly get angry; he had met the old woman in the path where he was taking a walk with his mistress, and Geneviève had taken upon herself to rate the young woman with a violence of language quite biblical. She, who had not the least fault to reproach herself with, would have cast the dirt from the roads in the face of sinning women. The notary's wife was very much terrified with this scene, and it is quite credible that the disdain and anger of the old protestant had something to do with her hurried departure.

As soon as Geneviève knew that shame had departed from La Noiraude, she quietly went to take again her position as supreme mistress. She only found there an additional child, little William. The thought of this child, when she was still living in the summer-house, had caused her a sacred horror; he was the child of sin, he might bring with him only misfortune, and perhaps the avenging God had caused him to be born in order to punish his father for his impiety. But when she saw the poor creature, in his pink and white cradle, she felt a sensation of tenderness hitherto unknown to her. This woman, whose feelings and passions had withered in the zealous virginity of a fanatic, experienced a vague sensation that there was awakening in her the yearning of wife and mother which exists in every maiden's nature. She thought herself tempted by Satan, and wished to resist the tenderness that was taking possession of her being. Then she gave up the struggle, and kissed William with a longing to recommend her soul to God, so as to protect herself against this child of sin on whom Heaven must have laid a curse.

And she gradually became a mother to him, but she was a strange mother whose caresses were never free from a sort of vague terror. At times, she would repulse him, then she would take him again into her arms with the bitter pleasure of a saint who thinks that he feels the devil's claw penetrating his flesh. When he was still quite small, she would look earnestly into his eyes, full of uneasiness, and asking herself if she was not about to find the light of hell in the pure clear gaze of the innocent creature. She could never bring herself to believe that he did not belong in a small degree to Satan, but her rough kind affection, though it felt the shock, was only lavished the more.

As soon as he was weaned, she sent the nurse away. She alone had charge of him. Monsieur de Viargue had handed him over to her, authorising her even, with his ironical philosopher's smile, to bring him up in whatever religion she pleased. The hope of saving William from the everlasting fire, by making him a zealous protestant, redoubled Geneviève's devotion. Up to the age of eight, she kept him with her in the room which she occupied on the second floor at La Noiraude.

William thus grew up in the very midst of nervous excitement. From the cradle he breathed the chilly air, full of religious terror, which the old fanatic shed around her. He saw nothing on awaking but this woman's face, fervent and speechless bent over him, he heard nothing but the shrill voice of this singer of chants, who would lull him to sleep at night by reciting in a lugubrious fashion one of the seven penitential psalms. The caresses of his foster-mother crushed him, her embraces suffocated him, and they were bestowed in shocks and with tears that would send the boy himself into a state of unwholesome tenderness. He acquired, to his hurt, the sensitiveness of a woman, and his nerves became so finely strung that his childish troubles were transformed into real sufferings. Often would his eyes fill with tears, for no apparent reason, and he would weep, not through anger, for hours, like a grown-up person.

When he was seven, Geneviève taught him his letters out of the big Bible with the iron clasps. This bible, with its paper yellowed with age and its forbidding appearance, used to terrify him. He could not understand the sense of the lines he had to spell, but the sinister tone in which his teacher pronounced the words, froze him to his chair. When he was alone, nothing in the world would have induced him to open the bible. The old protestant spoke to him about it as about God himself with awed respect. The child, whose intelligence was awakening, lived from that time in a sort of eternal dread. Shut up with the fanatic who talked to him incessantly of the devil, of hell, of the anger of Heaven, he passed days in a state of agonising terror: at night, he would sob, as he pictured to himself the flames running under his bed. This poor being who wanted nothing but play and laughter, had his imagination so unhinged that he did not dare to go into the park for fear of being damned. Geneviève would repeat to him every morning, in that shrill voice, the tones of which cut like sharp blades, that the world was an infamous place of perdition, and that it would be better for him to die without ever seeing the bright sun. She thought that by these lessons she was saving him from Satan.

Sometimes, however, in the afternoon, he would run about in the long passages at La Noiraude, and venture under the trees in the park.

The mansion, which was called La Noiraude at Véteuil, was a big square building, three stories high, and all dark and ugly, very much like a house of correction. Monsieur de Viargue disdainfully allowed it to fall into ruins. He occupied a very small portion of it; one room on the first floor and another at the top of the house, which he had made into his laboratory: on the ground floor, he had reserved himself a dining-room and a sitting-room. The other apartments in the spacious mansion, except those occupied by Geneviève and the servants, were completely deserted. They were never even opened.

When William went along the gloomy silent passages which traversed La Noiraude in every direction, he felt seized with secret terror. He hurried past the doors of the empty rooms. Filled with the horrible ideas which Geneviève put into his head, he fancied he could hear moanings and stifled sobs from these rooms; he would ask himself fearfully who could inhabit these apartments whose doors were always fastened. He preferred the walks in the park, and yet he did not dare to go far, such a timorous, cowardly mortal had the old protestant made him.

Occasionally, he met his father, but the sight of him made him tremble. Up to the age of five, he had hardly seen him. The count was forgetting that he had a son. He had not even troubled his head about the formalities he would have to go through some day if he wished to adopt him. The child had been necessarily declared as born of parents unknown. Monsieur de Viargue was aware the notary always pretended to be ignorant of the existence of his wife's bastard, and he promised himself some day to put William's position straight. As he had no other heir, he intended to bequeath his fortune to him. These thoughts, however, did not trouble him very much; he was absorbed in his experiments, more ironical and more haughty than ever: he listened impassively to the accounts that Geneviève gave him from time to time about the child.

One day, as he was going down to the park, he met him with the old woman, who was leading him by the hand. He was quite astonished to find him so big. William, who was entering on his fifth year, had on one of those delightful dresses of light bright-coloured material that children wear. The father, somewhat struck, stopped for the first time; he took hold of his son, and raising him up to his face, looked at him attentively. William, by a mysterious phenomenon of blood, was like the count's mother. The resemblance struck the father, and moved him. He kissed the poor little trembling fellow's brow.

From that day, he never met his son without kissing him. After his fashion, he loved him as much as he could love. But his embrace was cold, and the hasty kiss which he gave him at times was not enough to win the child's heart. When William could avoid the count, without the latter noticing it, he was nearly always delighted to escape his embrace. This stern man who haunted La Noiraude like a cold silent shadow, caused him more fear than affection. Geneviève, to whom Monsieur de Viargue had given orders to bring him up openly as his son, always represented his father to him as a terrible and absolute master, and this word father only awoke in his mind an idea of reverential dread.

Such was William's existence during the first eight years of his life. The strange teaching of the old protestant, and the terror with which his father inspired him, all contributed to make him feeble. He was doomed to keep with him through life the shudders and the unwholesome sensitiveness of his infancy. At eight years of age, Monsieur de Viargue sent him as a boarder to the communal school at Véteuil. He had, no doubt, noticed the cruel way in which Geneviève was bringing him up, and wished to remove him entirely from the influence of this disordered brain. At the school, William began in sorrow the apprenticeship of life: he was fatally doomed to be hurt at every turn.

The years that he spent as a boarder were one long martyrdom, one long ordeal that a neglected and deserted child has to pass through, trodden on by everybody and never knowing what he has dune wrong. The inhabitants of Véteuil nursed towards Monsieur de Viargue a secret hatred, which was the result of their jealousy and prudery: they never forgave him for being rich and doing as he liked, while the scandal of William's birth was an endless theme for their slanderous talk. Though they continued to bow humbly to the father, they avenged themselves for his disdainful indifference on the weakness of the son, whose heart they could break without danger. The boys of the town, those of twelve and sixteen, all knew William's history through having heard it told a hundred times in their families; at home their relatives would talk with such indignation of this adulterous child, that they looked upon it as their duty, now that he was their play-fellow, to torture the poor being who was cried out upon by the whole of Véteuil. Their very parents encouraged them in their cowardice, smiling slyly at the persecutions which they inflicted on him.

From the very first play-hour, William felt, from the jeering attitude of his new companions, that he was in a hostile country. Two big fellows, fifteen year old louts, came up and asked him his name. When he replied, in a timid voice, that it was William, the whole band jeered.

"Your name is Bastard, you mean!" cried a school-boy, amid the hoots and low jokes of these young scamps, who already had the vices of grown-up men.

The child did not understand the insult, but he began to weep with anguish and terror in the centre of this pitiless circle which surrounded him. He got a few shoves, begged pardon, which highly amused these gentlemen, and brought him a few more knocks.

The bent was followed, the school victim was found. During every play-hour, he caught a few thumps on the head, he heard himself saluted by the name of Bastard, which made the blood mount to his cheeks, he knew not why. The dread of blows made him cowardly; he spent his time in the corners, not daring to stir, like a pariah who finds a whole nation up against him and no longer dares to revolt. His masters banded secretly with his comrades; they saw that it would be a clever stroke of policy to make common cause with the sons of the big wigs at Véteuil, and they overwhelmed the child with punishments, themselves enjoying a wicked pleasure in torturing a feeble creature. William gave himself up to despair; he was a detestible pupil, brutalized with blows, hard words and punishments. Slow, sickly, stupid, he would weep in the dormitory for a whole night: this was his only protest.

His sufferings were all the keener for the poignant need that he felt of having somebody to love and only finding objects to hate. His nervous sensitiveness made him cry out with anguish at each fresh insult. "Good God," he would often murmur, "what crime have I committed?" And, with his childish sense of justice, he would try to find out what it was that could bring down on him such cruel punishments; when he could find nothing, he would be filled with strange dread, he would remember Geneviève's menacing lessons and think himself tormented by demons for unknown sins. On two occasions, he seriously thought of drowning himself in the school-well. He was then twelve years old.

On holidays he seemed to get out of a grave. The street children would often stone him to the gates of the town. He was now fond of the deserted park at La Noiraude where no one beat him. He never dared to speak to his father about the persecutions he had to endure. He complained only to Geneviève and asked her what was the meaning of that name Bastard which produced in him the burning sensation of a box on the ears. The old woman listened to him gloomily. She was annoyed that her pupil had been taken away from her. She knew that the school chaplain had induced M. de Viargue to let the child be baptised, and she looked upon him as positively doomed to the flames of hell. When William had confided to her his troubles, she exclaimed, without speaking directly to him: "You are the son of sin, you are expiating the crime of the guilty." He could not understand, but the fanatic's tone seemed to him so full of anger, that he never after made her his confidante.

His despair increased as he grew up. He at last arrived at an age when he knew what his fault was. His comrades, with their vile insults, had educated him in vice. Then, he wept tears of blood. They hit him through his parents, by telling him the shameful story of his birth. He knew of the existence of his mother by the coarse names which they gave to this woman all around him. The youngsters, once they set foot in the filth, wallowed in it with a sort of vanity; and the little dandies never spared the Bastard any of the vileness which they could invent out of the intimacy between the notary's wife and Mousieur de Viargue. William was seized at times with an outburst of wild rage; beneath the blows of his executioners, the martyr revolted at last, fell on the first he could lay hands on and tore him like a wild beast; but, as a rule, he remained passive under the insult and simply wept in silence.

As he was entering on his fifteenth year, an event happened, the memory of which he kept all his life. One day, as the school was walking out and passing along one of the streets of the town, he heard his comrades sneering round him and murmuring in their malicious tone:

"Eh! Bastard, look; there's your mother."

He raised his head and looked.

A woman was passing along the causeway, leaning on the arm of a man with a weak placid face. This woman surveyed William with a curious look. Her clothes almost rubbed against him as she passed. But she had no smile, and screwed up her mouth with a sort of sanctified and crabbed grimace. The placid expression of the man who was with her never changed.

William, who was nearly fainting, did not hear the banter of his comrades who were bursting with laughter, as if this little adventure had been the greatest joke in the world. He stood savage and speechless. This hurried vision had frozen his life-blood, and he felt himself more miserable than an orphan. For the rest of his life, when he thought of his mother, he would see before him the image of this woman passing by with a sanctimonious scowl, leaning on the arm of her cuckolded and happy husband.

His great grief, during these wretched years, was to be loved by no one. The savage tenderness of Geneviève frightened him almost, and he found his father's silent affection very cold. He would say to himself that he was alone, and that there was not a single being who had any pity for him. Crushed beneath the persecutions that he endured, he shut himself up with his inexpressible thoughts of kindness; his gentle nature carefully concealed, as a foolish secret at which people would have laughed, the treasures of love which it could not bestow at large. He would lose himself in the endless dream of an imaginary passion into which he would throw himself heart and soul for ever. And he would dream then of a blissful solitude, of a nook where there were trees and streams, where he would be all alone in company with a cherished passion; lover or comrade, he hardly knew which; he simply felt a longing desire for peace. When he had been beaten, and when still all bruised, he would summon up his dream, his hands clasped in a sort of religious frenzy, and he would ask Heaven when he would be able to hide himself and take his rest in a supreme affection.

Had his pride not sustained him, he would perhaps have become habituated to cowardice. But, fortunately, he had in him the blood of the De Viargues; the helpless weakness, to which he was a victim through his chance birth and the plebeian foolishness of his mother, would at times derive an accession of vigour from the pride which he had from his father. He would feel himself better, worthier and nobler than his tormentors; if he feared them, he had a calm disdain for them; under their blows his strength of pride did not desert him, and this exasperated the young brutes who did not fail to notice the contempt of their victim.

William, however, had one friend in the school. Just as he was promoted into the second form, a new pupil came into the same class as himself. He was a tall young fellow, vigorous and strongly built, and older than William by two or three years. His name was James Berthier. An orphan, with no other relatives than an uncle who was a lawyer at Véteuil, he had come to the school at this town to finish the studies which he had begun at Paris. His uncle wanted to have him near him, as he had learnt that his dear nephew was rather precocious and was already, at seventeen, running after the young ladies of the Latin quarter.

James bore his exile in excellent spirits. He had the happiest disposition in the world. Without any remarkable qualities, he was what you call a fine fellow. The frivolity of his nature was atoned for by a rough-and-ready sort of devotion. His entry into the school was an event; he came straight from Paris, and spoke of life like a youth who has already tasted the forbidden fruit. The pupils had a sudden respect for him when they learnt that he had slept with women. His easy manners, his strength, and his good fortune made him the king of the school. He would laugh aloud, he would gladly exhibit his powerful arms and protect the weak with the good-nature of a prince.

The very day of his arrival, he saw a big lout of a scholar hustling William. He marched up, and gave the fellow a good shaking, telling him at the same time that he would hear further from him if he bullied the youngsters like that. Then he took the victim's arm and walked about with him during the whole of play-time to the scandal of the scholars who could not conceive how the Parisian could choose such a friend.

William was deeply touched with the assistance and friendship which James offered him. The latter had been seized with a sudden feeling of sympathy for the pained face of his new comrade. When he had asked him a few questions, he saw that he was going to have to exercise an active protection and this decided him.

"Will you be my friend?" he asked as he held out his hand to William.

The poor fellow almost wept as he grasped this hand, the first which had been offered him.

"I will love you deeply," he replied in the timid tone of a wooer confessing his love.

The following play-time, a group of pupils came round the Parisian to tell him William's history. They counted on making him thrash the Bastard by informing him of the scandal of his birth. James listened quietly to the dirty jokes of his comrades. When they had finished, he shrugged his shoulders and said:

"You're a pack of idiots. If I catch one of you repeating what you have just said, I'll box his ears."

He only felt more sympathy for the pariah as he perceived the depths of his wounds. He had already had as a friend, at the Charlemagne college, a love-begot, a boy of rare and charming intelligence, who carried off all his form prizes and was beloved by his comrades and by his masters. This made him accept, as quite a natural thing, the story of the scandal which so raised the indignation of the young brutes of Véteuil.

"What geese those fellows are!" he said to William. "They are ill-natured blockheads. I know all; but come now, don't be afraid; if one of them touches you, tell me, and you'll see."

From that day, everybody felt a respect for the Bastard. One of the

ÉMILE ZOLA

fellows having ventured to salute him with this name, he got such a smack that the whole school saw that there was to be no more joking and sought another victim. William passed through the second class and the rhetoric class in profound peace. He became ardently devoted to his protector. He loved him with the love one has for a first mistress, with absolute faith and blind devotion. His gentle nature had at length found an outlet, his long pent-up tenderness was bestowed in its entirety on the deity whose hand and heart had befriended him. His friendship was mingled with a feeling of gratitude so warm that he almost looked upon James as a superior being. He knew not how to pay his debt, and his attitude towards him was humble and respectful. He admired his slightest movements; this big energetic noisy fellow filled him with a sort of respect, when he compared him to his own timid and piteous nature. His easy manners, the stories which he told of his life in Paris convinced him that he had for a friend an extraordinary man who was destined for the highest career. And there was thus, in his affection, a singular mixture of admiration, humility and love, which always left him a feeling at once tender and respectful for James.

The latter accepted, like the good fellow that he was, his protegee's adoration. He loved to show his strength and to be flattered. Besides, he was seduced by the devoted endearments of this weak proud nature who crushed the other pupils with his contempts. For the two years that they were at school together, they were inseparable.

When they had got through the rhetoric class, James set out for Paris, where he was to attend the lectures at the School of Medicine. William, left alone at Véteuil, remained for a long time inconsolable at the departure of his friend. He had lost all aptitude for work, living at La Noiraude as in the heart of a desert. He was then eighteen. His father sent for him one day into his laboratory. It was the first time that he had passed the threshold of this room. He found the count standing in the middle of the huge sanctum, his breast covered with a long blue workman's apron. He seemed to him terribly aged; his temples were bare, and his sunken eyes shone with a strange brilliancy in his thin face all seamed with wrinkles. He had always felt a deep respect for him; this day, he almost felt a dread of him.

"Sir," said the count, "I have sent for you in order to tell you my plans with regard to yourself. Be kind enough to tell me if, by chance, you feel an inclination for any occupation."

As William stood embarrassed and hesitating he went on:

"That is well, my orders will be the more easy for you to carry out. I wish you, sir, to follow no profession whatever, neither doctor, lawyer, nor anything else."

And as the young man looked at him, with an air of surprise, he continued in a slightly bitter tone:

"You will be rich, you will have it in your power to be a fool and a happy man, if you are fortunate enough to understand life. I regret already that I have had you taught something. Hunt, eat, sleep, these are my orders. Still, if you have a taste for fanning, I will allow you to dig."

The count was not joking. He spoke in a peremptory tone, in the certainty of being obeyed. He noticed that his son was casting a glance over the laboratory as if to protest against the life of idleness which he was imposing on him. His voice became threatening.

"Above all," he said "swear to me that you will never spend your time on science. After my death, you will shut this door and never open it again. It is enough that one De Viargue has buried himself here for a whole lifetime. I rely on your word, sir; you will do nothing, and you will try to be happy."

William was going to withdraw, when his father, as if touched with sudden grief and emotion, took him by the hands and murmured as he drew him towards him:

"You understand, my child, obey me; be a simple-minded man, if it is possible."

He kissed him hurriedly and dismissed him. This scene had a strange effect on William; he saw that the count must be suffering from a secret grief; in the few dealings that they had with one another, he showed him, from that day, a more affectionate respect. Besides, he conformed strictly to his orders. He stayed for three years at La Noiraude hunting, shooting, roving about the country, and taking an interest in trees and hills. These three years, during which he lived in companionship with nature, finished the work of predestination for the joys and sorrows which the future had in store for him. Lost in the green solitudes of the park, invigorated by the all-pervading thrill of nature beneath the foliage, he purified himself of his school-life, he increased in tenderness and pity. He took up the dream of his youth, he hoped again to find, on the brink of some fountain, a being who would take him in her arms and carry him away, kissing him like a child. Ah! what long reveries, and how sweetly the shadow and silence of the oaks fell on his brow.

But for the vague restlessness with which his unsatisfied desires filled him, he would have been perfectly happy. Nobody was persecuting him now: when he happened to pass through Véteuil, he saw his old comrades salute him with more cowardice than they had beaten him; it was known in the town that he would be the count's heir. His only dread, a strange dread mingled with painful hope, was of finding himself face to face with his mother. He did not see her again, and he was sad; the thought of this woman would recur to him every day; her complete forgetfulness of him, was for him an inexplicable monstrosity the cause of which he would have liked to discover. He even asked Geneviève if he ought not to try to see her. The old protestant answered him rudely that he was mad.

"Your mother is dead," she added, in her voice of inspiration; "pray for her."

Geneviève had always loved the child of sin, in spite of the terrors which such affection caused him. Now that this child had become a man, she put more guard on her heart. Yet at bottom, she was absolutely and blindly devoted to him.

On two occasions, James came to spend his student's holidays at Véteuil. These times were for William months of wild joy. The two friends were always together; they would shoot for whole days, or catch crawfish in the little brook that runs through the country. Often, in some secluded nook, they would sit down and talk about Paris, especially about women. James spoke lightly of them, as a man who had no very great regard for them, but who had the gallantry to look kindly on them, and not to speak all his mind on the subject. And William would then reproach him for his coldness of heart; he set woman on a pedestal, and made her an idol, before which he chanted an eternal song of fidelity and love.

"Oh! do be quiet," the impatient student would exclaim, "You don't know what you are saying. You will soon bore your mistresses, if you are always on your knees before them. But you will do as others do, you will deceive and be deceived. Such is life."

"No, no," he would answer in his obstinate way, "I shall not do as others do. I shall never love but one woman. I shall love her in such a way that I defy fate to disturb our affection."

"Rubbish! we shall see."

And James would laugh at the artlessness of his country friend. He almost scandalised him by the recital of his love adventures of one night. The journeys that he thus made to Véteuil cemented still more closely the friendship of the two young fellows. Besides, they used to write long letters to one another. Gradually, however, James's letters became less frequent; the third year, he had ceased to give any sign of life. William was very sad at this silence.

He knew, through the student's uncle, that his friend was to leave France, and he would have very much liked to bid him good bye before his departure. He was beginning to get mortally tired at La Noiraude. His father learnt the cause of his languid dejected ways, and said to him one night as he left the table:

"I know that you want to go to Paris. I give you leave to live there one year, and I expect that you will do some stupid thing or other. You shall have unlimited credit. You may start tomorrow."

Next day on his arrival in Paris, William learnt that James had gone away the day before. He had written a farewell letter to him at Véteuil which Geneviève sent on to him. In this letter, which was full of high spirits and very affectionate, his friend informed him that he had been gazetted as surgeon to our expeditionary army to Cochin China, and that he would be doubtless a long time away from France. William returned immediately to La Noiraude, distressed at this hurried departure and terrified at the thought of finding himself alone in an unknown town. He plunged again into his beloved solitude. But, two months later, his father again disturbed his loneliness by ordering him to return to Paris where he intended him to live for a year.

William went and took up his quarters in the Rue de l'Est, at the very hotel where Madeleine was already staying.

IV

When Madeleine met William, she was thinking of leaving the hotel and looking for a little room which she would furnish herself. In this house, open to all comers, full of students and young women, she did not feel sufficiently at home, and she found herself exposed to having to listen to horrible proposals which put her in mind cruelly of her desertion. After her removal, she intended to work and to utilise her talent for embroidery. Besides, her income of two thousand francs was sufficient for her needs. The future filled her with an indistinct feeling of anxiety; she foresaw that the solitude, to which she wished to condemn herself, would be full of perils. Although she had sworn to be brave, there were days that were so devoid of interest and so sad, that on certain nights, she would find herself in the midst of her dejection, entertaining thoughts of weakness that were unworthy of herself.

The night of William's arrival, she saw him on the staircase. He stepped aside against the wall with such a respectful air, that she was in a way confused and astonished at his attitude. Usually, the lodgers in the hotel almost walked over her feet and blew whiffs of tobacco in her face. The young man went into a room that adjoined hers, a thin partition separated the two apartments. Madeleine fell asleep listening, in spite of herself, to the step of the stranger who was taking possession of his quarters.

William, respectful as he had been, had not failed to notice his neighbour's pearly complexion and lovely golden hair. If he walked about a long time in his room that night, it was because, the thought of having a woman so near him caused him a sort of feverishness. He could hear her bed creak when she turned over.

Next day, the young people smiled at one another as a matter of course. Their intimacy made rapid progress. Madeleine gave way the more easily to her sympathy for this calm gentle young fellow, because she felt herself perfectly safe with him. She looked upon him somewhat as a child. She thought that if he should ever commit the folly of speaking to her about love, she would give him a lecture and easily get to know the motive of his desires. She felt confidence in her strength, and meant to keep her oath of widowhood. The following days, she accepted William's arm, and consented to take a little walk in his company. On their return, she went into the young man's room, and he went into hers. But there was not the least tender word, not the least smile to cause uneasiness. They treated one another as friends of a day's standing, with a reserve full of charming delicacy.

At bottom, their existence was disturbed in an indistinct kind of way. At night when they were alone in their rooms, they would listen to each other's step, and they would dream, without being able to read clearly the feelings that were disturbing them. Madeleine felt that she was loved, and she indulged the sweet thought, saying to herself all the while that she herself would not fall in love. To tell the truth, she did not know what real love was; her first intimacy had been so devoid of tenderness that she enjoyed William's attentions with infinite pleasure; her heart went out to him, in spite of herself, touched by a sympathy which was gradually ripening into affection. If she still happened to think of her wounds, she drove away the cruel memories by musing on her new friend; the passion of a sanguine temperament had dismayed her, the endearing affection of a nervous nature was filling her with a softening languor, and toning down her caprices one by one. As for William, he was living in a dream, he was worshipping the first woman he had met, and this was fatal. In the beginning he did not even ask himself where this woman came from, she was the first to smile on him, and that smile was sufficient to make him kneel down and offer her his life. He was joyously astonished at having found a sweetheart at once, he was in haste to open his heart so long closed, so full of restrained passion; if he did not embrace Madeleine, it was because he did not dare to, but he thought already that she was his.

Things went on like this for a week. William hardly went out; Paris terrified him, and he had taken good care not to go to one of the big hotels of which his father had given him the addresses. He congratulated himself now on having buried himself behind the Luxembourg in the heart of that peaceful neighbourhood where love was awaiting him. He would have liked to carry Madeleine off to the fields, far far away, not from a design of making her fall into his arms the sooner, but because he loved the trees, and wished to walk with her in their shade. She resisted, with a sort of presentiment. At last, she consented to go and dine with him at a little inn on the outskirts of Paris. There, at the restaurant in the Verrières wood, she surrendered herself.

Next day, when they returned to Paris, the two lovers were so astonished at their adventure, that they would at times speak to each other with a certain amount of ceremony. They even experienced a feeling of restraint, an uncomfortable sensation which they had not felt when they were simply comrades. By a singular sentiment of shame, they did not wish to sleep both of them in the hotel where, the day before, they had been almost strangers to each other. William saw that Madeleine would be pained by the smiles of the waiters, if she came to live in his room. He went at night to sleep in a neighbouring hotel. Besides, now that she was his, he wanted to have the young woman entirely to himself, in some retreat unknown to the world.

He acted as if he were on the point of getting married. The banker, on whom his father had given him unlimited credit, told him, when he made inquiries, of a quiet little house, which was for sale in the Rue de Boulogne. William hurried off to look at the place, and bought it at once. He put the workmen in immediately, and furnished it in a few days. The whole thing was the affair of a week at most. One night, he took Madeleine by the hand and asked her if she would be his wife.

Since the night they had spent in the restaurant in the Verrières wood, he came to see her every afternoon, like a betrothed young man paying his addresses to his lady-love; then he went away discreetly. His request touched Madeleine's heart, and she replied by throwing her arms round his neck. They went into the house in the Rue de Boulogne like two new married people, on the evening of their wedding day. It was there really that their nuptial night was spent. They seemed to have forgotten the chance circumstance which had thrown them suddenly, one night, into one another's arms: they seemed to think that this was the first time that they had been allowed to exchange kisses. Sweet and happy night when the lovers could picture to themselves that the past was dead for ever, and that their union had the purity and strength of an eternal bond.

They lived there for six months, severed from the world and seldom going out. It was a veritable vision of happiness. Lulled by their affection, they no longer reminded one another of what had preceded their love, nor were they uneasy about the events that the future might have in store for them. They were remote from the past and careless of the future, in a complete contentment of mind, in the peace of a happiness which nothing disturbed. The house, with its little rooms, carpeted and upholstered with bright material, offered them a lovely retreat, secluded, quiet, and cheerful. And then there was the garden, a little patch not much bigger than your hand, where they would forget themselves, in spite of the cold, chatting during the fine winter afternoons.

Madeleine used to think that her life only dated from the previous day. She did not know if she loved William; she only knew that this man brought happiness to her being, and that it was pleasant to repose in this happiness. All her wounds had been healed; she no longer felt those shocks and burning pangs which had torn her breast; she was filled with warmth, a genial unfluctuating warmth which gave rest to her heart. She never asked herself any questions. Like a patient recovering with reduced strength from a sharp attack of fever, she abandoned herself to the voluptuous languor of her convalescence, thanking him from the bottom of her heart, who had extricated her from her anguish. It was not the fond embraces of the young man which touched her the most; her senses were usually quiescent, and there was more maternity than passion in her kisses: it was the profound esteem which he showed for her, the dignity with which he treated her, like a lawful wife. This raised herself in her own esteem, and she could fancy that she had passed from the arms of her mother to the arms of a husband. This picture which her shame would draw, flattered her pride, and hampered all the modesty of her nature. She could thus hold up her head, and, above all, she enjoyed to the full her new affection, her peacefulness and smiling hopes, in the complete oblivion of the wounds which bled in her no longer.

William was in the seventh heaven. At last, the cherished dream of his youth and childhood was being realised. When he was at school, crushed by the blows of his comrades, he had dreamt of a happy solitude, a hidden secluded nook where he would pass long days of idleness, never beaten, but caressed by some kind and gentle fairy who would always stay by his side; and later on, at eighteen, when vague desires were beginning to throb in his veins, he had taken up again this dream beneath the trees in the park, on the banks of clear streams, replacing the fairy by a sweetheart, traversing the thicket in the hope of meeting the object of his affection, at every turn in the path. Today Madeleine was the kind and gentle fairy, the sweetheart that he had sought. She was his in the solitude that he had dreamt of, far from the crowd, in a retreat where not a soul could come to disturb his ecstasy. This, for him, was the highest bliss: to know that he was out of the world, to be no longer afraid of being hurt by anyone, to surrender himself to all the softened peace of his heart, to have by his side one being only, and to live on the beauty and love of this being. Such an existence consoled him for his youth of sorrow: a youth devoid of affection, with a proud ironical father, an old fanatic whose caresses frightened him, and a friend who was not enough to calm his feverish adoration. It consoled him for crushing persecutions, for a childhood of martyrdom and a youth of exile, and for a long series of sorrows which had made him ardently long for the shade and complete silence, for a total annihilation of his sorrowful existence in an endless happiness. Thus he reposed, and took refuge in Madeleine's arms, like a man weary and frightened. All his joys were joys of tranquillity. Such a peace seemed to him as never to end. He pictured to himself that the eternity of the last sleep was opening before him and that he was sleeping in the arms of his Madeleine.

It was with both of them a feeling more of repose than of love. You might have said that chance had drawn them together that each might staunch the blood of the other's wounds. They both felt a like need of repose, and their words of affection were a sort of thanks which they addressed to one another for the peaceful happy hours which they were enjoying together. They revelled in the present with the egoism of hungry souls. It seemed to them that they had only existed since their meeting; a memory of the past never entered their long lovers' talks. William was no longer uneasy about the years of Madeleine's life before she knew him, and the young woman never thought of questioning him, as women in love do, about his previous existence. It was enough for them to be by each other's side, to laugh, to be happy, like children who have neither regret for the past nor anxiety for the future.

Madeleine heard one day of Lobricbon's death. She merely remarked:

"He was a bad man."

She appeared quite unconcerned, and William seemed to take no interest in this news. When he received letters from Véteuil, he threw them into a drawer after reading them; his mistress never asked him what these letters contained. At the end of six months of this life, they knew as little of each other's history as they did the first day; their love had been bestowed without inquiries.

This dream came to a sudden end.

One morning, when William had gone to his banker's, Madeleine, not knowing what to do, began to turn over the leaves of an album which was lying in the room, and which had hitherto escaped her notice. Her lover had come across it the night before, at the bottom of a trunk. It only contained three portraits, one of his father, one of Geneviève, and one of his friend James.

When the young woman saw the latter, she uttered a cry of pain. With her hands resting on the open leaves of the album, erect and trembling she gazed at James's smiling face as if a phantom had risen before her. It was he, the lover of a night that had become the lover of a year, the man whose memory, long dormant in her breast, was awakening and hurting her cruelly, by this sudden apparition.

It was a thunder-bolt in her peaceful sky. She had forgotten this young fellow, she considered herself William's faithful wife. Why was James coming between them? Why was he here, in the very room where but a minute before her lover was holding her in his arms? Who had brought him to her to disturb her peace for ever? These questions set her distracted head reeling.

James was looking at her with a slightly mocking air. He seemed to be joking her on her softened heart; he was saying to her: "Good gracious! my poor girl, how you must be bored here! Come, let us go to Chatou, let us go to Robinson, let us go, quick! to where there is life and excitement—" She could fancy that she heard the sound of his voice and his burst of laughter; she thought that he was going to stretch out his arms to her in the old familiar way. Like a flash, she saw the past, the room in the Rue Soufflot, all that life which she thought so far off, and from which a few months only separated her. She had been in a dream then; the bliss of yesterday was not hers by right, she was false and dishonest. All the disgrace she had passed through rose to her heart and stifled her.

The photograph presented James in the careless attitude of his student's life. He was sitting astride an overturned chair, in his shirt sleeves, his neck and arms bare, and a clay pipe in his mouth. Madeleine could distinguish a mark that he had on his left arm, and she remembered how often she had kissed that mark. Her recollections caused her a hot burning sensation; in her suffering she could detect, as it were, the bitter dregs of the cup of pleasure which he had given her to drink. He was in his own room, half-undressed, and perhaps going to take her to his heart. Then she seemed to feel, around her waist, the clasp, that she knew so well, of her first lover. Fainting, she sank back in her chair, believing that she was prostituting herself, and looking round her with the frightened shudder of an adulterous woman. The little room had an appearance of demure quiet, of soft shade; it was full of that voluptuous peace which six months of love impart to a secluded cot; on a panel, above the sofa, hung William's portrait smiling tenderly on Madeleine. And Madeleine grew pale beneath this look of love, in the midst of that peaceful air, as she felt James take possession of her heart and fill her with pain.

Then she bethought herself. Before going away, the young doctor had given her his portrait, one exactly like this which a cruel fate had just put under her eyes. But, the day before she came to this house, she had religiously burnt it, unwilling to introduce the likeness of her first lover into William's home. And this portrait was coming to life again, and James was finding his way, in spite of herself, into her retreat! She got up, and took the album again. Then, behind the photograph, she read this inscription: "To my old comrade, to my brother William." William, James's comrade, James's brother! Madeleine, pale as death, closed the album and sat down again. With stony eyes and drooping hands, she remained a long time absorbed in thought.

She said to herself that she must be guilty of some great crime, to be punished so cruelly for her six months' bliss. She had surrendered herself to two men, and these two men loved one another with brotherly love. She pictured a sort of incest in her double affection. Formerly, in the Latin quarter, she had known a girl who was shared by two friends, and who went quietly from one friend's bed to the other's. She suddenly thought of this poor wretch, telling herself with disgust that she was as shameless as she was. Now she felt for certain that she would be haunted by the phantom as she devoted herself to William. Perhaps she would enjoy a horrid pleasure in the embraces of these lovers whom she would confound with each other. The anguish of her future seemed to her then so clearly defined, that she had an idea of fleeing, of disappearing for ever.

But her cowardice restrained her. The very night before, she had felt so happy in the genial, pleasant warmth of William's adoration. Could she not grow calm beneath the. young man's caresses, forget again, and think herself worthy and faithful? Then she asked herself if it would not be better to tell her lover everything, to confide to him her past, and to get his absolution. The thought of such a disclosure terrified her. How could she dare to confess to William that she had been his comrade's, his brother's former mistress? He would drive her away, he would banish her from his bed, he would never put up with the shame of such a partnership. She reasoned as if she were still James's mistress, so strong did she feel his influence over her even now.

She would say nothing, she would keep all the shame to herself. But she could not yet make up her mind to this decision; her straightforward nature revolted at the idea of an eternal falsehood, she felt that she would not have strength for long to live in her shame and anguish. It were better to confess at once, or flee. These agitating thoughts passed through her reeling head with painful noisy shocks. She examined her feelings without being able to come to a decision. Suddenly she heard the street door open. A rapid step mounted the staircase and William entered.

His face was quite agitated. He threw himself on the sofa and burst out sobbing. Madeleine, surprised and terrified, thought that he had got to know all. She rose up in a tremble.

The young man was still weeping, with his face buried in his hands, and shaking with the paroxysms of despair. At last, he held out his arms to his mistress, and said to her in a choking voice:

"Comfort me, comfort me. Oh! how I suffer!"

Madeleine went and sat down by his side, not daring to understand him, and asking herself if it was she who was making him weep like that. She forgot her own sufferings in the presence of a grief like his.

"Tell me, what is the matter with you," she asked her lover, as she took his hands in hers.

He looked at her like one distracted.

"I did not like to sob in the street," he stammered through his tears. "I ran, I was choking—I wanted to get here—Let me be, it does me good, it comforts me—"

He wiped his tears, then he almost choked afresh and burst out weeping again.

"My God! my God! I shall never see him again," he murmured.

The young woman thought she understood and was touched with pity. She drew William into her arms, kissed his forehead, wiped his tears, and soothed him with her broken-hearted gaze.

"You have lost your father?" she asked him again.

He made a sign of denial. Then he clasped his hands and in the meek voice of despair:

"My poor James," he said, seeming to address himself to a shadow seen only by himself; "my poor James, you will never love me more as you used to love me—I had forgotten you, I was not even thinking of you when you died."

At the name of James, Madeleine, who was still drying her lover's tears, jumped up with a shudder. James dead! The news fell with a dull thud on her heart. She stood stunned, asking herself if it was not she who, without knowing it, had killed this young fellow to get rid of him.

"You did not know him," William went on, "I have never spoken to you of him, I think. I was ungrateful, our happiness made me forgetful— He was a jewel, he had a nature full of devotion. He was the only friend I had in this world. Before meeting you, I had only known one affection, it was his. You were the only beings that had opened your hearts to me. And I have lost him—"

Here he was interrupted by a sob. He went on:

"At school, they used to beat me, and it was he who came to my aid. He saved me from tears, he held out to me his friendship and protection, to me, who lived like a pariah in the contempt, in the derision of everybody. When I was a child, I worshipped him like a god; I would have fallen on my knees before him, had he asked for my prayers, I owed him so much. I would ask myself with such fervour how I could pay him, some day, my debt of gratitude? And I have let him die far away. I have not loved him enough, I feel it."

His emotion choked him again. After a short silence he continued:

"And later on, what long days we passed together. We roamed the fields, hand in hand. I remember one morning we were searching for craw-fish under the willows; he said to me, 'William, there is only one good thing in this world, and it is friendship. Let us be devoted to one another, it will soothe us in after life.' Poor dear fellow, he is gone, and I am alone. But he will live always in my soul—I have nobody but you left, Madeleine, I have lost my brother."

He sobbed again, and again held out his arms to the young woman, with a gesture of utter despair.

She was in pain. The grief, the poignant regrets of William were causing her a singular feeling of rebellion; she could not hear from his month his passionate praise of James, without being tempted to exclaim: "Silence! this man has robbed you of your happiness, you owe him nothing." She had thus far escaped the anguish of being brought face to face with her past by the very man whose love compelled her to forget it. And she did not dare to close his lips, or to confess all to him, terrified by what she had just learnt, by that strong bond of friendship and gratitude which had united her two lovers. She listened to William's despair, as she would have listened to the threatening roar of a wave which was rushing towards her to swallow her up. Motionless and silent, her impassiveness was remarkable. She felt that her only sensation was one of anger. James's death irritated her. She had at first felt a sort of dull pang, and then she had revolted as she saw that his memory could not fade from her mind. By what right, since he was dead, did he come to disturb her peace?

William was still holding out his arms to her, and repeating: "My poor Madeleine, console me—You are the only one left to me in the world."

Console him for James's death; it seemed ridiculous and cruel to her. She was obliged to take him in her arms again, and dry the tears which he was shedding for her first lover. The strange part she was acting at this moment, would have made her weep too, could she have found tears. She was truly unfeeling and pitiless; no regret, no tenderness for him whom she had loved, nothing but a secret irritation at William's grief. She was still the daughter of Férat the workman.

"He loved him more than he does me," she thought; "he would cast me off if I were to declare what I think."

Then, for the sake of saying something, prompted too by bitter curiosity, she asked in a brief tone, how he had met with his death?

Then William told her how having to wait at his banker's, he had mechanically taken up a newspaper. His eyes had fallen on a paragraph which announced the wreck of the frigate Prophet which had been caught in a gale on nearing the Cape. The vessel had been dashed to pieces on the rocks and not a man had been saved. James, who was going out to Cochin China on this steamer, did not even repose in a grave where his friends could go to pray for him. The news was officially confirmed.

When the anguish of the lovers was allayed, during the night that followed, Madeleine meditated more calmly on the unexpected events of the day. Her anger had gone, and she felt herself dejected and sad. Had she heard of James's death under other circumstances, no doubt she would have had a choking sensation in her throat and the tears would have come. Now, alone in the recess where the bed stood, at the sound of the fitful breathing of her lover who was sleeping the heavy sleep of the wretched, she thought of him who was dead, of the corpse rolled and beaten against the rocks by the waves. Perhaps, as he had fallen into the sea, he had uttered her name. She remembered how one day he had cut himself rather severely, in the Rue Soufflot, and how she had nearly fainted at the sight of the blood trickling along his

ÉMILE ZOLA

hand. She loved him then, she would have sat up with him for months to rescue him from an illness. And now he was drowned, and she was feeling angry with him. Yet he had not become so indifferent to her as all that; she had him still, on the contrary, always in her breast, in every member; he had such hold on her that she thought she could feel his breath on her face. Then she felt the quiver which thrilled her in the old days, when the young fellow wound his arms round her body. She felt an inexpressible pang, as if a part of her being had been torn away from her. She began to weep, burying her head in the pillow, so that William might not hear. All her woman's weakness had come back to her; it seemed to her that she was more alone than ever in the world.

This crisis lasted for a long time. Madeleine prolonged it involuntarily as she called to mind the days of James's love; at each touching detail which came back to her from the past, she became more distressed, and she reproached herself with her petulant indifference during the day, as if it had been a crime. William himself, had he known her history, would have told her to fall on her knees and weep with him. She clasped her hands, she asked pardon of him who was dead, of him whom she evoked, of him whose cries of agony she fancied she could hear mingled with the roaring of the sea.

A violent desire suddenly seized her. She made no effort to struggle against this irresistible longing.

She got quietly out of bed, with infinite precautions, so as not to wake William. When she had put her feet on the carpet, she looked at him uneasily, dreading lest he should ask her where she was going. But he was asleep, his eyes still full of tears. Then, she went and looked for the night-lamp and passed into the sitting-room, trembling when the floor creaked beneath her bare feet.

She walked straight to the album, opened it on a little table, and sat down before James's portrait. It was James that she came to look for. Her shoulders covered with her loose hair, wrapping herself up shiveringly in her long nightdress, she gazed long at the portrait in the yellow flickering light of the lamp. A deep silence fell around her, and as she listened, starting with sudden and groundless fears, she could hear nothing but William's feverish breathing in the next room.

James no longer appeared to her to have his mocking look of the morning. His bare neck and arms, and his open shirt no longer irritated her memories. The man was dead; his portrait had assumed an indefinable softened expression of friendship and Madeleine felt soothed as she gazed on him. He was smiling at her with his old cordial smile, and even his careless attitude touched her deeply. The young fellow, astride on a chair, smoking his clay pipe, seemed to be forgiving her good-naturedly. He was as she had known him, a good fellow in death; he looked as if she had opened the door of their room in the Rue Soufflot, and James in his light-hearted, off-hand way was getting forgiveness for his peccadillos by his gay spirits.

Her tears became less bitter, she forgot herself in the contemplation of him who was no more. Henceforth this portrait would be a relic, and she thought she had nothing to fear from it. Then, she remembered her struggles of the morning, her indecision, her anxiety to know what to do. Poor James, at the moment of her distress at seeing him rise up between herself and her lover, had seemed to have sent her the news of his death to tell her to live in peace. He would come no more to disturb her in her new love; he seemed to authorise her to bury deep in her heart the secret of their intimacy. Why make William suffer? and why not seek for happiness again? She ought to keep silent out of pity, out of affection. James's portrait murmured: "Go, try to be happy, my child. I am no longer near you. I will never appear before you as your living shame. Your lover is a child. I have befriended him, and I implore you to befriend him in your turn. If you are good, just think of me sometimes."

Madeleine's mind was made up. She would say nothing, she would not be more cruel than fate which had wished to conceal her first lover's name from William. Besides, had he not said so himself? James's memory would live in his mind, and it must live there elevated and serene. It would be doing wrong to speak. When she had sworn to preserve silence, it seemed to her that the portrait thanked her for her resolution.

She kissed the likeness.

Day was breaking when she went back to bed. William, worn out, was still slumbering. She fell asleep at last, comforted, nursed by distant hope. They would forget this day of anguish, they would come back to their beloved state of bliss and love.

But their dream was over. The peacefulness of their first acquaintance was never more to lull them in their retreat in the Rue de Boulogne. During the days that followed, the rueful phantom of the shipwreck haunted the house, casting around them a gloomy sadness. They forgot their kisses, they would sit for a whole morning side by side, hardly saying a word, absorbed in their sad memories. James's death had entered into their genial solitude like an icy blast; now they shuddered, and it seemed to them as if the little rooms, where they had lived the day before on each other's knees, were large, dilapidated and exposed to every wind. The silence and the seclusion which they had sought, caused them a vague feeling of terror. They found themselves too lonely. One day, William could not restrain a cruel remark.

"This house is really like a grave," he exclaimed, "it is enough to stifle one."

He was sorry for it directly he had spoken, and, taking Madeleine's hand, he added:

"Forgive me. I shall forget him, and I will be yours again." He was in earnest, but he was not aware that the same dream rarely comes twice. When they had got over their dejection, they had lost the blind confidence of their early acquaintance. Madeleine especially was quite changed. She had just evoked the past, and she could no longer surrender herself to William's embraces like one who knew nothing. Life had inflicted a wound on her, it would do so again, and she must, she thought, be on her guard against the wounds that threatened her. Before, she hardly thought of the shame attached to her title of mistress; it seemed to her natural to be loved, she herself loved, smilingly, forgetting the world. Now, her pride had been hurt, she was feeling again the anguish she had felt in the Rue Soufflot, and she looked upon her lover as an enemy who was robbing her of her self-respect. There was a something which made her feel that she was not in her proper sphere in the Rue de Boulogne. The thought, "I am a kept woman," presented itself to her in all its nakedness and made her burn like a hot iron; she rushed off, and shut herself up in a room, and there wept bitterly, almost heart-broken.

William often made her presents, for he was fond of giving. At the beginning she had received these presents with the joy of a child at the gift of a plaything. The value of the object made little difference. She was happy that her lover was constantly thinking of her, and she accepted jewels as mere keep-sakes. After the shock which awoke her from her dream, she was strangely troubled at seeing herself dressed in robes of silk and adorned with diamonds that she had not paid for herself. Her life from that time was a continual bitterness, for she was hurt at the sight of this luxury which did not belong to her. She was pained by the lace-work and the softness of her bed, and by the rich furniture in the house. She looked upon everything about her as the price of her shame.

"I am selling myself," she would think sometimes, with a horrible oppression at her heart.

William, on one of their gloomy days, brought her a bracelet. She grew pale at the sight of the jewel and did not utter a word.

The young man, astonished not to see her fling her arms round his neck, as in the old days, said to her gently:

"You don't like this bracelet, perhaps?"

She was silent for a moment; then in a trembling voice she said:

"My dear, you spend a lot of money on me. You do wrong. I don't want all these presents and I should love you quite as much if you gave me nothing."

She restrained a sob. William drew her quietly towards him, surprised and vexed, yet not daring to divine the cause of her paleness.

"What is the matter with you!" he answered. "Madeleine, those are horrid thoughts—Are you not my wife?"

She looked him in the face, and her steady, almost stern gaze, said plainly: "No, I am not your wife." Had she dared, she would have proposed to him to pay for her food and dress out of her little income. Since her fall, her pride had become refractory; she felt that everything wounded her feelings and that irritated her all the more.

A few days after, William brought her a dress and she said to him with a nervous smile:

"Thank you; but, in future, let me buy these things. You don't understand anything about them, and they cheat you."

From that time she made her purchases herself. When her lover wanted to refund her the money that she had spent, she contrived a little plot to refuse it. Thus she was always on her guard, always making little attacks to defend her pride which was so easily wounded by a trifle. The truth was that life was beginning to prove unbearable to her in the Rue de Boulogne. She loved William, but she had made herself so wretched by her daily revolts, that she would fancy that she did not love him, though this could not prevent her from feeling greatly distressed when she thought that he might leave her as James had done. Then she would weep for hours and ask herself into what new shame she would fall then.

William could see perfectly well that her eyes were at times red with weeping. He could guess in part the wounds that she was inflicting on herself. He would have wished to be kind, to console her by becoming more affectionate towards her, and yet, in spite of himself, he was becoming more distressed and more feverish every day. Why did she weep like that? was she unhappy with him? was she regretting a lover? This last thought made him very wretched. He too was losing the faith and blind confidence he used to have. He was thinking of that period of Madeleine's past history of which he knew nothing, of which he wished to know nothing, and which however he could not help thinking of incessantly. The painful doubts that he had felt on the night of their walk at Verrières seized him again and tortured him. He felt anxious about the years gone by, he watched Madeleine in order to detect a confession in her gestures, or in her looks; then, when he thought that he could perceive a smile that he could not account for, he was distressed that she could be thinking of anything but himself. Now that she was his, she ought to be his without reserve. He would say to himself that his love ought to be sufficient to satisfy her. He would not admit of any ground for her reveries, and he felt himself painfully hurt by her passing fits of indifference. Often, when she was by his side, she was not listening to him; she would let him talk on, staring vacantly around, absorbed in secret thoughts; then he would stop talking, he would think himself slighted, and a sudden feeling of pride would change his love almost into disdain. "My heart is deceived," he would think; "this woman is not worthy of me; she has already seen too much of life to be able to reward me for my affections."

They never had an open quarrel. They continued in a state of tacit hostility. But the few bitter words they sometimes exchanged only left them more dejected and depressed.

"Your eyes are red," William would often say to Madeleine, "what is the cause of your secret weeping?"

"I don't weep, you are mistaken," the young woman would reply, trying to smile.

"No, no, I am not mistaken," was William's answer; "I can hear you quite well sometimes in the night. Are you unhappy with me?"

She would give a shake of denial with her head, and put on a forced laugh, or the look of a persecuted woman. Then the young man would take her hands in his, and try to infuse a little warmth into them, and as these hands continued lifeless and cold, he would let go of them exclaiming:

"I am a poor lover, am I not? I don't know how to win love—But there are some people who are never forgotten."

Such an illusion would have a painful effect on Madeleine. "You are cruel," she would reply bitterly. "I can't forget what I am, and that's why I weep. What can you be thinking of, William?"

He would hang down his head, and she would add, earnestly:

"It would, perhaps, be better for you to know my past history. Anyhow you would know what to do, and you would no longer think about shame which does not exist. Would you like me to tell you all?"

He would vehemently ask her not to, and take her to his heart, beseeching her pardon. This scene, which took place again and again, never went any further: but an hour after, they would forget it all, and go back to their old state: William, to his selfish despair at not possessing her entire affection, Madeleine, to the regrets prompted by her pride and to the dread of being hurt.

At other times, Madeleine would throw her arms round William's neck and shed tears unreservedly. These crises of weeping, which nothing could explain to him, were even still more painful to the young man. He did not dare to question his mistress, he consoled her, with a provoked air, which stopped her tears and made her assume a hard, implacable attitude. Then she refused to speak to him, and he had to relent so far as to sob, before they fell into each other's arms, distressing and consoling one another mutually. And they would have been unable to say what it was that was making them wretched; they were inexpressibly sad, they knew not why; it seemed to them that they were breathing a tainted air and that a lingering, unrelenting dejection was crushing them beneath its oppressiveness.

There was no termination to a situation like this. There was only one remedy—a frank explanation. But from this Madeleine shrank, for this William was too feeble. For a month, they lived this life of oppression.

William had got James's portrait richly framed, and this portrait, placed in the lover's bedroom, troubled Madeleine. When she retired to rest, it would seem to her as if the eyes of the dead man were watching her get into bed. During the night, she would smother her kisses that he might not hear them. When she was dressing, in the morning, she hurried on her clothes so as not to stand naked before the photograph in broad daylight. Yet, she loved this likeness, and there was nothing painful in the distress that it caused it. Her memories of the past were less hard, yet she no longer looked on James with the eyes of a lover, but from the standpoint of a friend of his who is ashamed of the past. She even felt more modesty with regard to him than before William, and was really pained at seeing him look on at her new passions. Sometimes she thought that she ought to ask his pardon, she would forget herself before his portrait, with no other feeling but one of solace. The days when she wept, or when she had exchanged bitter words with her lover, she gazed at James with a still gentler expression. She regretted him in a vague way, forgetful of her former sufferings.

Perhaps Madeleine would have wept at last before the likeness like an inconsolable widow, had not an event transpired to lift her and William from the sorrowful life they were leading. Another month, and they would doubtless have quarrelled outright, and cursed the day of their meeting. They were saved by circumstances.

William received a letter from Véteuil summoning him in all haste. His father was dying. Madeleine, touched at his grief, clasped him in a warm, affectionate embrace, and, for an hour, they sat once more hand in hand. He set out, full of anxiety, telling the young woman that he would write and that she was to wait for his return.

V

Monsieur de Viargue was dead. The truth had been concealed from William in order that the sad news might be broken gently.

Long after, the circumstances connected with this poor man's death would make the servants of La Noiraude shudder. The day before, the count had shut himself up as usual in his laboratory. As she did not see him come down at night, Geneviève seemed surprised; but he sometimes worked late, and took some food up with him, so the old woman did not disturb him for dinner. That evening, however, she felt a presentiment of something wrong; the window of the laboratory, which usually shone over the country, like one of the red mouths of the infernal regions, remained in darkness the whole night.

Next day, Geneviève, feeling very uneasy, went and listened at the door. She could hear nothing, not a sound, not a breath. Alarmed at this silence, she shouted out, but there was no reply. She noticed then that the door was simply closed; this detail terrified her, for the count always double locked it when he went in. She entered. In the middle of the room, Monsieur de Viargue was lying dead on his back, his legs all stiff, his arms apart and convulsed; the grinning head, disfigured with livid spots, was thrown back, exposing the neck which was covered also with long yellow marks. In the fall, the skull had knocked against the floor; a little stream of blood was trickling on and forming a tiny pool right under the stove. The death-struggle hardly seemed to have lasted more than a few seconds.

At the sight of the dead body, Geneviève fell back with a shriek. She leaned against the wall and mumbled a short prayer. What terrified her most, were the marks on the face and the neck which looked like contusions; the devil had strangled her master at last, the imprint of his fingers clearly proved it. She had long been expecting this event; when she had seen the count shut himself up, she had murmured: "He is going again to invoke the Accursed One: Satan will be even with him; one of these nights, he will take him by the throat and so have his soul at once." Her prediction was being realised, and she shuddered as she thought of the terrible struggle which must have brought about the death of the heretic. Her ardent imagination pictured the devil to her eyes, hairy and black, seizing his victim by the throat, tearing out his soul and then disappearing up the chimney.

The shriek she had uttered brought the servants. These domestics whom Monsieur de Viargue had carefully chosen from the most illiterate in the country, were convinced, like Geneviève, that their master had died in a conflict with the demon. They carried him down and laid him on a bed, with shudders of terror, as they trembled to see some unclean animal come forth from the black, open mouth of the corpse. It was firmly believed, for miles round, that the count was a sorcerer, and that the devil had carried him off. The doctor who came to inquire into the cause of death, explained it otherwise; he could see by the appearance of the livid spots which disfigured the skin, that it was a case of poisoning, and his curiosity as a medical man was singularly piqued by the strange nature of these yellow marks, the presence of which the action of no known poison could explain: he thought rightly that the old chemist must have poisoned himself by the aid of some new agent discovered by him during the course of his long researches. This doctor was a prudent man; he made a sketch of the marks from his love for science, and kept the secret of this violent death to himself. He attributed the decease to an attack of apoplexy, wishing by this to avoid the scandal there must have been, had any mention of Monsieur de Viargue's suicide been made. There is always an interested respect for the memory of the rich and the influential.

William arrived an hour before the funeral. His grief was great. The count had always treated him with coldness, and when he lost him, he could not feel that the snapping of the bonds of an affection which had never been very close could tear his heart; but the poor fellow was then in such a feverish state of mind that he wept bitterly. After the restless and painful days which he had just spent with Madeleine, the least sorrow would melt him to tears. Perhaps two months before, he would not have even sobbed.

On the return from the funeral, Geneviève took him up to her room. There, with the cruel calmness of her fanaticism, she told him that she had been guilty of sacrilege, in allowing his father to be buried in consecrated ground. Unfeelingly, she related to him, after her fashion, the story of that death which she attributed to the devil. Perhaps she would not have given these details over the hardly closed grave of the count, had she not wished to draw a moral from them; she adjured the young man, and solemnly implored him to swear that he would never form a compact with hell. William swore to everything she asked. He listened to her with a stupefied look, crushed by his grief, unable to understand why she spoke of Satan, and feeling himself going mad at the tale, uttered in her shrill voice, of his father's struggle with the devil. He listened quietly to what she said about the spots on the face and neck of the dead body, but he became quite pale, not daring yet to accept the thought which presented itself to his mind.

He was informed, just at this moment, that somebody wished to speak to him. In the hall, William found the doctor, who had investigated the cause of death. Then, this man, after beating about the bush for a long time, told him the horrible truth; he added, that if he had allowed himself to conceal it from the public, he had thought it his duty to declare everything to the deceased's son. The young man, chilled by such a confidence, thanked him for his concealment of the facts. He was not weeping now, he was looking before him with a fixed and gloomy gaze; it seemed to him that an unfathomable abyss was opening at his feet.

He was going away staggering like one drunk, when the doctor held him back. This man had not come simply, as he said, to inform him of the real truth. Impelled by an irresistible wish to penetrate into the count's laboratory, he had seen that a better opportunity would never occur: the son was to show him into that sanctuary, the door of which had always been closed to him by the father, during his lifetime.

"Excuse me," he said to William, "if I mention these matters to you at a moment like this. But I am afraid that tomorrow it will be too late to investigate certain details. The marks which I noticed on Monsieur de Viargue, were of such a peculiar nature, that I am totally ignorant of the poison which could have produced them—I beg you to be kind enough to allow me to visit the room in which the corpse was found; that will enable me, no doubt, to give you more precise information."

William asked for the key of the laboratory, and went up with the doctor. Had he been asked, he would have taken him anywhere, to the stables, to the cellars, without manifesting the least surprise, without knowing even what he was doing.

But, when he entered the laboratory, the look of this room astonished him so, that the shock roused him from his stupor. The big chamber was so strangely altered, that he hardly knew it again. When he had been in it before, about three years ago, the day that his father had forbidden him all work and all connection with science, it was in a perfect state of order and cleanliness: the tiles in the stove shone bright; the copper and glass-work of the apparatus reflected the clear light from the big window; the shelves that ran round the walls were covered with bottles, phials, and receivers of every description: on the middle of the table had stood piles of huge books, all open, and bundles of manuscripts. He still remembered the impression of reverential surprise produced on him by the sight of this study-workshop, littered methodically, so to speak, with quite a multitude of objects. There reposed the fruits of a long life of labour, the precious secrets of a philosopher who had questioned nature for more than half a century, never wishing to confide to anyone the results of his ardent curiosity.

As William penetrated into the laboratory, he expected to find again, in their place, the apparatus and the shelves, the books and the manuscripts. He entered into a veritable ruin. A storm seemed to have passed through the room, soiling and breaking everything; the stove, black with smoke, looked as if it had not been lit for months, and the heap of cold ashes which filled it had partly fallen out on to the floor: the copper of the apparatus was all bent, the glass broken: the phials and bottles on the shelves shivered into a thousand bits, lay piled in a corner, like those heaps of broken crockery one sees in slums; the shelves themselves were hanging down, as if they had been torn from their supports by some furious hand: as for the books and manuscripts, they were strewn, torn and half-burnt, in another corner. And this wreck was not of yesterday; the laboratory seemed to have been devastated for a considerable time; huge spider-webs hung from the ceiling, and a thick layer of dust covered the rubbish that lay scattered everywhere.

At the sight of such destruction, William felt an oppression at his heart. He thought he could account for it. His father had formerly spoken to him of science with secret jealousy and bitter irony. He must have looked on it as a lewd and cruel mistress sapping his life-blood with her charms: and so, from tenderness for her, and disdain for the world, he would have no one take her after him. And the young man drew a sad picture of the day when the old philosopher, seized with rage, had wrecked his laboratory. He could see him kicking the apparatus against the walls, smashing the phials on the floor, wrenching down the shelves, and tearing and burning his manuscripts. An hour, a few minutes perhaps, had been enough to destroy the researches of a lifetime. Then, when not one of his discoveries, not one of his observations remained, when he had found himself standing alone in the midst of his laboratory in ruins, he must have sat down and wiped his face with a terrible smile.

What horrified William above everything, was the thought of the frightful days which the man had passed afterwards, buried in this room, this tomb where slept his life, his toils, his loves. For months, he had shut himself up here as before, touching nothing, walking up and down, lost in the nothingness that he thought he had found. He would crush beneath his feet the fragments of his beloved instruments, he would kick away disdainfully the scraps of his manuscripts, the broken pieces of the phials that still contained a few atoms of the substances that he had analysed or discovered: or he would finish the work of destruction, upsetting a vessel still full, or giving a last stamp to an apparatus. What thoughts of supreme disdain, what bitter jeers, what a longing for death must have risen to his powerful mind, during the long hours that he spent in idleness musing on the self-made ruins of his labour!

Nothing remained. As William went round the room, he noticed at last, however, an object which his father's hand had spared; it was a sort of cupboard fastened in the wall, a little bookcase with glass doors containing small bottles full of liquids of different colours. The count, who had taken great interest in toxicology, had kept there certain violent poisons still unknown, and discovered by himself. The little bookshelf had come from a sitting-room on the ground-floor where William remembered to have seen it in his childhood; it was of foreign wood, ornamented at the corners with brass, and very chastely inlaid at the sides. This costly bit of furniture, of rich and wonderful workmanship, would not have disfigured a pretty woman's boudoir. The count had dipped his finger in the ink and written the word "Poisons" on each pane, in big black letters.

William was deeply touched at his father's cruel irony in preserving from all harm this cupboard and its contents. The whole life, the whole range of knowledge of the count was concentrated there, in a few phials of new poisons. He had destroyed his other discoveries, those which might have been useful, and out of his vast researches, out of the labours of his powerful mind, had bequeathed to humanity merely a few agents of suffering and death. This hit at learning, this sinister mockery, this disdain for mankind, this last avowal of sorrow, showed clearly what the death-agony of this man must have been, who after fifty years of study seemed to have found in his retorts nothing but the few drops of the drug with which he had poisoned himself.

William fell back to the door. Fright and disgust were driving him out. This filthy room, full of nameless rubbish, with its spider webs and its thick dust, exhaled a fetid odour which almost made him sick. The dirty heaps of broken bottles and old papers lying in the corners, seemed to him the filth of that science from which the count had estranged him, and which he seemed to have scornfully swept aside before dying, as one puts to the door a vile creature that one loves, with a contempt still full of longing desires. And as he opened the door of this poison cupboard, he fancied he could hear the pained laugh of the old chemist as he meditated for months on his suicide. Then, in the middle of the laboratory, he shuddered as he saw the narrow streak of blood which had come from his father's skull and trickled right under the stove. He could see too that this blood was beginning to clot.

Meantime the doctor was rummaging about. The moment he had crossed the threshold, he had understood all, and he had become really angry.

"What a man! what a man," he murmured. "He has destroyed everything, broken everything—Oh! if I had been there, I would have chained him up as a furious madman."

And turning towards William he went on:

"Your father was a very clever man. He must have made some wonderful discoveries. And see what he has left. It is madness, sheer madness—Can you understand it? A scholar who might have been a member of the Institute and yet preferred to keep to himself the result of his labours! Still, if I unearth one of his manuscripts, I will publish it, and it will be an honour both to him and myself."

He went and groped about among the heap of papers, regardless of the dust; but he soon began to moan:

"Nothing, not a single whole page. I never saw such a madman."

When he had visited the pile of papers, he passed on to the heap of broken bottles, and there continued to moan and cry out. He put his nose to the broken necks of the phials, sniffing, trying to discover the chemist's secrets. At last he came back to the middle of the room, furious at not having been able to learn anything. It was then that he noticed the cupboard containing the poisons. He rushed towards it with a shout of joy. But the key was not in the lock, and he had to be content with examining the phials through the panes.

"Sir," he said seriously, addressing himself to William, "I beg you as a favour to allow me to analyse these substances. I address this request to you in the name of science, in the name too of the memory of Monsieur de Viargue."

The young man shook his head, and pointing to the rubbish which strewed the floor, he replied:

"You see, my father has wished to leave no trace of his labours. Those phials shall remain there."

The doctor insisted, but he could not break his resolution. He began to walk round the laboratory again, more exasperated than ever. When he came to the streak of blood, he stopped and asked if this blood was Monsieur de Viargue's. When William replied in the affirmative, his face seemed to brighten. He bent down by the pool which had formed under the stove; then, with the tips of his nails, he tried, with delicate care, to detach a clot already almost dry. He hoped to be able, by submitting this blood to a minute analysis, to discover what poisonous agent the count had used.

When William understood for what object he was doing this, he advanced towards him with quivering lips, and, taking him by the arm, said to him in a peremptory tone:

"Come, sir, you can see very well that the place is stifling me—We must not disturb the peace of the dead. Let that blood alone. I insist on it."

The doctor left the clot with very bad grace. Urged on by the young man, he went out under protest. William, who had waited for him a moment with feverish impatience, breathed at last when he was in the passage. He shut the door of the laboratory, quite disposed to keep the oath which he had taken to his father never to set foot in it.

When he got downstairs, he found in the drawing-room on the ground-floor a magistrate from Véteuil. This gentleman explained to him, in a courteous tone, however, that he had come to put the seals on the deceased's papers, in case a legal will could not be shown him. He even had the delicacy to give the young man to understand that he was aware of the bond of relationship between him and the deceased, of his title of adoptive son, and to say that he did not doubt the existence of a will entirely in his favour. He ended his little speech with a gracious smile: this will would certainly be found in some drawer, but law was law, it might contain legacies of a private nature, and everybody must wait and see. William put a stop to his talk by showing him a will which left him sole legatee. The count had to wait for his son's majority in order to be able to adopt him and transmit to him his name; and as the adoption entailed the necessity of making his will, he had been allowed to treat his natural son as a legitimate child. The magistrate was full of excuses; he repeated that law was law, and withdrew, giving, with many bows, the name of Monsieur de Viargue to him whom a few minutes before he had addressed thoughtlessly as Monsieur William, though he must have known of the right which he had to assume the title of his adoptive father.

During the next few days, William was overwhelmed with duties. Not an hour was his own to think of his new position. On all sides, he was pestered with condolences, applications, and offers of service. At last he shut himself up in his room, requesting Geneviève to reply to the host of people who were importuning him. He left the management of his affairs entirely to her. The count, in his will, had left the old woman an income which would have permitted her to end her days in peace. But she was almost angry, refusing the money, saying that she would die on her legs and that she did not intend to give up her work. Really, the young man was very pleased to find some one who would relieve him of the material cares of life. His indolent and feeble disposition detested activity: the smallest annoyances of existence were for him big obstacles of vexation and disgust.

When at last he could find solitude, he was seized with sadness. His feverishness no longer buoyed him up, and he felt himself crushed by gloomy dejection. He had been able to forget for a few days the suicide of his father; now he thought of it again: he saw once more, in his ever-present thoughts, the laboratory wrecked and stained with blood, and the implacable remembrance of this sinister room brought with it, one by one, the cruel memories of his life. This recent drama seemed to him to be fatally connected with the long series of miseries which had already tortured him. He remembered with anguish his chance birth, his excited and terrified childhood, his boyhood of martyrdom, and his whole existence doomed to sorrow. And then his father must go and add to all this the horror of his violent death and the irony of his negations! The weight of all these sad circumstances pressing on the gentleness of this tender nature, was crushing its finer feelings and dismaying it in its need for affection and peace. William was stifling in this atmosphere heavy with sorrow which he had been breathing from the cradle; he was shrinking into himself, he was becoming more nervous, and more averse to action as events were bent on destroying his happiness. At last he looked upon himself as the victim of fate, and would have purchased the mournful tranquillity of forgetfulness at the price of any sacrifice. When he saw himself the possessor of a fortune, when he had to begin to play his part as a man, his hesitations and fears increased still more, for he knew nothing of the world, and he trembled before the future as he asked himself what new sorrows were awaiting him. During his hours of meditation, he felt a vague presentiment that his ways of life, the circumstances and surroundings in which he had grown up, were going to thrust him to the bottom of some gulf, the moment he ventured to take a step.

He thought himself very wretched, and this redoubled his love for Madeleine, and he began to think of her with a sort of religious devotion. She alone, he thought, knew his worth and loved him according to his deserts. Yet if he had examined himself more closely, he would have found within him a secret dread of that intimacy with a woman of whose past he was ignorant; he would have told himself that this again was one of the fatalities of his existence, one of the consequences of the circumstances which were influencing his life. Perhaps he would have even recoiled had he called to mind the history of his own mother. But he felt such a need of being loved, that he rushed blindly into the passion for the only being who had yet given him a few months of tenderness and peace. He wrote long letters to Madeleine every day, bewailing his loneliness and assuring her that their separation would soon cease. One moment, he resolved to go again and shut himself up with his mistress in the little house in Rue de Boulogne: then he bethought himself of the miserable days they had spent there, and he was afraid of never again finding their by-gone happiness. Next day, he wrote to the young woman begging her to come at once and join him at Vétenil.

Madeleine was delighted at this arrangement. She too dreaded the solitude of their little house, filled as it was with James's memory. During the fortnight that she had been living there alone, she had been wretched. The very first night, she had hidden the portrait of the man whose memory never left her; for by keeping it constantly in sight in her bedroom, now that she was free, she would have thought each night that she was surrendering herself to a phantom. She even felt angry sometimes with William for leaving her like that in a house inhabited by her former lover. It was with unfeigned joy that she shut the door of the little house, for it seemed as if she was imprisoning James's spectre within its walls.

William was waiting for her at Mantes. He led her a little way from the station to explain to her the plans of their new life. She was to appear as if she had come to make a short stay in the country, and he would pretend to let her the summer residence situated at the extremity of the park; there, he would come to see her whenever she wished. Madeleine shook her head; the idea of living yet with her lover was repugnant to her, and she tried to think of good reasons for refusing the hospitality which he was offering her. At last she told him that they would not be so free by both living almost in the same house, that this would give rise to gossip and that it would be better a thousand times to let her go into some little house near La Noiraude. The young man perceived the wisdom of these reflections, as he thought of the scandal produced in the country in former days by the intimacy of the count with the notary's wife. It was decided then between them that he was to return by himself in the carriage that had brought him, and that she was to take the coach so as to arrive at Véteuil as a stranger. Directly she had taken a house, she would let William know.

Madeleine had the good fortune to find what she was looking for immediately. The proprietor of the hotel where she put up, had a sort of farm about a mile from La Noiraude; he had a plain house built there, and he was very sorry for it now, for he hardly ever lived there and he regretted the money that it had cost him. When the young woman, on the night of her arrival, spoke of her wish to stay in the district, provided she could find in the neighbourhood of the town a house that suited her, he offered to let her his. The next morning, he got her to visit it. It was a one-storied summer residence with four rooms; the rains of the preceding winter had hardly discoloured the white walls, against which were fastened the grey window shutters; the red tiles of the roof appeared quite gay among the trees; a quick-set hedge surrounded the few yards of private garden; and a little way off, at about a stone's throw, was the farm, a collection of long black buildings, where she could hear the crowing of cocks and the bleating of sheep. Madeleine was delighted with her find, the more so that the house was let furnished, which allowed her to take possession of it at once. She rented it on the terms of five hundred francs for the six summer months, calculating that she would still have enough to pay for her daily expenses herself. That night, she was settled in her new home. She hummed a tune as she emptied her trunks, and she felt inclined to laugh and skip like a child. Since she had seen the little house with the red roof and grey shutters, white and smiling among the green leaves, she had kept saying to herself: "I feel that I shall be happy here in this secluded nook."

About nine o'clock, she had a visit from William to whom she had written in the morning. She did the honours of her house with a sort of joyous playfulness, taking him into every corner, not even forgetting a cupboard. She even wanted him to visit the garden, although the night was very dark. "There," she said with a look of pride, "there, I have strawberries; there, violets; here, I think I saw radishes." William could distinguish nothing; but, in the shadow, he had his arm round Madeleine's waist, he was kissing her bare arms, and laughing at her smiles. When they got to the end of the garden the young woman went on in a grave tone: "Just here, I saw a big gap in the hedge; this is the way you must come in every day, sir, so as not to compromise me." Then she insisted on the young man trying to see if he could get through the gap. It was long since the lovers had enjoyed such a pleasant time together.

Madeleine had not been mistaken; her life in this secluded spot was to be a happy one. It seemed as if a new love was filling her heart, a school girl's open smiling love. James's portrait was forgotten in the house in the Rue de Boulogne, where she had shut it up with all the painful memories of the years that were dead. At times, she would fancy that she had hardly left the boarding school, so joyous and free from anxiety did she feel. What charmed her most, was the thought of being at last in a home of her own; she would say: "My house, my room," with childish glee; she did the house-keeping, calculated the cost of the dishes that she ate, and became quite concerned if the price of eggs and butter went up. William had never made her so happy as on the days when he accepted her invitations to dinner; on these days, she forbade him to bring even fruit from La Noiraude, she wanted to take all the expense on herself, and she felt a delight at being able to give now in her turn instead of receiving. Henceforth she could love William on equal terms, for her affection was free; the shame in the idea that she was a kept woman could no longer shock the pride of her nature, and her heart expanded, without any relapse, at the sudden thought of her situation. When William came, she would throw her arms round his neck, while her smile, her look, and her unconstraint would say, "It is a free surrender of myself, there is no selling now."

Here was the explanation of the new affection of the lovers. William was surprised and delighted at thus finding in Madeleine a phase of her character which he had not known before. Hitherto she had been his mistress; now she had become his sweetheart. That is to say, that

ÉMILE ZOLA

hitherto he had loved her at his own house, now he went to pay her his addresses at hers. This difference was the key-stone of their happiness. Unconsciously, he was less free in the little cottage at Véteuil than he had been in the house in the Rue de Boulogne; he no longer felt himself master of the house and he was more grateful for the kisses which Madeleine allowed him to take. There was less coarseness in their intimacy; he experienced a sort of delicious restraint which redoubled his pleasures by giving them a new and delicate charm. His mind, prone to respectful love, enjoyed with exquisite relish the delicate touches of their now situation. There was a sensation of pleasure in visiting a woman as the lover of her choice; and he found in this house an unknown perfume of elegance and grace, and a genial warmth which was wanting at La Noiraude. Then he had to go there stealthily, for fear of malicious tongues; he went across country, tramping through ploughed fields, getting his feet wet in the dew on the grass, as happy as a truant scholar; when he thought somebody was looking at him, he would pretend to be gathering herbs, stooping down for flowers and grasses; then he would walk on again, looking round anxiously and breathless, happy already in the thought of his coming joys; and when he got to the garden, when he had crept like a burglar through the hole in the hawthorn hedge, he would throw his posy of wild flowers into Madeleine's skirt who was waiting for him to take him straight to the house, where she would present him at last her lips and cheeks, far from prying eyes. This little adventure, this walk, and the kiss of welcome became more charming to him every day. Had he been more free, he would perhaps have tired of it sooner.

And when they had shut the door, William would take a singular delight in telling himself that his happiness was unknown to everybody. He looked on each visit as a charming adventure, as an appointed meeting with a staid maiden. He was completely forgetting the months they had spent in the Rue de Boulogne. Besides, Madeleine was a different woman; she no longer had her fits of dreaming, she was bright and lively, and still she loved him; she loved him secretly, like a lady with a character to think of; she received him in her bedroom with sudden blushes, in that bedroom where he simply paid his visits now, and where the peculiar fragrance caused him at each visit a deep-felt emotion. He had nothing of his own in this room, not even slippers.

This pleasant life lasted the whole of the summer. The days glided by in happy peacefulness. The lovers were full of mutual gratitude and affection for the bliss they were conferring on each other, just as formerly they had nearly quarrelled as they felt that they were making each other unhappy.

Madeleine had taken the little house about the middle of April. She knew nothing of the country except a few nooks in the neighbourhood of Paris. Life in the open fields, for a whole summer, was for her a life of delight and health. She saw the trees bloom and the fruits ripen, standing by with happy surprise at the working of the soil. When she came, the bright green leaves were still tender; the country, still moist with the rains of winter, was bursting into life beneath the vernal rays of the sun, with the charming grace of a child just waking from sleep; from the depths of these pale horizons there came a sort of breezy and virginal freshness to her heart. Then, the caresses of the zephyrs became warmer, the leaves grew darker, the soil became a woman, an amorous and fruitful woman whose womb trembled with a mighty pleasure in the pangs of maternity. Madeleine, strengthened and soothed by the warmth of spring, felt the heat of the summer fill her with energy and give a steady strong flow to the blood in her veins. She thus found, in the sunshine, peace and vigour; she resembled one of those shrubs which though battered by the winter winds spring up again, which become young in order to grow afresh and unfold in the vigour of their foliage.

She felt a need of the free air, a love for the open sky which made her delight in long walks. Nearly every day she went out, and walked for miles and miles without ever complaining of fatigue. Usually, she met William in a little wood through which ran the brook where her lover had in former days hunted for crawfish. When they met each other, they walked away gently on the soft grass, hidden by the trees on both sides, ascending a sort of valley concealed by foliage and refreshingly cool. At their feet flowed the brook, a silver streak gliding noiselessly over the sand; here and there were little waterfalls whose crystal tones seemed as though they proceeded from a shepherd's flute. And, on both sides, rose the big tree-trunks, like the shafts of fantastical pillars, eaten away with a leprosy of moss and ivy; among these trunks, briars had sprung up, throwing out to one another their long prickly arms, and forming green walls which enclosed the valley and turned it into an interminable path of foliage. Above their heads, the vault was peopled with wrens, like big humming flies; in places, the branches became more open, which permitted them to catch a glimpse, through this green verdure, of the blue sky. William and Madeleine loved this secluded valley, this natural bower whose end they could never discover; they forgot themselves for hours as they followed its windings; the coolness of the water and the silence of the trees filled them with exquisite delight. With their arms round each other's waists, they clasped each other more closely in the hollows where the shade became thicker. At times they would play like children, running after one another, getting entangled in the briars and slipping on the grass. Suddenly Madeleine would disappear; she had hidden behind a bush; then her lover, who clearly saw a bit of her bright skirt, would pretend to hunt for her with an uneasy look; then, with a sudden spring, he would catch her and hold her on the ground, shaking with laughter, in his arms.

Sometimes, Madeleine would declare that she felt cold, and that she wanted to walk in the sun; the shade always became oppressive to her vigorous nature. Then they would go into the sun, the hot July sun. They would stride over the wall of briars and find themselves at the edge of immense corn-fields, undulating in bright waves right to the horizon, and lulled to rest in the heat of the mid-day sun. The atmosphere was sweltering. Madeleine walked comfortably in this burning furnace; she took a delight in letting the sun scorch her neck and bare arms; somewhat pale, her forehead beaded with little drops of perspiration, she revelled in the caresses of the orb of day. It gave her new strength, she said, when she was tired; she felt better under the crushing weight of the burning sky which pressed lightly on her strong shoulders. But William suffered a good deal from this heat; so when she saw him panting, she led him into the shady walk again, by the side of the clear cool brook.

Then they would resume their delightful walk, finding a fresh charm in this silence and coolness which they had left for a moment. Thus they came to a sort of amphitheatre where they usually stopped and rested. The valley grew broader, the brook formed a little lake with a surface as smooth as glass, the line of trees made a gentle curve, disclosing a broad belt of sky. It might have been thought a room made of verdure. At the edge of the pool grew tall waving reeds; then a carpet of grass was spread beneath the feet, reaching from the water to the foot of the trees, where it lost itself in the tall underwood which surrounded the opening with an impenetrable wall. But the charm of their wild and pleasant retreat was a spring which gushed from a rock; the enormous block, covered at the summit with over-hanging briars, projected out at the top a little, forming at its foot a sort of cavern filled with a pale blue tint; the slender stream glided, with the easy motion of an adder, from the further end of this grotto with its walls covered with climbing plants and oozing with moisture. William and Madeleine would sit here, listening to the drops as they fell one by one in regular cadence from the roof; there was in this sound an endless lullaby, a vague sensation of sleep and eternity which harmonised with their happy love. Gradually, they ceased to talk, overcome by the monotony of the continual music of the drops of water, fancying that they could hear the beating of their hearts, dreaming and smiling, hand in hand.

Madeleine always brought some fruit. She would forget her musing, and eat her supplies with hearty appetite, giving her lover a bite of her peaches and pears. William was enraptured to see her by him; each day, her beauty seemed more dazzling; he watched, with admiring surprise, the development of health and strength which the fresh air was imparting to her. The country was really making her another woman. She even seemed to have grown. Full of health and vigour and endowed with strong limbs, she had become a powerful woman, with a broad chest and a clear laugh. Her skin, though slightly tanned, had not lost its transparency. Her gold-red hair, carelessly tied up, fell on her neck in a thick glowing coil. Her whole body gave evidence of superb vigour.

William never grew tired of gazing at this healthy being, whose calm lusty kisses soothed his own feverishness. He felt that a supreme serenity was reigning in her; she had recovered her strength of will, she lived without agitation, obeying the native simplicity of her being; these surroundings of solitude and bright sunshine suited her, under their influence she was unfolding in grace and strength, becoming what she always would have been had her need for esteem and tranquillity been satisfied. During the long hours that they spent at the Spring, the name they had given to their retreat, William would gaze on Madeleine as she lay stretched on the ground, her neck all red with the reflection of her hair; he would trace, beneath her light dress, the firm lines of her limbs, and at times he would raise himself up to take her in his arms in a clasping embrace, with a sudden pride of possession. Still there was nothing of the animal in his love; it was calm and chaste.

On the days that the lovers did not visit the spring, they would drive out a few miles in a carriage, then leave their conveyance at some inn and tramp the country wherever the roads took them. They only chose the narrowest lanes, those that would lead them to the unknown.

ÉMILE ZOLA

When they had walked for hours, between two hedges of apple-trees, without meeting a living soul, they were as happy as marauders who had escaped the eye of the keeper. These broad Norman plains, rich and monotonous, seemed to them the image of their tranquil affection; they never grew tired of the same horizons of meadows and corn-fields. They would often ramble in the fields or visit the farms. Madeleine loved domestic animals; a brood of chickens pecking round their mother as she clucked and spread out her wings, would amuse her for a whole afternoon; she would go into cattle-sheds to stroke the cows; the young skipping kids filled her with delight; all the little denizens of a poultry yard held her charmed and filled with a longing desire to have at her own home hens, ducks, pigeons, and geese; and had not William's smile checked her, she would never have returned to Véteuil without carrying back some little animal or other in her skirts. She had another passion too, a passion for children; when she saw one rolling in a farm yard, on a midden, among the poultry, she would gaze at him in silence, somewhat pensively, with a softened smile; then, as if drawn to him, she would go up and take the little urchin in her arms, regardless of his face all smeared with dirt and jam. She would ask for milk, keeping hold of the child until she was served, making him skip and calling her lover to admire the dear creature's large eyes. When she had drank her milk, she would withdraw regretfully, turning round and casting a last glance on the child.

Autumn came. Dark clouds crossed the leaden sky driven on by icy winds; the fields were going to repose. The lovers wished to pay one last visit to the spring. They found their retreat very desolate. A shower of yellow leaves lay strewn on the grass; the walls of verdure were falling down; the amphitheatre, exposed to all beholders, was now only formed by the slender trunks of the trees whose branches stood out in rueful nakedness against the grey sky. The little lake and the spring itself were muddy, troubled by the last storm. William could see that winter was approaching, and that their walks would have to cease. He mused sadly on this death of summer as he looked at Madeleine. The young woman, seated in front of him, full of thought, was breaking the bits of dead branches with which the turf was strewn.

Since the previous night William had been thinking of proposing to his mistress to marry her. This idea of immediate marriage had occurred to him in a farm, as he had seen Madeleine fondling one of those little darlings that she adored. He had thought that if she should ever become enceinte, he would have a bastard for his son. The memories of his childhood always frightened him at this word bastard.

Besides, everything was tending without gainsay to marriage. As he used to say in the old days to James, he was fated to love one woman only, the first he met; he was fated to love her with his whole being, and to cling to this love, out of hatred of change, out of terror for the unknown. He had been lulled to rest in Madeleine's affection: now that he was warm, now that he was comfortable in this affection, he intended to stay there for ever. His inert mind and his gentle nature delighted in thinking. "I have a resting-place where I have taken refuge for life." Marriage would simply legalise an union which he already looked upon as eterna.

The thought that he might have a son only made him desirous of hastening an end that he had foreseen. Then, winter was coming, he would be cold, all alone in his big deserted château; he would no longer spend his days in the warm breath of his loved one. During these long cold months, he would have to run in the rain as he went to knock at Madeleine's door. What a happy warmth, on the contrary, if they lived in the same house! They would spend the days of bad weather in the chimney corner; they would pass their chilly honey-moon in a warm recess, which they would only leave in the following spring, to return to the sunlight. And there was too, in his resolution, the desire to love Madeleine openly, and to confer on her a mark of esteem which should touch her heart. He thought he could foresee that they would suffer no more from their intimacy, that they would no longer hurt each other's feelings, when there was a binding bond between them.

Yet at the bottom of the project which William fondly indulged in, there lay a vague feeling of dread which kept him uneasy, and hesitating. During the months of forgetfulness that they had just passed, he had never been a prey to the terrors about the future which the suicide of his father had awakened in him; events no longer crushed him; his love, after so many rebuffs, seemed to him a sovereign repose, a balm for his sufferings and fears. The fact was, he was living in the present, in the hours that glided by, bringing each its pleasure. But since he had begun to think of the future, the unknown in this future filled him with secret uneasiness. Perhaps he was trembling unconsciously on the brink of an eternal engagement with a woman whose history he did not know. Anyhow, he was full of conflicting thoughts, for his hesitations did not assume a definite form, while his heart urged him on to his project.

ÉMILE ZOLA

He had come to the spring, fully determined to speak. But the trees were so bare, the sky so gloomy, that he did not venture to open his lips, shivering at the first breath of winter. Madeleine was cold too; a kerchief on her neck, her feet well under her skirts, she was continuing to break the bits of dead branches on the turf, unconscious of what she was doing, gazing with a melancholy air at the clouds charged with rain that were silently drifting across the sky. At last, when it was time to return, William told her his project; his voice trembled a little and he seemed to be asking for a favour. Madeleine looked at him with a surprised, almost terrified air. When he had finished she said:

"Why not stay as we are? I don't complain, I am happy. We should not be any fonder of each other if we were married. Perhaps that would even spoil our happiness."

And as he was opening his lips to insist, she added in a brief tone: "No, indeed. It makes me quite afraid."

And she began to laugh, in order to tone down the hardness and strangeness of her words. Even she herself was surprised at having uttered them and with such stress. The truth was that William's proposal caused her a singular feeling of revolt; it seemed to her that he was asking for something impossible, as if she were not her own mistress and already in the possession of another man. Her voice and gesture had been like that of a married woman requested by a lover to live with him as his wife.

The young fellow, almost hurt, would have perhaps withdrawn his offer, had he not thought himself bound now to plead the cause of their love. He grew warm as he spoke, forgetting gradually the oppression of heart that he had felt at the point blank refusal of his mistress, and he melted into gentle and endearing words as he drew a picture of the calm and happy life they would lead when they were married. For some minutes, he thus poured forth his heart in his words, bending over Madeleine in an attitude of prayer and adoration.

"I am an orphan," he said, "I have no one in the world but you. Don't refuse to link your life to mine, or I shall think that Heaven continues to persecute me with its anger, and I shall tell myself that you do not love me enough to wish to assure my happiness. Oh! if you knew how I need your affection! You alone have soothed me, you alone have opened to me a refuge in your arms. And today I know not how to thank you; I offer you everything that I have, which is nothing in comparison with the happy hours you have given me and will give me again. Come now, I feel that I shall always be your debtor, Madeleine. We love one another, and marriage cannot increase our affection; but it will permit us to adore each other openly. And what a life ours will be! a life of peace and pride, a confidence without bounds for the future, an affection constant in the present. Madeleine, I implore you."

The young woman listened, as if seized with distressing thoughts, with a curbed impatience which gave to her lips the appearance of a peculiar smile. When her lover could find nothing more to say and stopped, with a choking sensation in his throat from the emotion which was overpowering him, she sat silent for a moment. Then in an unfeeling tone, she exclaimed:

"You cannot however marry a woman of whose past you know nothing. I must tell you who I am, where I came from, and what I have done before knowing you."

William was already on his feet and putting his hand on her mouth.

"Don't say a word!" he answered with a sort of terror. "I love you, and I want to know nothing more. Come now, I know you quite well. You are perhaps better than I am; you certainly have more will and strength. You can't have done wrong. The past is dead; I am speaking to you of the future."

Madeleine was struggling in his clasping embrace of supreme tenderness and absolute faith. When she could speak she said:

"Now listen, you are a child, and I must argue for you. You are rich, you are young, and some day you will reproach me for having accepted your offer too hastily. As for myself, I have nothing, I am a poor girl! but I am anxious to keep my pride, and I should not like you to turn round and accuse me later on of having entered your house as a fortune-hunter. You see, I am frank. I can make you an adorable mistress; but if I were to become your wife, you would say to yourself next day that you ought to have married a girl with a better dowry and more worthy of you than myself."

If Madeleine had wished to make William more in earnest, she could not have devised a better method. The suppositions that she was making almost made him weep. Now he had the anger of a child, and swore to overcome his mistress's resistance at all cost.

"You don't know me, Madeleine," he exclaimed, "and you hurt my feelings. Why do you talk like that? Are you not aware what I have been thinking of and dreaming of, for the whole year that we have been living together? I should like to go to sleep on your breast and never awake. You know very well that that is the desire of my whole being; you do wrong to think that my thoughts are like other men's. I am a child, you say; ah well! so much the better! you can't be afraid of a child who trusts in you."

He went on in a gentler tone, and fell again into his tender beseeching accents. He spoke so much that his heart was full. Madeleine was giving way. She was touched by this trembling voice which was offering her so humbly the pardon and the esteem of the world. Yet, deep in her heart, there still continued the vague feeling of revolt. When her lover wound up by saying, "You are free, why refuse me this happiness," she gave a sudden start.

"Free," she replied in a strange voice, "yes, I am free."

"Well!" added William, "say nothing more of the past. If you have loved before, that love is dead, and I am marrying a widow."

Madeleine was struck by this word widow, and became slightly pale. Her hard brow and grey eyes had an expression of painful anxiety.

"Let us go back," she said, "night is coming on. I will give you an answer tomorrow."

They went back. The sky had become dark, and the wind was howling mournfully in the trees that overhung the path. When William left Madeleine, he pressed her silently to his heart. He could find no words to say to her, and he wished to take possession of her being by this last embrace.

Madeleine passed a sleepless night. When she was alone, she reflected on her lover's proposal. The thought of marriage flattered her feelings, and yet caused her a sort of terrified surprise. A thought of this ceremony had never occurred to her. She had never ventured to indulge in such a dream. Then, as she thought of the calm and worthy life which William offered her, she was very much surprised at feeling so averse to it. At the recollection of the young man's endearing words, she felt ashamed of having shown so much unfeelingness: she asked herself what secret thought had induced her to refuse such an union, which she ought to have accepted with humility and gratitude. Why those fears, those doubts? Was she not free as William had said? What necessity was making her disdain the unexpected happiness which was coming to her? She became bewildered in these questions, and could only feel herself troubled with a vague sense of disquietude. She could have given herself an answer, but it seemed foolish and ridiculous, and she avoided it. The truth was she was thinking of James. She had felt the memory of this man springing up again confusedly in her being, while her lover was speaking. But it could not be this memory which troubled her. James was dead, and she owed him nothing, not even a regret. By what right had he come to life again in her thoughts to remind her that she was his? The doubts which she felt now about her liberty irritated her deeply. Now that the phantom of her first lover stood before her, she struggled with him in the flesh, she wished to overcome him in order to show him that she was his no longer. And she had a consciousness, in spite of her disdainful smiles, that it was James alone who had been able to make her harsh towards William. This was monstrous, inexplicable. When these thoughts presented themselves clearly, in the night-mares of her sleeplessness, she made up her mind with all the impulsiveness of her nature, that she would silence the dead by marrying the living. Then she fell asleep at day-break. She dreamed that the shipwrecked man was rising out of the livid waves of the sea, and coming to snatch her from her husband's arms.

When William came in the morning, trembling and anxious, he found Madeleine still asleep. He took her gently in his arms. Madeleine awoke with a start and threw herself on his bosom, as if to take refuge there and tell him; "I am thine." Then came the long kisses, and the passionate embraces. They both seemed to feel a need of abandoning themselves to each other's caresses, to each other's arms, so as to be convinced of the strength of their union.

That afternoon, William went to arrange about the formalities of the marriage. When, at night, he announced to Geneviève that he was going to marry a young lady in the neighbourhood, the protestant looked at him with her malicious eyes, and said:

"That will be better."

He saw that she knew everything. People had no doubt noticed him with Madeleine, and gossip travelled fast in the country, Geneviève's remark made him hasten the wedding-day. A few weeks were enough. The lovers were married at the beginning of winter, almost secretly. Five or six inquisitive Véteuil folks alone watched them enter their carriage as they left the mayoralty and the church. When they were back at La Noiraude, they thanked their witnesses and shut themselves up. They were at home, united for life.

ÉMILE ZOLA

VI

The four years that followed were calm and happy. The newly-married couple spent them at La Noiraude. They had made plans, the first year, for travelling: they had wished to air their love in Italy or on the banks of the Rhine, as is the fashion. But they always held back at the moment of starting, finding it useless to go and seek so far away for a happiness which they had at home. They did not even pay a single visit to Paris. The memories which they had left in their little house in the Rue de Boulogne, filled them with uneasiness. Shut up in their beloved solitude, they thought themselves protected against the miseries of this world and defied sorrow.

William's existence was one of unmixed bliss. Marriage was realising the dream of his youth. He lived an unchequered life, free from all agitation, a round of peace and affection. Since Madeleine had come to live at La Noiraude, he was full of hope, and thought of the future without a fear. It would be what the present was, a long sleep of affection, a succession of days like these and equally happy. His restless mind must have this assurance of uninterrupted tranquillity: his dearest wish was to arrive at the hour of death like this, after a stagnant existence, an existence free from events, an existence of one unbroken sentiment. He was at rest, and he felt an aversion to quit this state of repose.

Madeleine's heart too was at rest. She was enjoying a delicious repose from the troubles of her past in the calm of her present life. There was nothing now to hurt her. She could respect herself, and forget the shame of the past. Now she shared her husband's fortune without scruple, and reigned in the house as legitimate wife. The solitude of La Noiraude, of this huge building, all black and ruinous, pleased her. She would not allow William to have the old house done up in modern fashion. She simply permitted him to repair an apartment on the first floor, and the dining and drawing-rooms down stairs. The other rooms remained closed. In four years they never once climbed the staircase to the attics. Madeleine liked to feel all this empty space round her; it seemed to isolate her all the more, and protect her against harm from without. She took a pleasure in forgetting everything in the spacious room on the ground floor: a silence which calmed her seemed to fall from the lofty ceiling, and the dark corners of the room made her dream of immensities of peaceful shade. At night, when the lamp was lit, she was deeply soothed at the thought of being alone, and so small in the midst of this infinity. Not a sound came from the country: the secluded sanctity of a cloister, that seclusion one finds in a sleepy province, seemed to have settled on La Noiraude. Then Madeleine's thoughts would recur at times to one of the noisy evenings she had passed in the Rue Soufflot with James; she would hear the deafening rumble of the carriages on the pavement in Paris, she would see the harsh glare of the gas-lamps, and she would live again, for a second, in the little hotel-apartment full of the fumes of tobacco, chinking of glasses, bursts of laughter and kisses. It was only a flash, like a whiff of warm and nauseous air coming right into her face, but she would look round, terrified, stifling already. And then she would breathe freely again as she found herself in the sombre and deserted big room: she would awake from her bad dream, trustful and comforted, to bury herself once more with greater pleasure, in the silence and shade around her. How sweet this placid life was for her straightforward and cold nature, after the agitations of the flesh to which fate had exposed her! She would thank the cold ceiling, the dumb walls and all this building which enveloped her in a winding-sheet: she would stretch out her hands to William, as if to return thanks to him: he had brought her true joy by restoring to her her lost dignity, he was her beloved deliverer.

They thus passed their winters in almost complete solitude. They never left the drawing-room on the ground-floor, a big fire of logs of wood blazed in the huge fireplace, and they stayed there the whole day long, spending each hour alike. They led a clock-work life, clinging to their habits with the obstinacy of people who are perfectly happy and fear the least agitation. They hardly did anything, they never grew weary, or at least the feeling of gloomy weariness in which they indulged seemed to them bliss itself. Yet, there were no passionate caresses, no pleasures to make them forget the slow march of time. Two lovers will shut themselves up sometimes, and live for a season in each other's arms, satisfying their desires and turning days into nights of love. William and Madeleine simply smiled on each other, their solitude was chaste; if they shut themselves up, it was not because they had kisses to conceal, it was because they loved the still silence of the winter, the tranquillity of the cold. It was enough for them to live alone, side by side, and to bestow on each other the calm of their presence.

Then, directly the fine days came, they opened their windows and went down to the park. Instead of isolating themselves in the huge

ÉMILE ZOLA

room, they would hide in some thicket. There was no change. In this way they lived in the fine weather, wild and retired, shunning the noise. William preferred winter, and the warm moist atmosphere of the hearth, but Madeleine was always passionately fond of the sunshine, the blazing sunshine which scorched her neck and made her pulse beat steady and strong. She would often take her husband into the country, they would go and revisit the spring, or follow the open space by the brook reminding each other of their walks in the days gone by, or they would visit the farms again, rambling about, striking into the fields, far away from the villages. But the pilgrimage they loved best was to go and spend the afternoon in the little house where Madeleine had lived. A few months after their marriage, they had bought this house, for they could not bear the idea of its not belonging to them, and they felt an unconquerable desire to go in, whenever they passed by it. When it was theirs, their minds were at rest, and they said to themselves that no one could enter and drive away the memories of their affection. And when the air was mild, they used to go there nearly every day, for a few hours. It was like their country-house, although it was only ten minutes' walk from La Noiraude. Their life there was even more solitary than at La Noiraude, for they had given orders that they were never to be disturbed. They sometimes even slept there, and on these nights they forgot the whole world. Often would William say:

"If any calamity ever overtakes us, we will come here and forget it; here we shall be proof against suffering."

In this way the months glided by, in this way season succeeded season. The first year after their marriage, a joyful event had happened—Madeleine had given birth to a daughter. William welcomed with profound gratitude this child which his lawful wife, and not his mistress, as might have happened, had presented to him. He saw in this retardation of maternity a kind design on the part of Heaven. Little Lucy peopled their solitude herself. Her mother, strong as she was, could not suckle her herself, and she chose for her nurse a young woman who had been in her service before her marriage. This woman, whose father managed the farm by the little house, thus suckled the child quite close to La Noiraude. The parents used to go to inquire about her every day, and later on, when Lucy had grown, they would leave her for weeks at the farm, where she used to like to stay and lived a healthy life. There they would see her every afternoon, when they went to seclude themselves in their little house. They would take her with them, enjoying an exquisite pleasure in surrounding this little fair head with their happy memories. The dear girl gave a perfume of childhood to the little rooms where they had loved each other, and they would listen to her prattle with melting affection, in their meditation on the past. When they were all three together in their retreat, William would take Lucy with her laughing rosy lips and blue eyes on his knees and say gently:

"Madeleine, here we have the present and the future."

Then the fond mother would smile serenely on them both. Maternity had given the finishing touch to the equilibrium of Madeleine's temperament. Up to that time, she had retained her girlish impulsiveness, and her young woman's amorous gestures; her golden hair fell down her back in wanton freedom; her hips were too obtrusive in their movements, and in her grey eyes, or on her red lips would play bold expressions of desire. Now, her whole being had toned down, and marriage had imparted to her a sort of precocious maturity; there was a slight rotundity in her figure, her movements were more gentle and dignified; her golden-hair, carefully tied up, was now merely a charming token of strength, a vigorous setting for the picture of her now calm face. The girl was giving place to the mother, to the fruitful woman, settled in the plenitude of her beauty. What especially gave to Madeleine her dignified bearing, her noble expression of peace and health, her complexion clear and smooth as tranquil water, was the internal contentedness of her being. She felt herself free, she lived proud and satisfied with herself; her new existence was a suitable atmosphere in which her better part was rapidly developing. Before this, during the first few months that she had spent in the country, she had expanded in joy and strength; but then she had not been free from a something that seemed coarse, and this coarseness was now being transformed into serenity.

Madeleine's smiling vigour was a great solace for William. When he pressed her to his heart, he felt invigorated with a share of her strength. He loved to lay his head on her bosom, to listen to the steady beat of her heart. It was this beat which regulated his life. A fiery and nervous woman would have put him into a state of keen anguish, for his body and mind shrunk from the slightest shock. Madeleine's regular and steady breathing on the contrary strengthened him. He was becoming a man. His timid weakness was now simply gentleness. His young wife had absorbed him: he was now a part of her. As happens in every

ÉMILE ZOLA

union, the strong nature had taken undisputed possession of the weak one, and henceforth William was hers who ruled him. He was in her power in a strange way, in a way which affected his whole being. He was continually influenced by her, subject to her joys and sorrows, following her in each change of her nature. His own identity was disappearing, and he could no longer assert himself. He would have wished to revolt against thus being led captive by Madeleine's will. But from henceforth his tranquillity depended on this woman, and her life was irrevocably destined to become his. If she was at peace, he too would live in peace; if she became agitated, his agitation would be as strong as hers. It was a complete fusion of body and mind.

Besides, a broad peaceful future was opening before them, and the husband and wife could look forward to it without fear. The four years of bliss were removing from their minds all apprehension of calamity. William was contented to abandon himself to Madeleine's will, and to feel himself breathing freely, and growing stronger in this submission; he would say to her sometimes with a smile: "It is you Madeleine who are the man." Then she would kiss him, half-abashed at this power which she was acquiring, in spite of herself, by the force of her character. Had you seen them going down to the park, with little Lucy between them, each holding one of her hands, you could not have failed to guess the happy serenity of their union. The child was like a bond which united them. When she was not with them, William seemed almost timid by Madeleine's side; but there was so much affection in their lingering gait, that the thought of an event to mar the happiness of these two smiling beings would never have occurred to anyone.

During these first years of their married life, they received very few visitors. They knew scarcely anybody, and were slow to form connections, having no love for new faces. Their most frequent guests were two neighbours, Monsieur de Rieu and his wife, who lived in Paris during the winter, and came to spend the summer at Véteuil. Monsieur de Rieu had formerly been the most intimate friend of William's father. He was a fine old gentleman, of aristocratic bearing, stiff and ironical; his pale lips were at times lit up by a faint smile, a smile that looked as sharp as a blade of steel. Almost completely deaf, all the keenness of the wanting sense had concentrated in his look. He saw the smallest things, even those that went on behind him. Yet, he seemed to see nothing, his proud bearing never relaxed; not a crease in his lips would show that he had seen or heard. On entering a house, he would sit down in an arm-chair, and stay there for hours together, as if absorbed in his eternal silence. He would throw his head back, never relaxing the rigidity of his features, and half close his eyes as if asleep: the truth was, he was carefully following the conversation, and studying the smallest play of features on the faces of the speakers. This amused him wonderfully; he took a savage delight in this pastime, noting the coarse and wicked thoughts that he fancied he could detect on the faces of these people who looked on him as a post, before which they could without fear confide to each other the most important secrets. For him, smiles, and pretty delicate expressions did not exist; he had no eye for anything but grimaces. As he could hear no sounds, he thought every sudden contraction, every playful turn of the features grotesque. When two people were talking in his presence, he watched them curiously, as if they were two animals showing their teeth. "Which of the two will eat the other," he would think. This continual study, this observation and this science of what he called the grimaces of features had given him a supreme contempt for mankind. Soured by his deafness, which he would not admit, he would tell himself sometimes that he was fortunate in being deaf and able to isolate himself in a corner. His pride of birth was turning into pitiless raillery; he appeared to think himself living in the midst of a race of wretched puppets, splashing in the dirt like stray dogs, crouching with a skulk at the sight of the whip, and worrying one another for a bone picked up on the dung-hill. His proud impassive face protested against the turbulence of other faces, and his keen-edged laughs were the bitter jeers of a man delighted with infamy, and disdaining to feel angry at brutes deprived of reason.

Yet he felt a little kindness towards the young couple; but this did not go so far as to disarm his derisive curiosity. When he came to La Noiraude, he looked at his young friend William, with a certain amount of pity; the latter's attitude of adoration in Madeleine's presence did not escape his notice, and this spectacle of a man at a woman's knees had always seemed to him monstrous. Still, the young couple, who talked but little, and on whose faces sat an expression of relative placidity, seemed to him the most sensible beings he had yet met, and his visit to them was always one of pleasure. His victim, the eternal subject of his bitter observation and mockery, was his own wife.

Hélène de Rieu, who nearly always accompanied him to La Noiraude, was a woman above forty. She was a little dumpy person, with an insipid fair complexion, and, to her great despair, slightly inclined to stoutness. Picture a chubby-cheeked doll transformed into a woman. Affected, with a passionate love for puerility, she had a quiverful of pouts, glances, and smiles; she played with her face as on an exquisite instrument, whose celestial harmony was to seduce everybody; she never allowed her features to remain at rest, hanging her head down in a languishing fashion, raising it to the sky with sudden feints of passion and poetry, turning it, nodding it, according to the exigencies of attack or defence. She made a vigorous resistance to age, which was bringing flesh and wrinkles: smeared with unguents and pomades, laced up in stays that choked the breath out of her, she fancied herself growing young again. These were only her follies; but the dear woman had vices. She looked on her husband as a dummy whom she had married to give herself a position in the world, and she thought she ought to be easily excused for never having loved him. "What! talk about love to a man who can't hear you!" she would say to her friends. And then she would put on the air of an unhappy and misunderstood woman. The truth was, she did not stint herself of consolation. Not wishing to forget the love phrases which she could not utter to Monsieur de Rieu, she rehearsed them to people who had good ears. She always selected lovers of a tender and delicate age, eighteen to twenty at the most. Her girlish tastes must have young fellows with rosy cheeks, who had not yet lost the odour of their nurses' milk. Had she dared, she would have debauched the collegians that she met, for there was in her passion for children, an appetite of shameful pleasure, a wish to teach vice, and to taste strange delights in the soft embraces of arms still weak. She was fastidious; she liked timid kisses, which tickled her cheeks without bearing a deep imprint. Thus she was always to be seen in the company of five or six young sparks; she hid them under her bed, in the wardrobes, everywhere where she could put them. Her happiness consisted in having half-a-dozen tractable lovers fastened to her skirts. She soon tired them out, changing them every fortnight, and living in a perpetual renewal of followers. You would have thought her a boarding-school mistress, dragging her pupils about. She was never without admirers, she got them anywhere, from that crowd of young idiots whose dream is to have a middle-aged married woman for a mistress. Her forty years, her silly girlish airs, her insipid white skin which repelled men of riper years, were an invincible attraction for the young rascals of sixteen.

In the eyes of her husband, Hélène was a singularly curious little machine. He had married her on a day that he felt bored, and he would have driven her away from his house the next, if he had thought her worth getting angry about. The laborious toil that this coquette made her physiognomy undergo, gave him the greatest pleasure, for he tried to find out the secret wheels that set the eyes and lips of this little machine in motion. This pale face, plastered with paint, which was never at rest, seemed to him a mournful comedy, with its winks, its contortions of the mouth, all its rapid and, to him, silent play. It was after a long contemplation of his wife, that he had come to the conclusion that humanity was composed of wicked and stupid marionettes. When he pried into the wrinkles of this aged doll, he discovered, beneath her grimaces, thoughts of infamy and foolishness which made him look on her as a creature that he ought to have whipped. Yet, he preferred to amuse himself by studying and despising her. He treated her as a domestic animal; her vices left him as indifferent as the caterwauling of a tabby-cat after a tom; setting his honour high above the shame of such a creature, he sat still, with superb disdain and cold irony, at the procession of young sparks marching into his wife's room. One might have thought that he took a pleasure in showing off his contempt for mankind, his denial of every virtue, by thus tolerating the vices that were taking place under his own roof, and by seeming to accept debauch and adultery as quite usual and natural things. His silence, his cruelly derisive smile said plainly: "The world is a vile hole of filth; I have fallen into it, and I have to live there."

Hélène did not stand on ceremony with her husband. She spoke to her lovers in his presence, in the most off-hand, familiar way, convinced that he could not hear her. Monsieur de Rieu could read these familiar expressions on her lips, and he then displayed an exquisite politeness to the young men, amusing himself at their embarrassment, and obliging them to shout gracious answers into his ears. He never manifested the slightest astonishment at seeing his drawing-room filled with new faces every month; he welcomed Hélène's boarders with a paternal good nature, which was a cloak to his terrible sarcasm. He asked them their ages, and made inquiries about their studies. "We are fond of children," he would often say, in a tone of bantering kindness. When the drawing-room was empty, he would complain of the way in which young people forget their elders. One day even, as his wife's court was not very well attended, he brought her a young fellow of seventeen, but he was hump-backed, and Hélène speedily dismissed him. Sometimes Monsieur de Rieu would be even more cruel still; he would hurriedly

　　　　　　　　　　　　　　　　ÉMILE ZOLA

enter his wife's room, and keep her panting for an hour, talking to her about the fine weather or the rain, while some poor, simple creature was stifling under the bed-clothes, which had been hastily pulled over him at the unexpected entrance of the husband. The title, (title, by the way, which is found in every little town) of cuckolded husband was bestowed on him at Véteuil; having caught his wife in the very act with a collegian who had slipped out of bounds, he had simply said to this young lover, in his cold, polite voice: "Ah, sir, so young, and without being forced to it! you must be very courageous." But Monsieur de Rieu was not the man to thrust his nose into a place where he was likely to catch his wife at this sort of thing; he tried to appear blind as well as deaf; for this allowed him to preserve his haughty bearing, and his terribly calm attitude. What made his enjoyment more delicious, was the stupidity of his wife, who thought him simple enough not to suspect anything. He pretended to be a good-natured fellow, made scathing allusions with exquisite politeness, enjoying, like a connoisseur, the bitterness of the double-pointed words that he addressed to her, words the refined cruelty of which he alone understood. He played with this woman every hour, and would have been really annoyed if she had repented. At bottom, Monsieur de Rieu wished to know how far disdain can go.

There had been between this ironical nature and the disordered mind of Monsieur de Viargue, a sort of sympathy which explained the previous friendship of the two old men. Both had reached the same degree of disdain and denial; the philosopher, as he thought he had put his finger on nothingness; the deaf man, as he fancied he had discovered, beneath the human mask, the mouth of a lewd beast. During the count's lifetime, Monsieur de Rieu was the only person who entered his laboratory, and they often spent a whole day there together. The suicide of the chemist did not appear to surprise his old friend. He came back the following year to La Noiraude, as unmoved as ever; only, he took the liberty of introducing his wife, accompanied by her young gentlemen.

William and Madeleine had been married a few months, when Hélène brought them her last conquest, a young fellow from Véteuil, whom she had taken into her house to while away the leisures of her residence in the country. This youth's name was Tiburce Rouillard: he was rather ashamed of the Rouillard, and very proud of the Tiburce. The son of a man who had been a cattle-dealer, and who was to leave him a pretty round sum, Monsieur Tiburce had an unbounded ambition: he was vegetating at Véteuil, and intended to go and push his way in Paris. Boorish, crafty, and capable of any act of cowardice likely to prove useful to him, he was already beginning to feel his strength. He was of those scamps who say to themselves, "I am a millionaire ten times over," and who always end by getting their ten millions. Madame de Rieu, when she took him in his youth, had thought, as usual, that she was taking a child in hand. The truth was, the child was already steeped in vice; if he pretended ignorance and timidity, it was because he had an interest in showing himself ignorant and timid. Hélène had at last found a master. Tiburce, who had seemed to throw himself thoughtlessly in her way, had long calculated his thoughtlessness. He told himself that an intimacy with such a woman, carefully worked, would take him to Paris, where she would open every door to him; he made himself indispensable to the debauched appetites of his mistress; whether she would or not he would make her the instrument of his fortune the day he had her under his thumb as a submissive slave. If this scheme had not been the motive of his actions, he would have burst out laughing in Hélène's face at their first meeting. This old woman, who had filthy tastes, and yet talked about the ideal, seemed to him a grotesque creature; her embraces took his breath away, but he was a youth with courage, who would have wallowed in a gutter, in order to pick up a twenty-franc-piece.

Madame de Rieu appeared delighted with her young friend. He charmed her as yet with his most delicate flattery and was remarkably docile. She had never found a candour more spiced with budding vice. She adored the rascal to such a degree that her husband had to take a thousand precautions so as not to catch them every minute with their arms round each other's necks. She trotted Tiburce out like a young dog, calling for him, and coaxing him with look and voice. When she introduced him to La Noiraude, he looked upon that as a first service that she was rendering him. He had been at the school at the same time as William, and had shown himself one of his most cruel tormentors: younger than William by two or three years, he took advantage of the latter's terrors as an outcast to enjoy the malicious delight of beating a boy bigger than himself. Today, he was sorry for this error of his youth: for he had laid it down as a maxim that people ought to beat the poor only, those whose services they are not likely to want in after life. Before becoming acquainted with Hélène, he had schemed in vain to get into La Noiraude. William hardly returned his salute. When his mistress had brought him in the folds of her skirt, he humbled himself to the dust in the presence of his former victim; he called him "De Viargue" without the Monsieur, laying stress on the aristocratic "de," just as formerly he had laid stress on the name Bastard which he had been so ready to cast in his face. His plan was to set up at Véteuil as a person living on familiar terms with the rich and noble in the country. He would not have objected besides to utilise William and Madeleine for his future career. He even tried to make love to the young wife: he knew, in an indistinct way, the history of her secret intimacy with William, which made him think her of easy virtue. If he had been able to seduce her, he would have had two women instead of one in his service. He dreamed already of turning their rivalry skilfully to account so as to stimulate their zeal and make them bid against each for his love. But Madeleine received his proposals with such disdain that be had to abandon his project.

The young couple saw with repugnance Tiburce Rouillard come to La Noiraude. There was, besides, at the bottom of this crafty nature, a provincial foolishness, and an obtrusive stupid pride which William could hardly tolerate. When the coxcomb called him his friend, with a sort of personal satisfaction, he could hardly resist his longing to show him the door. It would certainly have come to this, had he not been afraid of causing a scandal which would have affected Monsieur de Rieu. Madeleine and he then put up with the intrusion as patiently as they could. Besides, they scarcely had a thought for anything but the tranquillity of their affection, and they troubled their heads very little about their visitors and forgot them immediately the door was shut behind them.

Once a week, every Sunday, they were certain to see the three coming to spend the evening with them at La Noiraude. Hélène, leaning on Tiburce's arm, would come first; while Monsieur de Rieu followed with a serious, uninterested look. Then they all went down to the park; and it was a sight to see, under the arbour of foliage where they sat, the languishing looks of the lady and the respectful attentions of the young man. The husband, in front of them, watched them with half-closed eyes. By certain despicable and cruel smiles, which curled Tiburce's beardless lips, he had guessed the vile character and evil designs of this youth. His science, as an observer, told him that his wife had fallen into the hands of a master who would beat her some day. The drama promised to be a curious one, and he enjoyed beforehand the rupture that was to take place between these two puppets; he fancied he could see the claws on the yet caressing fingers of the lover, and he awaited the hour when Hélène would raise a cry of anguish as she felt these claws enter her neck. She would be punished by vice; she would tremble and humiliate herself at the feet of a child, she who had revelled so much in young flesh. Monsieur de Rieu, in his silent, sneering fashion, pondered over this vengeance which fate was sending him. At times, Tiburce's cold face with its aped affection almost frightened him too. He treated him with great cordiality and seemed to take care of him like a bull-dog that he was training to bite people.

Madeleine, who knew of Madame de Rieu's amours, always looked at her with a sort of astonishment. How could this woman live peaceably in her sins? When she asked herself this question, she really thought that she had to deal with a monster, with a diseased and exceptional creature. The fact is, Madeleine had one of those sound, cool temperaments which can only accept clearly-defined positions. If her feet had slipped into the mud for a moment, it was by accident, and she had long suffered from the effects of her fall. Her pride could never have become inured to the agitations of mind and the cruel wounds inflicted on the senses by adultery: she must live surrounded by esteem and peace, in an atmosphere where she could walk with her head erect. As she looked on Hélène, she could not help thinking of the fears with which she must be harassed when she was hiding a lover in her bed. As she was not passionate herself, she could not understand the keen charms of passion; she saw only its sufferings, the terror and the shame in the presence of the husband, the kisses, often cruel, of the lover, and the existence troubled at every hour by the affection and anger of these two men. Her open nature would never have accepted such an existence of baseness and falsehood, and she would have revolted against it at the first feeling of anguish. It is feeble characters and weak bodies that submit to blows, and end at last by building themselves a luxurious nest in anxiety itself, where they willingly go to sleep. As she looked at Hélène's sleek, shining face, Madeleine would think: "If I ever surrender myself to any other man than William, I will kill myself."

For four summers, the visitors came to La Noiraude. Tiburce's father had placed him with a lawyer and unfeelingly kept him at Véteuil, where the young fellow chafed bitterly at not being able to follow his mistress to Paris. Hélène was so touched by his grief, that on two occasions she passed several of the winter months at Véteuil; yet, each spring, she took him again with renewed eagerness, for the woman doted on him and found no other lover who satisfied her. Tiburce was beginning to feel a singular detestation for her. When she turned up, in the middle of December, he felt half disposed to turn a deaf ear to her, for he cared not a straw for her kisses that took his breath away, and was growing desperate at not being able to turn her to advantage. Four summers of useless love-making to this woman, who might have been his mother, had so irritated him, that he would, some day, have eased his feelings by insulting and beating her and then leaving her to chance, if the old cattle-dealer had not had the happy idea of dying from a fit. A fortnight afterwards, young Rouillard was on his way to Paris in the same compartment as Hélène, more respectful, more affectionate than ever, while Monsieur de Rieu carefully surveyed the couple through his half-closed eyes.

When the De Rieus were away, especially during the long winter nights, William and Madeleine found themselves alone with Geneviève. She lived with them on a footing of equality, sitting down at the same table, and occupying the same rooms. She was then ninety; still perfectly straight, though lanker and more bony, she had relaxed none of the gloomy fervour of her mind; her pointed nose, her sunken lips, and the wrinkles that seamed her face, gave to her appearance the harsh outlines and deep shadows of a sinister mask. At night, when the work of the day was over, she would come and sit in the room where the husband and wife were, she would bring her Bible with its iron clasps, open it wide, and, under the yellow light of the lamp, read through the verses in a sing-song undertone. She would read thus for hours together, with a dull continual murmur, broken only by the rustling of the leaves as she turned them over. In the silence, her droning voice seemed as though it were reciting the prayers for the dead; she drawled along in mournful lamentations, like the monotonous murmur of the waves. In the huge room one felt quite shivery at this hum which seemed to proceed from invisible mouths hidden in the gloom of the ceiling.

Some nights, Madeleine was seized with secret terror, as she caught a few words of Geneviève's reading. She chose for preference the gloomiest pages of the Old Testament, narratives of blood and horror, which excited her feelings and gave to her accents a sort of restrained fury. She spoke with implacable joy of the anger and of the jealousy of the terrible God, of that God of the Prophets, who was the only Deity she knew of; she would represent him crushing the earth at His will, and chastising with His cruel arm both beings and things. When she came to verses about murder and fire, her voice would proceed more slowly, in order that she might dwell with longer pleasure on the terrors of hell, and the displays of the unrelenting justice of Heaven. Her big Bible always showed her Israel prostrate and trembling at the feet of its Judge, and she would feel in her flesh the sacred shudder that shook the Jews, and in her excitement she would give stifled sobs, fancying that on her shoulders were falling the fiery drops of the rain of Sodom. At times, she would resume her reading in a sinister tone: she would condemn the guilty as Jehovah did; her pitiless fanaticism took a delight in casting sinners into the abyss. To smite the wicked, kill them, burn them, seemed to her a sacred duty, for she looked on God as an executioner, whose mission was to whip the impious world.

This hard-hearted woman filled Madeleine with dejection. She would become quite pale, as she thought of the year of her life that needed absolution. Pardon had come, and she had thought herself absolved by William's love and esteem, and now in the very midst of her peace she heard these inexorable words of chastisement. Had not God then blotted out her faults? Was she to remain till death crushed beneath the burden of the sin of her youth? Would she have to pay some day her debt of repentance? As these thoughts disturbed her peaceful life she would think of the future with secret disquietude; she grew alarmed at her present tranquillity, at this smooth water which fed her hope; abysses were forming perhaps beneath this clear peaceful surface, a breath would suffice to throw it into a raging storm and to engulf her in its cruel waves. The heaven which Geneviève disclosed to her eyes, this sombre tribunal of judges, this chamber of torture, where there were cries of agony and odours of burnt flesh, seemed to her like a vision of blood. In her early days, when she was at the boarding-school, she had been taught, at her first communion, that paradise was a delightful confectioner's shop, full of sweetmeats, distributed to the elect by white and pink angels. In after life, she had been amused at her girlish credulity, and she had never afterwards set foot in a church. Today she saw the confectioner's shop changed into a court of justice; she could no more believe in the eternal sweetmeats than in the eternal red fires of the fallen angels; but the mournful pictures which the disordered brain of the fanatic evoked, if they did not make her afraid of God, filled her with strange uneasiness as they caused her to think of her past life. She felt that the day Geneviève learnt her sin, she would condemn her to one of the punishments of which she spoke with such delight; strong

ÉMILE ZOLA

and proud in her life of purity, the old woman would be implacable. At times, Madeleine would fancy that Geneviève was looking at her in a fierce way; then she would hang her head; she would almost blush, and tremble like a guilty person who can hope for no pardon. While she could not believe in God, she had a belief in powers and fatal necessities. The old woman would stand erect, severe and unrelenting, pitiless and cruel, and declare to her: "You bear in you the anguish of your past existence. Some day this anguish will rise to your throat and strangle you." It seemed to her that fatality lived at La Noiraude, and surrounded her path, chanting mournful verses of penitence.

When she was alone with William, in their bedroom, she thought of her secret shudders of the evening, and spoke in spite of herself of the terror which the protestant caused her.

"I am a child," she said to her husband, with a forced smile, "Geneviève has frightened me today. She was muttering horrible things by the side of us. Could you not tell her to go and read her Bible somewhere else?"

"Nonsense!" William answered, laughing frankly, "that would vex her perhaps. She thinks she is assuring our salvation in giving us a share in her readings. However, I will ask her tomorrow to read not quite so loud."

Madeleine, seated on the edge of the bed, with a far-off look, seemed to see again the visions evoked by the fanatic. Her lips quivered with a slight movement.

"She spoke of blood and anger," she went on in a slow voice. "She does not possess the indulgent good nature of old age, she would be inexorable. How can she be so hard-hearted, when she lives with us, in our happiness, in our peace? Really, William, there are moments when this woman makes me afraid."

The young man continued to laugh.

"My poor Madeleine," he would say taking his wife to his arms, "you are nervous tonight. Come, get into bed, and don't have bad dreams. Geneviève is an old fool, and it is wrong of you to mind her gloomy prayers. It is all habit; formerly, I could not see her open her Bible without being terrified; now, I should feel something was wanting if she did not lull me with her monotonous murmur. Don't you feel greatly soothed, at night, as we sit lovingly in this silence, tremulous with complaints?"

"Yes, sometimes," replied the young wife, "when I don't catch the words, and her voice moves along like a breath of wind. But what stories of horror! what crimes and punishments!"

"Geneviève," William went on to say, "is a devoted creature; she saves us a great deal of trouble and annoyance by looking after everything in the château; she was with us when I was born and when my father was born too. Do you know that she must be more than ninety years old, and that she is still strong and straight? She will work till she is more than a hundred... You must try to like her, Madeleine; she is an old servant of the family."

Madeleine was not listening. She was rapt in an uneasy reverie. Then, with sudden anxiety, she asked:

"Do you think that Heaven never pardons?"

Her husband, surprised and saddened, then kissed her, as he asked her, in a voice touched with emotion, why she had doubts about pardon. She did not give a direct reply but murmured:

"Geneviève says that Heaven will have its reckoning of tears—There is no pardon."

This scene occurred several times. It was, however, the only trouble which disturbed the serenity of the young couple. In this way they passed the first four years of their marriage, in a seclusion scarcely disturbed by the visits of the De Rieus, and in a state of happiness, the smooth course of which even Geneviève's lamentations were powerless to trouble seriously. It would have taken a greater calamity than this to rack their hearts again.

It was at the beginning of the fifth year, in the early part of November, that Tiburce accompanied Hélène to Paris. William and Madeleine, certain of not being disturbed again, settled down to spend their winter in the large quiet room where they had already lived so peacefully for four seasons. At one time, they spoke of going to live in Paris in their little house in the Rue de Boulogne; but they put off this project to the following winter, as they did every year; they could not see any necessity for leaving Véteuil. For two months, from November to January, they lived their secluded life, enlivened by the prattle of little Lucy, who was now growing up. A peaceful tranquillity shed on them its balm, and they thought that they would never be disturbed in their bliss.

ÉMILE ZOLA

VII

About the middle of January, William had to go to Mantes. A matter of importance which could not very well be attended to by anybody but himself called him to this place, and was likely to keep him there the whole evening. He set off in a fly, telling Madeleine that he would be back, about eleven o'clock, so she waited up for him along with Geneviève.

After dinner, when the table was cleared, the protestant brought out her big Bible, as usual, and began to read a few pages here and there at random. Towards the end of the evening, the book opened at that touching narrative of the sinning woman pouring ointment on the feet of Jesus, who forgives her and tells her to go in peace. It was very seldom that the fanatic chose a passage from the New Testament, these stories of redemption, these parables full of tender and exquisite poetry could not satisfy the gloomy fervour of her mind. But this night, whether it was that she yielded to the fate that had opened the Bible at a passage full of compassion, or because she was touched by a vague and unconscious feeling of tenderness, she droned aloud the story of Mary Magdalen in a meditative, almost tender voice.

On the silence of the room fell the murmur of the words: "And, behold, a woman in the city, which was a sinner, when she knew that Jesus sat at meat in the Pharisee's house, brought an alabaster box of ointment, and stood at his feet behind him weeping, and began to wash his feet with tears, and did wipe them with the hairs of her head, and kissed his feet, and anointed them with the ointment."

Thus she went on, raising her voice, letting the verses fall one by one, slowly, like suppressed tears.

Up to this, Madeleine had done her utmost not to listen, for an evening spent in close company with the old woman frightened her. She was even glancing over a book, in the chimney corner, trying to busy herself in her reading, and waiting impatiently for William. The few words of Geneviève's sing-song that she caught in spite of herself, filled her with discomfort. But when the protestant began the story of the repentant and pardoned sinner, she raised her head and listened with eager emotion.

The verses were drawled out one by one, and Madeleine fancied that the big Bible was speaking about her, about her shame, her tears, and the fragrance of her affection. As the story unfolded, interrupted, so to speak, by deep sighs, sighs of remorse and hope, she gradually felt pervaded by a feeling of unspeakable tenderness. Sentence by sentence she followed the narrative, waiting with fervency for the last words of the Saviour. At last came the gracious promise that, inasmuch as she had loved greatly and shed bitter tears, Heaven would permit her to taste the joys of the redemption. She thought of her past life, of her intimacy with James, and the memory of this man which still, at times, caused her cheeks to burn, filled her now with but a tenderness of repentance. All the ashes of this love were cold, and a breath of compassion had now carried them away. Like the Magdalen, whose name she bore, she could live in the desert, and become purified in her love. It was a supreme absolution that she was receiving. If at times, as Geneviève had read, she had fancied she could hear invisible mouths, hidden in the gloom of the spacious room, threatening her with a terrible punishment, she thought, at this moment, that she could catch, from endearing voices, assuring words of pardon and bliss.

When the protestant came to the verse: "Then said Jesus to the woman, thy sins are forgiven," a smile of heavenly joy passed over Madeleine's lips. She felt her eyes filling with tears of gratitude and could not help telling Geneviève of all the happy feeling which she had just experienced.

"What a charming story that is," she said to her, "I am so pleased to have heard it—You shall read it to me again sometimes."

The fanatic had raised her head, and was looking at the young wife with her stern expression, without replying. She seemed surprised and displeased at her taste for the touching poems of the New Testament.

"How I prefer that narrative," Madeleine went on, "to the cruel pages that you nearly always read! Now you must confess that it is pleasant to grant pardon and pleasant to receive it. Why! the sinning woman and Jesus himself tell you so."

Geneviève had risen. Her nature protested against Madeleine's tender accents; her eyes grew dark, and closing the Bible with a bang, she exclaimed in her voice of condemnation: "God the Father cannot have pardoned her."

These terrible words, full of savage fanaticism, this blasphemy which denied every spark of tenderness, froze Madeleine to the soul. It seemed to her as if a lead cloak had fallen on her shoulders. Geneviève was pushing her back, with her unfeeling cruelty, into the gulf from which

ÉMILE ZOLA

she had just escaped: Heaven had no pardon, and she was a foolish creature for having dreamt of the tenderness of Jesus. She was seized at this moment with heart-felt despair. "What have I to fear?" she thought, "this woman is, mad." And yet, in spite of herself, the presentiment of a calamity that might have threatened her, make her cast an uneasy glance round. The huge room had an air of repose in the lamp's yellow light, and the fire was shining on the hearth. Everything around her, this oppressive silence of a winter's night, and this subdued light which pervaded the room, seemed to conceal an unfathomable calamity.

Geneviève had gone to the window.

A red flash of light had passed across the panes, and the sound of a carriage pulling up in front of the steps had caught her ear. Madeleine, who, only a few minutes before, had been impatiently expecting her husband, sat still in her chair, instead of rushing to meet him, watching the door with strange anxiety. Her heart was beating painfully, but why, she could not say.

William burst into the room. He seemed very excited, but it was an excitement of joy. He threw his hat on to a chair in the corner, and wiped his brow, although it was bitterly cold outside. He walked up and down, and at last stopped in front of Madeleine. As soon as he recovered his breath, he asked her with an overpowering desire to tell her his secret straight off:

"Guess whom I have found again at Mantes."

His young wife, still seated, did not answer. The boisterous glee of her husband surprised her, frightened her almost.

"Come now, guess—try—I give you a thousand chances," he repeated.

"Really, I don't know," she said at last, "we have no friend that you could have met to make you so pleased."

"You are mistaken, I have met a friend, the only, the best—"

"A friend," she replied with a vague sensation of dismay.

William could not keep his good news any longer. He took his wife's hands and suddenly exclaimed in a burst of triumph:

"I have found James again."

Madeleine raised no cry, and sat without moving a limb. But she became terribly pale.

"It is not true," she murmured, "James is dead."

"Oh no! he is not dead. It is quite a little story, and I will tell it you—When I saw him at Mantes station, I was afraid of him. I took him for a ghost."

And he began to laugh, a happy laugh like a pleased child's. He had let go Madeleine's hands and they had fallen lifeless on her knees. She was crushed, speechless, almost insensible under this terrible news. She would fain have got up and fled, but she could not stir a limb. In the stupor that pervaded her whole being, she could hear nothing but Geneviève's cruel words, "God the Father cannot have pardoned her." And, indeed, God the Father had not pardoned her. She felt certain that the calamity was hanging over her, ready to strangle her. In her stupefaction, she gazed on the walls, as if she did not know the huge room; its calm seemed terrible to her, now that fear caused her brain to throb with a deafening noise. At last she fixed her eyes on the protestant and said to herself: "It is that woman who rules the decrees of fate, it is she who has brought James to life again in order to put him between my husband and myself."

William, who in his delight failed to notice Madeleine's agitation, had gone up to Geneviève.

"We must have the blue room got ready," he said.

"Is James coming tomorrow?" asked the old woman, who always spoke of the doctor as a young boy.

This question rang in Madeleine's ears in spite of her stupor. She rose, with staggering step, and leaning on the back of her chair, said rapidly in a feverish voice:

"Why should he come tomorrow? He won't come—He saw William at Mantes, and that is all he wanted—He has gone to Paris, has he not?—He must have business there, and people to visit."

She stammered out her words, not knowing what she was saying. William burst into a fit of joyous laughter.

"Why James is outside," he said, "he will be here in a second. You may be certain that I did not let him go—He is helping to unyoke the horse that has hurt itself—The roads are frightful, and the night is pitch dark!"

Then he went and opened the window and shouted:

"Hallo! James, make haste."

A strong voice from the darkness of the yard answered:

"All right, all right!"

This voice went to Madeleine's heart, as if she had been struck with a piece of iron. She dropped down again on to her chair, with a sigh like the rattling of the death-agony. Oh! how gladly she would have died! What was she going to say when James came in, what attitude would

ÉMILE ZOLA

she take up between these two brothers, her husband of the present and her lover of the past? She was becoming mad at the thought of the scene that would take place. She would weep with madness and grief, she would bury her face in her hands, while William and James stood aloof in disgust; she would crawl to their feet, like a woman crazed, not daring now to take refuge in her husband's arms, and driven to despair at the thought of having cast her shame like a gulf between these friends of boyhood. And she kept on repeating the words: "James is outside, he will be here in a second." Every second that passed was for her an age of anguish. She fixed her eyes on the door and closed them at the slightest noise, so as not to see. In this situation, this waiting which lasted at most a minute, were contained all the sufferings of her life.

William was continuing to walk joyously up and down the room. At last he noticed Madeleine's paleness.

"Why, what is the matter with you?" he asked as he went up to her.

"I don't know," she stammered, "I have not been well all the evening."

Then, with a vigorous effort, she got up, and tried to summon every bit of energy she had left, in order to run away and put off the terrible explanation.

"I am going to bed," she said in a somewhat firmer tone. "Your friend would keep us up talking a long time and I really am worn out. My head is splitting—You shall introduce him to me tomorrow."

William, who was looking forward to bringing together the only two beings he had loved in his life, was annoyed at his wife's sudden indisposition. All the way from Mantes he had whipped his horse on without mercy, and the poor beast had even dislocated a leg by slipping in a rut. He had felt as eager as a child to be at La Noiraude; he had already wanted to push open the door of the dining-room, picturing to himself, with emotions of joy, the touching scene that would take place. One moment, he thought, with childish glee, of acting a little comedy; he would introduce James as a stranger, and enjoy Madeleine's confusion, when she learnt the unknown man's name. The fact is, he was really crazed with pleasure; his heart hereafter was going to be full, full of love and friendship which would make his existence one long series of happy events. He could see himself joining James and Madeleine's hands saying to the one: "This is your sister," and to the other: "This is your brother, love one another, let us all three love one another to the last breath." This picture delighted his timid affection.

He tried to get his wife to stay, for it was hard for him to put off till next day the enjoyment that he had been promising himself all the way from Mantes. But Madeleine seemed so unwell, that he allowed her to retire. She was going to pass through the door that opened into the entrance-hall, when she thought she heard the noise of footsteps. She drew back, with a sudden terrified movement, as if she had wished to escape from somebody who was suddenly forcing his way in; then she hastily disappeared through a door that led into the drawing-room. She had hardly closed this door when James entered.

"Your horse is very badly hurt," he said to William. "I am a bit of a veterinary surgeon and I think the beast is lamed for life."

He said this simply for the sake of talking, as he looked enquiringly round the room with an inquisitive glance. As he knew a little about love after his scape-grace fashion, he was very curious to know what sort of a wife his friend could have married, that friend with the tender, almost womanish heart whose enthusiastic love ideas had made him laugh so in the past. William understood the mute interrogation of his glance.

"My wife is not well," he said, "you shall see her tomorrow."

Then, turning towards Geneviève, who had not yet left the room, he continued:

"You must be quick and have the blue room got ready. James must be worn out with fatigue."

The protestant had noticed Madeleine's heart-felt emotion, and an ardent curiosity alone had retained her in the room. For a long time her inquisitorial mind had scented the young woman's sin. This strong handsome creature, with her red hair and rosy lips, had seemed to her reeking with a carnal, hellish odour. In spite of the repugnance of her religion to pictures, the fanatic had in her room an engraving representing the temptation of Saint Antony, and its demoniacal medley delighted her visionary nature. Those imps who were tormenting the poor saint with their frightful grimaces, and that mouth leading to the infernal regions which was yawning to swallow up virtue the moment it made the least slip, were a faithful symbol of her religious beliefs. In one corner, there were women exposing their naked breasts before the virtuous hermit, and, as chance would have it, one of these women bore a faint resemblance to Madeleine. This resemblance struck Geneviève's ardent imagination very forcibly, and she was seized with dread as she fancied she could see in William's young wife, the bold smile and wanton hair of the courtesan, of the monster belched forth by the abyss. She would even, in her mind, often call her, with the feverish excitement of an exorcist, by the Latin epithet "Lubrica" which was written on the margin of the engraving below this she-devil. All the lower part of this picture, which was coarsely printed, was covered in like manner with figurative names personifying some vice in each demon. When, on the news of James's coming to life again, Madeleine's face had become suddenly agitated, Geneviève was convinced that it was the devil with which she was possessed who forced her in spite of herself to make these grimaces of pain. She thought she could perceive at last the unclean animal hidden beneath this pearly skin, in this flesh of perdition, and she would scarcely have been surprised to see the superb voluptuous body of this young creature change into a monstrous toad. If she did not understand the details of the drama which was racking the mind of the unfortunate woman, she felt certain that it was sin that was choking her. Thus she determined to watch her so as to give her no chance of doing any harm, in case she should try to introduce into La Noiraude that Satan who had left it with Monsieur de Viargue's soul, by the laboratory chimney.

She was about to go upstairs to prepare the blue-room, when James cheerily took her shrivelled hand. He made excuses for not having noticed her on coming in, and renewed his acquaintance with her. He complimented her on looking so well, told her that she was growing young again, and actually brought a smile to her pale lips. He had the somewhat clumsy heartiness of a young fellow in capital health who has lived a free and happy life, and never felt a pang at his heart. When Geneviève had withdrawn, the two friends sat down by the fire which had half died out. A few red coals were burning on the ashes. The vast room seemed filled with an air of repose.

"You are half asleep already," said William with a smile, "but I will not keep you long. Ah, my dear James, how pleasant it is to meet again. Let us have a little chat, will you? Let us talk as we used to do by this fire-place, where we warmed our frozen hands on returning from our famous fishing excursions. What craw-fish we did catch!"

James was smiling too. They talked of the days gone by, of the present, of the future; their memories and hopes were at their conversation's beck.

Already, on the way from Mantes to Véteuil, William had overwhelmed his friend with questions, on how he had been rescued from the waves, on his long silence, on what he intended to do in the future. He knew James's story, and made him repeat it to him with fresh additions and fresh wonders.

The paper that William had read had made a mistake. Two men had escaped alive from the wreck of the Prophet, the doctor and sailor, who had the good fortune to hang on to a boat which was floating on the waves. They would have died of hunger, if the wind had not driven them ashore. There they were dashed with such violence on the shingle, that the sailor was crushed to death, and James was found in a fainting condition, with his ribs half broken. He was carried into a neighbouring house, and stayed there, at the point of death, for nearly a year; the ignorant doctor who attended to him nearly killed him ten times over. When he was well, instead of returning to France, he continued his voyage, and calmly went on to Cochin China, where he resumed his duties. He wrote once to his uncle, enclosing another letter for William, which the Véteuil lawyer was to take to La Noiraude. But the worthy man had died, leaving his nephew an income of some ten thousand francs James's correspondence had been lost, and he had never had sufficient courage to write again, for like all men of action, he had a horror of ink and paper. He did not exactly forget his friend, but he put off from day to day the few words that he wanted to send him, and at last said to himself, in his charming, happy-go-lucky, careless way, that it would be time to tell him about himself when he got back to France. The news of his fortune produced very little impression on him, for he was then in love with a native woman, whose strange beauty held him enraptured. Later on, he grew tired of her, and feeling disgusted with his duties, he resolved to come back and enjoy his income in Paris, and had disembarked the previous day at Brest. However, he had only reckoned on staying one day at Véteuil; he was going on in all haste to Toulon where one of his comrades, who had just come back from Cochin China to this port, was dying. As this young fellow had once saved his life when he was in danger, he felt it his duty to go and watch by his bedside.

William, who could fancy he was listening to one of the stories of the Arabian Nights, was very much amazed at these details. He could never have imagined that so many events could take place in such little time, it seemed incredible to a man like himself, whose existence of late had been one long dream of tranquillity and affection. His gentle and indolent nature was even somewhat startled at this multiplicity of occurrences.

ÉMILE ZOLA

The two friends went on with their merry cordial chat.

"What!" exclaimed William, for the twentieth time perhaps, "you are only staying with me one day, you come and you are off again—Come, let me have you for a week."

"It is impossible," replied James; "I should look upon it as a sin to leave my poor comrade alone at Toulon."

"But you will come back?"

"Most certainly, in a month, in a fortnight, perhaps."

"And never to go away again?"

"Never to go away again, my dear William. I will be at your service, entirely at your service. If you wish it, I will spend next summer here—Meantime, however, I take the train tomorrow night. You have one day of my company, do what you like with me."

William was not listening; he was looking at his friend with tender affection, and seemed to be indulging in a happy reverie.

"Listen, James," he said at last, "I have just been drawing a little picture which you can realise; come and live with us. This house is so big, that we sometimes feel quite lost in it; half the place is uninhabited, and these empty rooms, which used to terrify me formerly, still make me feel uncomfortable somehow. When you are here, I feel that La Noiraude will no longer seem lonely. You shall have a whole storey if you wish, and live there exactly as you like, as a bachelor. All I ask of you is your presence, your happy smiles, and your hearty greetings: and in return I offer you our calm happiness, and our uninterrupted peace. If you only knew how cozy and nice it is in the nooks where two lovers are hiding! Don't you feel tempted to come and repose in our secluded nest? Come and live in this house, I beg of you; tell me you will spend years here, far from the bustle and noise of the world: learn to enjoy our placid sleep, and you will see that you will never want to awake again. You will bring us your happy spirits, and we will share with you our blissful reverie. I will continue to be your brother, and my wife shall be your sister."

James was listening smilingly to William's impassioned words. His whole attitude was one of slight raillery. His only answer was: "Why, just look at me!"

He took the lamp and turned the light on to his face. His appearance had become, so to speak, cross and hard: the sea breezes and the bright sun had imparted to it a swarthy tan, and his features had lost their delicate outlines through the rough life he had led. He seemed to have grown and to have become stouter; his square shoulders, broad chest, and strong limbs almost gave him the appearance of a wrestler with enormous fists and an animal's head. He had come back slightly coarse: his trade as limb-cutter had deadened the few finer feelings of his childhood; he had eaten so much, laughed so much, and lived such a jolly animal life, during the years he had spent in the army, that he now felt no need of tenderness, and was content to gratify his flesh. Yet at the bottom he was a good-natured fellow, but incapable of understanding friendship, after William's passionate, arbitrary fashion. His idea of life was to have definite pleasures, an existence free from every tie, spent here and there, in the cosiest corners, and at the best tables. His friend, who had not yet examined him closely, was surprised to find him so matured, and so manly in his appearance; he felt like a feeble child by the side of him.

"Well! I am looking at you," he replied with an uneasy air, foreseeing what he was driving at.

"And you don't renew your offer, isn't that it, my dear William?" answered James with a hearty laugh. "I should die in your calm surroundings, I should certainly have a fit before the end of the first year."

"No, no, happiness keeps one alive."

"But your happiness would never be mine, child that you are! This house would be a living tomb to me, and your friendship would not save me from the overpowering weariness of those big empty rooms you talk to me about—I am speaking my mind frankly, for I know we cannot offend one another."

And as he saw William quite distressed at his refusal, he continued: "I don't say that I will never accept your hospitality. I will come and see you, and spend a month with you from time to time. I have already asked permission to come and stay with you next summer. But directly the cold comes, I shall be off to Paris for warmth. Bury me here under the snow! Oh! no, my good fellow."

His lusty voice and sanguine spirits hurt poor William, who was quite disconsolate at seeing his dream dispelled.

"And what do you intend to do in Paris?" he asked.

"I don't know, nothing probably," replied James. "I have had a good long spell of work. And since my uncle has been so good as to leave me an income, I am going to enjoy it in the sunshine. Oh! time will not hang heavy on my hands. I shall eat well, drink plenty of wine, and have

ÉMILE ZOLA

more pretty girls to amuse me than I shall want. What more would you have, my dear boy?"

He burst into another merry laugh. William shook his head.

"You will not be happy," he said. "If I were you, I should get married and come and live in this peaceful retreat, where happiness is certain. Listen to this stilly silence which surrounds us, and look at the peaceful light of that lamp; this is my idea of life. Just think what a pleasant life you would live in this perfect calm, if you felt your heart full of affection, and had before you to satisfy this affection, days, months, years, all alike and equally tranquil—Get married and come."

This idea of marriage and seclusion in a monastery of love, according to William's description, seemed singularly comic to the doctor.

"Ah! what a curious creature a man in love is," he exclaimed. "He will not believe that he is the only person on earth with ideas like himself— But, my good friend, husbands like you are not made now-a-days. If I were to get married, I should perhaps beat my wife at the end of a week, although I am not a bad fellow. You must understand that we are quite different men. You have a ridiculous respect for woman, while I look upon her as a dainty feast where one must not get indigestion. If I were to get married and live retired here, I should sincerely pity the sad creature whom I was shutting up in my company."

William shrugged his shoulders.

"You make yourself blacker than you are," he said. "You would adore your wife, and look on her as an idol the day she presented you with a child. Don't make sport of my ridiculous respect; it will be so much the worse for you if you never have any. A man ought to love one woman only in his life, the woman that loves him, and they ought both to live in this mutual affection.

"That is a remark I recognise again," replied James, in a somewhat ironical tone, "you have made it to me before under the willows by the brook. Why, you are just the same, and I find in you the enthusiast of former days. But then, I have not changed either, only I look at love in another light. A life-long connexion would make me afraid, and I have always avoided being bewitched by a petticoat, and my mind is so constituted that I desire every woman without loving one—Pleasure has its bright side, my dear hermit."

He stopped a moment, then he suddenly asked in his blunt, cheery voice:

"Are you happy, yourself, with your wife?"

William, who was just on the point of pleading in behalf of his sentiments of life-long affection, was calmed by this personal question, which awoke in him the delicious remembrance of his last four years of happiness.

"Oh, yes, I am happy, perfectly happy," he replied in a softer tone. "You, who refuse to taste it, cannot picture such bliss. It is an endless sensation of being lulled to rest; I can fancy I have become a child again and that I have found a mother. For four years we have been living in this unalloyed happiness, and I only wish you had been there to learn how to love. This silence and this shade which frighten you have made our life a heavenly dream, from which we shall never awake, my friend; I feel the certainty and foretaste of an eternity of peace."

As he spoke, James was watching him curiously. He had a great wish to question him about his wife, about the kind soul who had consented to drown herself in such a river of milk.

"Is your wife pretty?" he blurted out.

"I don't know," replied William. "I am very fond of her. You shall see her tomorrow."

"Did you get to know her in Véteuil?"

"No, I met her in Paris. We fell in love with one another, and I married her."

It seemed to James that a slight blush had mounted to his friend's cheeks, and he had a vague inkling of the truth. He was not a man to refrain from putting any more questions.

"Was she your mistress before she became your wife?" he asked.

"Yes, for a year," William simply replied.

James got up and took a few steps in silence. Then he came and planted himself in front of his friend and said in a serious tone:

"In the old days, you used to listen to me when I scolded you. Allow me for a moment to assume my old character of protector—You have been very foolish, my good fellow; no one thinks of marrying his mistress. You don't know anything about life; some day you will see your mistake and you will remember my words. Marriages of this kind are delightful, but they always turn out badly; the husband and wife worship one another for a few years, and then detest each other for the rest of their days."

William had now jumped up.

"Hold your tongue," he exclaimed with sudden firmness, "I love you very well as you are, but I don't want you to judge of us from other married people. When you have seen my wife, you will repent of your words."

"I repent already if you wish it," said the doctor in his still grave tone. "Let us say that experience has made me sceptical and that I am unable to understand the refinements of your affection. I have simply spoken my mind. It is somewhat late to give you advice; but, if the time should come, you will be able to derive some advantage from my warning."

Then there was a painful silence. At this moment a servant came to announce that the blue room was ready. William's face recovered its genial smile, and he held out his hand to his friend with a cordial and endearing movement.

"You shall go to bed," he said. "Tomorrow it will be light and you shall see my wife and my little Lucy—Come now, I will convert you! I will make you marry some good girl, and you will end by coming and burying yourself in this old house. Happiness is patient, and it will wait for you here."

The two young fellows chatted as they walked. When they were in the hall, at the foot of the staircase, James took his old comrade by the hand.

"Don't be offended at me for my remarks," he said with great effusion: "I desire nothing but your welfare—You are happy, are you not?"

He was already going up the steps to the first floor.

"Oh, yes!" replied William with a last smile, "everybody is happy here—Good night."

As he was going back into the dining-room, he saw Madeleine standing in the middle of the room. The young wife had heard the whole of the conversation between the two friends. She had remained behind the drawing-room door, rooted to the spot by James's voice. This voice, whose smallest inflexions she knew again, produced a strange effect on her. She followed the sentences, calling to mind the gestures and movements of the head with which the speaker must be accompanying them. The door which separated her from her former lover did not exist for her; she fancied that he was before her eyes, living, moving, as in the days when he would take her to his breast in the Rue Soufflot. The presence, the vicinity of this man caused her a bitter pleasure; her throat choked with anguish at his hearty laughs, while her body burned with the feverish excitement which he had been the first to cause her to know. She felt, though with secret horror, attracted towards him: she would fain have fled, but she could not, and she enjoyed an involuntary pleasure in seeing him brought to life again. Several times she stooped down with an instinctive movement, trying to peep through the keyhole, so as to get a better view of him. The few moments that she stood like this, fainting, and leaning her hands against the door, seemed to her an eternity of torments. "If I fall," she would think, "they will come, and I shall die of shame." Some of James's remarks went to her heart; when he declared that a man never ought to marry his mistress, she began to sob, stifling her tears, afraid of being heard. This conversation, these projects of happiness which she was going to dash to the ground, and these confidences which wounded the very depths of her being, were for her an unspeakable torture. She could hardly catch William's gentle voice; her ears were filled with James's scolding accents which burst with terrible fury in the midst of her calm sky. She felt thunderstruck.

When the two friends went to the foot of the staircase, she made a supreme effort, telling herself that all this must end. After what she had just heard it was impossible for her to accept such a situation till tomorrow. Her straightforward nature revolted at the idea of it. She came back into the dining-room. Her red hair had fallen down; her face, horribly pale, was covered with sudden twitches, and her dilated eyes seemed the sullen vacant eyes of a mad-woman. William, surprised to find her there, was terrified at seeing her disorder. He hurried up to her, asking:

"What is the matter with you, Madeleine? have you not been to bed?"

She replied in a hollow voice, pointing to the door of the drawing-room.

"No, I was there."

She took a step towards her husband, put her hands on his shoulders, and looking at him with her cold eyes asked in a brief tone:

"Is James your friend?"

"Yes," replied William with astonishment, "you know very well he is, I have told you what a strong bond unites us—James is my brother, and I want you to love him as a sister."

At this word sister a strange smile came over her face. She shut her eyes for a moment: then opening them again, she replied, paler and more resolute:

"You are dreaming of getting him to share our life; you want him to come and live with us, so as to have him always by your side?"

"Certainly," said the young man, "that is my dearest wish—I should be so happy with him and you, as I should live between the only two beings in the world who love me—In our young days, James and I swore to have everything in common."

"Ah! you took that oath," murmured Madeleine, struck to the heart by her husband's innocent remark.

Never had the thought of being shared by James and William caused her so much distress. She had to keep silent: her throat was dry, and she could only have uttered cries to confess the truth. At this moment Geneviève entered the room without attracting the notice of the young couple: she saw their trouble and stood erect in the shade; her eager eyes shone bright, and her lips were moving silently, as if she was pronouncing words of exorcism in an undertone.

During the whole of Madeleine's confession, she stood there, motionless and implacable, like the rigid and mute figure of Fate.

"Why do you ask me these questions?" said William at last, with a vague feeling of terror at his wife's attitude.

Madeleine did not reply at once. She continued to lean with her hands on her husband's shoulders, looking at him closely in his eyes with ruthless fixedness. She hoped that he would read the truth in her face, and that she would thus be spared the pain of having to confess her shame aloud. The thought of immediate avowal was horribly distressing to her. She did not know how to begin, and yet she must do it.

"I knew James in Paris," she said, slowly.

"Is that all?" exclaimed William, failing to understand. "You frightened me—Ah well! if you knew him in Paris, he will be an old acquaintance for both of us, that's all—Do you suppose that I dream of blushing on your account? I have already told our history to our friend, I am proud of our intimacy."

"I knew James," repeated the young wife, in a hoarser tone.

"Well?

The blindness, the absolute confidence of her husband distressed Madeleine. He would not understand, he was compelling her to blurt out the truth. She felt an outburst of fury, and exclaimed violently:

"Listen, you have implored me never to speak to you of my past. I have obeyed you and almost forgotten it. But now the past is coming to life again, and crushing me, wretched me, who was living so peacefully here. I cannot, however, keep silent. I must tell you about it, so that you may prevent James from seeing me—I knew him, do you understand?"

William sank down on a chair in the chimney corner. He thought he had received a blow on the skull, and stretched out his hands as if to cling to something in his fall. His whole body turned cold. The nervous trembling which had made his legs give way shook him from head to foot, and set his teeth a-chattering.

"Him!—Oh! wretched woman! wretched woman!" he repeated in a broken voice.

He clasped his hands in an attitude of prayer. His hair slightly erect on his temples, his eye-balls dilated, his lips white and quivering, his whole face agitated by poignant anguish, seemed to be praying to heaven not to smite him with so much cruelty. There was more fear than anger in his mind. This was the attitude he used to have at school when his comrades were coming to beat him, and he would shrink despairingly into a corner, asking himself what wrong he could have done. He could find in his bleeding heart, not one reproach, not one insulting word to cast at Madeleine to ease his grief: he could do nothing but gaze at her in silence, with a beseeching terrified look in his big child's eyes.

Madeleine hoped he would strike her. Her temper would have risen under his blows, and all her energy would have come back. But his looks of despair, and his imploring attitude made her cast herself panting at his feet.

"Forgive me," she stammered, throwing herself prostrate on the ground, weeping, her hair all down, and shaken with paroxysms of sobs. "Forgive me, William. You are in pain, my poor fellow. Oh! God has no pity. He punishes His poor creatures like a jealous and implacable master. Geneviève had good cause to tremble before Him, and to be afraid of His anger. I would not believe the woman, and I hoped that heaven did pardon sometimes. But He never pardons. I used to say: The past is dead, I can live in peace. The past was the man who had been swallowed up by the sea. He was buried with my shame deep beneath the waves, rolled in the depths of the ocean, beaten against the rocks and lost to sight for ever. But, oh no! he comes to life again: he returns from the gulf with his hearty laughter: fate casts him ashore, and sends him to rob us of our happiness—Can you understand it, William? He was dead, and yet he is not dead—It is horrid and cruel enough to kill one—It is only miracles like this that Providence performs. He would not kill James all at once, for He wanted this ghost to punish me with— But what have we done wrong? we have loved one another, and we have been happy. It is for our felicity that we are being punished. God wills not that His creatures should live peacefully. It would do me good to blaspheme—Geneviève is right—The past, the wrong never dies."

"Wretched woman! wretched woman," repeated William.

"Remember, I did not want to accept the marriage you offered me. When you besought me to unite my life to yours, you remember, that gloomy evening in autumn, by the side of the spring then muddy with the rains, a voice cried to me not to reckon on the clemency of Heaven. I said to you: 'Let us stay as we are; we love one another, and that is enough: perhaps we should love each other less if we were married.' And then you insisted, saying that you wanted to have me all to yourself, and to live openly with me: you spoke to me of a life of peace, in words that told of esteem, of life-long affection, and a home in common. Oh! how unmerciful I was to disregard the secret warning of terror! You would have accused me then of not loving you; but today I should be escaping from James's presence, and disappearing from your existence, without sullying your trustful affection, without dragging you with me into the dirt. I thought that if I remained your mistress, I should never become infamous in your eyes, and if we ever were brought face to face with my shame you could drive me away as a worthless creature, and train your disgust to forget me. I should still be an abandoned wretch passing from one man's bed to another's, and put to the door by my lovers, at the first blush my ignominy brought to their brow. And now we have a little daughter. Oh, forgive me, my good fellow. I was a base woman to give way to you."

"Wretched woman! wretched woman!" was all William could repeat.

"Oh yes! it was base, but you must understand everything. If you knew how weary I was, what a need of repose I felt—But, I am not pretending to be better than others; only, I know that I did not lose my pride; I gave way out of need for respect, out of a desire to heal the wounds which my self-esteem has sustained. When you gave me your name, it seemed to me that you were cleansing me from every stain. Yet, it appears that filth leaves spots which cannot be washed out—However, I did not yield without a struggle, did I? I passed a whole night asking myself if I should not be committing a base action in accepting your offer. I had made up my mind to refuse in the morning. But you came before I was awake, and took me in your arms; I remember, your clothes had the fresh smell of the morning air: you had walked through the wet grass in order to arrive sooner, and all my courage fled. Yet, James had appeared to me in my sleepless dreams. The spectre had told me that I was his still, that he would be present at our marriage, and live in our bedroom—I revolted, I wanted to prove that I was free, and I was base,

base, base—Oh! how I must wring your heart; how you do right to hate me."

"Wretched woman, wretched woman!" repeated William in a feeble monotonous tone.

"Later on, I was a fool, and congratulated myself shamelessly on having committed a cowardly action, For four years, Heaven has had the cruel mockery to reward me for my misdeed, wishing to deal the blow in the very midst of my calm, so as to render the wound fatal—I lived at peace in this room, persuading myself at times that I had always lived here, and I thought myself pure when I kissed our little Lucy— What days of genial love, what kind caresses, what rapturous affection and happiness all stolen. Yes, I stole it all; your love, your esteem, your name, the serenity of your life, and my girl's kisses. I deserved nothing good, nothing worthy. Why could I not see that fate was sporting with me, and that some day or other it would snatch away from me these joys which were not meant for a creature like me? No, I gloried, like a fool, in my bliss, in my theft; and at last I imagined that these happy days were mine by right; I was simple enough to tell myself that they would last for ever. And then the crash came—Well, it is nothing but justice, for I am a wretch. But, William, you must not suffer. I won't let you suffer, do you hear?—I will go away; you shall forget me, and never hear of me again."

And then she began to sob, burying herself in her dress, and brushing away the hair that had stuck to her cheeks with the tears. The despair of this strong woman, whose habitual energy had been crushed by a sudden blow, was full of a suppressed undertone of anger. She humbled herself, but she would be seized at times with a sudden attack of fury, and then she would fain have railed at fate itself. She would have become calm all the sooner if her pride had not suffered so much. One gentle thought only really softened her mind: she pitied William. Her knees had given way, and she found herself on the ground: as she spoke in the fitful tones of a delirious dying woman, she raised her eyes to her husband, with a beseeching glance, as if to implore him not to give way so to his anguish.

William, bewildered and stupefied, looked at her with a mournful expression, as she lay on the floor. He had taken her head between his hands, repeating "Wretched woman, wretched woman," rocking his head like an idiot who could find no words but these in his empty brain. Indeed, there was nothing but this plaint in his poor aching being. He

ÉMILE ZOLA

knew not now why he suffered: he was soothing his mind with this mournful litany, with these words whose meaning had escaped him. When his wife's voice choked with grief, and she ceased to speak, he seemed quite surprised at the profound silence which reigned around him. Then he remembered, and a shudder of unspeakable suffering passed through his body.

"Yet, you knew that James was my friend, my brother," he said, in a strange voice, a voice no longer like his own.

Madeleine shook her head with an air of supreme disdain. "I knew all," she replied, "I have been base, I tell you, base and infamous. You remember the day when you came back to the Rue de Boulogne in tears, and brought the news of James's death? Well, just before you came, I had discovered this man's portrait. God is witness that I would have fled that day, to spare you the pain of knowing that you shared me with your brother—It was fate that tempted me. Our history has been Heaven's sinister sport. When I thought that the past was dead, when I learnt that James could not come between us, I grew weak, I had not the courage to sacrifice my affection, and, to excuse myself, I said that I ought not to make you wretched by leaving you. And, from that hour, I have lied, I have lied by my silence—Yet, shame did not choke me. I should have kept the secret for ever, and you would have died perhaps in my arms without knowing that I had clasped your brother to my breast—But today you would recoil with a shudder at my kisses, and you are thinking now with disgust of our five years of love. And yet, I accepted all this infamy. But then I am wicked."

She suddenly stopped, holding her breath and listening: there was an expression of sudden fright on her anxious face. The door of the room leading into the hall had remained half open, and she had fancied she could hear the noise of steps in the staircase.

"Listen," she whispered, "James is coming down—Do you know that he might come in any moment?"

William looked as if he had woke up with a start. Filled with the same anxious thought, he, too, listened. Thus they remained for a moment, both leaning forward, deafened and stifled by the beating of their hearts. You would have thought an assassin was there, in the darkness of the hall, and that they expected to see him every instant burst open the door, and rush on them, with a knife in his hand. William trembled even more than Madeleine. Now that he knew the truth, he could not bear the idea of meeting James face to face, and an immediate explanation made his delicate and feeble mind shrink with revolt. His wife's supposition, the thought that his friend was going to come downstairs again perhaps, almost made him mad, after the crisis which had just crushed him. When he had listened without hearing anything, he fixed his eyes again on Madeleine and gazed on her at his feet with a feeling of deep dejection and abandonment. His whole being felt a supreme need of consolation.

With an instinctive movement he glided into the arms of his young wife, and she took him and pressed him to her bosom.

Thus they wept for a long time, seeming to wish to unite themselves together in one embrace, to cling so closely to each other that James might never be able to separate them. William had clasped his hands behind Madeleine's back, and he sobbed like a child, with his head on her shoulder. His tears were a pardon, this sudden loss of control over himself, which had thrown him into her arms, proved his forgiveness. His want of moral force said: "You are not guilty: it is fate which had done all this. You see I love you still, and do not think you unworthy of my affection. Speak no more of parting." And it said, too: "Comfort me, comfort me: take me to your bosom and lull me so as to soothe my suffering. Oh! how I weep and what a need I feel of finding a refuge in your arms! Do not leave me, I implore you. I should die if I were alone, I could not bear the weight of my grief. I would rather bleed from your blows than lose you. Heal the wounds you are causing me, be kind now and love me." Madeleine could understand all this in her husband's silence and stifled sighs. She felt she must take pity on his nervous nature and console it. Besides, her heart was filled with sweet comfort by this absolute pardon, and this mute forgiveness, a forgiveness of tears and kisses. Had her husband said: "I pardon you," she would have shaken her head in sadness: but he said nothing, but fell into her arms and hid himself on her breast. He trembled with fear as he asked her to protect him with her affection, and she grew calm by degrees, and soothed at feeling him so absorbed in her, and so grateful for her caresses.

Madeleine was the first to tear herself away. It was already an hour past midnight, and they must make up their minds to something.

"We can't wait till he wakes up," she said, avoiding the mention of James's name. "What do you intend to do?"

William looked at her with such an air of consternation that she saw it was hopeless to expect him to take any energetic measures in his present distress. She added, however:

"If we were to tell him everything, he would go away, and leave us in peace. You might go upstairs."

"No, no," stammered William, "not now, later on."

"Would you like me to go up to him?"

"You!"

William pronounced this word with dismayed astonishment. Madeleine had offered to go up herself, urged by her straightforward and courageous nature. But he could not understand the logic of her proposal, and looked upon it as really monstrous. The thought of his wife being alone with her former lover hurt his finer feelings, and tortured him with a vague sensation of jealousy.

"What must we do then?" asked Madeleine.

He did not reply at once. He fancied he had heard the sound of footsteps again on the staircase, and he listened, pale with anxiety, as he had done at the previous scare. James's near presence, the idea of his coming and holding out his hand, caused him an anguish which became more and more violent. One thought only filled his head, to flee, and avoid an explanation, and to take refuge in some solitude where he could grow calm. It was always his nature, in painful situations, to seek to gain time and go further away in order to resume his dream of peace. When he raised his head, he said in a whisper:

"Let us go away; my head is splitting, and I can't possibly make up my mind to do anything just now—He is only going to spend a day here. When he is gone, we shall have a month before us to recover and establish our happiness."

This proposal of flight was repugnant to Madeleine's straightforward nature. She saw that it would settle nothing and leave them as agitated as before.

"It would be better to have it all over," she replied.

"No, no, come; I beg of you," whispered William, earnestly—" We will go and sleep in our little house; we will spend the day there tomorrow, and wait till he has gone—You know how happy we have been in this secluded nook: the warm air of this retreat will soothe us: we will forget everything, and make love to one another as we did in the days when I used to pay you my secret visits.—If either of us sees him again, I feel that our happiness is gone."

Madeleine gave a movement of resignation. She was quite upset herself, and she saw her husband was so agitated that she did not dare to demand any courageous decision from him.

"Very good," she said, "let us start. Let us go where-ever you like."

They looked round them. The fire had gone out, and the lamp only gave a yellowish flickering light. This vast room, where they had spent so many comfortable evenings, appeared gloomy, cold, and mournful. Outside, a strong wind had got up, and was blowing hard against the rattling windows. It seemed as if a winter hurricane was passing through the place, carrying away with it all the joy, all the peace of the old home. As William and Madeleine were making towards the door, in the shade they perceived Geneviève, erect and motionless, following them with her gleaming eyes.

During the long scene of despair which she had just witnessed, the old woman had never relaxed her rigid and implacable attitude. She felt a savage delight in listening to these sobs and these cries of the flesh. Madeleine's confession had opened to her a world of desires and regrets, of sorrows and griefs which had never touched her virgin heart, and this picture made her think of the cruel joys of the damned. She said to herself that they would have to laugh and weep like those who were licked by the flames and caressed by their flaming tongues. And yet, with her horror there was mingled an ardent curiosity, the curiosity of a woman who has grown old in household duties, without ever knowing a man, and suddenly hears the story of a life of passion. Perhaps even for a moment she envied the bitter pleasures of sin, and the burnings of hell with which Madeleine's breast was racked. She had not been mistaken; this woman was one of Satan's creatures, and Heaven had placed her on this earth for the damnation of men. She watched her writhe and cringe as she would have watched the pieces of a mutilated serpent wriggle in the dust; the tears that she shed seemed to her the tears of rage of a demon who sees himself unmasked; her dishevelled red hair, her sleek white neck swollen with sighs, and her limbs sprawling on the ground seemed to her to reek with carnal and nauseous odour. This was Lubrica, the monster with the plump breasts, and the enticing arms, the infamous courtesan concealing a heap of infectious filth beneath the satiny exterior of her pearly voluptuous skin.

When Madeleine advanced towards the door, she stepped back to avoid touching her.

"Lubrica, Lubrica," she muttered between her teeth—"Hell has belched you forth, and you are tempting the saint by exposing your impure nakedness. Your red hair and your red lips are still burning with the eternal fire. You have bleached your body and your teeth in the flames of the abyss. You have become fat on the blood of your victims. You are lovely, you are strong, you are lewd because you feed on flesh— But a breath of God will bring you to the dust, Lubrica, cursed woman, and you will rot like a dead dog by the roadside—"

William and Madeleine could only catch a few of these words which she mumbled with feverish excitement, as if they were a prayer of exorcism to protect her against the attacks of the demon. They thought that everybody in the house was in bed, and they were surprised and terrified to find her there.

She must have heard everything. William was going to beg her not to say a word, when she anticipated him, asking him in her cold sermonizing tone:

"What shall I say tomorrow to your friend? Shall I tell him of your shame?"

"Silence, madwoman," shouted William with secret irritation.

"The woman is right," said Madeleine, "we must explain our absence."

"Well! let her say what she likes—I really don't know—Let her pretend that one of your relatives is dead, or that some unexpected bad news has obliged us to set out immediately."

Geneviève looked at him full of sadness. She answered:

"I will tell a lie for your sake, my child. But my falsehood will not save you from the torments which you are bringing on yourself. Take care! hell is opening, I have just seen the abyss yawning before you, and you will fall into it if you give yourself up to the impure—"

"Silence, madwoman," shouted William again.

Madeleine recoiled beneath the fanatic's searching glance.

"She is not mad," she stammered, "and you would do well to listen to her voice. William—Let me go alone; it is I who ought to tramp along the roads this winter's night. Listen to the howling of the wind—Stay, forget me, and do not vex Heaven by wishing to share my infamy."

"No, I will not leave you," replied the young man, with sudden energy. "We will suffer together, if we are to suffer. But I am hopeful, and I love you. Come, we will console each other and we shall be pardoned."

Then Geneviève's voice rose, in its brief damnatory tone:

"God the Father never pardons!" she said.

These words which she had heard, like a presage of calamity, before James's arrival, and which she now was hearing again, at the moment when she was going to seek for oblivion, froze Madeleine to the soul with a shudder of terror. All the force which had hitherto kept her up, now fled. She staggered and leaned on her husband's shoulders.

"Do you hear," she murmured, "God never pardons, never—We shall not escape the punishment."

"Don't listen to that woman," said William, dragging her along; "she lies; Heaven is kind, and has pardon for those who love and weep."

She shook her head and repeated:

"Never, never—"

Then with a deep cry of anguish she exclaimed:

"Oh! the memories are let loose, I feel them pursuing me."

They crossed the entrance hall, and left La Noiraude with a vague sensation of the cruel folly of such a flight. But in their fright at the sudden blow which had just crushed them, they could not resist the instinctive movement of wounded animals, of going and hiding themselves in some corner. They were no longer led by reason. They were escaping from James and leaving him their home.

VIII

The night was as black as ink It was cold, wet and dirty. The wind which had risen was driving along torrents of rain in blinding showers; far away in the gloomy darkness, it howled mournfully as it twisted the trees in the park, and its sighs resembled the lamentations of human voices, the death-rattle in a thousand throats. The soaked ground, covered with pools of water, yielded beneath the feet like a carpet of decaying filth.

William and Madeleine, huddling together, struggling against the wind which blew in their faces with its piercing breath, slipped in the pools and fell into the holes. When they were out of the park, they instinctively turned their heads, and looked towards La Noiraude; they were both anxious to assure themselves if James was sleeping, and that the windows of the blue room were not lit up. They saw nothing but the darkness, nothing but the black impenetrable mass of gloom; La Noiraude seemed to have been carried away in their rear by the storm. Then they began to walk on, painfully and in silence. They could not distinguish the ground, they were entering into fields where they sank up to their ankles in the soil. The road to the little house was quite familiar to them, but the darkness was so complete that it took them nearly half-an-hour to cover a distance of at most three quarters of a mile. They lost their way twice over. Just when they were reaching the door, they were caught in a downpour which wet them to the skin and nearly blinded them. In this state they entered their retreat, muddy and shivering, half poisoned by the odour of that sea of dirt through which they had just passed.

They had the greatest difficulty in lighting their candle. Then they shut themselves in, and went up to their bedroom, on the first floor. It was here that they had spent so many happy nights, here that they hoped to recover the genial calm of their love. But when they had opened the door of this room they stood almost heart-broken on the threshold, for they had forgotten the previous day to close the window, and the rain had been driven in by the wind, forming a large pool of water in the middle of the floor. This they had to mop up with a sponge, and yet the wood remained wet. Winter had taken up its quarters in this room into which it had been entering at will since the previous day; the walls, the furniture, and all the nick-nacks that lay about were oozing with damp. William went down to look for some wood. At last they had a bright fire burning in the grate, and then the young couple hoped they would get dry and comforted again in the warm and silent atmosphere of their solitude.

They always left a few articles of clothing there, and when they had a change of linen, they sat down by the fire. The thought of going to lie down side by side, still shivering and terrified, in the cold bed where they had formerly passed so many nights of burning love, caused them a secret repugnance. When three o'clock struck, William said:

"I feel that I could not sleep. I shall wait in this chair till the day breaks—But you must be worn out, Madeleine, so go to bed."

His young wife shook her head slightly to signify her unwillingness, and then they relapsed into silence.

Outside the tempest was howling more violent and fiercer than ever. Gusts of wind beat against the house with the roar of a wild beast, rattling the windows and the doors; you might have thought that a pack of wolves was besieging the little cot and shaking it from top to bottom with their furious claws. At each fresh gust it seemed as if the frail dwelling must be carried away. Then the clouds would burst, discharging torrents of rain which appeased for a moment the clamour of the wind and fell on the roof with the dull continued beat of the muffled drums at a funeral. The young couple suffered from the crashes of the storm; each shock, each howl filled them with a vague sensation of distress; they were seized with sudden anxiety, and listened as if they had heard the moan of human voices down below on the road. When a more than usually violent blast made every bit of wood-work in the house creak, they looked up with a start and gazed round with alarmed surprise. Could this be their beloved retreat, which used to be so warm, so fragrant? It seemed to them that the furniture, the hangings, even the building itself had been changed. They cast looks of distrust on each object, recognising nothing. If a memory of the past came back to them, this memory hurt them; they thought that they had tasted in this room delightful pleasures, yet the sensation they felt of the far-off distance of these pleasures assumed the shape of poignant bitterness. William used to say formerly, as he spoke of the little house: "If any calamity ever falls on us, we will go and forget it in this solitude." And today when a terrible blow was crushing them and they had hurried to take refuge in this retreat, they found in it only the mournful spectre of their love, and they sat overwhelmed beneath the weight of the present and the painful regret for the past.

Little by little, a gloomy prostration pervaded their whole beings. The tramp through the mud, in the wind and rain, had calmed their excitement, and cleared their heads of the feverish feeling that had filled them. Their hair, drenched with rain, had hung almost like pieces of ice on their burning brows. Now, the heat of the fire made their tired limbs feel quite heavy. As the warmth from the hearth penetrated their flesh, which a minute before had been quite numb with cold, it seemed as if their blood became thicker and flowed with greater difficulty. Their sufferings, now less acute, revolved in their minds like slow-moving millstones. They felt nothing but a continual crushing; the keen burning sensations, and the sharp excruciating pains had passed, and they abandoned themselves to this torpor, as a weary man gives way to his feeling of sleep. Yet, they were not sleeping; their thoughts were drowned in their stupor, but they were still floating, confused and heavy, turning over, and filling their brain with vague pangs of pain.

They could not have uttered a word without incredible fatigue. Seated before the fire, they had sunk down in their chairs, as silent as if they had been a thousand miles from each other.

Madeleine, when she had changed her clothes, had taken off her skirts and muddy stockings. Then she had put on a dry chemise, and simply wrapped herself up in a long dressing-gown of blue cashmere. The lappets of this dressing-gown had fallen back on the arms of the easy-chair where she sat, and disclosed her naked limbs on which the flame cast a ruddy glow. She had just slipped her toes into her little slippers, and her feet reflected the rosy tints of the bright fire. The dressing-gown had fallen open higher up too, disclosing her bosom beneath the half-open chemise. Thus she sat staring at the blazing logs, and dreaming. You would have thought she was not aware of her nudity, and that she could not feel the burning caresses of the fire on her skin.

William was surveying her. Bit by bit, he let his head fall on the back of his chair, and in this position he half closed his eyes, appearing to slumber, but never taking his looks from Madeleine. He was absorbed in the spectacle of this half naked creature, whose plump firm frame awoke in his mind but a painful sensation of uneasiness: he felt no pangs of desire, her attitude seemed to him that of a courtesan, and her hard heavy look that of a woman cloyed with pleasure. The flame which fell askant on her face, formed deep shadows, rendered all the blacker by the shining outlines of the nose and forehead; her features stood out harshly, and her whole countenance, mute and curdled, so to speak, had an appearance of cruelty. And down the cheeks right to the chin, her red hair, still matted with the rain, fell in heavy masses, forming a setting of stiff lines to her face. This cold mask, this corpse-like forehead, these grey eyes and red lips over which passed no brightening smile, caused William an uncomfortable sensation of astonishment. He hardly knew this face which he had seen so smiling, and so childlike. It was as if a new being were before him, and he questioned each feature so as to read the thoughts which were producing such a transformation in his young wife. When he allowed his eyes to wander lower down, on the breast and naked limbs, the yellow gleam from the hearth that played on them, caused him a sort of fright. The skin was fair; and at certain moments, you would have said that it was covered with stains of blood, which flowed rapidly over the curves of the breasts and knees, disappearing, and then re-appearing again to speckle this tender and delicate exterior with red spots.

Madeleine leaned forward, and began to poke the fire, still absorbed in thought, and hardly knowing what she was doing. In this attitude she remained some time, with her face almost in the flames. Her flowing dressing-gown which had nothing to keep it up, had slipped down her shoulders, to the middle of her back.

And William then felt an oppression at his heart, at the sight of this majestic nudity. He followed the supple strong movement of the exposed bust, and the flexible lines of the bent neck, and falling shoulders; thus his eyes went on down the curve of the spine, and passed around the body and under the arm, till they caught a glimpse of the pink nipple of the breast through the shade of the arm-pit. The whiteness of the skin, that milky whiteness, peculiar to the skin of red-haired women, set off a little black mark which Madeleine had at the bottom of the neck. And he stopped with pain as his eyes fell on this mark, which he had so often kissed. All this lovely bust, this pearly white flesh, with its delicate curves of exquisite tints, tortured his heart with unspeakable anguish. The fact, was, that in spite of his stupor, his recollections were awakening, not like the quick flashes of memory, but like heavy masses which moved slowly in his brain. He was half asleep, and this semi-conscious state made him mentally repeat a hundred times the same phrase. His waking dream was a crushing nightmare of which he was unable to rid himself. He thought of the five years that he

ÉMILE ZOLA

had passed, with Madeleine in his possession, of the happy nights he had spent sleeping warmly on her white bosom, and he called to mind the rapture of their mutual embraces and kisses. In the old days he had given himself up to her entirely, and his tenderness and faith were absolute; never had the thought occurred to him that he might not be all in all to this woman, for he judged of her by himself, and he felt that she was all-sufficient for him, and that the world disappeared, when he was sleeping on her breast. And now a horrible doubt preyed upon his mind; he saw himself kissing those soft shoulders, he felt beneath his lips the quiver of that skin, and he asked himself with anguish, if it was his lips alone, which made her quiver, and if she was not still warm and panting with the caresses of another. His heart was free when he surrendered himself to her, and he could never confound with his present pleasure, the ever-living sensation of pleasures that were past; but Madeleine's heart was not free like his; when their lips met, she felt again, doubtless, the rapturous excitement which her first lover had caused her to know. Certainly, she must be thinking of this man when she was in his arms, and he even said to himself, that she might perhaps feel a monstrous pleasure in evoking the delights of the past, so as to double those of the present. What infamous and cruel dupery! While he had thought himself the husband, the only being that she loved, he was no doubt only a passing lover whose mouth simply gave a new zest to the sweet burning sensation of the old kisses that had hardly become cool. Who knows? perhaps this woman played him false every hour with a phantom? or made use of him as of an instrument whose amorous sighs reminded her of melodies that she had known long ago; no doubt he faded from her mind, and she lived in thought with the absent one, and showed her gratitude to him for so many hours of pleasure. This vile comedy had gone on for four years; for four years he had acted, unknown to himself, an odious part, and had allowed himself to be robbed of his heart, and his flesh. As he thought of these things, as he was led away by this horrible reverie, with which the nightmare was filling his brain, he gazed on the nudity of his young wife with supreme disgust; he fancied he could see on her bosom, and her white shoulders, impure spots, and ineffaceable bruises all bleeding.

Madeleine was still poking the fire. Her face had lost none of its impenetrable rigidity. At each movement of her arm, as she stirred the ashes, the dressing-gown had gradually slipped down.

William could not remove his eyes from this body, which was becoming exposed by each motion, and displaying itself in all its wanton and superb fulness. It seemed to him a profusion of impurity. Each action of the arms made the fleshy muscles of the shoulder stand out, and produced on him the effect of a lascivious spasm. He had never suffered so much. He thought: "I am not the only one who knows these little cavities formed below her neck, when she holds out her hands." The idea of having shared this woman with another man, and of only having come second, was unbearable. Like all delicate and nervous temperaments, he had a refinement of jealousy which was wounded by the merest trifle. He must have complete possession. The past terrified him, because he dreaded to find rivals as he looked back upon it, secret rivals, that he could not get at, and against whom he could not contend. His imagination then carried him away, and he dreamed of horrible things. To complete his misery, Madeleine's first lover must be James, his friend, his brother. It was this that tortured him. He would have been simply irritated at any other man; but against James, he felt an indefinable feeling of painful and helpless revolt. The previous intimacy of his wife with the man whom he had looked upon as a god in his youth, seemed to him one of those supremely infamous actions at which human reason is confounded with horror. He saw in it incest and sacrilege. He pardoned James, and wept tears of blood for him; he thought of him with a vague sensation of terror, as of a being out of his reach, who had mortally wounded him unknowingly, and to whom he would never return wound for wound. As for Madeleine, in the excitement of his bad dreams, which intensified the most transient sensations, she seemed dead to him for ever; by a strange subversion of the reality, he told himself that she was James's wife and that he must never more touch her with his lips. The mere thought of a kiss filled him with horror; this flesh was repulsive in his eyes, for it seemed to him to belong to a creature whom he could only take to his arms in a desire for debauch. If his young wife had called him to her, he would have recoiled as if to avoid committing a crime. And he continued to forget himself in the painful sight of her nudity.

Madeleine dropped the poker. She threw herself back in the armchair, concealing her back and displaying her breast. With gloomy face she preserved her silence, and began to look vacantly at a bronze cup which stood at one end of the mantelpiece.

But, if William pardoned James, the wounds that he had inflicted were none the less painful. He had been betrayed in the only two love-passions he had known; fate had delighted in making its cruelties more acute, by wounding him in all his affections at once, by preparing long ago, with unheard-of refinement, the drama which today tortured his flesh and his brain. Now he had no one to love; the fatal knot which had already been tied between James and Madeleine seemed to him so strong, so living, that he accused them of adultery, as though they had, the night before, surrendered themselves to each other. He drove them with indignation from his memory, and again found himself alone in the world, in the chilly solitude of his youth. Then all the sufferings of his life came back to his mind; he felt Geneviève's terrifying breath pass over his cradle, he saw himself again at school, covered with bruises, and he thought of his father's violent death. How could he have deceived himself to such an extent as to believe that Heaven was becoming merciful? Heaven had sported with him by caressing him for an hour with a dream of peace. Then when he was beginning to be comforted, when he was looking forward to an existence of warm affection, Heaven had suddenly thrust him into a black and chilly abyss, thus making his fall the more cruel. He felt now that all this was the work of fate, that everything was dooming him to anguish. His history, which had seemed to him a crying injustice, was only a logical chain of facts. But he did not accept without revolt the continual crushing weight of events. His pride was being roused. He always retreated alone to his solitude, and this was because he was better, and of a more sensitive and delicate nature than other men. He knew how to love, and the world only knew how to wound. This thought of pride consoled him; he derived from it real energy which buoyed him up, and made him ready to fight again against fate. When the certitude of his nobleness came back to him, he grew calm to some extent, and looked at Madeleine's shoulders with a remnant of disdain blended with tender pity.

His young wife was still absorbed in thought, and William asked himself what she could be thinking of like that. Of James doubtless. This idea filled him with extreme pain, and he vainly tried to read on her face the thoughts that kept her motionless and silent. The truth was that Madeleine was thinking of nothing; she was half asleep, with her eyes open; she was crushed, hearing nothing but the confused hum of her anguish, which had now become calmer. Thus the young couple stayed till morning, in their silent motionless attitude, and never exchanging a word. A feeling of total loss of energy made the solitude they had come to seek perfectly oppressive. In spite of the fire which scorched their legs, they felt icy blasts passing over their shoulders. Outside, the storm was subsiding with softened and prolonged lamentations, like the plaintive howls of a suffering beast. It seemed a night without end, one of those nights of bad dreams, when we ardently wish for the dawn which seems as though it would never come.

Day came at last, a dirty wretched day, breaking slowly and gloomily. First, a dirty haze shed a pale light on the window panes; then the room became slowly filled with a yellowish vapour, which enveloped the furniture, leaving it as indistinct as before, and giving a dirty faded look to the hangings. You might have thought that a stream of mud was flowing over the carpet. The candle, now nearly out, grew pale in this dense mist.

William got up and went to the window. The outlook was miserable and disheartening. The wind had completely fallen, and the rain too was beginning to cease. The country was transformed into a veritable sea of mud, and the sky, covered with low hanging clouds, had the same gray tint as the fields. The dull landscape was like a huge hole, in which lay scattered, like nameless rubbish, muddy trees, blackened houses, and rounded hills, whose rough edges had been worn away by the rain. It seemed as if a furious hand had kneaded up the entire plain into a filthy mixture of putrid water and brown clay. There was something so equivocal, so underhand, in the dirty appearance of the wan lustreless daylight which was struggling for existence over this foul immensity, that it filled the beholder with disgust.

This cloudy daybreak of a winter's morning is a painful hour for people who have spent a sleepless night. William gazed upon the dull horizon in a stupor of grief. He was cold, he was coming to his senses, and he felt a discomfort both of body and mind. He seemed as if he had been beaten and had hardly recovered consciousness. Madeleine, weary, dispirited, and shivering like himself, came to look out too. She could not restrain a cry of distress as she saw everything so muddy.

"What dirt!" she murmured.

"There has been a lot of rain," remarked William, hardly knowing what he said.

After a short silence, during which they continued to stand by the window, Madeleine exclaimed:

"Look, the wind has broken a tree in our garden—The earth has run down into the walks from the borders—You might think it was a cemetery."

"It is the rain which has ruined everything," replied her husband, in his monotonous tone.

They dropped the little muslin curtains which they had lifted up, unable to bear the sight of such a sink any longer. A sudden shiver came over them, and they went towards the fire. The daylight had become clearer, and their room seemed miserable, filled as it was with the gloomy rays from the outside. They had never seen it in this sad state. They felt an oppression at the heart, for they knew that this feeling of disgust and wretchedness proceeded not only from the dull sky, but also from their own misery, and from the sudden collapse of their happiness. The gloomy future gave a taste of bitterness to the present, and spoiled the pleasures of the past. They thought: "We did wrong to come here; we ought to have fled for refuge to some strange room where we should not have found the cruel living memory of our former love. If this bed where we have slept, if these chairs in which we have sat, no longer seem to us to be possessed of the warmth of former days, it is because our bodies themselves have turned them cold. Everything is dead in us."

Yet they were becoming more reconciled to their fate. Madeleine had drawn her dressing gown over her shoulders, and William was forgetting his nightmares and coming back to a calmer estimate of real life. In his frightful dreams when he had been a prey to the excitement of that semi-consciousness which magnifies the smallest sufferings, he had been carried away by horrible thoughts, thoughts that overstepped the bounds of possibility and wandered into the region of infamous suppositions. Now, the cool morning air was lifting him out of his stupor, and his mind, now somewhat relieved, was being freed of its visions. He was being brought to his senses by the ordinary course of events. He no longer saw Madeleine in James's arms, he no longer tortured his mind by evoking the spectacle of this strange adultery which locked his wife and friend in such a close embrace. Each detail was fading in the perspective, and the drama was losing its painful reality. He saw the lovers in a vague way, in the distant past, but they were too far off to cause his flesh to revolt. From this time his position seemed acceptable; he could fall back into the ordinary course of existence, he could live again with Madeleine as her husband, beloved by her, and ready to fight in order to keep her in his possession. He still suffered from the terrible blow which had almost driven them both mad, but the first crushing pain was passing away. His frozen heart was thawing and he was passing with ease over obstacles which had at first seemed odious and insurmountable.

Thus he began to hope again. He looked with sad smiles at Madeleine, in whom a similar change was taking place. Still there was at her heart a heavy lump which stifled her and which she could not get rid of. She encouraged herself to thoughts of hope, but there was always this lump to bar the way. It was like a fatal weight which was to remain in her breast till it caused her death. The smiles which she gave William resembled the smiles of a poor invalid who feels the hand of death already on her face and is yet unwilling to distress those around her.

They sat a part of the morning before the fire chatting about one thing and another. They avoided all mention of their yet raw wounds, putting off till later on the trouble of coming to a decision. For the moment, they wished simply to give a little breathing space to their sufferings. In the middle of their chat, William had a sudden inspiration. The day before, Lucy's nurse had come to look for the little child at La Noiraude; she was going to begin the baking for the farm, and this amused the girl, who was a little glutton in the way of cake. As a rule, she never missed being in at this event. Her father, thinking that she was doubtless still there, close by them, felt an ardent wish to see her, and to place her between Madeleine and himself, as an earnest of peace. In his anguish, he had forgotten their child, and he felt a great comfort in looking upon her again as a living bond which united them to each other. Was she not a pledge of the eternity of their union? One of her smiles would suffice to heal their wounds, and to prove to them that nothing in the world could separate them.

"Madeleine," he said, "you ought to go and look for Lucy at the farm—She might spend the day with us."

His young wife saw his meaning. She too had not given a thought to her daughter, and her mere name had caused her a sensation of the profoundest joy. She was a mother, and she would forget everything, even this weight which was stifling her.

"You are right," she answered. "Besides, we can't spend the day without eating—We will have a breakfast of eggs and milk."

She laughed, as if they were going to have a nice party. She was saved, she thought. Two minutes were enough for her to put on warmer clothes; she slipped on a skirt, threw a shawl over her shoulders, and ran off to the farm. Meanwhile, William drew a little table up to the fire and threw a cloth over it. These preparations for a tête-à-tête breakfast with

ÉMILE ZOLA

his wife, carried him back to their happy love-days, when she used to offer him some light refreshment in her little house. The room appeared to re-assume its former modest charms; it was secluded, warm, and filled with perfume. He forgot the dirt outside, telling himself that they were going to be quite warm, that they would spend a delightful day, far from the world, alone with their dear Lucy. Even the grey gloomy morning seemed to add to his pleasure.

Madeleine was a long time away, but at last she came back. William went down to meet her and to relieve her of the milk and bread with which she was loaded. Little Lucy herself was carrying a large piece of cake and holding it with all her might close to her breast.

The child was then three and a half years old. She was very tall for her age, and her thick short limbs made her look like a country girl, who had shot up without restraint in the open air. Fair like her mother, she smiled with childish grace, and this happy smile gave a softened expression to her face, otherwise inclined to be harsh. Precociously intelligent, she chattered for days together, already mimicking fine folks, and making requests and putting questions which made her parents weep with laughter. When she saw her father at the foot of the stairs, she shouted:

"Take me, carry me upstairs."

She would not let go her cake, and did not venture to climb the steps without clinging to the balustrade. William took her in his arms, with smiles and fond looks, delighted to have her with him. This little warm body leaning against his shoulder, sent his blood glowing to his heart.

"Just fancy, this young miss had not got up," said Madeleine, "and it took me a whole quarter of an hour to get her to come with me. They had promised, she said, to roast her some apples this morning. I have had to put two in my pocket and give her my solemn word that I would roast them here on the hearth."

"But I'm going to roast them myself," replied Lucy; "I know quite well how to do it."

As soon as her father had put her down on the carpet, in the room upstairs, she toddled round her mother until she had succeeded in thrusting her hand to the bottom of the pocket in her skirt. When she had got the two apples, she stuck them on to the point of a knife, and bent down as seriously as could be before the fire. She cleared a little place in the cinders, put the fruit on to the rib, and then set down to watch them, never taking her eyes off them. Her big piece of cake she had carefully placed on her knees.

William and Madeleine smiled as they looked at her. The thoughtful look of a busy housewife which she assumed highly amused them. They had such need to seek for rest in the innocent ways of this child after the agitations to which they had been subject! They would willingly have played with her, so that they might forget the past and pretend to be still little and innocent themselves. Lucy's childish serenity, and the fresh fragrance of her breath, softened their hearts and shed around them a balmy tranquillity. And they were full of hope, telling themselves that the future would be peaceful and pure; the future was contained in this dear creature, this good angel of peace and purity.

They had sat down at the little table and were eating with good appetites. They even ventured to speak of the morrow, making plans, and already seeing their daughter grown up, married and happy. The memory of James had been driven away by the child.

"Your apples are burning," said Madeleine laughing.

"Oh, no! they are not," replied Lucy, "I am going to toast my cake."

She had raised her head, and was looking at her mother with a serious expression which made her features prematurely old. When she was not smiling, her lips became firm, almost harsh, and there was a slight contraction of the eyebrows. William looked at her, and gradually grew pale as he examined her with increasing curiosity.

"What is the matter with you?" asked Madeleine in an uneasy tone.

"Nothing," he replied.

And he still continued to gaze on Lucy, unable to take his eyes from her, and leaning back in his chair, as if to avoid a sight which frightened him. There was an expression of restrained, terrible suffering in his face. He even vaguely waved his hand, as if he were trying to put the child aside. Madeleine, alarmed at his paleness, and unable to understand the cause of this agitation, pushed the little table back and came and sat on the arm of his chair.

"Tell me," she said, "what is the matter with you? We were so peaceful—You were smiling just now—Why, William, I thought our happiness had returned, and that we were beginning a new life. Tell me the bad thoughts that are coming back to your mind. I will send them away, I will make you better. I do want to be happy."

He shook his head and trembled.

"Look at Lucy," he said in a whisper, as if he were afraid somebody might hear him.

The child, still seated on the carpet, in front of the fireplace, was toasting her cake quite seriously with a fork. With contracted lips and frowning eyebrows, she seemed quite absorbed in the importance of her work.

"Well, what is there?" asked Madeleine.

"Don't you see?" replied William in a voice more and more changed.

"I don't see anything."

Then the young fellow hid his face in his hands and wept. At last he appeared to make an effort and stammered:

"She is like James."

Madeleine shuddered. Her eyes, dilated with frenzy, were fixed on her daughter with an anxiety which caused her whole body to tremble. William was right; Lucy bore a faint resemblance to James, and this resemblance became quite striking when the child pursed her mouth and brow. This half-frown like that of a practical man, was the usual expression on the doctor's face. The young mother refused for the moment to acknowledge this terrible truth.

"You are mistaken," she murmured. "Lucy is like me. We should have noticed what you say before now, if it really was so."

She avoided the mention of James's name. But William felt her shuddering by his side, and he answered:

"No, no, I am not mistaken. You know it is so—The child is growing, by and by she will be his exact image. I have never seen this serious look on her face before—I am going mad."

He really was losing his head, wiping the cold sweat which flowed down his temples, and holding his brow with his hands as if to prevent it from splitting. His wife did not dare to speak; she leaned on his shoulder, unable to hold herself up, and continuing to look at Lucy who paid no attention to what was going on around her. Her apples were hissing, and her smoking cake was putting on a lovely brown colour.

"Were you thinking of him?" asked William in a hollow voice.

"I thinking of him?" stammered Madeleine.

She saw what he meant. He thought that she had evoked the memory of James, at the moment when she was conceiving Lucy between his arms. The nightmares of the young husband were springing up again in his distracted brain; he was thinking again of that strange moral adultery of which his wife must have rendered herself guilty, in allowing her imagination to accept her husband's kisses for her lover's. Hence, the resemblance of her daughter to this lover. Now, he had a proof; he could no longer doubt the odious part that he had played. His child was not his; she was the fruit of Madeleine's shameful connexion with a phantom. When the young wife had guessed these accusations in his wild look, she went on:

"Why, it is monstrous, what you are thinking of. Be reasonable, and don't make me more infamous than I am. I have never thought of this man, when I was with you."

"Lucy is like him," repeated William pitilessly.

Madeleine wrung her hands.

"I don't know how it is," she said. "Fate is against me. Oh! I have never, never done what you think. It is vile." William shrugged his shoulders. His obstinacy was the unfeeling obstinacy of suffering. The thought that Lucy's resemblance to her mother's first lover was a pretty frequent case, depending on certain physiological laws as yet unknown, could not occur to him in such a moment of anguish. No such explanation came to relieve his tortured mind. Madeleine's whole nature was indignant. She would have wished to persuade him of her innocence, but she saw with despair that it was impossible to give a proof. He was accusing her thoughts, and she had only protestations and adjurations to defend herself with. For some minutes, they both preserved a silence full of sobs and suppressed cries.

"Oh! my apples are done!" suddenly said little Lucy.

Up to this time she had sat in a meditative attitude of ecstacy, silenced by the sight of her apples and her cake. She then rose, clapping her hands, and took a plate from the table, and went back in order to place her apples tidily on it. But they were so hot that she was obliged to wait. She sat down again on the carpet watching them smoke with a longing that made her from time to time touch them with the tips of her fingers. When they seemed all right for eating, she was seized with a scruple. She reflected that perhaps it would be the proper thing to offer some to her parents. There was a short struggle between her greediness and her generosity; then she approached her father and held out the plate.

"Will you have some, papa? "she asked in a hesitating voice that craved a refusal.

Since she had been attending to her cooking, with the busy look of a woman overwhelmed with work, see had not raised her eyes.

When she saw her father weeping and looking at her in a despondent way, she became quite serious. She put her plate on the ground, and continued:

"You are crying, you have not been good."

And she approached William and put her little hands on his knees. She raised herself on tip-toe, and tried to get to his face by the help of an arm of the chair. The sight of the doleful group that her parents formed, frightened her somewhat; she hardly knew whether she ought to laugh or cry. She stood for a moment in anxious thought, with her face raised, looking at her father with an expression of tender pity. Then she put out her hands.

"Take me," she said with an endearing inflexion of the words which she often used.

He was still looking at her, leaning back in his chair, more pale and shivering than ever. How she was like James, especially when she put on the expression of a little thoughtful girl. He felt her childish hands burn his knees, and he would have liked to thrust her away, so as not to torture himself any more by examining each of her features. But Lucy had an object in view; she wanted to put her arms round his neck and console him. Besides, she was beginning to feel rather afraid, and would have gladly taken refuge in his arms. When she had repeated several times:—"Take me, take me," without seeing him lean towards her, she made up her mind to climb up. She had already succeeded in getting her elbows on the chair, when William, losing his head, repulsed her rather violently.

She slipped back staggering, and fell backwards. The carpet broke her fall. She did not burst out crying immediately; the surprise was such that she simply looked at her father with wondering fear. She screwed her lips, and pursed her brows, just like the doctor.

Madeleine had rushed towards her, as she saw her fall. The child's head had passed within an inch or two of the table, where she might have got a nasty blow.

"Oh! William," exclaimed the young mother, "you are cruel—I did not know that you were a bad fellow—Beat me, but do not beat this poor creature."

She took Lucy to her bosom. Then the child burst into sobs, as if she had been beaten. She had not hurt herself, but the mere fact of getting pitied was sufficient to make her think it her duty to shed a torrent of tears. Her mother walked up and down the room with her, and tried to appease her, telling her it was nothing, that she was all right again, and kissing her noisily on the cheeks.

William felt deeply sorry for his brutal conduct. Directly he saw Lucy reel, he began to sob himself, with shame and grief. Why, he was killing children, now! His gentle nature grew indignant at his cruelty, and he felt more keenly than before the sufferings which had made him so hasty and violent. When he came to think that the little girl's head might have come into contact with the table, he shivered as if he been an assassin. And yet Lucy's tears irritated him, and Madeleine's kisses seemed to him monstrous. He could not get rid of the idea that she was kissing James as she kissed her daughter. Then, unable to stand, and crushed by this latter thought, he went and threw himself on the bed, hiding his head in the pillow so as to avoid every sight and sound. There he lay motionless and heart-broken.

But he did not sleep. In spite of himself he could not help following Madeleine's footsteps. In the night, full of waking visions, he could always see Lucy's pouting expression, and her firm lips and contracted brows. He would never again dare to kiss this childish face, on which at times sat the serious expression of a man; he would never again be able, without horrible suffering, to see his wife caress this fair head. He had now no daughter, no living bond to unite him to Madeleine. His last hope of safety was changed into supreme grief, and for the future it would be folly to seek for happiness again. These thoughts beat like a funeral knell in his anguish-stricken brain. At last he was worn out with despair and fell asleep.

When he awoke, it was quite dark. He got up, with a feeling of pain, hardly knowing what it was that could have bruised his body so. Then he remembered, and suffered again. But his suffering now was like a heavy sensation, for the crisis was past, and he felt nothing but a silent, hopeless dejection. There was no candle lighted in the room, and the yellow gleam of the fire cast but a faint light on the gloomy corners. He saw Madeleine, reclining in an armchair in front of the hearth; she was looking at him fixedly with her large open eyes. Lucy was not there; her mother must have taken her back to the farm, and William made no inquiries about what had become of her. He seemed to have forgotten that she existed.

"What time is it?" he asked his wife.

"Eight o'clock," she answered in a calm voice.

Then there was a short silence.

ÉMILE ZOLA

"Have you been asleep?" he asked again.

"Yes, a short time."

Madeleine, in fact, had dozed for a few minutes. But what a long, sorrowful afternoon! She had just spent hours of pain, in this room where she had slept so peacefully in the old days. Now she gave up the struggle, not knowing how to fight against her fate. "I will kill myself tomorrow, if it is necessary," she thought; and the certainty of being able to escape from shame and suffering whenever she wished, had almost given her back her peaceful frame of mind. She spoke in a gentle tone, like a resigned woman at the point of death, who gives herself up into God's hands, knowing that nothing can increase her troubles.

William took a few steps round the room, and drew aside the window curtains. The weather had cleared up, and he could see, in the fields, the sombre block of building of La Noiraude. There was no light, except in the windows on the ground floor, so James must have gone.

Then the young man went up to his wife, who was still seated before the fire. He seemed to reflect and hesitate for a moment, and then said:—

"We will go and spend a month in Paris."

Madeleine scarcely moved or raised her head. The proposal seemed to have no surprise for her.

"We will start in an hour,"

"Very good," she replied, simply.

What did it matter to her whether she went to Paris or stayed at Véteuil? Was she not doomed to suffer from her wound everywhere? She saw that William wished to avoid seeing Lucy for some time, and she fell in with his idea of going to seek for forgetfulness. At the end of a moment, this thought of a journey even awoke in her a vague hope of finding a cure; at first she had accepted it passively, now she clung to it, as to a last hope of safety.

As they shut the door, the young couple felt a painful oppression at their hearts. They had rushed here to find the peace of their former affection, and they left it more heart-broken and dejected than before. And they asked themselves where this blast of misfortune that persecuted them was going to drive them.

At La Noiraude they learnt that James had only been gone half an hour at most. They dined in haste, hardly touching the dishes. Geneviève did not speak a word, but simply looked at Madeleine with a gloomy expression. As nine o'clock struck, William ordered the carriage to be got ready. It was too late to go by train, and the young fellow, in a whim of his disorded brain, had a fancy to go to Paris by night, in his own conveyance. The silence of the dark road would calm them, he thought. He told Madeleine to wrap herself up warmly, and a few minutes later they were on the way to Mantes.

IX

It was bitterly cold. The wind of the previous night had dispersed the clouds, and it was freezing again almost keen enough to crack the stones. The moon shining like polished steel lit up the whole sky with her full-orbed brightness. In this pale blue light, limpid as the clear water from a spring, every little object stood out with singular clearness as far as the eye could see. Caught by the frost, the country seemed to have stiffened during the last blasts of the storm, forming sharply-defined edges, pools of congealed mud, and, here and there, a rigidness like that of a corpse frozen by the hand of death in its last dying convulsions. The smallest black branches, the least little white stones on the walls stood out with great boldness, as if they had been so many bits of colour pasted on to the vast and uniform background of grey.

William had selected a carriage with just room for two and covered with a leather hood that could be lowered at will. He had bought it some time before so drive about the country with Madeleine; in these excursions he did not care to take the coachman, but preferred to drive himself. There was only room for himself and his mistress on the narrow seat, and as he had urged on his horse with gentle encouragement, he used to feel her warm limbs nestling up to his. What pleasant drives they had in his carriage, and how they used to laugh as a sudden jerk would knock them against each other! But tonight it travelled smoothly and monotonously over the road; in the silence of the frozen fields the young couple could hear nothing but the metallic click-clack of the horses shoes on the hard ground. On each side of the road, now white with a frosty dust, the lamps threw two long streaks of yellow light, which hurried over the ditches with occasional sudden leaps, and these rays, as they traversed the clear country, grew pale beneath the moon, like the flame of a candle in the dawn.

William and Madeleine had pulled a large grey woollen rug over their knees. He was driving without saying a word, simply addressing from time to time a little exclamation to his horse, which caused it to prick up its ears. She seemed to be asleep in her corner of the seat. She was wrapped up in furs, her feet were warm with the woollen rug, and her hands were covered up, hence she only felt cold in the face; besides, the keen air, that made her eyes and lips tingle was not unpleasant; it kept her awake, and cooled her burning brow. She stared vacantly at the streaks of light from the lamps, as they ran rapidly over the road. Her mind was wandering in a reverie with starts like the sudden leaps of these rays. She was deeply amazed at the scenes which had just passed. How could she have lost her senses as she had done? Her usual life was one of straightforward will, and she was seldom carried away by her imagination or her feelings. A moment's thought would perhaps have sufficed to put everything straight, and she had become crazed all at once, she who was always so full of calm deliberation. Certainly James must be the cause of her sudden derangement; but she did not love James now; she could not understand why his memory refused to die in her flesh, or why his resurrection had so unhinged her mind. She tried to explain it, examining first one fact and then another, and becoming lost in the apparent contradictions of her nature. Yet, deep down in her heart, she felt a vague inkling of the truth; but she recoiled before the strange nature of the sensations that she experienced.

When Madeleine had forgotten herself in James's arms, her virgin flesh had received the ineffacable imprint of the young fellow's nature. It was then that the close life-long union of her marriage had been consummated. She was at that time in her full vigour, and at the age when the organism of a woman becomes matured and fecundated at the contact of a man; her powerful body, her firm constitution allowed itself to be the more deeply penetrated that it was full of rich, healthy blood; she surrendered herself with all her calm, with all her freedom, to the fusion of flesh between herself and her lover, so much so that her dispassionate nature became a new cause which rendered more complete and more lasting the possession of her whole being. It might seem as if James, in pressing her to his bosom, had moulded her after his own likeness, had given her his bones and muscles, and made her his for life. Fate had thrown her in this man's way, had kept her in his embrace, and while she was with him, by mere chance, and always on the point of being separated from him, the fatality of physiological laws had bound her closely to him, and filled her blood with his. When, after a year of this secret exchange of blood and life, the doctor went away, he left the young woman with the eternal impression of his kisses on her lips, and so possessed with his being that she was no longer the sole mistress of her own body; she had in her another nature, and virile elements which gave the finishing touches of strength to her being. All this was a purely physical phenomenon.

Today the bond of affection was broken, but the bond of flesh was as close and firm as ever. If her heart no longer loved James, her body found it hopeless to try to forget him; it could not shake him off. In vain did the sentiment of affection die out, for the feeling that he had possession of her flesh lost none of its force; the traces of the intimacy which had made her a woman survived her love. She was still James's wife, although she had now but a feeling of secret hatred, as it were, towards him. William's caresses, and the five years she had spent in the embraces of another, had been unable to drive from her members the being that had entered them at the hour of her puberty. Her nature was formed and made virile for ever, and the kisses of a multitude would have sought in vain to efface the memory of the first kisses that she had received. Her husband was in possession really of nothing but her heart; when her lips were offered him, they were not a gift, but a loan.

She had simply lent herself to him since her marriage, and of this she had a living and irrefutable proof in the fact that little Lucy was like James. Even when he had a daughter by her, William had been unable to give her his likeness. Although she had received the seeds of maternity from her husband, the young wife had given to her child the features of the man whose imprint she could not get rid of. There was no doubt that James's blood had a large share in her impregnation; he who had made the virgin a woman was the first father.

Madeleine was fully aware of her bondage the day that William had offered to marry her. She was not free, and there was an instinctive revolt of the flesh at the thought of a fresh marriage to which she could not give herself up wholly. A blank refusal had risen to her lips in spite of herself, and then her affection had been astonished at this refusal. Did she not love William, and had she not lived with him for a year? She would not listen to the cry of her being, to the rebellion of her blood which warned her that if she had been allowed to take a second lover, it was forbidden her to made a life-long union with any other than James; and, for not having obeyed this cry of her captive body, she was now weeping tears of blood.

There was in all this a phenomenon that concerned her so closely, and was yet so full of strangeness and terror, that Madeleine was as yet aghast at such an explanation. The certainty of being possessed for ever by a man she no longer loved, would have driven her mad; she would rather at once have thrown herself under the wheels of the conveyance, terrified at the thought of the frightful sufferings that were awaiting her; if it were so, she would have to drag on a wretched existence with an enslaved body, she would always feel in her James' detested blood, and she would never be able to forget herself in William's beloved arms without the thought that she was prostituting herself. Besides, she knew not of the fatal bond of the flesh which sometimes unites a virgin to her first lover in such a cruel way that she can never after free herself from the effects of this chance marriage, and must accept for life the husband of an hour, under pain of living one long existence of adultery. In order to calm herself, she thought of the four years of peaceful affection that she had just spent. But she felt that James had never left her, that he had simply lain dormant deep in her heart, and that less than a second had sufficed to awake him in all his life and vigour. Here was the cause of Madeleine's sudden derangement, here was the secret of this calm and energetic turb her sound judgment and her usually dispassionate senses; he clung to her heart strings, and the sound of his voice or the mere thought of him would throw her into a state of excitement. When he had risen before her, she had lost her head, and she would do so again each time she felt her flesh under his influence. This intuition, that her peace no longer depended on her-creature's agitation. James alone was able to disself, produced on her mind a singular effect of dread; she, who delighted in the tranquility of her dispassionate nature, looked back on her shudders of the previous day with terror and disgust, and grew desperate as she thought that these shudders would seize her again, if ever she met James. Epileptics do not feel a more heart-rending dread at the thought of the crisis which hang over them. She was, like them, gloomy and horror-struck, and always liable to horrible convulsions.

Huddled in the corner of the conveyance, watching the yellow light of the lamps flit over the white road, Madeleine did not put these thoughts to herself in all their harsh clearness. On the contrary, she avoided coming to a definite decision, and her mind was losing itself in questions that she was unwilling to solve. She was weary, and she put off to some future date the examination of her conscience; then she would take energetic measures to make a bold stand. She only thought of these things because she could not help thinking of them. It was a vague and fitful reverie, lulled somewhat violently by the jerks of the conveyance. The young wife felt her hands and feet quite warm; she buried herself, unknowingly, in the warmth of the grey woollen rug, and in the softness of the seat cushions. She would have fallen

ÉMILE ZOLA

asleep contentedly, but for the sharp air, that stung her lips and eyes; and when she looked ahead, over the horse's ears, she saw the stiff and frozen country stretching out before her like a withered corpse under the shroud of the moon. The stiff outlines of these silent fields made her dream of the joys of eternal rest.

William thought that Madeleine was asleep. He was driving unconsciously, listening to the silence of the night, and happy at finding himself on this lonely road in the cold dry air that calmed his fever. All the way from Véteuil he had been thinking of James's remark:—"A man ought never to marry his mistress." This remark seemed to have been brought back to his mind, he hardly knew why, from the depths of his memory, and it forced itself on his attention with singular pertinacity. He discussed it, turned it over, and found himself secretly alarmed at its meaning, and yet refusing all the time to look upon it as a necessary rule of conduct.

He had never entertained the foolish idea of trying to redeem a fallen woman. In marrying Madeleine, he had never dreamt for a moment of restoring, or, as we say, re-making her virginity, by the help of his esteem and love. He had married her because he loved her, and for no other reason. His nature was too nervous, and he obeyed his affection with too much delightful pleasure, to trouble his head about the ridiculous considerations of a moralist. He had simply followed the dictates of his heart, and had not set himself a task from high motives, a task, besides which his complete want of control over body and mind would have prevented him from accomplishing. Certainly, he regretted his loved one's past history, and would have wished her to forget it, but it was from a feeling of selfishness, and from a rebellion of his nature, which made the thought of not possessing her entirely to himself unbearable. It is only young simpletons or old sinners cloyed with pleasure, that form sometimes the project of redeeming a soul. William knew nothing of life, and yet he was never led astray by any false ideal. He had never thought at any time that Madeleine's soul needed saving; he had merely sought to win her love, seeing in this world the necessity simply of absolute and life-long affection. If the thought of a restoration to purity had presented itself to his mind, he would not have dwelt upon it, for he would have reflected that love of itself washes away every stain.

Thus he did not quite understand the words:—"A man ought never to marry his mistress." Why? It seemed to him on the contrary that it was good for him to repose in the arms of a woman that he knew and adored. His nightmare of the previous night had failed to dispossess him of this belief. If he had suffered, it was through the cruelty of fate. He felt that Madeleine still loved him, and he did not regret having married her. One wish only filled his heart, the wish to show himself better, kinder and more considerate towards her, now that she was in sorrow. He no more judged her guilty than imprudent. Trouble had come upon them and they must cling more closely to each other, and console themselves in each other's arms, and then their affection would save them:

Step by step, his whole being, which had been frozen by suffering, became thawed as he indulged in new hopes. The extreme pain was causing a reaction which was throwing him on to Madeleine's bosom, with an ardent desire there to hide and seek for shelter against all harm from without. He could still only look upon her by his side as the woman whose embraces could make him forget the woes of life. Forgetting that she was the cause of his recent anguish, he dreamed of looking to her for supreme joys, joys intense enough to absorb him wholly and set at naught the rest of the world. And what did they want to accomplish this dream? A secluded nook where they might both be permitted to bury themselves in their affection. And he gave himself up to this dream of a solitary existence which he had indulged in since his youth, and which appeared more and more pleasant as the blows dealt by the hand of fate became more and more cruel. His need of calm was growing greater, and his desire not to lose Madeleine's love was even turning to cowardice; at certain moments he would have clung to her neck begging her to dry his tears even if she had beaten him. Yet his feelings of pride would revive from time to time to isolate him and make him think with dread of the solitude of his heart; his shy affection condemned him to live apart from the world, in an unsatisfied desire after serene nobleness and absolute love.

As he dreamed of the new life they were going to lead in Paris, William felt himself penetrated by the increasing warmth of Madeleine's body. Their legs had become interlaced under the grey rug, and the warm touch of his young wife had no small part in the dream of tranquility and affection which he was indulging in again. Unknown to himself, his hope proceeded from the delight at finding her again so near him. She was keeping him warm. The gig was rolling on in the frosty night, surrounded by the deep stillness of the cold air.

The travellers were approaching Mantes. They had not opened their

ÉMILE ZOLA

lips since leaving Véteuil, both absorbed in their reverie, and looking in the distance at the patches of clear white, cast by the moon on the ploughed fields. As they were passing in front of a house built by the side of the road, a dog began to howl in a doleful way, and Madeleine trembled.

"Were you asleep?" asked William.

"Yes," she replied, as she felt how oppressive her long silence must have been to her husband. "That animal woke me up—Where are we?"

He pointed to a few roofs in the distance, on which the moon was casting a blue light.

"That is Mantes," he said, whipping on his horse.

Just at this moment, a woman who had been hidden behind a hedge came out on to the road and ran after the gig. When she caught it up, she held on to one of the lamps and ran by their side muttering some indistinct words, which the noise from the wheels prevented them from hearing.

"She is some beggar or another," said Madeleine, leaning over and noticing the woman's miserable dress.

William threw her a five franc piece. She caught it in its fall, but she did not quit her hold of the lamp all at once. When Madeleine leaned over, she had raised a stifled cry, and she was now looking at her with strange eagerness.

"Off you go," shouted William, feeling the trembling of his wife at the woman's fixed look.

When she had at last consented to leave go, he as-assured Madeleine.

"Oh, I was not afraid," said his companion, still all of a tremble. "But why did she look at me like that? I could not make out her features for the handkerchief tied round her face, but she seemed old, didn't she?"

"Yes, replied her husband, "I have heard speak of a girl of the district who ran away to Paris, and has come back half crazed—It is perhaps she."

"How old might she be?"

"On my word, I don't know—Do you suppose that she knows us?—She was simply asking us for another five franc piece"

Madeleine did not speak. She felt a vague, uncomfortable feeling, as she thought of the earnest gaze that the beggar had fixed on her. She leaned her head out of the gig, and still saw her still running a few yards from the wheels. It caused her a real terror, but she did not venture to speak to her husband about her again.

The conveyance was now entering the streets of Mantes, and William was nursing a project which had suddenly come to his mind. It was just on the stroke of eleven, and he thought that they would hardly reach Paris before daybreak. This long night journey was beginning to fill him with dismay; perhaps it would be more prudent to sleep at Mantes, in an inn. When this idea had occurred to his mind, he fell in with it at once, impelled by his secret desire to have Madeleine to himself in some unknown retreat. The previous night, when their thoughts of the past had been torturing them in the little house near to La Noiraude, he had wished to inhabit an unknown room, where they would have nothing to remind them of their previous history. This dream which had come to him again on the lonely road could be easily realised now. He had only to knock at the door of the first hotel he came to; there he would find the usual room, the chance apartment, where he might try to find oblivion. The idea of sleeping at Mantes, which had been dictated at first by prudence, thus became one of his dearest wishes.

"Would you like to stop here?" he asked Madeleine. "You must be tired, and we will start off again tomorrow morning."

His young wife fancied that she could still hear the steps of the poor beggar running after the gig, and she jumped eagerly at William's proposal.

"Yes, yes," she replied, "let us stay the night here. I am dying of sleep."

Then William tried to find his whereabouts. He knew of a vast inn, close by the gates of Mantes, where he was certain to find a room. This inn, known as the "Big Stag," had its day of celebrity among the waggoners and commercial travellers, before the making of the railway. It was almost like a little village, with its stables, sheds, yards, and its three blocks of buildings of unequal height. Traversed by endless passages, intersected by innumerable staircases connecting the different stories in all sorts of odd places, it used to be filled in days gone by, with the life of a little world of travellers. Today, it was nearly always empty. The proprietor had tried to turn it into a hotel, fitted up after the modern fashion, but he had only succeeded in making the furniture of his bedrooms and sitting-rooms perfectly ridiculous. He saw all his old customers leave him and go to take up their quarters with one of his fellow landlords, who had just built, near the station, a sort of furnished house, decorated with mirrors and cheap clocks, after the Paris fashion.

William had an instinctive liking for unpretentious and solitary houses, so he made for the "Big Stag." Next day was market day, and the people in the inn had not yet gone to bed. A waiter came and threw the door that led into the principal yard wide open. William got down in order to lead his horse in himself by the rein. The waiter had gone to look for a candle and the key of a bedroom, as the new-comers had expressed their wish to retire at once. Madeleine did not alight till they were in the yard, and she hardly stayed there two minutes. Still shaken by the jerks of the gig, and trembling at their adventure on the road, she looked round with an air of uneasiness. She thought she recognised this strange house to which her husband was bringing her. In front of her rose a pigeon-cote built of red brick, which she must have seen somewhere; and there was, too, a stable door, painted yellow, which seemed an old acquaintance. But her weariness and her vague feeling of terror, made her recollections very confused, and it would have been impossible for her to make a vigorous appeal to her memory. These black walls, these gloomy masses of building, lit up by white patches of moonlight, assumed in the night a curious, sad appearance, and she felt certain that she was looking on them for the first time. The stable door and the pigeon-cote astonished her, even frightened her by their existence in a place where she never remembered having been before. Yet, it was only a flash, a rapid sensation of uneasiness which redoubled her uncomfortable feeling, and her secret fears.

The waiter came back in haste, and led the travellers up a labyrinth of little staircases, whose well-worn steps leaned in an alarming fashion. He made excuses and said that if the gentleman and his wife had come in on the kitchen side they could have got to their room by the principal staircase. Madeleine was still looking round her, but she recognised nothing in this maze of floors and passages.

At last the waiter opened the door. He thought he must make excuses again. "This room looks into the yard," he said, "but it was quite ready, and you seemed so anxious to retire at once—Besides, it is a good bed."

"All right," replied William, "only let us have a fire, for it is enough to freeze one here."

The waiter put a few logs in the grate, and there was a good supply of wood in the corner. Madeleine and William walked up and down the room somewhat impatiently, waiting for him to go. The young wife had taken off her hat, and the handkerchief which she had tied round her neck. When the waiter, who had been bending down by the fire and noisily blowing the flame with his mouth, got up, he suddenly stopped in front of her, examining, with surprise, her face lit up by the full light of the candle. Madeleine had her eyes fixed on the tips of her boots, which she was holding out to the fire, consequently she did not notice his astonishment. He gave a sort of knowing smile and looked at William with a roguish expression.

"Take good care of my horse," said the latter, dismissing him. "I shall come down, I daresay, before going to bed, to see if he has everything he wants."

The room in which the young couple were going to spend the night was a spacious, square apartment. The paper on the walls seemed to have lost its colour ages ago; it was now turning a dingy grey, and it was almost impossible to trace the faded roses with which it must have been decorated. There was a big crack in the ceiling; this crack, which was oozing with damp, was bordered with rust-coloured spots, and the bare cold plaster was thus divided, from one end to the other, by a yellow-looking streak. The room was paved, too, with broad tiles painted blood red. As for the furniture, it consisted of a pot-bellied chest of drawers, with brass knobs, a huge wardrobe, a bed, remarkable narrow for two persons, a round table, and a few chairs. The bed and the windows were hung with curtains of blue cotton material, fringed with a garland of white flowers. On the bare marble top of the drawers, stood a clock made of blown glass, one of those childish wonders which country people hand down, with precious care, from father to son; this clock represented a mansion all dotted with windows, and adorned with galleries and balconies, and through the windows one could see, in the interior, parlours and drawing-room in which little dolls lay reclining on sofas. But all the objects of luxury had been reserved for the decoration of the chimney-piece. Here were displayed two bouquets of artificial flowers, carefully placed under glass globes, then a dozen or so of teacups all of different patterns, arranged in perfect order on the edge of the shelf, and in the centre, between the bouquets, rose a singular construction, a sort of monument made of those boxes won at a fair, with pink shepherds and shepherdesses on the lid; there were quite a dozen of them, of different shapes and sizes, the little ones on the bigger, very skilfully arranged one above the other, so as to form a kind of tomb of fantastical architecture. The fine arts were represented, too, in the room, by a series of pictures relating the story of Pyramus and Thisbe; framed with narrow black rods, and covered with glass all full of green knots; these pictures, eight in number, went right round the room, dotting the walls with yellow, blue, and red spots; the stiff, glaring colours, laid on in big daubs, set off the pale tints of the paper in a curious fashion, while the childish simplicity of the drawing smacked of the country design; at the bottom of each picture was a long legend, and it would have taken a good hour to read the whole story.

This room, which the inn-keeper had fancied he was making so comfortable by spreading a strip of carpet under the round table, had that indefinable odour so peculiar to all furnished hotels. It smelled close and fusty, and there was a lurking perfume of old linen, cast-off clothes, and damp dust. Huge, shabby, and chilly, it resembled a public-room where the whole world might have come, and no one left a trace of his presence or his habits; it had the dreary cheerlessness, the vulgar nakedness of a barrack sleeping-room. Young and old, men and women had slept for a night in this narrow bed, which remained as cold as a stone seat in a porch. A world of sorrow, or a world of joy had perhaps lived here for a few hours, but the, room had preserved no trace of the tears and auglier that must have peopled it. Its vulgarity, its gloom, and its silence were full of a sort of ashamed sadness, a sadness that pervades the little rooms of wretched prostitutes into which enter the kisses of a whole neighbourhood. An inquisitive searcher might have found at the bottom of one of the cups on the mantle-piece a stick of cosmetic, forgotten by some young spark of a commercial traveller, and behind another cup a few hair pins which had fastened up the chignon of some lady from a gay neighbourhood in Paris, who had been led astray in Mantes.

William had dreamed of a more genial solitude, and a more fitting retreat. He was distressed for a moment at the sight of this shabby room; but there was no choice, and, besides, he had found what he wanted, a nook unknown to the world, where no one could come to disturb his peace. He gradually recovered from his dejection, and smiled at last as he thought that they had left La Noiraude, to come and sleep in such a hole. He had seated himself by the fire and drew Madeleine on his knees as she sat holding out her feet to the flame, absorbed in thought, and seeing nothing around her.

"You are weary, my poor Madeleine?" he asked, in an endearing tone.

"No, she replied. "I felt chilly as we were coming up the steps, and I am just going to warm my feet before getting into bed."

She was shivering, and thinking still, in spite of herself, of the poor creature who had followed their conveyance.

"You are not very angry with me for having brought you here, are you?" asked William again. "We shall sleep very badly, I daresay, but we will start off early tomorrow morning—I feel pretty comfortable myself in this room. Are you not happy at the peaceful calm and the still silence that surrounds us?"

"She did not answer, but whispered:—

"That woman frightened me just now on the road. She stared at me with such an ill-natured expression.

"Good gracious! what a child you are," exclaimed her husband. "You were afraid of Geneviève, and now it is a poor beggar that terrifies you. And yet, you are not usually nervous. Come now, that woman is quietly sleeping by some ditch-side."

"You are mistaken, William. She followed us, and I thought I saw her come into the inn at the same time as ourselves."

"Ah well! She came to ask to be allowed to sleep in the stable. Come now, calm yourself, Madeleine, and consider that we are alone, separated from the world, in each other's arms."

He had clasped his hands round her waist, and was holding her closely to his breast. But she sat gloomily and lifeless in his embrace, watching the logs burn with an anxious expression, and giving no reply to the look of adoration that he was fixing on her. The flames cast a red gleam on them both, and the candle, set on a corner of the drawers, shed only a speck of flickering light in the vast, damp room.

"How peaceful everything is here," William continued in a gentle tone. "We cannot hear a sound, and we might think ourselves in some happy solitude. Might we not? You could fancy we were in one of those old monasteries where men buried themselves for a whole lifetime, listening to the monotonous sound of the bell. This deserted house ought to appease the fevers of the heart. Don't you feel more tranquil, Madeleine, since we have been breathing the chilly air of this room?"

His young wife was thinking of the pigeon-cote of red bricks and the yellow door of the stable.

"It seems to me," she murmured, "as if I had seen a yard somewhere like the one belonging to this inn—I don't know now—It must have been a long time ago."

She stopped, full of uneasy thoughts, as if she had dreaded to ransack her memory. Her husband smiled slightly, and said in his tender voice:—

"You are asleep and dreaming, Madeleine. Cheer up, now, we are in our solitude. Ever since yesterday, I have been dreaming of exiling

ÉMILE ZOLA

ourselves like this, of getting away from the world. This room is somewhat cheerless, but it has for us a great charm; it speaks to us but of the present, and soothes us with its bareness and its shabbiness. I congratulate myself on having thought of stopping on the way. Tomorrow we shall have found our happiness again. Cheer up, Madeleine."

She shook her head and stammered, without taking her eyes from the fire:—

"I don't know what is the matter with me. I feel as if I were going to choke, and strangely uncomfortable. I have been frightened, you see, and think myself not out of danger yet."

William pressed her more affectionately, and the gaze which he fixed on his wife's frightened face, became exquisitely tender.

"What are you afraid of?" he continued. "Are you not in my arms? No one here can come to dismay us. Oh! what a joy I feel in telling myself that not a being on earth knows that we are in this room. To be forgotten by all, to live on like this in a hidden retreat, to be able to say that not a creature, friend or foe, can come and knock at our door, is not this the supreme peace we have need of? I have always dreamed of living in the desert, and many a time have I sought in the country to find some quiet corner in which to bury myself. When I could see no more country people or farms, when I found myself alone beneath the sky, certain of being noticed by no passerby, I used to feel sad, sad unto death; still my sadness was pleasant to me, and kept me there for hours. And I am here with you, Madeleine, as I used to be alone in the fields in days gone by. Smile on me again with your kind affectionate smile."

She shook her head afresh, putting her hand to her brow, as if to dispel the secret disturbing memories that kept her so cold and dejected. William continued:—

"I have always had a dislike and a dread of the world, that world which is capable of nothing but harm. As we came away from Véteuil, I had an idea of going to Paris, so that the bustle of the street might deafen the noise of our sufferings; but how much more beneficial the calm of this solitude is!—In this room there are only two beings who love one another. Look, I hold you in my arms, and can forget and forgive everything. There is no one here to prevent me with his deriding glances from pressing you to my heart, nobody to jeer at the surrender which I make you of my whole being. I want our love to be elevated far above the vulgar and conventional love of the crowd, and I desire our affection to be absolute, with no anxious thought about the miseries and shames of this lower world. What has the past to do with us, and why need we be concerned about harm from without? It is enough that we love one another, that we live in each other's embraces, absorbed in ourselves, and never seeing what is passing around us. So long as a corner remains in which we can hide ourselves, so long shall we be allowed to look for and find happiness. Let us tell ourselves that we no longer know anybody, that we are alone on the earth, without relations, without child, without friends, and let us bury ourselves in the thought of our solitary affection. We are now the only people in the world, Madeleine, and I give myself up entirely to you; I am happy in my weakness, and in telling myself that I love you still—You have made my life disconsolate, and I love you Madeleine—"

His heart had gradually warmed to his words. His voice, tender and earnest, had the fervour of prayer it had flowed on, now with sudden humility, now with a gentle, penetrating vibration. He was in one of those hours of reaction when the heart melts and overflows after a long period of firm purpose. As he said, he loved solitude because it allowed him to abandon himself to his want of moral force without fear of interruption. If Madeleine had then returned his look of adoration, the weakness of his passion would have impelled him, perhaps, even to fall down on his knees before her. He felt a strange delight, after his sufferings of the previous day, in surrendering himself to the arms of this woman, far from every prying eye. This dream that he continually indulged in, of becoming entirely absorbed in her, of forgetting the rest of the world on her bosom, this vision of an existence of affection and repose was the eternal cry of his nervous, tender nature, that had been hurt at each moment by the rude shocks of life.

Slowly, yet surely, Madeleine felt herself comforted by the murmur of affection and the warm embraces of her husband. Her grey eyes grew brighter, and her lips lost their harsh contraction and pale hue. Still she did not smile on William. She simply felt pervaded with great peacefulness at seeing herself loved with such absolute faith. She ceased to stare at the fire and turned her head towards him. When their looks had met, he continued with greater tenderness:—

"If you wish it, Madeleine, we will go on like this along the road, travelling from day to day, sleeping where fate leads us to, and setting off again next day for the unknown. We will leave France, and make short journeys towards the countries of sunshine and pure air. And, in this continual change of landscape, we shall feel ourselves more alone,

ÉMILE ZOLA

and more un ted. Nobody will know us, and not a single being will have the right to speak to us. We should never sleep more than a night in the inns we found by the road-side; our love could have no fixed abode there, and we should isolate ourselves from the whole world only to cling more closely to each other. I dream of exile, Madeleine, of an exile when I should be permitted to live on your breast, I should desire to take no one but you, to feel myself battered with the wind, and to make myself a pillow on your bosom, where the storm had driven me. Nothing would exist for me but that fair bosom on which I should listen to the beating of your heart. Then, when we were lost among a people whose language we knew not, we should hear nothing but our own talk, and we could look on the passers-by as deaf and dumb animals; then should we be isolated indeed, we should pass through the crowds without thinking of the creatures that formed it, just as, during our walks in the days gone by, we passed with careless step through the flocks of sheep that were browsing on the stubble. And we should go on like this for ever. Do you consent, Madeleine?"

A smile had gradually risen to his young wife's lips. The rigidity of her being was relaxing, and she was surrendering herself freely to William's caresses. She had passed one arm round his neck, and was looking at him with a softened expression.

"What a child you are!" she murmured. "You are awake and yet dreaming, my dear, and we should be tired in a week of this journey that you are proposing to me. Why not get one of those caravans made at once that the gipsies have?"

And a slight and tender joking smile passed over her face. William would perhaps have been annoyed if she had not accompanied this smile with a kiss. He shook his head gently and continued:—

"It is true, I am a child, Madeleine, but children can love. I feel that solitude is now necessary to our happiness. You speak of gipsies, these gipsies are happy people, who live in the sunshine, and I envied them more than once when I was at school. On the days when we were allowed to go out, I nearly always used to see bands of them just outside the town camped on a waste bit of ground, where the wheelwrights of the neighbourhood had their woodyards. I used to amuse myself by running along the long beams laid on the ground, watching the gipsies as they boiled their pots. The children rolled about on the ground, the men and the women had odd faces, and the interior of the caravans, into which I sought to pry, seemed to me like a world of fantastical objects.

And I would stay there, walking round these people, and opening wide my inquisitive and startled eyes. I still felt on my shoulders the bruises which my comrades had given me with their fists the day before, and I would dream sometimes of going far, far away in one of these travelling houses. I would say to myself:—'If they beat me again this week I will go off next Sunday with the gipsies, and I will beg them to take me away into the heart of some country where I shall be free from blows.' My childish imagination delighted in this dream of being continually on the move in the open air. But I never dared. Don't make light of me, Madeleine."

She was still smiling and giving a look of encouragement to her husband as he thus unbosomed himself. This childish talk calmed her and made her forget for a moment the drama which was torturing both their minds.

"I must tell you," William continued cheerfully, "that I was a singularly wild child. The blows had made me gloomy and unsociable. At night, in the dormitory, when I could not sleep, I could see, when I shut my eyes, little nooks of landscape and strange solitary places, confusedly jumbled together in my head, and these I arranged afterwards, bit by bit, as my shy and tender nature would have them. I generally saw deep valleys filled with rocks; down below, at the bottom of the black gorges roared angry torrents; on each side rose steep grey hills towards a sky of cloudless blue, where eagles soared on steady wing; and amongst the enormous blocks at the edge of the abyss I would place a white flag-stone where I saw myself in thought, seated and dead as it were, in the midst of this desolation and unsheltered glare. At other times my reveries were of a gentler nature; I would create a tiny island, situated in the middle of a broad and tranquil river; I could hardly distinguish the distant banks, which were like two green belts lost in the mist; the sky was of a pale grey, and the poplars of my island rose up straight in the white mist from the water; then I saw myself reclining on the soft grass, lulled by the subdued and continual murmur of the river, and refreshed by the rich breath of this moist soil. These landscapes which I evoked, and which I delighted to modify incessantly, taking away a rock, or adding a tree, used to appear to me with singular clearness; they consoled me and transported me into unknown countries, where I thought I lived a whole life of silence and peace. When I opened my eyes, when everything faded away, and I found myself again in the gloomy dormitory, lighted by the pale rays of a night lamp, my heart felt

ÉMILE ZOLA

oppressed with anguish, and I listened to the breathing of my comrades, dreading to see them get up and come and beat me as a punishment for having escaped them in my dreams."

He stopped to return to Madeleine the kisses that she was bestowing on his brow. She was touched by the story of the sufferings of his youth. In this hour when he was opening to her his heart, she could fathom the gentleness of this nervous constitution, and she solemnly swore to love William as he deserved, with refined and absolute affection.

"Later on," he continued, "when I felt the inclination to run away with these gipsies, I was simply yielding to the hope of finding along the roads the landscapes which I had seen in my dream. I firmly believed that I should discover them somewhere, and I fancied that I had pictured them as they really existed. It was doubtless some good angel who had revealed them to me, for I scorned the idea of having been able to create them entirely, and I should really have felt deeply troubled, if it had been proved to me that they had only existed in my brain. They beckoned to me, they called me to go and repose amongst them, and promised me a life of eternal peace." He stopped again, hesitating, not venturing to continue. Then, with a timid smile, with the embarrassed look of an upgrown man who is confessing some childish folly, he murmured:—

"And shall I tell you, Madeleine? I still believe that they exist, those landscapes where I have spent so many nights of my childhood. During the day I was a martyr, and I looked on the cold walls of the school with the despair of a prisoner shut up in the room where he is to be tortured; but at night, I wandered over the fields and revelled in the free air, tasting a heart-felt pleasure in no longer seeing the uplifted fist ready to fall on my head. I lived two lives, each as real as the other. No, Madeleine, my dreams cannot have deceived me. If we search, we shall find somewhere on earth, my gorge filled with rocks, and my island situated in the middle of a broad and tranquil river. And this, Madeleine, is why I wish to go where chance may lead us, convinced that I shall find some day the solitudes I have dreamed of. Oh! if you knew how pleasant and peaceful they were in my dreams. There we should repose in happy rest, there we should live for ever far from the world, far from everything that has harmed us. It would be life transformed into a dream. Are you willing for us to start in search of these happy nooks? I should know them, and say to you:—'It's here that we must love each other.' And don't laugh, Madeleine; they do exist, for I have seen them."

His young wife was not laughing now. Her eyes were filling with tears, and her lips were quivering with emotion. William's words, and the gentle murmur which he was pouring into her ear were making her weep. How he loved her, and what depth of ineffable tenderness she found in his heart! Unconsciously the thought that she could not give herself to him entirely and without reservation redoubled her emotion; but she did not think then that it was only the soothing effect of these words falling one by one on her heart that she was feeling. She kissed her husband's face from time to time as he spoke, and surrendered herself to his arms, yielding to his embraces and clasping him closely round the neck. The burning logs which threw off large, yellow flames, cast on them a warm light. And, behind them, the huge strange room was sunk in repose.

"Child, child," repeated Madeleine. "Come now, if we are unable to realise your dream, we can always, however, love one another."

"Why not flee?" answered William, eagerly.

Again a slight smile passed over her lips.

"Because we cannot go and live in your castles in the air, my dear poet," she replied. "Happiness must exist in ourselves, and it is useless for us to rely on fate for finding it. I see that you have forgotten everything, and I feel that I am forgetting too; we still have many happy hours to live together."

And as her husband was beginning to look sad, she added cheerfully:—

"Now, we shall be happy everywhere. I defy sorrow—I don't know what the feeling of fear was that came over me on the road. I was half asleep, and the cold must have affected me. Then this inn produced a strange feeling of repugnance on me—But since we have been here, warming ourselves and chatting, I have seen that you are right; we are very comfortable here, surrounded by this deep silence. Your words have calmed my anguish—Now I am hopeful."

William was soon consoled as he heard her talking in this strain.

"Yes, hope on, Madeleine," he said. "See how united we are to each other. Nothing now can separate us."

"Nothing," replied the young wife, "if we love each other as we are doing. We may return to Véteuil, or go to Paris, but we shall find our love everywhere—Love me without ceasing, as you have loved me tonight, and I will bring back your happiness, I swear it to you—I am yours, do you hear, yours entirely."

ÉMILE ZOLA

They clasped each other in a closer embrace, and exchanged silent kisses for several minutes. The clock struck twelve.

"Midnight already," exclaimed Madeleine. "We really must go to bed, if we wish to awake early."

As she jumped up from William's knees, he left his chair, saying:—

"I am going down for a moment to the stable. I want to see how that young fellow has attended to my horse—You will not be afraid of being left alone in the room, will you?"

They exchanged a last kiss; then William went down leaving the key in the door.

When Madeleine was by herself, she stood for a moment, lost in thought, staring at the fire with the blank smile which her husband's tender words had brought to her lips. As she had just said, she felt greatly comforted, and lulled with new hopes. Up to this moment, she had hardly bestowed a look on the room; as she had entered, she had come straight to the fire-place to warm her feet, and had remained there, seated on William's knees. When her fit of musing had passed away, she felt a desire, before getting into bed, to set in order the few packages that the waiter had brought up, and dropped at random. She raised her eyes and looked round her.

Then all her uncomfortable feeling came back, nor could she explain to herself why this vague sensation of terror was creeping over her. She was distressed by the same feeling of repugnance and uneasiness which she had already experienced in the yard. She seemed to recognise the room again; but the candle cast such a feeble light on the walls that she could distinguish nothing clearly. She said to herself that she was silly and afraid, thinking that she was dreaming awake. She pushed the packages into one corner, trying all the time to re-assure herself. There was a carpet bag missing, and she looked for it all round, finding it at last on the marble top of the drawers, where the waiter had dropped it down. It had entirely hid the glass clock. When Madeleine had got the bag and discovered this clock, she stood rooted to the spot, and horribly pale.

She had not been mistaken; she knew the inn, and she knew the room, for she had slept here with James. The student was passionately fond of boating, and he would often go all the way to Rouen by the river, with a few friends who were taking their mistresses with them. Madeleine had come with him on one of these trips, but when she had got as far as Mantes, she had felt unwell, and the whole party had made for the "Big Stag."

Rooted to the spot, and stupified, the young wife examined the clock. An object like this could leave no doubt in her mind, for castles in blown glass are not often met with, and she recognised again the little galleries and the open windows, through which were seen the bedrooms and parlours in the interior. She remembered, too, that James and she had a long laugh at the little dolls that inhabited these apartments, and that they had even taken off the globe and amused themselves by putting the dolls into fresh rooms. It seemed to her that all this had taken place the day before, and that she was looking on the clock again after an absence of a few hours. The candle, placed by the side of this frail construction, penetrated with its rays the slender colonnades, and the narrow rooms with their transparent walls, casting a point of light on each drop of the molten glass that had trickled down, and transforming the rails of the balconies into needles of flame. It might have been thought a fairy palace, a palace lit up with green and yellow flames by millions of invisible lamps. And Madeleine gazed on these flittering stars with a look of terror, as if this fragile toy had enclosed some terrible and threatening weapon.

She drew back, lifted up the candlestick, and took a turn round the room. At each step, she found a memory. One by one she recognised the coloured pictures that told the story of Pyramus and Thisbe. Certain spots in the faded paper attracted her attention, and each piece of furniture spoke to her of the past. When she came to bed, she fancied that the clothes had not even been changed, and that she was going to sleep with William in these sheets that were still warm with James's body.

It was this thought that distressed her. She had traversed the room like a person walking in his sleep, with her eyes wide open, and her lips firmly closed, examining every object with the minuteness of a mad woman, and seeming to attach an immense interest to allowing no detail to escape her notice. But when she had touched the blue cotton curtains, with their border of pale flowers, and suspended by a rod above the bed, she felt her legs give way all at once, and she had to sit down. Now her thoughts were fixed on this narrow bed, arched in the middle like the white headstone of a grave, and she said to herself that she would never sleep there with William.

She put her hands to her brow, fancying that her head was going to split, and she felt a secret feeling of rage rising to her heart. The unrelenting pursuit and attack of her memories was filling her with

ÉMILE ZOLA

exasperation. Would she never more then be able to pass a peaceful night, would she never be allowed to forget? James was finding her out even in this out of the way place, even in this inn bedroom, where chance had driven them. And she had been fool enough to hope, and to pretend that she felt appeased and comforted. She ought rather to have listened to her fears, and to the uncomfortable feeling which had warned her of the blow that was threatening her. This time, she would be driven mad. What was she going to say to her husband, to that man whose tender words had lulled her with a false dream, a few minutes before? would she have the courage to exclaim: "Come away, you have made a mistake, this room is accursed, for I have slept in it with my first lover." Or would she say nothing, would she consent to prostitute herself in William's arms, while thinking of James? In her anxiety, she kept looking at the door, and listening to the faint sounds in the house, dreading to hear her husband's footsteps, and shuddering at the idea of seeing him come in, and not knowing what to say to him.

As she listened, it seemed to her that somebody was walking softly along the passage, and stopping at her door. There was a wary tap.

"Come in," she shouted absently, hardly knowing in her trouble what she was saying.

The door opened, and in walked—James!

X

When James woke up at La Noiraude, he was very much surprised at the sudden departure of William and his wife, for he had not the least suspicion of the terrible drama that his presence had brought about. In a few words, Geneviève told him the story of the sudden death of a relative, which had obliged her master and mistress to set out in the night. He could not think for a moment of questioning the veracity of this account. "Oh! very well!" he said to himself, "I shall see my turtle-doves when I come back from Toulon." And he thought of nothing more but of killing the day in the pleasantest possible manner.

He started out to air his vexation in the little silent streets of Véteuil, but he was unlucky enough not to come across a single one of his old schoolfellows, and the hour of departure seemed as if it would never come. Towards evening, as he had only a few minutes left to catch the coach, he was accosted by a worthy fellow who uttered an exclamation on recognising him and began to tell him a long story about the last moments of his uncle, and when he had let him go, the coach had gone. James lost an hour in looking for a conveyance that he might hire, and got to Mantes just in time to hear the whistle of the train starting off. This delay was very vexatious, but having learnt that he could take an early train next morning which would bring him to Paris in time to catch his train at the Lyons station, he made up his mind to stay at the Big Stag, where in days gone by he had some very pleasant parties.

He felt quite at home there; the people were nearly the same, and the waiter who showed him to his room took the liberty of reminding him, with the familiarity of hotel servants, of the short stay he had made in the inn in Madeleine's company; and he remembered the lady quite well, he said, a fine girl, with her purse always open.

It might be then ten o'clock, and James had forgotten the flight of time in smoking by his fire till past eleven. Just as he was going to bed he heard a scratching at his door and went to open it. The waiter entered with a singular expression on his face. He had something to tell the gentleman, he stammered, but he hardly dared, and the gentleman must promise beforehand to pardon him for his indiscretion; besides, if he was interfering in other people's affairs, it was because he thought he was doing a kindness to the gentleman, of whose recent return to France he was aware, and who would, he dared say, not be sorry to learn about a certain person. James lost his patience and begged him to explain himself.

Then, becoming as unreserved as he had been cautious just before, the waiter informed him of the presence of Madame Madeleine in the inn, where she had just arrived and a man with her. He gave a little knowing smile as he added that he had given the travellers room number seven, which the gentleman had good reason for remembering. The young doctor could hardly help smiling too, but his delicate feelings had become too deadened by his love adventures for him to think of feeling hurt by such a confidence. He even put two or three questions to the waiter, asked him if Madeleine was still pretty, if her companion seemed old, and at last dismissed him with the assurance that the proximity of the young woman was not going to prevent him enjoying a sound sleep.

But this was merely a boast, for when the waiter had gone he began to walk up and down the room, pondering in spite of himself, over his old love. He was not of a meditative nature, and during his long absence the memory of his former mistress had hardly troubled his head. Yet he could not learn without a certain emotion that she was there, in an adjoining room, in company with another man. She was the only woman with whom he had lived as husband for a year, and the certainty that she had been a virgin when she came to him, made her different in his eyes from the numerous creatures that he had made love to for a night and cast off next morning. However, he told himself philosophically that such was life, and that he hardly could have expected anything else than to find Madeleine leaning on another man's arm. The thought never occurred to him for a moment of accusing himself of having been the cause of the young woman's loose life; she was travelling about and must have fallen in with a rich lover. His reverie ended in an ardent wish to shake her hand like an old comrade; he was not in love with her now, it was true, only he would have felt it a real pleasure to chat with her for a few minutes. When the thought of this friendly grasp of the hand had occurred to him, he forgot the little touch of regret that he had just experienced, and thought solely of devising an excuse to get near Madeleine for a moment. This interview appeared perfectly natural and it fell in with his jovial good natured disposition. He expected, too, that his former mistress would throw herself into his arms again. The idea that she could be married, if it had occured to him, would have seemed very ludicrous, for he could always see her in his mind's eye at his lodgings in the Rue Soufflot surrounded by his friends smoking their clay pipes. He resolved simply to act prudently, so as not to compromise her in the mind of her new lover.

His room was at the end of the passage, three doors away from number seven. He had half opened his door, and stood listening and considering on the difficulty of putting his project into execution. As he had to start early next morning he was beginning to despair of accomplishing his object, when he heard the noise of the opening of a door. He put his head out and caught a glimpse in the shade of a man leaving number seven and going away in the direction of the staircase. When the noise of his footsteps had died away, he had a quiet laugh to himself as he thought:

"The gentleman has gone out, now is the time to go and pay my respects to the lady."

And he came stealthily and knocked at Madeleine's door. When he was inside the room, and she saw him before her, she jumped up with a sudden start. However, this apparition did not give her the violent shock that the unexpected sight of him under other circumstances would have done, for she was almost expecting him. Since she had recognised the room, since the memories of the past had been driving her mad again, she could fancy that her former lover was before her. And now he was come, and it seemed quite natural to her, for he was in his own room. She did not even ask herself how it came about that he was at the Big Stag or how he had learnt that she was there too. She simply felt her whole being turn cold. Erect and motionless, with her eyes fixed on James, she waited, in a strange calm attitude, for him to speak first.

"Oh yes, it is Madeleine; there is no doubt about it," he said at last lowering his voice.

He was smiling and looking at her with a pleased expression.

"This Joseph has an excellent memory—You remember, he was the young fellow who waited on us, when we stayed in this inn—He has just told me that you were here, and that he had recognised you again—I wanted to shake hands with you, my dear girl."

And he advanced towards her, with his hands stretched out cordially, and still smiling. The young woman drew back.

"No, no," she whispered.

He seemed surprised at this refusal, but he did not lose his cheerful humour.

"You won't let me shake hands with you?" he went on. "Why? You surely don't suppose that I am coming to interfere in your new love. I am a friend, Madeleine, an old comrade, and nothing more—I have waited till the gentleman went out, and I will be off before he comes back. Is it big Ralph?"

Big Ralph was the student who had offered to take Madeleine into his lodgings, a few minutes after the doctor's departure. She shuddered at the man's name. James's supposition, the possibility of an intimacy between her and one of his old friends, hurt her deeply. "If I were to tell him all?" she thought. Driven into a corner, and bleeding at heart, she was recovering the vigour and decision of her character; she was going, in a few short words, to confess the truth to her first lover, and beg him never to try to see her again, when James went on in his merry tone:

"Won't you answer me—Good gracious! how reserved you are!—Was it you that chose this room?—You remember this room, don't you?—Ah! my dear girl, what jolly happy days we had!—But do you know, you are playing this gentleman rather a scurvy trick by bringing him here?"

He burst into a loud laugh, while Madeleine, crushed and dejected, looked at him with an air of utter stupor.

"I was never very particular," he added, "and I believe that you have perfectly forgotten me—Yet I should not like to be in this gentleman's place—I say now, between ourselves, why on earth did you choose this room?—Won't you answer me? We parted bad friends, then?"

"No," she said, in a hollow tone.

She was reeling, and leaning against the mantelpiece to prevent herself from falling. She felt that she would not have the courage to speak now; she would never dare to mention William's name, now that James had made sport of the man who was to spend the night with her in the room where they had formerly made love to each other. And then he must go and suspect her, in the unfeeling joke of a man of pleasure, of having chosen this room purposely. It seemed to her that her first lover was throwing her back, by one word, into the mire that she ought never to have left. She thought herself sullied with a stain so ineffaceable, that she lowered her head in shame like a guilty woman. Besides, James's presence was producing on her the effect of alarm, which, the day before, had made her lose her usual imperturbability and energy; her sanguine temperament was liable to sudden periods of agitation, and this strong-minded young fellow to whom she would always belong by the close bonds of the flesh, broke down her will by the mere sound of his voice, and with one look overcame all her resistance and made her weak and nervous. When she felt in her being this enervation of submissiveness, she was afraid of her first thoughts of resistance, and gave way entirely. James knew nothing, it was fate which had thrown him in her way, so she would bear her shame to the bitter end, and wait till he had gone.

The young fellow could not guess the thoughts which were making her shudder and turn pale. He imagined that she was supposing him capable of waiting for the man she was with, and then making a ridiculous scene.

"Don't tremble;" he said, continuing to laugh. "Do you take me for an ogre? I have told you already that I simply wanted to shake hands with you. I am here and off again directly—Really, I have no desire to see this gentleman. The sight of him would not interest me in the least. At the faintest noise, I am off—"

He went and listened at the door which he had left open. Then he came, losing none of his cheeriness at Madeleine's attitude. This original interview amused him, and he felt nothing of its cruel and coarse side.

"Do you know," he continued, "that I nearly stayed over in yon country, in a comfortable bed at the bottom of the sea? But the fishes would have nothing to do with me—I have come back to live in Paris. Oh! I am certain to come across you there, and I am sure that you won't make that frightful face at me—And you, Madeleine, how has the world treated you? What are you doing?"

"Nothing," she replied.

She had no energy left, and listened and answered quite mechanically. She told herself that he was going to go away, and that she would reflect afterwards. In her scare, the thought that her husband might come up any moment did not occur to her mind now.

"Ah," he said, somewhat abashed, you are doing nothing Good gracious! how cool you are! And I really thought that you would rush into my arms—You love him then?"

"Yes."

"So much the better! I hate people that have no heart. And have you been with him long?"

"Five years."

"The deuce! that is quite a serious affair—It is not big Ralph, you are sure? George then? No—Ah! perhaps it is Julian Durand, the little fair fellow?—No, not he either?—Then it is somebody that I don't know?"

ÉMILE ZOLA

She grew pale again, and felt a shudder which caused an expression of unspeakable suffering to pass over her face. James thought that she fancied she could hear her lover's footsteps.

"Come, don't shudder like that," he continued, "I have promised you that I would be off the moment he comes back. It is a pleasure to me to chat with you a bit—Then you don't see the fellows now at all that I have just mentioned?"

"No."

"They were jolly dogs, comrades of a day that I have thought about sometimes, far away from France—Do you remember the merry days we spent with them? We used to start out in the morning for Verrières wood, and come back at night, loaded with lilac boughs. I remember yet the enormous dishes of strawberries we used to eat, and especially the little room where we slept so often; I used to open the shutters by five o'clock, and the sun would wake you up by shining on your eyes—I always thought that one of my excellent friends must have taken my place in your heart."

Madeleine gave a beseeching gesture. But James was at last becoming somewhat piqued by her cold attitude, and he continued unfeelingly:

"Come now, you may confess the truth, and I shall not be annoyed— It must have been so, so don't say no—Well! such is life; meetings, partings, and meetings again. There is not a week that I don't come across some old—You make a mistake to look at things on the tragic side and to treat me as an enemy—You used to be so bright and reckless."

He was looking at her, and wondering to see her so stout and healthy looking, in the full bloom of her beauty.

"It is no use your pulling long faces at me," he said jokingly, "I think you are quite charming. You have become a woman, Madeleine, and you must have been happy—Come, just give a look at me; ah! my lovely red hair, and my soft pearly skin!"

He had moved nearer to her, and a flash of desire passed across his eyes.

"Come now, won't you give me a kiss before I go away?"

Madeleine threw herself back to escape his hands which he was stretching out towards her.

"No, let me alone, I implore you," she stammered in a feeble tone.

James was struck with the despairing accent of her voice. He suddenly became serious, for the good nature that lay at the bottom of his character was moved, and he felt a vague consciousness of having been brutal and cruel unintentionally. He took a few steps towards the door. Then stopping and turning round, he said:

"You are right, Madeleine. I am a fool, and I was wrong to come here—Pardon my jokes as I pardon your coldness. But I am afraid that you have neither heart nor memory. If you really love this man, don't stay with him in this room."

He spoke in a serious tone, and she kept back her sobs as he pointed to the walls of the room with a vigorous gesture.

"I am a gay rogue, myself," he continued. "I love a little everywhere, without any very nice scruples. And yet I can still hear this bed, this furniture and the whole room speaking to me of you—Remember, Madeleine."

The thoughts that he was evoking brought a new flash of desire to his eyes.

"Come," he said approaching her again, "one shake of the hand, and I am off."

"No, no," repeated the young wife quite crazed.

He kept her for a few seconds trembling before him; then he shrugged his shoulders and left the room. He went away looking on her as a fool. His transient regret, at having come and shown himself perhaps somewhat brutal, had been drowned in a secret irritation at his former mistress, who had refused even to shake hands with him. If he had felt a spark of sentimentality as he had pointed to the walls of the room, this tender emotion sprung from a vague feeling of jealousy which he would have blushed to avow openly.

When Madeleine was left alone she began to walk mechanically up and down in the room, moving the packages about, scarcely knowing what she was doing. There was in her being a sort of deafening rumble which prevented her from hearing her thoughts. For an instant, she entertained the idea of running after James and telling him of her marriage with William; she thought, now that she saw him no longer before her, that she felt strong enough to make such a confession. Yet, she was not urged to this act of courage by the thought of succouring her husband, or of assuring him a peaceful future; she thought but of herself, for she was revolting at last beneath the familiar and mocking contempt of her first lover, and wished to show him that she was living as a virtuous woman, and that she ought to be respected. This rebellion of her pride concealed from her the real situation, and she was no longer asking herself what she should say to William when he came upstairs again. Exasperated by the merciless persecution of fate, she was simply becoming angry, and feeling a selfish need of soothing herself in an immediate and violent fashion.

As she was walking up and down with sudden gesticulations, she heard behind her the creaking of the door which James had left half open, and she turned round, thinking it was her husband who was coming back. Then she saw on the threshold, the beggar they had met on the road, the woman in rags who had followed the conveyance right to the Big Stag.

The woman came nearer, looking earnestly at her. Then she said: "I was not mistaken. I recognised you, Madeleine, although your face was in the shade. Do you know me?"

Madeleine had stepped back in sudden surprise on seeing the poor woman's face in the full light. She drew herself up in a stiff and unpitying attitude.

"Yes, I know you, Louise," she replied, in a tone in which she gave vent to all the anger and all the revolt of her being.

The apparition of this woman was the last straw that was wanting to turn her crazed. Louise was that old companion who had taken her to see her daughter, a few miles out of Paris, the day before James went away. She was known in the Latin quarter under the nickname of Verdigris, a title she had earned by her fondness for absinthe and the greenish tints of her flabby and sickly-looking cheeks. Verdigris used to be pointed out in those days as a celebrity, whose favours the school-truants wrangled for. She had a wild look, and had become quite hysterical with drink, and, at the public dances, she would throw her arms round the necks of all the men: she was a sad spectacle of drunken, down-at-heels debauchery, utterly regardless of the stink of the gutter in which she was wallowing. For a moment, when she had a daughter, she had seemed to reform a little. As James rather liked her low vulgar ways, he had felt no scruples in introducing her to Madeleine for a companion, the more so, as she was at that time the mistress of one of his friends: she wanted to turn over a new leaf, she said, and live with one man only. Then she had relapsed into the mire again, unable to take a serious view of her duties as a mother, and even chaffing herself for having believed in this stupid nonsense for a few months. When Madeleine was living in the Rue de l'Est, she had seen her one night staggering along the causeway, dead drunk, between two abusive students, and this vile creature had remained in her memory as the most horrible recollection of her former life.

Today, Verdigris seemed to have sunk into the very last stage of shame. She must have been thirty and some odd years old, but she might easily have been taken for fifty. She had on a wretched dress, all in rags, and her tattered, short skirt exposed the old pair of men's boots on her feet: she had a tartan shawl tied round her body, but it was too scanty to cover her arms, half-bare and blue with cold. Her face, encircled with a handkerchief fastened under her chin, bore an expression of abject stupidity, for drink had transformed it into a sottish mask, with colourless sagging lips, and bleary blinking eyes. She spoke in a hoarse whisper, with frequent hiccups, and accompanied her remarks with a running commentary of vague gesticulations, in which lingered a trace of the ribald graces of her old disreputable dancing days. But the saddest feature of this vile, debauched creature, was her look of wild vacancy, and the continual shuddering which shook her whole frame: absinthe had made terrible ravages, both on her mind and body, and she moved and spoke in a sort of stupor, broken, now and again, by hysterical laughter, or sudden fits of excitement. Madeleine remembered what her husband had told her about this woman, wandering about the roads like an escaped lunatic. She looked upon her as quite mad, and only felt all the more horror.

"Yes, I know you," she repeated, in a harsh tone. "What do you want with me?"

Louise was still looking at her with her vacant eyes. She gave a maniac's laugh and replied:

"You are talking to me like a fine lady, you are proud!—Is it because I have not got a silk dress like yourself?—But you know quite well, my dear girl, that there are ups and downs in life? Tomorrow you may be as wretched as I am today."

Each of her words went to Madeleine's heart, and increased her irritation. All her past rose before her, and she told herself that this woman was right, and that she might sink to this depth of shame."

"You are mistaken," she replied, vehemently. "I am married—Don't interfere with me."

But the madwoman continued:

"You have been really lucky. Such things don't happen to me— When I saw you in the carriage with a man, I thought that you had a millionaire in tow—Then he is your husband, that gentleman who threw me a five franc piece?"

Madeleine did not reply; she was in terrible agony. Meantime Verdigris was cudgelling her brains and debating a scruple which had just seized her. At last she fumbled about in one of her pockets, and stammered:

"Wait a minute, I am going to give you back your five francs—It is a husband's money and sacred—I thought this gentleman was your lover, and there was no harm, was there, in accepting five francs from an old friend's lover?"

The young wife shook her head with a gesture of refusal. "Keep the money," she said "it is my gift—What do you want with me yet?"

"What do I want? nothing," replied Louise with a vacant stare. Then she suddenly bethought herself and began to chuckle.

"Ah, yes," she exclaimed, "I remember now—But, on my soul, Madeleine, you are very unkind. My head is not over strong, and you are upsetting me with your fine airs. I wanted to chat and be merry, and talk about the good old times—I was delighted when I saw you in that gig. I followed you, because I did not dare to shake hands with you before the gentleman who was there, and I was very wishful to be with you by yourself, you may be sure. For, in this part of the world, I never see any of our old friends. I am delighted to see you looking so well and happy."

She had taken a chair, and was whining out her words in her husky voice, chatting away with a familiarity that grated on Madeleine's finer nature. Her gesticulations were without animation, and she sat huddling in her rags, fixing on her old friend a dull vacant stare enlivened now and again by the maudlin smile of a drunkard. Her harsh accent, into which she strove to infuse a little warmth of endearment, and the cordial attitude of her enervated body, made her a disgusting, unbearable object.

"You see," she continued, "I have had no luck—I fell ill in Paris, I had taken too much absinthe, it seems: my head felt empty, and I trembled all over like a leaf. Look at my hands, they are always trembling—In the hospital I was afraid of the young saw-bones, for I heard them saying that it was all over with me and that I had not much more life left. Then I asked for my discharge, and they let me leave. I wanted to come back to Forgues, a little village about three miles from here, where my father was a wheelwright. One of my old lovers paid my railway fare."

She stopped to take breath, for she could only speak in short sentences now.

"Just fancy," she proceeded, "my father was dead. His business had gone badly. In his place I found another wheelwright who showed me the door. It will soon be six months since. I should have liked to get back to Paris, but I had not a penny left, and my clothes would hardly hold together—I was used up as they had said at the hospital. The men would not have touched me with the tongs. Then I stayed in the neighbourhood. The people are not bad, for they give me something to eat—Sometimes, on the roads, the urchins run after me throwing stones at me."

Her voice had become melancholy. Madeleine stood listening to her, chilled to the soul, with the heart no longer to send her away. Verdigris recovered and tossed her head with a careless air; the chuckle which usually showed her yellow teeth came back to her lips and she continued:

"But no matter, I have had my day, my dear—Do you remember how the men used to run after me? We have had some jolly parties together at Verrières. I was very fond of you, because you never used to abuse me. I remember, however, one day when I made you sulky out in the country; my lover had kissed you, and I pretended to be jealous. You know, I rather made fun of him."

Madeleine grew frightfully pale, for the memories evoked by this creature nearly choked her.

"By-the-bye," asked Verdigris suddenly, "your lover, that fine young fellow, Peter, James, or something or other, what have you done with him? He was a jolly man, if you like. I must tell you something, he used to come after me, for he thought me rather a brick. You cannot feel annoyed now when you hear of this—Do you ever see him?"

Madeleine was losing all patience, finding it impossible to bear any longer the anguish that this woman's presence caused her. Her anger was coming back again, and she felt thoroughly exasperated.

"I have told you that I am married," she replied. "Do go away, do go away."

The mad-woman became afraid, and she jumped up as if she had heard the shouts of the boys throwing stones at her in the fields.

"Why do you tell me to go away?" she stammered. "I have never done you any harm, I have been your friend, and we did not part on bad terms."

"Go away," Madeleine was still repeating. "I am a different woman from what I was when you knew me. I have a little girl."

"So have I, or at least I had. I don't know now whether I have or not, I forgot to give the nurse her monthly pay, and she has been taken away from me. You are not kind you receive me like a dog. I was right when I used to say that you were a minx, with your finical airs."

And as Madeleine in drawing nearer her made her retreat slowly towards the door, her madness declared itself openly and she shouted in a shrill voice:

"You ought not to despise others because you have been lucky yourself. You were no better off than myself once, I give you to understand, when we were both living in the same neighbourhood. If your fine gentleman had come across me, it would have been my luck to be wearing your silk dresses today, and you would be wandering about barefoot. Just think of that, my dear girl."

Just at this moment, Madeleine heard William's footsteps in the passage. Seized with sudden passion, she grasped Louise by the wrist and dragged her forcibly into the middle of the room, exclaiming:

"Stop, you are right. Here is my husband coming up. Stay and tell him that I am a wretch."

"Oh, no!" replied the other freeing herself. "The fact is that you made me angry at last. You are too proud, you know—I am going. I don't wish to cause you any bother."

But as she was going to leave the room, William entered. He stood still in surprise at the sight of the beggar, and cast an inquiring glance on his wife. Madeleine stood leaning against the big wardrobe, where her exasperation had drawn her up erect and firm. There was no blush on her brow, no agitation of shame in her expression; cold, resolute, her face contracted with a threatening look of energy, she seemed to be getting ready for a struggle.

"This is one of my old friends, William," she said in a brief tone. "She has come up to have a talk with me. Invite her to come and see us at La Noiraude."

These words fell painfully on William's ears. He could see, by the sound of Madeleine's voice, that their peace was gone again. An expression of mute anguish passed over his gentle face, and approaching Louise he asked her in a low tone of emotion:

"Did you use to know Madeleine?"

"Yes, sir," replied the poor woman "But don't listen to her. If I had known, I should not have come up."

"Do you want money?"

She shook her head disdainfully in refusal.

"No, thank you. If you were my lover, I don't say—I am going, good-night."

When she had shut the door, the young couple looked at each other for a moment in silence. They felt that an inevitable blow was going to fall on them, and that they could not open their lips without inflicting a fatal wound on each other; they would have wished not to speak, and yet, in spite of themselves, they were going to be compelled to meet the new sorrows that were threatening them. There was a cruel moment of distrust and anxious suspense. In the painful surprise which this unforeseen calamity caused him, William stood waiting in a resignation full of terror. He had left Madeleine, peaceful, smiling, and dreaming of a future teeming with affection, and he found her trembling and irritated, with her eyes fixed on him with a hard implacable expression; the difficulty he felt in explaining this sudden change redoubled his uneasiness, and made him anticipate some terrible blow whose rebound he could not avoid. He moved nearer to his wife, seeking to make her relent, and throwing into his gaze all the pitying tenderness that still existed within him. But she stood exasperated by the two rapid scenes which, one after the other, had just crushed her: ten minutes had been enough to bring before her all her past history, and now the only sensations she felt were those of unconcern and alarm produced on her by the apparitions of James and Verdigris. Since her former lover had left the room, she had not felt concerned about the misery that her husband would endure, she simply tried to find an outlet for the revolt of her whole being. The visit of Verdigris had produced in her the fierce selfishness of suffering. One thought alone throbbed in the tumult of her anger. "Since I am a wretch, since there is no pardon for me, and everything seeks to crush me, I will be what Heaven wishes me to be."

She was the first to speak.

"We have been cowards," she said to William, bluntly.

"Why do you say so?" he asked.

She shook her head disdainfully.

"We ought not to have run away like guilty criminals. We should have been strong in our right, in our five years of affection. Now the time has gone by to make any resistance, we are overcome, and our peace is gone."

William wished to know all, and replied:

"Why, what has happened, Madeleine?"

"Can't you guess?" exclaimed his young wife; "did you not see that poor wretch? She has reminded me of that past which stifles me and which I strive in vain to forget."

"But she has gone now; calm yourself. There is nothing in common between this creature and you. Don't I love you?"

Madeleine gave a short laugh and shrugged her shoulders as she replied:

"Nothing in common! I should like you to have been here. She would have told you that I should be walking the streets of Paris at this very moment, if you had not picked me up."

"Silence, Madeleine, don't speak like that. You are forgetting yourself; you ought not to sully our affection."

But his young wife grew excited by the hard words she felt rising to her lips. She was irritated to see her husband defend their love, and sought, in a feeling of anger, for crushing proofs of her shame, in order to cast them in his face and prevent him from trying again to calm her. Yet all she could say was:

"I have seen James."

William did not understand. He looked at her with a stupefied expression.

"He was here just now," she continued, "he spoke to me familiarly as he used to do, and wanted to kiss me."

And she looked straight at her husband who was turning pale.

He sat down on the table and stammered:

"But James has gone."

"Oh! no, he is sleeping in an adjoining room. I have seen him."

"Is this man everywhere, then?" said William, in an outburst of anger and alarm.

"Good heavens!" replied Madeleine, with a supercilious gesture of certainty. "Do you really hope to kill the past? Ah! indeed, this room seemed to you a secluded nook, a quiet retreat where nobody could come to stand between us; you told me that we were alone, out of the world, and elevated above the crowd, and that here we were going to spend a night of peaceful love. But, after all, the shade and silence of this room were false, and anguish awaited us in this strange inn where we were only to remain a few hours."

Her husband was listening in an attitude of utter dejection. His eyes were fixed on the ground and he despaired of arresting the furious torrent of her words.

"And I, poor fool," she continued, "was credulous enough to believe that there are places where oblivion can be found. I lulled myself with your dreams. But you see, William, that there is not a spot where we can be alone. It is vain for us to flee, and hide ourselves in the most secret retreats, for fate can reach us, and even there we should find my shame to drive us mad. The fact is, I carry sorrow with me, and a breath of air will be enough now to open my wounds. You must confess that we are tracked like wounded beasts which from thicket to thicket seek in vain for shelter, and die at last in some ditch."

She stopped for a moment, and then resumed, in a more irritated tone:

"It is our own fault, I say so again. We ought not to have been so cowardly as to run away. As we left La Noiraude, the night this man came, bear in mind, I told you that the memories of the past had been let loose and that they would pursue me. They are the howling pack that is on our track. I heard them running furiously behind me, and now I feel them worrying me and digging their claws into my flesh. Oh! how I suffer; these memories are tearing me limb from limb."

As she uttered this cry, she put her hands to her breast as if she had really felt the teeth of the dogs entering her flesh. William was weary of suffering: the cruel words of his wife were beginning to cause him a sort of nervous impatience. The bitter pleasure that she took in crying out against fate wounded his inert nature and his need of tranquillity. He was becoming irritated himself, and would have wished to silence her. Still he thought that he ought to try once more to calm her; but the attempt he made was very feeble.

"We will forget everything," he said, "and we will go farther away and seek for happiness."

Madeleine began to laugh. She clasped her hands and stretched forward her pale face.

"Ah! you think," she exclaimed, "that I shall be able to get hurt at every step and yet keep my head cool and sound. I don't feel that I have strength enough for that. I must have peace, or I cannot answer for my reason."

"Come now, don't stand out against me like that," replied her husband, coming nearer and trying to take her by the hands. "You see how I suffer. Spare me, and let us put an end to this cruel scene—Tomorrow, when we are calm, we shall perhaps find some remedy—It is late, let us go to bed."

He had lost all hope, and wished simply to isolate himself in the darkness and silence of the night; it seemed to him that he would suffer less when the candle was blown not, and he was in bed, no longer listening to Madeleine's grating voice. He went to the bedside, drew aside the curtains, and turned down a corner of the clothes. Madeleine, who was still leaning against the big wardrobe, watched him do this with a strange expression on her face. When the quilt was turned down and she saw the dazzling whiteness of the sheets, she said:

"I shall not go to bed. I will never sleep there with you."

He turned round in surprise, not understanding the reason of this fresh outbreak of resistance.

"I have not told you," she continued, "that I have already occupied this room with James—I have slept there in his arms."

And she pointed to the bed with a significant gesture. William fell back, and came and sat down on the table again. He uttered not a word, for this time he was utterly prostrate, and surrendered himself to the will of fate, for it seemed as if everything was crushing him more cruelly than he could bear.

"You must not be vexed with me if I am speaking the truth," replied Madeleine, harshly. "I am sparing you a feeling of shame. You refuse, don't you, to embrace me in the bed where I have already slept in James's arms? We should have horrible dreams, and, perhaps, I should die of anguish."

The name of her first lover, which she had just mentioned for the second time, brought her mind back to the recent interview. Her brain was wandering, and her thoughts only came in sudden rushes.

"He was with me just now," she said. "He jeered and insulted me. I am, in his eyes, a poor, abandoned woman, an abandoned woman whom he has the right to abuse. He does not know that I am respected now, and he has never seen me leaning on your arm—One moment, I wished to confess the truth to him. And I could not—Do you wish to know why I could not, and why I let him laugh, and speak familiarly to me? No, I can't tell you this—Oh! how carefully I ought to conceal it from you. But you must know all, and then you will not speak to me again of finding a remedy for all this sorrow—This man suspected me of having dragged a fresh lover into this room in order to taste a vile pleasure in evoking the past."

William had ceased to shudder, for he was growing enfeebled beneath all these blows.

"Oh, I know this room well," murmured Madeleine, after a short silence.

She came away from the wardrobe against which she had been leaning since the beginning of the scene, and stepped forward into the middle of the room. Here, full of mute rage, her neck swollen with suppressed violence, she began to stare slowly round with terrible fixedness. William, who had raised his head on hearing her footsteps, was alarmed by the expression of her eyes, and could not help saying:

"You frighten me, Madeleine; don't look at the walls like that."

She shook her head, and continued to turn round where she stood, examining each object at a distance.

"I know them, I know them all," she repeated in a low sing-song voice. "Oh! my poor head is splitting. You must forgive me, William, you must. The words came to my lips, in spite of myself; I should like to keep them back, but I feel them slipping out. I am filled with the memory of the past—It is a frightful thing not to be able to forget—Oh! for mercy's sake, kill my thoughts, kill my thoughts!"

She had raised her voice, and was shouting now:

"Oh! how I should like to be able to think no more, to be dead, or to be alive and mad!—Oh! to lose one's memory, to exist like a stone, to listen no longer to the frightful noise of the thoughts of my brain!—All this is escaping me in spite of all I can do; my thoughts torture me without respite, they flow through my body with the blood of my veins, and I can hear them vibrating at the tips of each of my fingers—Forgive me, William, I cannot keep silent."

She took a few strides with such a wild expression that her husband thought she was really going mad. He stretched out his hands, calling her by her name and endeavouring to keep her back.

"Madeleine, Madeleine," he said in a beseeching tone.

But she paid no heed. She had approached the wall, which fronted the fire-place, and was still repeating:

"Oh! that I could think no longer, for my thoughts are horrible, and I am expressing them aloud—I know everything here."

And she raised her eyes and gazed on the wall before her. The reappearance of James, of that man whose presence filled her with such deep emotion, had brought about in her a crisis both of body and mind; this crisis had gone on increasing, and now it was exciting her nature and producing on her a singular hallucination. The young wife, forgetting the presence of her husband, and filled with the memory of the past, thought herself back again in the days gone by; a feverish agitation had totally upset her usually calm being, and the smallest objects that surrounded her produced on her a keen, unbearable sensation which made her give utterance to each of her impressions in words and exclamations. She was living again the hours that she had spent in this place with James, and, as she had said, she was living them aloud, in spite of herself, as if she had been alone.

The blazing fire threw a bright red light on the walls. William's figure alone, as he still sat on the table, threw a shadow, which rose, black and colossal, from the floor to the ceiling; all the rest of the room, even the smallest corners, was brightly lit up by the shine. The bed, half exposed where the clothes had been turned down, lay white and inviting in the ruddy warmth from the fire, the angles and edges of the furniture shone with bright threads of light, and little miniature flames danced on the panels: the clear rays from the hearth brought out the harsh, glaring tones of the pictures, the red and yellow garments of Pyramus and Thisbe, stained the faded paper, with splashes of blood and gold, and the glass clock and the frail castle were illuminated from cellar to attic, as if the little dolls that lay reclining in the rooms had been holding a merry festival.

And in this clear brightness, Madeleine was going along in fits and starts by the side of the walls, her brown travelling dress rustling against the furniture, her face deathly pale, and her hair as red as if it were ablaze. She was examining one by one the pictures that related the unfortunate love-story of Pyramus and Thisbe.

"There ought to be eight," she said, "I counted them with James, and I stood up on a chair, and read him the inscription at the bottom of each picture. These little narratives seemed to him very funny, and he laughed at the bad grammar and the ridiculous wording of the sentences—I remember that I was annoyed at the way he poked fun at them, for I thought these artless love-stories full of charming simplicity—Ah! there is the wall that separated the lovers, and the crack through which they confided to each other their affection. Is it not delightful, that wall full of chinks, that obstacle which could not keep two hearts asunder? And then what a terrible ending! Here is the picture where Thisbe finds Pyramus bathed in blood: the young fellow thought that his loved one had just been devoured by a lioness; he has stabbed himself, and Thisbe, finding him lying dead on the ground, stabs herself too, and falls on his body to die—I should like to die like that—James laughed at me. 'If you were to find me dead,' I asked him, 'what would you do?' He came and took me in his arms, and kissed me, laughing louder than before, and answering: 'I would kiss you like that, on the lips, to bring you to life again.'"

William rose, full of feverish excitement and secret irritation. The thoughts and the sights which his wife was bringing before his eyes caused him a feeling of unbearable anguish, and he would have wished to stop her mouth. He took her by the wrists, and drew her into the middle of the room, shouting:

"Hold your tongue, hold your tongue. You are forgetting that I am here. You are too cruel, Madeleine."

But she escaped from him, and ran towards the window.

"I remember," she said, drawing aside one of the little muslin curtains, "this window looks into the yard. Oh! I recognise everything again, one streak of moonlight is enough—There is the pigeon-cote built of red bricks: in the evening, I used to stand with James watching the flights of pigeons coming back home, and stopping for a moment, on the edges of the roof, to plume their feathers, before disappearing one by one through the narrow round holes; they used to utter little plaintive coos and peck one another—and that is the yellow door of the stable which used to stand wide open; we could hear the horses breathing, and see the hens coming out cackling and scratching at the bits of straw they had found inside. It seems to me as if it were yesterday. I had to stay in bed for the first two days, because I was very unwell. Then, when I was able to get up, I came to this window. I thought this outlook of walls and roofs very melancholy, but I love animals, and I amused myself for hours together by watching the greedy habits of the hens, and the billing and cooing of the pigeons. James smoked all the time, and walked up and down the room. When I called him with shouts of laughter to come and see a chicken running off with a worm in its beak, followed by the others, all eager to share the dainty morsel, he would come and bend down to put his arm round my waist—he had a way of kissing me on the neck, light, quick kisses, so as to imitate with his lips, which hardly touched me, the cackling of the chickens. 'I am pretending to be a young chicken,' he would say jokingly."

"Hold your tongue, hold your tongue," shouted William, violently.

Madeleine had come away from the window, and was standing by the bed, staring at it, with a strange expression on her face.

"It was summer time," she went on in a lower voice, "and the nights were very hot. The first two days, James slept on the floor, on a mattress. When my illness had passed away, we put this mattress on to those I had slept on. At night, when we lay down, we found the bed full of lumps, and James pretended, in fun, that if we were to put twenty mattresses one on the top of the other we should not sleep any softer. We left the window partly open, and drew these blue cotton curtains aside, so as to get a breath of air. They are just the same as they were, and I see a rent there, that I made with a hair-pin. I was strong even then, and James was no weakling, and the bed seemed very narrow."

William, beside himself with exasperation, came and planted himself between Madeleine and the bed. He pushed her towards the fire-place, with an almost unconquerable longing to seize her by the throat, and strike her on the mouth, to reduce her to silence.

"She is going mad," he stammered, "and yet I cannot beat her."

The young wife stepped backwards to the table, looking on her husband's pale face with a stupefied expression. When she felt herself touching it, she suddenly turned round, and began to inspect it, throwing the light of the candle on to the greasy wood, and examining every spot that she noticed.

"Stay, stay," she muttered, "I must have written something here—It was the day before we went away. James was reading, and I was feeling bored at my own thoughts. Then I dipped the tip of my little finger in an inkstand that there was, and I wrote something on the wood. Yes, I shall find it, for it was very distinct and cannot have been rubbed out—"

She turned round, and bent down so as to see better. After a search of a few seconds she raised a cry of triumph. "I knew," she said, "stop, read this:—'I love James.'"

While she was looking, William had been thinking of the gentlest way he could devise of keeping her silent. His pride, and the selfishness of his love, were so deeply hurt that he felt as if he could not help being brutal. His fists doubled in spite of himself, and his arms were preparing to strike. If he did not use blows, it was because he had not yet completely lost his head, and because the little reason he had left revolted at the thought of beating a woman. But when he heard Madeleine reading, "I love James," and giving to the words the tender emphasis which she must have given in the days gone by, he drew himself up behind her with his fists in the air as if to hit her.

It was all done like a flash, yet his young wife, feeling a vague presentiment of what was happening, turned suddenly round and exclaimed:

"That's right, beat me—I want you to beat me."

Had she not turned round, in all probability William would not have restrained his anger. This enormous chignon of red hair, and this bold neck where he fancied he could still see the red imprints of James's kisses, made him pitiless. But when he saw before him Madeleine's pale and delicate face, he suddenly relented, and drew back with a gesture of the utmost despondency.

"Why do you hold back?" said his wife, "you see very well that I am mad and that you ought to treat me as a beast."

Then she burst out sobbing, and this crisis of tears suddenly subdued her excitement. Since the beginning of this strange hallucination which had made her live over again the days of the past, she had felt her head filled with a flood of tears.

She would not have spoken if her sobs had come freely. Now that her anguish and anger were melting in hot tears, she gradually became more and more herself again; she felt her being relent, and she saw all the cruelty of her madness. It seemed as if she were just recovering from the effects of a nightmare during which she had related aloud the frightful sights with which her disordered brain had been haunted. And she became astonished and blamed herself for the words which had just escaped from her lips. Never would she be able to recall these words, never would her husband forget them. Henceforth there would be, between herself and William, the memories of this room, the living reality of an episode of her intimacy with James.

Full of despair, and terrified by the idea that she had avowed everything of her own accord, without any request for confession on the part of William, she went up to him with her hands clasped in the attitude of a suppliant. He had just dropped into a chair, hanging his head and hiding his face in his outspread hands.

"You are in pain," she stammered, "and I have said things which are making your heart bleed—I know not why I told you all that. I was mad—Still I have not lost all my goodness of heart. You remember our happy evenings, when I had forgotten everything and thought myself worthy of you. Oh! how I loved you, William—And I love you still. I dare not swear to you that I love you always, because I feel that you will not believe me. It is the truth, however—In this room the memories seized me by the throat again, and I should have choked if I had not spoken."

He said nothing, but sat still, prostrate in a despair without bounds. "Very well," continued Madeleine, "I see all is over between us. Nothing remains now for me but to vanish out of sight—Death must be pleasant."

William raised his head.

"Death," he murmured, "death already—No, no, everything cannot be over yet."

He was looking at his wife, deeply touched at the thought of seeing her dead. He could hope no longer, and he felt himself struck by a mortal wound which could never be healed, yet all his nervous want of courage grew alarmed in presence of an immediate and abrupt ending. He might wish to live longer, but it was not because he dreamed of trying to seek for happiness again; it was because, unknown to himself, he found a bitter pleasure in suffering for this love which had been the joy of his life. In the grave, he would not even feel the wounds that Madeleine had caused him.

"Well! be open," said his wife, falling back into her harsh tone. "Don't be afraid of being cruel. Have I spared you?—Henceforth there will be some one between us—Would you dare to kiss me, William?"

There was a moment of silence.

"You see, you can't give me an answer," she continued—"Flight is impossible. I have no wish to lay myself open to the chance of meeting women in rags on the road, who speak to me as if I were a partner in their shame, and I have no wish to stop at inns where I shall run the risk of bringing to life again the days that are dead—It is better to have done with everything at once."

She was walking up and down, now suddenly stopping, now as suddenly starting again, looking vaguely round her for some means of putting an end to her life. William carefully watched her, not knowing what to say. Had she killed herself at that moment, he would have offered no resistance. But she suddenly stopped: the thought of her child had just presented itself to her mind, but she would not confess to her husband the cause of her hesitation. She said, simply:

"Listen, promise not to seek to prevent me from dying, the day our life becomes intolerable—Will you promise me this?"

He nodded his head in assent. Then he rose and put on his hat.

"You don't want to stay in this room till tomorrow, do you?" asked Madeleine.

"No," he replied, with a slight shudder, "we are going away."

When they had collected their belongings, they cast a farewell look on the room: the fire was dying out: the half-displayed bed-sheets were quite pink: the pictures of the loves of Pyramus and Thisbe hung now on the walls like black patches: and the glass clock was becoming quite blue in the shade. And the young couple told themselves that they had entered this room with hope at their hearts, and that they were leaving it in despair. As soon as they were in the passage they trod softly, almost unconsciously, so as to deaden the sound of their footsteps. James might hear them going away.

Madeleine even turned her head and looked towards the end of the landing with an instinctive movement.

When they were in the yard, they had to wake the servant, who got up in a very bad humour. It was two o'clock in the morning, and this sudden departure seemed to him extremely singular. Then he imagined that there must have been a little scene of jealousy between Madame Madeleine's two gentlemen, and this made him forget his bad temper. When William and Madeleine were in the gig he shouted out in a bantering tone:

"A pleasant journey. Good-bye, till we see you again, Madame Madeleine."

The young wife began to weep in silence. William let the reins hang loose and the horse took the road to Véteuil of its own accord. The thought that they had started to go to Paris no longer troubled them, for they preferred now to go and staunch their bleeding wounds in the calm and silence of La Noiraude. And they travelled back, mechanically, over the road they had come, like wild beasts smitten to death and dragging themselves to their holes to die in peace. This return journey was almost heart-rending. The country lay spread out with a more forbidding aspect under the slanting rays of the moon, which traced out colossal shadows along the road now white with the frost. From time to time William gave an encouraging exclamation to his horse, quite unconscious that he did so, and Madeleine had begun again to stare vacantly at the yellow reflection of the lamps flitting over the ditches. Towards morning the cold became so keen that her hands were quite numb under the grey woollen rug.

XI

At La Noiraude the young couple resumed their uneventful existence, and shut themselves up again in the silent shade of the vast dining-room. But their solitude had lost its previous smiling peace; it was gloomy and full of despair. Only a few days ago, they had spent their time in the chimney-corner, hardly speaking a word to each other, and content with the mere exchange of happy glances: today, their long silent tête-à-têtes depressed them with crushing weariness and vague fear. Nothing seemed changed in their life; it was the same calm, the same clock-work regularity, and the same solitary trance. Only, their hearts were closed, their looks no longer met with exquisite tenderness, and this was enough to make everything around them seem cold and forbidding. The big room had now a funereal aspect, and they lived there in a continual shudder, saddened by the cheerless wintry sunshine, and fancying themselves buried in some tomb. They would get up sometimes and go to the window, but, after casting a disconsolate glance at the bare trees in the park, they would come back with sudden shivers, to spread out their cold hands to the fire.

They never spoke of the drama which had crushed them. The few words that they exchanged never went beyond the commonplace and trivial expressions of ordinary intercourse. They sank prostrate in their ennui, with hardly the energy to think openly of their sufferings. The crisis which had overtaken them at the Big Stag seemed to throw them into a state of stupor and unworthy inaction: they had come out of it with aching brains and weary limbs, and they gave way to a feeling of heaviness in the gloomy tranquillity that surrounded them. If a painful thought came suddenly to disturb their sleepy existence, they would tell themselves that they had still a month before them. James had given them a thirty days' peace, and they might slumber till his return. And they would fall back into their trance, striving to become callous, and musing from morn till night on trivial matters, on the fire that refused to burn, on the weather, or on what they were going to have for dinner.

They plunged more deeply every day into this animal life. Still, they enjoyed good health. Madeleine grew stout; her cheeks became fuller, and assumed the flabby paleness of a nun's. She was becoming inordinately fond of good things, and felt a keen pleasure in all physical enjoyments. William gave way like his wife to the stupor of his grief, and spent hours in picking up with the tongs the little bits of burning wood that fell on to the ashes, and putting them behind the logs.

The month of sleepy inaction which the young couple had before them seemed as if it would never finish. They would willingly have consented to end their life in this blank inactivity in which they found themselves, and, for the first few days especially, they felt filled with a peaceful feeling of calm. But this stupor could not last: it was soon disturbed by sudden and painful transports of sorrow. The least event which drew them from their state of dejection caused them unbearable anguish. Geneviève was not long in making them undergo martyrdom: it was she who first drove them back to their suffering. She stood like a phantom before Madeleine, and crushed her with her presence.

Strong in her life of virtue and toil, the old fanatic showed herself without pity for the sinner. The thought of carnal joys exasperated this woman, this woman who had lived a life of strict virginity. Thus she could not forgive the young wife her career of love, and the quivering of pleasure that would still set her flesh vibrating. She could always see her passing from the arms of James to the arms of William, and this double surrender of herself seemed to her to be a diabolical prostitution, and to indicate a desire for coarse debauch. She had never loved Madeleine, and she now began to detest her with a disdain mingled with dread. This strong young woman, with a fair skin and red hair, frightened her as if she were a ghoul thirsting for the blood of young men; if she hated her to the very depths of her being, she trembled in her presence, and stood on the defensive through dread of seeing her spring at her throat. She would not have hated the devil more thoroughly, nor taken greater precautions against him.

She continued to live in close intimacy with the young couple, always taking her meals with them and passing the evenings in their company. Her rigid and threatening attitude was an eternal protestation: she treated them as guilty criminals, looked on them with the eyes of an implacable judge and clearly showed them every hour the disgust and anger that their union caused her. She tried especially to make Madeleine feel how much she despised her. When the young wife had touched any object, she avoided making use of it, wishing by this to show that she looked upon it as polluted. Every night she began to drawl the verses of her big Bible. William had requested her once to go and read it in her bedroom, but she had given him to understand that her sacred reading purified the dining-room and drove away the demon. And she had become so doggedly persistent as to stay there till bed-time, filling the shade with her droning voice. Day by day, she read in a higher tone and selected passages more reeking with blood: the narratives of guilty women brought to chastisement, the fire of Sodom, or the pack of dogs worrying Jezebel's entrails were continually on her lips, and then she would cast a look gleaming with fierce joy on Madeleine. Sometimes too she would add a few observations on the text, and threaten with horrible torments a criminal, not mentioned by name, but sufficiently designated by her eyes. In these extemporary comments, which were muttered in a deep voice, she set forth in all their terror the punishments of hell, the caldrons of boiling oil, the long tusks of the demons turning over on the red hot ashes the frizzled bodies of the damned, and the rain of fire falling throughout all eternity, every drop marking as with a searing iron the shoulders of the howling denizens of the abyss. Then she demanded of God speedy justice, and besought him not to let a single guilty soul escape, but to rid the earth at once of its pollution.

Madeleine had no wish to listen, but the mumbled hissing words entered her ears in spite of herself. At last she became superstitious, though hitherto she had not been able to bring her mind to believe in any form of faith. At certain periods of the disorder of her brain, she fancied that this hell, this chamber of torture, of which the fanatic always drew such a frightful picture, really did exist. From that time she lived in a perspiration of anguish which stood in beads on her brow, when the thought of death presented itself to her. She looked upon herself as guilty and doomed to eternal punishment. This old woman, who spent her days in causing her to feel the horror of her crime and the cruelty of the punishment which heaven was reserving for her, so far deranged her reason that she became as timid as a child: she hardly knew where she was, and thought of the devil as she had thought of Old Mother Broomstick when she was a little girl. And she would say to herself: "I am a wretch, and Geneviève is right in treating me as a sinner: I bring a stain on this house by my presence and I deserve the most cruel torments." Then, in the evenings she listened to the old protestant's reading with terror and excitement, fancying she could catch the sound of the clanking of chains and the hissing of the flames in the murmur which pervaded the room. And she would think that if she happened to die during the night, she would wake up next morning in the heart of a blazing furnace.

But she did not always submit without resistance, to the influence of these horrible sensations which Geneviève's attitude produced on her, and at times she would feel quite irritated at the continual presence of this pitiless woman. When she saw her reject the bread that she had just cut, or met the fierce look that followed her everywhere, she would at last fall into a blinding passion, for she still preserved an occasional burst of pride which made her revolt against the unceasing attacks of the old protestant. Then she would declare that she intended to be mistress in her own house and become almost furious.

"Out you go," she would yell at the old woman. "Leave this house immediately. I'll have no lunatic here."

And, as William hung his head, not venturing to breathe a word, she turned towards him and added violently:

"What a coward you are! You stand by and let people be disrespectful to your wife—Rid me of this mad creature, if you have any love left for me."

Geneviève gave a strange smile and rose, erect and rigid, fixing on Madeleine her round eyes flashing with suppressed fire:

"He is no coward," she said in her cracked voice, "he is well aware that I am not insulting anybody—Why do you make such a violent objection, when it is God who speaks?"

She pointed, with a fiendish expression on her face, to her Bible. Then she too, became furious, and continued, raising her voice:

"That is always the way—Impurity wishes to raise its head and bite honest women. It would be a fine thing, indeed, for you to drive me from this house where I have toiled for thirty years, you who have only come to bring sorrow and sin—Just look at me, and then look at yourself. I shall soon be a hundred years old: I have grown grey in devotion and prayer, and I have not a single fault to reproach myself with when I look back at my long life. And you want me to bend before you, and to be fool enough to give up my place to you! Where do you come from, and who are you? You are still quite young, and yet the hand of death is on you already; you come from the abode of evil, and you are fast approaching your punishment—I can pass my judgment on you to your face, and I ought not to obey you."

She uttered these words with an accent of indomitable pride, and with deep conviction, for she looked upon Madeleine as a thief, who

ÉMILE ZOLA

had stolen by surprise into La Noiraude, and sought to filch respect and peace. The young wife grew exasperated at each of her thrusts.

"You shall go," she repeated vehemently. "Am I mistress in this house or not?—It would be preposterous if I were to be obliged to give up my home to a servant."

"No, I shall not go," replied Geneviève, flatly. "God has placed me in this house to watch over my son William, and to punish you for your faults—I shall stay till he is delivered from your arms, and I see you crushed beneath the anger of Heaven."

This stubbornness, and the shrill voice of this woman subdued Madeleine's will. She gave way, not daring to offer any further resistance to the centenarian, and unable to devise a means of getting rid of her presence. She sank into her chair, and repeated in a harrowing tone:

"How I suffer! How I suffer!—You don't see that you are killing me by inches with your persecutions. Do you think that I don't feel the icy thrill of your glances that are always fixed on me? And every night, when you are reading, I can perceive very well that you are addressing yourself to me only—Do you want me to repent?"

"Repentance is useless, for God never pardons crimes of the flesh."

"Very well then, leave me in peace: speak to me no more of your devil and your God: cease to fill me, each night, with bad thoughts that hold me panting till next morning—You may stay, it is all the same to me: but I do not wish to see you again, and I beseech you to go and live somewhere else, in another room—Even yesterday you were speaking of hell with sinister delight: I passed a frightful night—"

She shuddered, and Geneviève watched her grow pale, with a singular expression of satisfaction.

"It is not I," she said, "who cause you these bad dreams. If you cannot sleep, it is because the demon is in your body and torments you, the moment you have put out your candle."

"You are mad," shouted Madeleine, whiter than a sheet, "and you are trying to frighten me as if I were a child—But I am no coward, and I don't believe in your nursery tales."

"Yes, but you do," repeated the fanatic with the conviction of hallucination, "you are possessed—When you cry, I see Satan puffing out your neck. He is in your arms that are never still, and in your cheeks that quiver with nervous contractions—There now! just look at your left hand at this moment: do you see the convulsions that are contorting the fingers: Satan is there! Satan is there!"

She raised a cry, and recoiled as if before an unclean beast. Madeleine looked at her hand, and there really was a nervous twitching of the fingers. She became silent, for she could not utter another word of protestation or anger. "Geneviève is right," she thought. "It is not she that frightens me, the fright is in myself, in my guilty flesh. At night when I have bad dreams, it is my memories that are choking me." Then she became resigned and tolerated the presence of the old servant. All their wranglings ended like this, and Madeleine was only more terrified than ever after each one. In her terror she confused James, whose presence never left her, with the demon whom the protestant pretended to see writhing under her skin. The disdain which the latter heaped on her, and the holy horror which she seemed to feel at the sight of her, plunged her into bitter reveries: "I must be very infamous," she would say, "that this woman should refuse to touch the objects I have made use of. She shudders at the sight of me as if she saw a toad, and she would gladly crush my head with her heel. I must, indeed, be a miserable creature." And she would become alarmed at herself, and look with loathing at her fair skin, fancying that she saw it reeking with a pungent odour. It seemed to her as if her beauty were a mask behind which was concealed some monstrous animal. When the religious mania of the fanatic had so far disordered her brain, she had no clear consciousness of her existence, and spent hours together in listening if she could not really hear Satan in her breast.

William was too nervous to save her from Geneviève's clutches, for this woman exercised a strange influence over them both, by her age and her almost prophetic attitude. The young husband would gladly have welcomed the courage to send her to live alone in the little house on the edge of the park. But he did not dare to put any pressure on her. She had nursed his father, she had looked after his own bringing up, and he could not drive her away. When she quarrelled with Madeleine, he kept out of the way, trying not to get crushed between these two angry women. But it was in vain, for he always arrived just at the moment when each of them was making a thrust at him; Madeleine reproached him for tolerating Geneviève's incredible liberty of speech, and Geneviève accused him of rushing willingly into damnation by living with sin. Assailed on both sides, and too feeble to come to a decision that would require energy, he would beseech them to be quiet and not distress his life so cruelly. Directly he saw them near each other, the dread of hearing them commence an attack made him feel extremely uneasy, and if they happened to exchange a few sharp words he went and tapped on the windows, full of anxiety, and feeling the storm gathering over his head.

What produced the most painful impression on the young couple, was Geneviève's idea that she was trying to bring about William's salvation. She wished to tear him from Madeleine's arms and to purify him so that he might not go to hell. She busied herself in this conversion with all the obstinacy of her nature. Every hour, she found means of recurring to her fixed idea, and the smallest incident served to make the conversation turn on this subject.

"Listen, my son," she would say, "you ought to come, at night, and say your prayers in my room, as you used to do when you were little. You remember; you used to clasp your hands and repeat the words one by one after me. This would save you from the snares of the demon."

William paid no attention, but this only made the protestant the more earnest, and she explained straight out what she meant.

"You can still escape the clutches of Satan," she went on. "You are not contaminated and condemned for ever. But, take care! if you continue to repose in the arms of the impure one, she will carry you off one of these nights into the abyss—A prayer would redeem your soul—If when you are on this woman's breast, you will repeat three times a prayer which I am going to teach you, she will raise a loud cry and fall into dust. Try, you will see."

Madeleine was by, listening with terror to the old lunatic.

Then Geneviève slowly recited the prayer which was to make the young wife crumble into dust. "Lubrica, daughter of hell, return to the flames which thou has left for the damnation of men. May thy skin become black, may thy red hair spread over thy whole body and cover thee with a beast's fur. Disappear in the name of Him at whose word thou tremblest, disappear in the name of God the Father."

This adjuration had doubtless been composed by the fanatic herself. She accompanied it with certain instructions; it was to be pronounced three times, and each time a cabalistic sign was to be made on the body of the impure one, the first time on the left breast, the second time on the right, and the third on the navel. It was after this third sign, that this snowy body would change into vile filth.

As the young couple listened to Geneviève's terrible vagaries, they thought that they had raised a phantom which could never be laid. This medley of religion and sorcery made them lose all proper judgment of things. Madeleine felt carried away by a sort of diabolical whirlwind, and her sense of right wavered more and more each day beneath the ttacks of the old woman. Like his wife, William led a terrible life of shocks to his nerves and foolish fears. For a month, they lived in this atmosphere of dread, and La Noiraude was filled with the exorcisms of old Geneviève. The droner of canticles paced the long passages muttering her prayers, and often at night humming psalms which filled the silence with their mournful echoes. You might have thought that she was fully bent on driving her master and mistress stark mad.

The young couple had another ground too of anguish. They were cruelly pained by the serious expression on little Lucy's face which made her look so like James. She was now compelled to stay at La Noiraude, because her nurse had just gone into service in a tradesman's house at Véteuil. William did not dare to confess that she frightened him and that they would have to send her away. He tried to forget her presence during the days that she spent by his side in the huge room. Lucy hardly played at all now; she would sit on the floor, mute and motionless, like an important person buried in thought. With that intuitive notion about affection which is so inherent in children, she could see that her father did not take to her; she had not yet reached her fourth year, and could not attempt to give any explanation for the way he neglected her, but she felt that she lived in a cooler atmosphere of love, and she grew sad to find that they were forgetting to kiss her. Seeing that her noisy games pained her husband, Madeleine had so often told her in a stern voice to keep quiet, that she had become quite timid. She would walk on tip-toe, trying to avoid making the least noise, and her boisterous enjoyment had given place to a sort of terrified meditation. Her favourite position was to sit crouching before the fire; she would put her little hands on her legs, and, sitting in this attitude, rock herself for hours. Then she fell into a brown study and gazed at the flames, perfectly motionless. She must be musing on her chilly surroundings, and her thoughts, as yet scarcely formed, were lost doubtless in the big sorrow that her undeserved misfortunes caused her. At times, for no apparent reason, she would suddenly wake up from her reverie, and raise her head, looking at William straight in the face. Then she would screw up her lips and frown as she examined her father with a steady gaze, as if to read in his face what it was that he could have to reproach her with. William would then think that it was James who was before him, and he would leave the chimney corner and walk excitedly up and down the room.

And, as he thus tramped backwards and forwards, he felt that the child's eyes were fastened on him. As she seemed to wake up from these brown studies, Lucy's face had the look of a little old woman; her pale features seemed wrinkled and became strangely serious, and she appeared to be thinking of things beyond her age. Her father fancied then that she understood everything and that she guessed what it was that estranged him from her. Her attitude like that of an important person, and her eyes full of sad thoughts touched him with an indefinable emotion, as if he had always expected to hear her argue like an upgrown woman and speak to him about her resemblance to James.

Often Lucy would not be content with simply looking at her father, but would get up gently and approach him holding out her arms. Then in a beseeching tone she would repeat her favourite expression, "Take me, take me," urged by that irresistible need for kisses that children sometimes feel. And as William did not kiss her/she insisted, and a nervous twitching would pucker her little face. When her father had managed to escape touching her hands, she went and threw herself with tears into Madeleine's arms. Her mother was grieved at the sadness of her daughter; yet she did not dare, when she saw her in an attitude of meditation, to take her on her knees and play with her to drive away her resigned expression of martyrdom, for she was afraid of irritating her husband. But every time that the child, on being repulsed by her father, came to ask her for consolation, she could not resist the wild longing that she felt to press her to her heart. She dried with her kisses the big silent tears that filled her eyes, and walked about with her for a moment, speaking softly to her, and striving to give her for a few seconds the affection which she usually denied her.

One day, Lucy had been repulsed by her father with a hasty movement and she ran sobbing to her mother. When she was on her knees, she stammered:

"Papa has beaten me. He is very naughty and I won't have anything more to do with him."

William had gone near to her, sorry for his brutality.

"Look now," said Madeleine to the little girl as she rocked her on her knees, "your father is here. He will kiss you if you are good."

But the child threw her arms round her mother's neck, with a shudder of fright. When she thought herself safe, she raised her eyes towards her father and looked at him with a serious expression, sobbing:

"No, no, I won't have anything more to do with him."

And she accompanied these words with a little pout of reluctance that made the young couple cast a singular glance at each other. William's eyes said clearly to Madeleine: "You see, she refuses to be my daughter, for she has blood in her veins which is not mine." The presence of this poor little being was thus a source of continual pain, for it seemed to them that James was always there, by their side. They made martyrs of themselves, giving to trivial matters a significance of terror and suffering. The young husband especially seemed to take a horrible pleasure in imagining monstrous things. He still loved his child with a strange affection, an affection subject at times to a sudden accession of dread. Sometimes he felt a desire to press her to his bosom, to obliterate her features with his kisses, so as to make her entirely his. He would look at her earnestly, seeking for a spot on her face that bore a resemblance to himself, in order to plant his kisses on it. Then he gradually became frightened, as he saw the child, troubled by this scrutiny, screw up her mouth and contract her brows. And then he would lose himself again in his old thoughts: he was not this little thing's only father, he had made a total surrender of himself to Madeleine, and had only been able to have by her a daughter whose form had been fashioned in the embraces of another man. The sight of Lucy, as she looked upon him with the dreamy expression of a person of importance, the thought that fortune had simply made him an instrument to assist in giving birth to James's child, former affection for this man and the jealous hatred with which he now felt pervaded, all this produced in him a sensation of unbearable anguish, and heartrending revolts of body and mind.

"I am the dupe of life," he would think bitterly. "I have been robbed of everything, body, heart, and reason. Events and men have tortured me unceasingly. I have loved two beings, James and Madeleine, and these two beings are turning against me at the present moment. Nothing remained for me but to undergo this incredible grief, the grief of being robbed of my child—My kisses have brought James to life again: I have put Lucy, I have put this man between Madeleine and myself."

Another event transpired to increase his woes. One evening, Lucy, who had been crouching before the fire as usual, fell asleep, with her head leaning against her mother's knees. But her slumber was very much disturbed by sudden starts and rambling complaints, and when

Madeleine took her in her arms to put her to bed, she noticed that her face was quite red. This alarmed her, for she thought that the child was threatened with some kind of fever, and she insisted on her little bed being removed and set up in her own room, and made up her mind to stay by her, telling William to lie down. But he did not sleep a wink the whole night, for he could not take his eyes from his wife who was watching with uneasy anxiety. The room, lit up by the pale light of, a night-lamp, seemed to him indistinct and veiled as in a dream. He lost all consciousness of himself: thoroughly worn out, and with his eyes wide open, he seemed to be passing a night of ghastly dreams. Each time that Madeleine leaned over the cot of the little patient, he fancied he could see a phantom rise by the bed-side of his dead child. Then as Lucy tossed about in the delirium of the fever, he was astonished at hearing her still complaining, and fancied he was watching an endless death agony. This sight of his wife clad in a white dressing gown, anxious and silent, bending over the shivering child, whose red face he saw clearly among the bed clothes, had in the stilly silence of the night and the flickering flame of the lamp an air of painful desolation. He lay crushed and terrified till morning.

When the doctor came about nine o'clock he found Lucy in a very alarming state. The illness had declared itself, the child had the small-pox. From this moment her mother never left her: she passed the whole day by her bedside and had her meals, which she scarcely touched, brought up to her: at night, she snatched an hour or two's rest on a long chair. For a whole week, William lived in a sort of stupor: he kept going and coming from the bed-room to the dining-room, and stopping in the passages to reflect, without being able to find a single thought in his empty brain. But it was the nights especially that were so terrible: in vain did he turn over in his bed, he only succeeded in falling off, towards morning, into a feverish sleep, out of which the least groan from Lucy awoke him. Every night as he lay down, he dreaded to see her die under his eyes. The air of the room, pervaded with the odour of drugs, stifled him, and the thought that a poor creature was suffering by his side caused him a continual anguish by exciting his nervous sensibilities. If he could have read clearly the cause of his trouble, he would have wept with shame and rage. Unknown to himself, he was feeling irritated at Madeleine who seemed to have quite forgotten his existence, and he was angry with her for becoming so entirely absorbed in the safety of this child whose face pained them. Perhaps she was simply watching over her because she was like James: she wished to keep constantly before her the living picture of her first lover. If the little thing had been like him, her father, his wife would not have been so distressed. He did not acknowledge to himself these frightful suppositions, but they revolved vaguely in his brain with a sensation of torture. One day, when he was alone in the dining-room, he asked himself all at once what would be his feelings if Madeleine were to come down and tell him the unexpected news of Lucy's death. His whole being replied that this news would console him greatly. Then he was beside himself, and thought he had discovered in his nature the cruelty of an assassin. Today he was wishing for his daughter's death, tomorrow doubtless he would kill her. His stupor was thus subject to sudden crises of madness.

Geneviève, in her character of implacable judge, redoubled his anguish. From the very first commencement of Lucy's illness, she had seized every opportunity of entering the room where the poor child lay suffering. When she was by her side, she never ceased to predict her death, and to mutter that heaven would take her away from her parents to punish them for their sins. She never assisted Madeleine to nurse her, she never gave the little patient her medicine or smoothed her pillow, without some ominous remark. Exasperated by these continual thoughts of death and punishment which forbade all hope, the young mother soon drove her from the room and gave her orders never to set foot in it again. Then the old protestant haunted William's footsteps with her mournful remarks; whenever she could catch him in a passage or in the dining-room, she kept him for an hour listening to her vagaries, pointing to the hand of God in the illness of his daughter and to the certainty of punishment for himself in the near future. These interviews crushed what little hope the poor man had.

Not daring to remain in the bedroom and dreading to meet the fanatic if he left it, he knew not where to spend his days. In her delirium Lucy kept calling "Papa, papa," in a strange tone which pierced his heart. "Is she really calling for me?" he would ask himself. Then he would go near and lean over the little patient's bed. The burning eyes, enlarged and inflamed by the fever, would fasten on him with terrible earnestness. She hardly seemed to see him, and her gaze was lost in space. Then she suddenly turned her head, and stared at another point of the room, still shouting "Papa, papa," in a more panting tone. And William would say, "She does not hold out her arms to me, she is not calling for me at all." At other times, Lucy would smile

ÉMILE ZOLA

in her fever; there was nothing irregular or fitful in her delirium, she rambled peacefully from one subject to another, chattering away with an occasional stifled murmur of complaint: she would lift her little wasted hands from beneath the bed clothes, and wave them feebly, as if she were asking for invisible toys. It was a heart-rending sight and Madeleine could not refrain from weeping as she tried to tuck her up again. But the child refused to lie down, and sat up in bed chattering all the time in disconnected words. William, thoroughly unnerved, made towards the door.

"Stay, I beg you," Madeleine would say, "she often calls for you, and it would be better if you were always by."

Then he would stay and listen with nervous shudders to Lucy's sweet yet painful prattle. Since the very first day that the small-pox had declared itself, he had taken a strange interest in following the ravages of the disease on the child's face. The pimples first attacked the forehead and the cheeks which they covered almost entirely with a mass of sores; then by a curious freak the spread of the pustules stopped leaving a space round the eyes and mouth. The face looked almost like a hideous mask, with holes in it through which appeared a delicate mouth and soft childish eyes, In spite of himself William kept trying to discover if the pimples would not efface the resemblance to James on these altered features. But invariably, through the holes of the mask, in the contraction of the lips and the play of the eyelids, he fancied he could detect still the portrait of Madeleine's first lover. Yet, in the height of the fever, he saw with unconscious joy that the resemblance was disappearing, and this calmed him and permitted him to stay by Lucy's side.

One morning the doctor announced that he could at last assure them of the child's recovery. Madeleine could have kissed his hands, for she had felt thoroughly worn out for a week. Yet the improvement in the patient was very slow, and William was a prey again to a secret feeling of anxiety. He began once more to study his daughter's face, feeling an oppression at heart as each pustule disappeared. Gradually the mouth and eyes which had been attacked in the later stages of the disease became clear of sores, and the young father told himself that he was going to see James brought to life again once more. One gleam of hope remained. One day as he was showing the doctor out, he asked him at the door:

"Do you think that any marks will remain on the child's face?"

Madeleine overheard this question, although it had been put in a whisper. She rose up very pale, and went to the door.

"Set your mind at ease," replied the doctor. "I think I can promise you that the pimples will leave no trace."

William started with a movement so pronounced of regret and dejection that his wife looked him in the face with an expression of deep reproach. Her eyes seemed to say: "Then you would have your child's face disfigured in order to escape a little pain!" He hung his head and felt oppressed with one of those mute feelings of despair to which he was subject when he found himself giving way to cruel thoughts of selfishness. The longer he lived, the more cowardly he felt himself in presence of suffering.

The little patient's cote stayed in her parents' bedroom a fortnight longer. Lucy gradually regained her strength. The hopes of the doctor were realised; the pimples had entirely disappeared, and William now hardly dared to look at his child. For some time too, a new source of anguish had been springing up in his breast; for his restless disposition, exaggerating the smallest circumstances, seemed to take a cruel delight in self-torture. Having noticed one day a little gesture in Madeleine which reminded him of a movement of the hand which James made every minute when he was talking, he began to watch his wife and to study each of her attitudes and each of the inflections of her voice. He was not long in convincing himself that she had preserved something of the ways of her former lover. This discovery was a terrible blow to him.

It was no dream, for Madeleine had at times certain points of resemblance to James. In former days when she had been sharing the young man's life, and living under his influence, she had almost unconsciously fallen in with his tastes and mode of life. During a whole year, she had received from him a sort of physical education which had fashioned her after his image; she repeated the words of his ordinary conversation, and reproduced, unknown to herself, his familiar gestures and even the intonations of his voice. This propensity to imitation, which gives to every woman, after a certain time, a sort of kinship of manners to the man in whose arms she is living, brought about the modification of certain of her features and changed the character of her face into James's ordinary expression. This was a result that must necessarily follow from the physiological laws of their union; as her virginity was ripening under his influence, as he was making her his for life, he was transforming the virgin into a woman and stamping this woman with his imprint. At this period Madeleine was unfolding in the full bloom of puberty; her limbs, her face, even her look and smile were transformed and expanded by the action of the new blood which the young fellow was infusing into her veins; she became one of his family, and took his likeness. Afterwards when he went away, she forgot his gestures and inflexions of voice, though still remaining his wife, his submissive kinswoman. Then William's kisses had almost obliterated James's features from her face, and five years of forgetfulness and peace had made this man's blood stagnant. But since his return, it had become brisk again, and Madeleine, by living continually in thought and dread of her first lover, was assuming again, under the influence of this one idea, her attitudes, accent and features of former days. All her former intimacy seemed to be coming to life again in her outward appearance. She began to walk, talk and live at La Noiraude, as she had formerly lived in the Rue Soufflot when she was James's submissive mistress.

William trembled sometimes as he heard her pronounce a word. He would raise his head in alarm, and look before him, as if he had expected to behold his former friend. And he saw his wife who would remind him of the doctor by the freaks of the features of her face. She had a turn of the neck and a shrug of the shoulders that he recognised. Certain special words too which she repeated every moment, gave a painful shock to his nerves, for he remembered having heard them from James's lips. Every time now that she opened her mouth or moved a limb, he could see that she was full of and quivering with her first love. He could guess how far she was under the influence of this passion. Had she wished to deny the possession of her whole being, her body itself and its smallest movement would have declared what a slave she was. She was not simply thinking of James now, she was living with him in the flesh, in his embraces; she was confessing every instant that he possessed her still and that she would never lose the imprint of his kisses. Nothing could have induced William to clasp her in his arms, when he saw that she could not shake off the impression of his comrade and his brother; he always ended by looking on the two as inseparable, and he would have thought himself guilty of a monstrous desire, if he had taken her then to his breast. When he felt certain that Madeleine was becoming James's submissive spouse, he grew absorbed in the study of this strange change, and in spite of himself, though such an inspection caused him terrible sufferings, he hardly took his eyes off his wife, and he stood by at the awakening of the old love, noting each fresh resemblance that revealed itself. His hourly observations nearly drove him out of his senses. Not only was his daughter the picture of this man, the thought of whom brought a burning sensation to his cheeks, but to complete his misery his wife must be continually speaking of him by her voice and by her gestures.

In the transformation of her being Madeleine went back too to some of the habits she had when a young woman. The gentle and thoughtful serenity which five years of esteem and affection had imparted to her nature departed at the reappearance of the emotions of her former life. She lost the soft pink tint of her complexion, her bashfulness, the modest grace of her carriage, and all that chaste appearance which marked her out as a woman of the better class. Now she would remain half-dressed for mornings together, as in the days when she lived in the Rue Soufflot; her red hair fell down her neck, and her dressing-gown would be open at the top, disclosing her plump white neck, inflated with voluptuousness. She put no restraint on her actions, mixing up in her conversation words that she had never heard uttered at La Noiraude, indulging in gestures that she had learnt from her old friends, and becoming almost vulgar unconsciously by virtue of her memories of the past. William looked on, with sorrowful dismay, at this debasement of Madeleine's character; when he saw her walking with an ungainly waddle, as if her hips were too heavy for her limbs, he hardly recognised her for the strong healthy woman whom he had as his wife for four years. He looked upon himself now as married to a girl reeking with the filth of her past. The fatal concomitants of a life such as Madeleine had led had fallen upon her in his arms, as if to show him that his kisses were powerless to save her from the consequences of her former intimacy with James. It was vain for her to lull herself in a dream of peace, for she awoke at the first quickening of her blood, and fell back into the shame which she had formerly accepted, and which she was now to complete.

Madeleine had no clear perception of her present state, no consciousness of the way in which she was relapsing into her former habits. She simply suffered at the thought of being possessed by James whom she was unable to drive from her thoughts. She was not in love with this man now, and would gladly have removed him from her breast, and yet she would always feel his embraces and his influence. It was like a continual violation of herself, against which her mind revolted and to which her body consented, finding no effort of will strong enough

ÉMILE ZOLA

to deliver her from it. This struggle between her captive flesh and her desire to belong entirely to William was for her an unending cause of excitement and dread. When she had exerted every energy, when she believed that she had rid herself of the memory of her lover, and heard, at the moment when she thought she could at last surrender herself in peace to her husband's kisses, this memory cry out in her being with a more tyrannical voice, she was seized with a despair without bounds, giving up every form of resistance, and allowing the past to prostitute her in the present. The thought of being thus unceasingly at the beck of a man for whom she now felt no affection, the certainty that she loved William and that she deceived him against her will every hour, inspired her with a deep disgust of herself. She could not explain to herself the fatal physiological laws which placed her body out of reach of the action of her will; she could not fathom that secret quickening of her blood and nerves which had made her James's wife for life; when she wished to reason with herself on the strangeness of her sensations, she always ended by accusing herself of monstrous tastes, as she saw her powerlessness to forget her lover and love her husband. Since she detested the one, and adored the other, why should she be subject to such painful pleasures in James's imaginary embraces, and why could she not testify her affection freely to William? When she asked herself this insoluble question, which contained the key to the trouble of her existence, which would have explained the enigma of the special malady from which she was suffering, she fancied she was a prey to some horrible and unknown disease, and told herself that Geneviève was right and that the devil must be in her body.

During the day, she still resisted the influence of James's memory and succeeded in forgetting him. She no longer sat as she had done, prostrate with dejection, in the chimney corner: she moved about, finding work for her hands, and when there was nothing to be done, she would talk excitedly on any subject so as to deaden her thoughts by the sound of her words. But at night she belonged entirely to her lover. Directly she began to drop asleep, directly her strength of will became relaxed in vague dreams, her body lost all control of itself and relived the old love. Every night, she felt the horrible sensation coming on: scarcely had a slight drowsiness come over her weary flesh, when she thought herself already falling into James's arms: she was not quite asleep, and would fain have opened her eyes, or moved her limbs, to drive away the vision; but she had not strength enough, for the warmth of the bedclothes enervated her senses and this caused her to surrender herself more easily to the embraces she fancied she was receiving. And she would gradually drop into a feverish sleep, preserving her attitude of resistance, even in the midst of her pleasures, and making every effort to free herself from James's clasp, and tasting, after each of her vain struggles, a faint pleasure in allowing herself to fall overcome on this man's breast. Since she had ceased to watch by Lucy's bedside, not a night had passed without this horrid dream. On waking up in the morning, a burning blush would mount to her cheeks, and a painful feeling of disgust would almost choke her as she saw her husband looking at her. She made a solemn vow never to go to sleep again, and to keep her eyes always open, so as never again to commit, by William's side, this adultery into which her sleep betrayed her.

One night, William heard her moan, and thinking she was unwell, he sat up in bed, and moved away from her a little so as to see her face by the light of the night-lamp. The young couple were alone in the room, for they had Lucy's bed carried back to its own place. Madeleine had ceased to moan, and her husband, bending over her, was examining her face with anxious earnestness. In raising himself up he had pulled back the bedclothes and partly uncovered her white shoulders: a quiver was passing over her pearly skin, and her lips were half-open with a tender smile, and yet she was fast asleep. Suddenly she seemed moved with a sort of nervous shock, and she uttered another soft and poignant moan. The blood had rushed to her neck, and she was stifling and murmuring, "James, James," in a tender voice and with faint sighs.

William, pale and frozen to the soul, had jumped on to the floor. With his naked feet in the thick rug, and his hands leaning on the edge of the bed, he leaned over, watching the agitation of Madeleine, in the shadow of the curtains, as if he had been looking at some monstrous sight which nailed him to the spot with horror. For nearly two minutes he stood aghast, unable to turn away his eyes, and listening, in spite of himself, to the stifled murmur of his young wife. She had thrown back the clothes and was stretching out her arms, with the smile still on her lips and repeating, "James, James," in an endearing tone that gradually died away.

At last William flew into a passion. He felt, for a moment, as if he must strangle this creature whose mouth was uttering the name of another and whose neck was inflated with pleasure. He placed his hand on one of her bare shoulders and shook her roughly.

"Madeleine, Madeleine!" he growled, "wake up."

She woke up, with a start, panting for breath, and bathed in perspiration.

"What? What is there?" she stammered, sitting up in bed and looking round with a wild expression.

Then she saw that she was half-naked, and perceived her husband standing on the rug. The earnest look that he was fixing on her panting breast told her all, and she burst into sobs.

They did not exchange a word. What could they have said? William felt a wild desire to fly into a passion, and to treat his wife as the most infamous of wretches, as a prostitute who was defiling their bed; but he restrained himself, for he felt that he could not accuse her for her dreams. As for Madeleine, she could have beaten herself: she would fain have defended herself for the faults of which her sleep alone was guilty, yet not finding any suitable words, and seeing that nothing, all innocent as she was, could purify her in the eyes of William, she was seized with a veritable madness of despair. The smallest details of her nightmare came back to her mind; she had heard herself calling James in her sleep, and she remembered how she had felt the sighs and quiverings of love. And her husband was there listening and looking on. What shame, what infamy!

William had got into bed again, and was lying at the very edge, avoiding all contact. His hands beneath his head, and his eyes fixed on the ceiling, he seemed buried in an unrelenting reverie. Madeleine was still sitting up and sobbing. She had covered her shoulders, and tied up her red hair, in an instinctive feeling of modesty. Her husband was becoming a stranger to her, and she was ashamed of her disorder and of the quivers that were passing over her bare skin. The silence and stillness of her husband depressed her, and, at last, she grew terrified at seeing him muse like that. She would have preferred a quarrel which would have thrown them, perhaps, weeping and forgiving, into each other's arms. If they said nothing, if they tacitly accepted the anguish of their situation, all would be over between them for the future. And she shuddered in her night-dress, which she had drawn over her knees: she gave a deep sigh, yet William never seemed to notice that she was suffering by his side.

Just at this moment, the singing of a psalm descended from the storey above. This singing, muffled by the thickness of the ceiling, filled the silent room as if with a dying groan. It was Geneviève who, unable to sleep doubtless, was working out her own salvation and that of her master and mistress. Tonight, her voice died away in lamentations that were strangely ominous. Madeleine listened, seized with terror; she could fancy that a funeral procession was passing through the corridors of the house, and that the priests were coming with the singing of psalms to take her and bury her alive. Then she recognised the shrill voice of the old protestant, and she had a still more horrible nightmare. Seeing William still silent, with firmly closed lips and fixed staring eyes, she said to herself that Geneviève's chants were going to remind him perhaps of the prayer of exorcism which this woman had taught him. He would lean over her, and make a cabalistic sign on her left breast, another on her right breast, and a third on her navel, repeating three times: "Lubrica, laughter of hell, return to the flames which thou hast left for the damnation of men. May thy skin become black, may thy red hair spread over thy whole body and cover thee with a beast's fur. Disappear in the name of Him at whose word thou tremblest, disappear in the name of God the Father." And, who knows? perhaps then she would crumble into dust. In her fright at this gloomy hour of the night, and still shuddering at the thought of her bad dreams, she looked upon the vagaries of the fanatic as realities, and asked herself if a prayer would not be enough indeed to kill her. She was seized with childish terror, and lay down quietly, covering herself with the bed-clothes. Her teeth chattered and she dreaded every instant to feel William's fingers tracing signs on her skin. If he was lying thus with his lips closed and his eyes open, it was, doubtless, because he was waiting till she was asleep, to assure himself if she were a woman or a demon. This foolish, yet overwhelming fear, kept her awake till morning.

Next night the young couple occupied separate beds, by tacit agreement. From this moment there was divorce between them, for the scene of the previous night had as it were annulled their marriage. Since James's reappearance, everything had been gradually tending to this separation. They had been infatuated enough to wish to drive away the memory of this man by mutual embraces, and they had only declared themselves vanquished when they had found it impossible to continue the contest any longer, William feeling that he had no courage left to sleep by Madeleine's side when she was subject to her nightmares, Madeleine unable to devise means to keep herself awake. Their divorce brought them some consolation. The most strange thing was that they still loved each other with deep affection, and their mutual pity was even mingled with a mutual desire. The abyss, which the powers of fate had placed between them, only separated them in the flesh, for they stood on the brinks of the gulf adoring each other from afar. Their fits of anger and disgust were thus full of an affection which was powerless to bridge over the abyss between them. They felt that they were separated for ever; but if they despaired of a reunion and of resuming their tranquil life of love, they still felt a sort of bitter pleasure in living under the same roof, and this pleasure prevented them from seeking a remedy for their sufferings in a violent and immediate termination of them.

They always shrank from deciding what they would do when James came back. They had at first put off till next day the unpleasant task of making up their minds. And every day they deferred till the next the conversation that they wished to have on this subject. The difficulty of coming to a rational decision, and the pain which such a discussion must cause them, frightened them and gave rise to their endless delays. As the weeks passed by they felt themselves more cowardly and more incapable of openness and energy. Towards the end of the first month, the days that they spent were most trying, for they fancied continually that they could hear James ringing at the door. They had not even the courage to confide to each other their fears, or to seek for comfort by talking of what alarmed them both; all they did was to turn pale, and exchange terrified glances at each pull of the bell. At last, in the latter part of February, William received a letter from the doctor, in which their old friend told them first about the death of his poor comrade in the hospital at Toulon: then he would up jovially by explaining to them how a young lady, whom he had met in this port and afterwards followed to Nice, prevented him from returning to Paris, as soon as he would have wished. He would stay in the south a fortnight or perhaps a month longer. William silently handed this letter to Madeleine, watching for the emotion that it would produce on her face. But she sat perfectly unmoved; a slight contraction of the lips only betrayed any feeling. The young couple, free now from immediate danger, told themselves that they had still time before them and again put off the unpleasant task of making up their minds.

Yet their stay at La Noiraude was becoming unbearable, for everything seemed to be dogging their footsteps. One sunny morning as they had gone down to the park, they noticed, peering through the railings that bordered the road to Mantes, the hideous face of Verdigris following them with her vacant eyes. Some accident had doubtless brought this rover to Véteuil. She seemed to recognise Madeleine; a smile displayed her yellow teeth, and she began to sing the first verse of a song with which the two young women had in the old days made the echoes ring in Verrières wood, as they returned from their pleasure parties, in the chilly dusk.

Her husky voice screeched out:

> *There was a rich pasha*
> *Whose name was Mustapha,*
> *He bought for his harem*
> *A certain Miss Wharem.*
>
> *And tra la la, tra la la la.*
> *Tra la la la, la la, la la.*

The refrain had a sound of terrible irony in her mouth, and the "tra la la's" which she repeated with renewed volubility died away in a hysterical laugh. Madeleine and William hastened towards the house as if haunted by this vile song. But from that day, the young wife could not set foot out of doors without finding Verdigris clinging to some bar of the railings. The poor woman was always prowling about La Noiraude, with brute obstinacy; she had no doubt recognised her old friend, and she came to see her as a matter of course, without thinking of any harm. For hours together, she walked like children do, on the stone coping into which the iron railings were fixed; thus she went on, clinging to the bars, then stopping all of a sudden, and putting her hands on the top to look, with prying eyes and open mouth, into the park. She was often heard on the road, singing, behind some wall, the story of Miss Wharem; she would repeat the verses ten or a dozen times over, with the pertinacity of a disordered brain which delights in saying over and over again the few phrases that it can remember. Every time that Madeleine saw Verdigris from the windows she felt a shudder of repugnance, for it seemed as if her past life were prowling around her. This ragged woman, running behind the railing and sticking her face to the bars, appeared to her like some unclean animal trying to break out of its cage so as to get near her and pollute her with its slaver. For a moment she thought of getting her driven out of the country; but she was afraid of a scandal and preferred to condemn herself to stay in the house and not even go to the windows.

When the young couple thus found themselves driven to bay at La Noiraude, they determined to flee to Paris. There they would be out of the way of Louise's songs, out of the way of Geneviève's canticles, and their daughter's serious face. The two months of anguish that they had just spent, had made their solitude unbearable. Since James still gave them three or four weeks' peace, they wanted to spend this time in trying to forget their grief, or in looking for some happy chance event. As soon as Lucy was quite well, they set out, about the middle of March.

XII

For nearly five years the little house in the Rue de Boulogne had been unoccupied. William had never wished to let it, intending always to come and spend a few months in it in the winter. Soon after his marriage, he had sent an old servant from La Noiraude to look after it in the capacity of lodge-man. The old fellow lived in a sort of superior sentry-box built of red bricks by the side of the gate at the entrance from the street. All he had to do was to open the windows one morning a week, and let a little fresh air into the rooms. It was a sort of sinecure for the old servant as a reward for his long services.

Having received notice of the coming of his master and mistress the evening before, he had spent a part of the night in dusting the furniture, and when William and Madeleine arrived they found a fire lighted in every room. These blazing hearths were a pleasant surprise, and seemed to fill the old retreat with the comfortable warmth of former days. During the journey from Véteuil to Paris, they had felt a secret pang of pain at the thought of coming back to this little house, where a few months of their past life had been spent in such happy seclusion; they remembered the last few weeks of their stay, with its hours of sorrowful anxiety, and they dreaded to awaken the bitterness of their memories, as they had already done in their country house near to La Noiraude. Thus they seemed surprised and delighted with the cheeriness of their home, for the nearer they had approached Paris, the more gloomy and desolate had their excited imagination expected to find it. One thing only occurred to mar William's happiness; on entering their bedroom he saw James's portrait, which the old housekeeper must have discovered in some corner, hanging against the wall. He tore it down hastily and threw it into the bottom of a wardrobe before Madeleine came up.

Yet, the young couple had no intention of isolating themselves in this little house. These snug rooms, which they had chosen before, as a secluded nest in which to cradle their budding love, now seemed too small to hold them both. They would always be treading on each other's heels, almost living in each other's arms. Their whole nature revolted today at the sight of these little sofas, where, in the old days, they had sat so happy in each other's embraces. They had come to Paris fully determined never to stay at home, and to drown their thoughts out of doors; their wish was to mix in the crowds and to feel themselves as

ÉMILE ZOLA

much separated as possible. The very next day they went to call on the De Rieus, who lived close by in the Rue la Bruyère. They were not at home, but the same night their friends returned their call.

The three came in the usual order, Hélène leaning on Tiburce's arm, and the husband last. Monsieurde Rieu seemed unwell; he had long been a martyr to disease of the liver; but his face, though yellow and shrunk with his complaint, had lost none of its haughty scornfulness, and his eyes twinkled as ironically as ever. Tiburce, who had entirely shaken off his provincial rusticity, had the bored and irritated air of a man engaged in an irksome duty; his face, with its thin lips, did not even attempt to conceal a sort of fury, and a secret desire to be brutal. As for Hélène, she was so changed that William and Madeleine could not restrain an exclamation of surprise when they saw her. She seemed to have lost all pride in herself, and to have entirely given up the use of her paints and powders. She was no longer a child's doll transformed into an old woman, with paint-be-daubed cheeks, and hysterical simpers: she was a poor wretch whose grey hairs and wrinkled face showed but too clearly the coarse and shameful melancholy at her heart. The excessive use of pomades and toilet requisites had played sad havoc with her complexion; her sickly face was all covered with blotches, her eyes had become quite bloated and her lips were as flabby as if they had been pounded. You might have thought that the mask she had worn had fallen off, and that the real face was now appearing from under the borrowed features. And the worst was that this face still preserved some of the painful graces of the mask; for the half-washed wrinkles still retained the rosy tints of the unguents, and the faded hair was streaked with threads of various colours. Hélène was hardly forty-five, and she seemed to be quite sixty. She had apparently lost too her giddiness and her maidenish gracefulness; full of shrinking fear, and with every finer feeling deadened, she looked round as if she were in continual dread of being beaten.

As they came into the room, Tiburce rushed towards William with that effusive demonstration of friendship which he always showed him. Fancying that Hélène, who had just left his arm, was not moving aside quickly enough to let him pass, he trod on her dress, and looked at her angrily, as he gave her a somewhat rude shove. The little woman who was paying her compliments to Madeleine and making her one of her old childish bows, went and crouched in a chair by the wall with a frightened expression on her face, forgetting completely to finish her compliment and assuming her previous look of stupor. Monsieur de Rieu had taken in the whole of this rapid scene, the push Tiburce had given to his wife, and the terrified movement of the latter; but he stood with his eyes half-closed, and a pleasant smile on his lips, as if he had seen nothing.

Everybody sat down. After a few minutes of general conversation about the dreariness of the country in the winter and the pleasures to be found in Paris at this time of the year, William proposed to Tiburce that they should go and smoke a cigar in the next room. The sight of Hélène really distressed him. When the ladies were alone with Monsieur de Rieu, they could not find what to say. The old man seated in a big arm-chair, with his hands crossed on his knees, was looking straight in front of him with that vague expression peculiar to deaf people, whose thoughts never seem to be troubled by any noise; he even appeared to have forgotten where he was. At times, he would gently lower his eyelids, and a little sharp glance would escape from the corner of his eyes, with singular irony, and fasten itself on the face of the two women who had no suspicion that they were being subjected to this scrutiny.

They sat in silence for a few minutes. Then Hélène, in spite of herself, made a remark about Tiburce. All she could talk about now was this young fellow who had her completely under his thumb. Everything brought her back to this topic, for she had soon exhausted all other subjects, and she always returned after a certain number of sentences to the life of terror and pleasure that her lover led her. In her moral debasement, she had gradually lost sight of that self-respect, that sort of modesty which hardly ever leaves a woman and is the result of her prudence and pride, that sense of decency which forbids her to confess her shame openly. This woman, on the contrary, took a delight in laying bare every detail of her intimacy with Tiburce; she unbosomed herself to the first-comer, with no consciousness of her infamy, and perfectly contented, provided she was talking about the man who was now everything to her. It was quite enough for her if she was allowed to confess her sins without being interrupted too much; then she plunged with exquisite delight into the story of her debauch, passing on of her own accord to shameful confessions, and seeming to wallow in her own words, forgetful that she was speaking to anyone. The truth was she was speaking for herself alone, in order to re-live the filthy pleasures she was relating.

She told Madeleine everything. A simple sentence served as

a pretext for passing from their trivial chat to the confession of her adultery, and she did this so naturally that Madeleine was able to listen to her story without a frown. When she had mentioned Tiburce's name as a lover whom her friend must have known of for years, she added in a snivelling tone:

"Oh! my dear, I am cruelly punished. This man, who used to be so tender and affectionate, has become cruel and unfeeling—He beats me. I know that is a shameful confession to have to make, but I am so wretched, and I feel such a need of consolation. How lucky you are to have never gone astray and to be able to live in peace! But poor me! I have to endure all the torments of hell—You saw how Tiburce pushed me just now. He will kill me perhaps one of these days."

Yet she thoroughly enjoyed her sorrows, and her voice had an undertone of pleasure as she spoke of the blows she received. It was easy to see that nothing in the world would have induced her to change her life of martyrdom for the existence of chaste tranquillity whose joys she pretended to sigh for. This was an easy way of expressing herself, for her sham repentance permitted her to relate her story at length, and the recital caused her nervous shocks and excitements which made her feel more deeply the bitter pleasures of her life. She cared very little about baring her wounds, provided she was talking on her favourite topic; she even delighted in magnifying the horribleness of her position, and in setting up as a victim, since this gave her license to pity herself. If anybody was complaisant enough to listen to her she would whine like this for hours, regretting the days of her innocence which were too far off to be recalled, and plunging into her mire with the gratification of a beast which licks the hand that strikes it.

Although she spoke in a low tone, Madeleine was afraid that Monsieur de Rieu might hear. Hélène caught her looking at him with an uneasy expression.

"Oh! don't be afraid," she continued, in a more distinct voice and with calm cynicism. "My husband cannot hear me—I am much more to be pitied than he is. He knows nothing, and he never sees my tears which I carefully conceal from him. In his presence, I always appear smiling, even when Tiburce treats me to his face as the vilest of women. Even yesterday, he slapped me on the cheek in my own drawing-room, because I found fault with him for running after girls. This slap made quite a noise, and yet Monsieur de Rieu, who was bending over the fire, did not turn round till a few seconds after. He never moved a muscle of his face, for he had heard nothing. Although my cheek quite burned I pretended to be smiling—There is no need to stop talking. Look at him, he is half asleep."

Indeed, Monsieur de Rieu did seem to be partly asleep, yet his half-closed eyes were shooting out keen glances all the time. By the twitching of his fingers that were crossed together on his knees a closer observer would have guessed that his thoughts must be occupied with some secret and delightful topic. No doubt, he was reading on his wife's lips the story of the slap.

Madeleine thought it her duty to show some compassion for her friend out of politeness. She expressed astonishment that Tiburce's love should have waned so quickly.

"I really cannot account for his unkindness," replied Hélène. "He loves me still, I am sure—But there are times when he behaves very badly—Still, I am devoted to him; I have already exerted myself a good deal on his behalf, in order to give him the position in Paris that he deserves; it is true that some unexplainable bad luck has attended my efforts so far—I am old. Do you think he only loves me out of interest?"

Of course, Madeleine said that she could not imagine such a thing.

"This thought grieves me very much," continued Madame de Rieu, hypocritically, for she knew perfectly well how things stood.

Tiburce had not shrunk from telling her the truth, and she was not blind to the fact that he only intended to use her as a tool. Yet she cared very little for this, provided she could only get payment out of him for her services. But she had not yet sunk so low as to confess openly that she was willing to purchase the young man's love rather than not have it. She was attached to the fellow with the passion of a woman at the change of life, who finds herself, at this critical period, subject to the feelings of excitement incident to puberty. He had become indispensable, and, if he left her, she would probably not find another lover so obliging. She would have kept him at the price of any shame or sacrifice.

"I wish I could be of service to him," she continued, following almost consciously the thread of her thoughts. "Perhaps, he would be grateful, I still hope—You have found me very much changed, have you not? I have no energy left to spruce myself up. I suffer so!"

She sank back, limp and nerveless, into her chair. The truth was that debauch had made her so worn out that she never felt more than half-awake. She had lost all interest in everything, even in her toilet. The very woman who had made a vigorous struggle against the advances of age, now felt a disinclination even to wash her hands. She would sit for days together, listless and unoccupied, ruminating like an animal on the pleasures of the previous day and dreaming of those she would enjoy the next. The lewd beast only remained, the woman was dying out in her, with her desire to please, her longing to appear always young and to be always loved. So long as Tiburce satisfied the gluttonous passions of her old age, she demanded from him neither affection nor compliments. Her only idea was to keep him in her arms, and she had no thoughts now of making him her slave with her smiles, her affectations and her painted face: she reckoned that her vile passions and her filthy debasement would be enough to attach him to her.

Madeleine looked at her with sorrowful pity. She could not fathom the bottom of this vile sink of iniquity, and she fancied that it was Tiburce's brutal conduct alone that caused this ruin of body and mind. Thus she could not restrain from declaring indignantly:

"Why, a man like that ought to be driven out of the house!"

Hélène raised her head with a scared look on her face.

"Driven out, driven out!" she stammered with secret terror, as if her friend had spoken of cutting off one of her legs.

Then she calmed down, and added quickly:

"But, my dear, Tiburce would never consent to go away. Ah! you don't know him! If I were to talk to him of separation, it is quite likely he would beat me to death. No, no, I am his, and I must bear it to the end."

She was telling a most shameless lie, for that very afternoon her lover had threatened never to set foot in her bedroom again, if she did not find him at once some honourable post.

"Ah! how I envy you," she said again, "and how pleasant it must be to be virtuous!"

And she began to whine once more, never giving Madeleine a chance of speaking, and varying her lamentations with curious smiles as she remembered her pleasures. For nearly an hour, it was a horrible drivel of silly regrets, and sudden longings for debauch, of avowals of tranquil cynicism, and supplications which asked for help and pity from all honest people. At last Madeleine felt her feeling of uncomfortableness increasing every moment as she listened to these moans; this unreserved confession embarrassed her, yet she said nothing, simply answering by a nod or a shake of the head. Occasionally she would cast an uneasy glance at Monsieur do Rieu; but there was always the same vague smile on his lips, always the same expression of ironical assurance on his face. Then, as Hélène repeated for the tenth time, the same dirty story, the young wife looked on her own history; she thought of the drama which was crushing herself and William: and she half began to wish to see her husband, deaf and idiotic, sitting rooted in his chair, and to find herself so sunk in the mire that she no longer felt any pricks of conscience, but wallowed peacefully in her shame.

While the two women had been talking in this fashion, William and Tiburce had retired into a little adjoining room which was used as a smoking room. William, who now sought every opportunity of talking on ordinary topics of conversation, asked his old schoolfellow if he liked his stay in Paris. Whether he did or not, was perfectly indifferent to him, for he detested the fellow, but he was not sorry to have him near him to help him to forget his trouble. Tiburce replied in a somewhat irritated tone, that he had no success as yet. William's innocent question had touched his wounds to the quick.

He began to smoke excitedly, and then after a few minutes' silence he gave full scope to his latent fury. He confessed to William as his mistress had confessed to Madeleine, but with far more energy in the coarseness of his words. He spoke of Madame de Rieu in the terms that men only use among themselves when they are talking about prostitutes. This woman, he said, with barefaced cheek, had taken a mean advantage of his youth; but he did not intend that his life should be wrecked for a ridiculous love affair like this, and he was fully determined to tear himself from the arms of this shrew, whose kisses filled him with disgust. What he did not confess was the vexation he felt at his blighted ambition. All his present distress proceeded from the reflection that he had received hitherto such little profit from his kisses. This allowed him to set up as a young man led astray through his inexperience by the wiles of an old woman. If Hélène could have got him a government appointment, or a post as attaché to some embassy, he would have had nothing for her but mealy-mouthed praises, and he would have sought to justify the relationship between them. But, you see, his caresses were not even paid for, and Tiburce Rouillard was not the man to confer favours for nothing.

He was not unaware, however, that the poor woman had left no stone unturned. But her ardent desire to be of service to him went for very little; he wanted results, and his mistress by a sort of fatality had obtained none as yet. This fatality was nothing else than the hand of Monsieur de Rieu. The old fellow, seeing that the comedy would lose half its charm if Tiburce were to receive the price of his kisses, made stealthy moves in his wife's rear, and counteracted each fresh attempt and undermined her cleverest schemes. This Was a splendid way of rousing the exasperation of the lovers against each other, and to cause between them those terrible scenes over which he smacked his lips like a connoisseur. When he had contrived to spoil a specially good move on the part of his wife, he feasted his eyes for hours together on Hélène's cringing fears and Tiburce's irritated attitude. The young fellow would come, with clinched lips and pale face, doubling his fists and trying to get his mistress into a corner so as to bully her. But, on these days, he could never get her far away from her husband; she would look at him with tear-strained eyes and trembling lips, as if imploring him to have mercy. And the old man would pretend to be deafer than usual and look on with an air of contented imbecility. Then when Tiburce had succeeded in getting Hélène to the other end of the room, when he had so far lost his temper as to shake her roughly, although the deaf man pretended to be turning his back, he seemed to hear everything, both words and blows. His face could not be seen, but it had an expression of diabolical cruelty.

Thus Tiburce was beginning to think that his mistress had no influence, and that she was unable to be of any service to him, and this was making him quite ruthless. He had now only one idea in his head, and this was to avenge himself for his four years of useless service, and to cast one parting shaft at Hélène as he gave her the slip. Hitherto, he had not dared to leave her entirely, since he could not make up his mind to give up all hope of the benefits he might derive from an undertaking which had already cost him such painful efforts. He had always come back to the grindstone, trusting to Providence, and telling himself that heaven would be very perfidious if it did not reward him for his constancy. But today all hope had left him and he was firmly resolved to break with his mistress.

William listened compassionately to Tiburce's violent words. He was of course somewhat disgusted with the young man's intimacy with Hélène, but he allowed himself to be talked over by his comedy of regrets and indignation. The other was simply making this confession to ease his mind, and also as a sort of rehearsal before his friend, whom he knew to be somewhat nice and prudish, of the apology he would make to the world for his ridiculous connections with Madame de Rieu. He felt that if this woman did not succeed in procuring him a position in the world, he would be jeered at and despised for having shared her bed; success would have made him a clever man, worthy of every favour, but failure was ruining him for life. Thus he wanted to anticipate the scorn and raillery of the world and pose as a victim who has a claim to pardon. He played his cards with remarkable skill, and William actually offered to assist him and lend him the support of his name and fortune. If he wished, he said, he would recommend him to an old friend of his father's, and he strongly approved of his determination to break with his mistress. Besides, William himself was acting a part, for he was trying to feel an interest in a story, about which he did not care a straw, hoping by this means to forget his own affairs by busying himself in those of others.

Their cigars being finished, William and Tiburce returned to the drawing-room. Hélène, interrupted in the middle of her mournful lamentations, suddenly stopped short, casting a glance of terror at her lover, as if she were afraid he would ill-treat her for having dared to complain. She sat uneasily, venturing on a word now and then, but only to be taken up sharply by Tiburce, who interrupted all her remarks, giving her clearly to understand that she did not know what she was talking about, and making no attempt to conceal his irritation from the company. You might have thought he was trying to show William how little he cared for her. Everybody seemed relieved when the visit came to an end. Just before going away, Monsieur de Rieu, who had scarcely opened his lips during the whole evening, spoke, in his cold tone, at considerable length in praise of Tiburce, this fine young fellow whose friendship was so precious to himself and his wife: he was not like those hare-brained dandies, who were always running after pleasure, he had a love and respect for old age, and he wound up by asking him to go and look for a cab. He usually treated him like a servant, and never gave orders to be fetched, when he left home. It was raining. Tiburce came back splashed up to the knees. Monsieur de Rieu leaned on his shoulder from the house to the cab, and then sent him to fetch his wife, who was sheltering under the awning at the top of the stone steps. He almost asked him then to mount the box with the driver.

William and Madeleine saw that visits like this one would not be sufficient to prevent them from brooding over their sorrows. They could not think of receiving company at their own house in the Rue de

Boulogne, which was too small, and hardly allowed them to invite the De Rieus to a friendly party. Thus they determined to go out and spend the evening at other people's houses, in the noisy commonplace chatter of those drawing-rooms, where a few dozen men and women, who are perfect strangers to each other, meet together and sit simpering and twirling their thumbs from nine o'clock till midnight. The very next day, Monsieur de Rieu gave them an introduction to seven or eight houses, which were only too delighted to give a hearty welcome to the name of De Viargue. From one end of the week to the other, the young couple soon had every evening engaged. They left home together at dusk, got their meals in different places like strangers on a journey, and only came back to sleep.

At first, they felt relieved, for the blank of this existence calmed them both. It mattered little what house they went to: every drawing-room was the same for them. Madeleine would take a seat at the end of a sofa with that vague smile on her lips so peculiar to every woman who has not one idea in her head: if there was music, she stared at the piano as if in ecstasy, although she was not paying the slightest attention to the piece; if there was dancing, she accepted the invitation of the first person that asked her, and then sat down again, unable to say whether her partner was fair or dark. Provided she was surrounded with abundance of light and abundance of chatter she was perfectly content. As for William, he was quite lost among the black coats. He sat for whole evenings in the embrasure of a window, staring, with haughty gravity, at the rows of bare shoulders that sat, shivering and shining, in the glaring light of the candles; or he would plant himself near a card-table, seeming to be enormously interested in certain tricks, though he understood nothing whatever of the game. He had always detested society, and he had only entered it in despair, in order to lose Madeleine in the crowd for a few hours. Then, as the parties broke up, the young couple ceremoniously withdrew, and as they descended the staircase, they would fancy that they were strangers to each other rather more than they were when they had come.

But though their evenings were always engaged, their days were still a blank. Then Madeleine threw herself feverishly into Parisian life; she trotted from shop to shop, visited dressmakers and milliners, became quite coquettish, and tried to take an interest in the new inventions of fashion. She formed a friendship with a silly creature, who had left the convent and just got married, and was fast ruining her husband with all the avidity of a Magdalen. This little woman took her off to the churches to hear the sermons of the chief preachers in vogue, and from there they went to the Park where they discussed the toilets of the girls. This life of bustle, which was a round of silliness and excitement, produced in Madeleine a sort of intoxication, which gave her the besotted smile of drunkards. William, too, was leading the life of a rich bachelor cloyed with pleasure; he lunched at the café, rode in the afternoon, and tried to become conversant with the thousand trifles which are discussed for days together at the clubs. Now, he only saw his wife at night, when he was taking her to a party.

The young couple led this sort of life for a month. They were trying to look on their union from the standpoint of fashionable people who get married from expediency, to increase their fortune or perpetuate their name. The young bridegroom gets a position, and the bride gets her liberty. Then, after one night together, they occupy separate beds, and exchange more bows than words. The gentleman goes back to his bachelor life, the lady commences her life of adultery. Very often all intercourse ceases between them. A few, the more amorous, have a passage that connects their bedrooms. From time to time, the husband pays a visit to his wife's bedroom, when he feels inclined, just as he would pay a visit to a house of ill-fame.

But William and Madeleine were too subject to passion to put up with such an existence for long. They had not been brought up in the selfish ways of the world, and they could not learn those little habits of ceremonious politeness, and that indifference to affection and feelings which permit a husband and wife to live side by side like strangers. The way in which they had become acquainted, their five years of solitude and affection, and even the mutual pain that they had inflicted would not allow them to forget one another, or live apart. It was all in vain that their efforts were tending to a complete separation of their existence, their joys, and their sorrows, for they always found themselves with the same feelings, and the same thoughts. Their lives were irrevocably united in every place, and in everything.

They had not had three weeks of this separation before their painful feelings came back again. Their change of habits had, it is true, been able to divert them for a moment from their fixed ideas. They had allowed themselves to be deceived by the excitement of this new existence. These parties, where they had lost sight of each other, had produced in them, at first, a sort of pleasant stupor: they had been dazzled by the glitter of the candles, and the hum of voices had deadened their tumultuous feelings. But, when the first surprise had worn away, when they had grown accustomed to these lights, and to this smiling and gaily-dressed crowd, they retired within themselves, for it seemed to them that the world was disappearing, and that they were falling back into their solitude. From this time, they carried their sufferings with them every night. They continued to go from party to party, in a sort of stupor, and spending hours surrounded by thirty or forty people, seeing nothing and hearing nothing, entirely taken up with their anxiety of body and mind. And if, to forget their feelings, they tried to interest themselves in what was taking place around them, their sight was dimmed, and they fancied that a grey smoke filled the air, and that each object was tarnishing and becoming faded and sullied. In the harmonious movements of the dances, in the sweet notes of the piano, they found the nervous shocks that were assailing them. The painted faces seemed red with tears, the seriousness of the men terrified them, and the bare shoulders of the women became, in their eyes, a sort of indecent show. The surroundings in which they lived were no longer exciting enough to lull them with their smiling luxury, nay, on the contrary, they themselves were imparting to these surroundings a portion of their dejection and despair.

Besides, they had now got over the effect of the surprise, and they could estimate the true characters of the people whose honeyed words had at first relieved them. The nothingness and the silliness of society bored them. They lost all hope of finding a remedy for their troubles in the company of such puppets. They seemed to have been at a play, where in the first act, they had allowed themselves to be carried away by the glitter of the lights, the richness of the dresses, the exquisite politeness and the pure language of the characters; then, the illusion had passed away, and they saw in the following acts, that everything was sacrificed for the sake of scenery, and that the characters had empty heads and were only repeating ready-made sentences. It was this deception which made them fall back on their own thoughts. They began to suffer again with a sort of pride, for they preferred their anguish and their life of passion to this emptiness of head and heart. Soon they were quite familiar with all the little scandals of the corner of Paris which they frequented. They knew that such and such a lady was admired by such and such a gentleman, and that the husband knew of and winked at the intimacy; they learnt that another husband was living with his mistress at his wife's house, which gave this latter a license to bestow her favours wherever she thought. These stories astounded them. How could these people live peacefully in such infamy? They themselves had almost been driven out of their minds by a single memory of the past, and they had nearly died of anguish at the mere thought that they had not grown up in each other's arms. They must be of a more delicate nature, their hearts must be prouder and nobler than those of other couples whose egotistic peace nothing troubled, not even shame. From this time they avenged themselves for their suffering, by feeling a sovereign disdain for this society, which was more guilty than they were, and yet showed a smiling face in its infamy.

One day, in a moment of anger, the same thought occurred to both William and Madeleine. They each told themselves that they ought to bestow their love elsewhere, in order the better to forget each other. But at the very first attempts of this nature, their whole beings revolted. Madeleine was at this time in the full bloom of her beauty, and wherever she went she bad a host of admirers. Young fellows, with dainty gloves and irreproachable collars, were most assiduous in their attentions, yet they were for her but so many ridiculous puppets. As for William, he had allowed himself to be carried off to a supper where his new friends had laid a scheme to make him choose a mistress, but he came away disgusted at the sight of young minxes who dipped their fingers into the sauce and treated their lovers like lackeys. The bond of sorrow between the young couple was too close for them to be able to break it; if the rebellion of their nerves did not permit them to be affectionate towards each other, their very sorrows permitted no mutual forgetfulness; they felt themselves inseparably united as man and wife, but with no heart for close intimacy. The efforts that they were making to bring about a violent separation were only rendering their wretchedness more unbearable.

At the end of a month, they gave up all further struggle. As their divided life, the going out during the day, and the hours that they spent at night surrounded by the crowd, brought them no respite, they gradually broke off these new habits of existence and shut themselves up in the little house in the Rue de Boulogne. Here the certainty of their inability to live without each other overwhelmed them. William felt at this time how closely his life was bound up with Madeleine's. From the very first few days of their intimacy, she had exerted a sway over him by her stronger and more vigorous temperament. As he used to say smilingly, it was he who was the wife in the house, the feeble being who obeyed and whose mind and body were influenced by his partner's. The same phenomenon which had filled Madeleine with James, was filling William with Madeleine, for he was becoming fashioned after her model, and imitating her voice and gestures. Sometimes he would say to himself in terror that he was filled both with his wife and her lover, for he fancied that he could feel their influence throughout his whole being. He was a slave, and belonged to this woman who herself belonged to another. It was this double possession which plunged them both in hopeless anguish.

William's existence was necessarily one of passive obedience, and he was subject to all Madeleine's moods. He was influenced by her excitement and felt the effects of each shock to her nerves. Calmer at the moments when she was calm, he fell back again into his grief and pain directly she became agitated. She would have made his life tranquil and serene, just as she was now troubling it. Thrown towards her by fate, absorbed in her by the force of circumstances, with no other courage, no other wish than hers, his heart beat responsive to each pang, each throb of his wife's. At times, Madeleine would look at him with a strange expression.

"Ah!" she would think, "if his nature were more energetic, we should perhaps find a remedy for our wretchedness. I wish he would domineer over me, and even get so angry as to beat me, for I feel that a thrashing would do me good. If I were lying helpless on the floor, I think I should suffer less, if he had made me feel his power. He ought to drive James's memory out of me with his fist, and he would, if he were strong."

William could read these thoughts in Madeleine's eyes. He saw how he would doubtless have been able to save her from her memories, if he had the energy to treat her as a master and to clasp her in his arms until she forgot James. Instead of shivering at her shivers, he ought to have remained calm, to have lived superior to the troubles of his wife, and filled her with the serenity of his mind. When these thoughts occurred to him, he accused himself of all the mischief, and gave way to despair all the more, treating himself as a coward and yet helpless to battle with his cowardice. Then, the young couple would sit gloomily silent for hours, Madeleine with a faint curl of suffering and disdain on her lips, and William shrinking into that nervous pride, that certainty of the nobleness and affection of his heart, which was his last refuge.

A few days after their resolve to pay no more useless visits to other people's houses, they felt such a sensation of wretchedness in the solitude of the Rue de Boulogne, that they determined to set out for La Noiraude. Yet they were returning without the least prospect of solace, for such a hope would have seemed ridiculous. Since the night they had run away from James's presence, they had been driven as it were by a wind of mad terror which gave them no chance to stop and take breath. Their repugnance to come to a decision and their continual delays had plunged them into a heavy stupor in which their wills felt a great reluctance to be disturbed. They had gradually become accustomed to this state of anxious suspense, and they no longer felt the strength to escape from it. Apparently indifferent and torpid, they allowed the days to pass by in blank and gloomy silence. They did not fail to tell themselves that James might return any day, they were even uneasy at not bearing from him, for they fancied he was already back in Paris. But they so far forgot themselves in their stupor that they sought no remedy, and this would have gone on for years, without their ever thinking of freeing themselves from their wretchedness by some violent effort. A fresh calamity would have to befall them before they could rouse themselves. Meantime, they were living in a sort of pain, and going wherever their instinct led them. They were returning to La Noiraude more with the intention of changing their residence than of running away from James. The troubles of their minds were making this cloistered life unbearable which had formerly lulled them so pleasantly. The thoughts of a journey and of a hurried removal had some charm for them. Besides, it was now the middle of April; the mornings were getting warm, and people were beginning to think of leaving Paris for the country. Since they were not cut out for society, they preferred to go back and suffer in the silence and peace of La Noiraude.

The evening before their departure they paid a farewell visit to the De Rieus whom they had not seen for some time. On reaching the house, they learnt that Monsieur de Rieu was very ill, and they were just on the point of going away when a servant came to tell them that the old gentleman requested them to go upstairs. They found him in bed in a big gloomy room. The liver complaint from which he suffered had suddenly taken a serious turn, which left him no doubt about his approaching end. Besides, he had asked his doctor to tell him the whole truth, in order, he said, that he might put certain affairs in order before his death.

When William and Madeleine entered the huge room, they saw Tiburce standing, with a troubled expression on his face, at the foot of the bed. Hélène, seated in an arm-chair at the bed-head, seemed also under the effect of some unforeseen calamity. The glances of the dying man, as sharp as steel blades, were passing from one to the other; his yellow face, terribly wrinkled by his suffering, had its usual smile of supreme irony, and his lips were contracted with that peculiar curl which made them so conspicuous when he was enjoying the anguish of his wife. He held out his hand to the new comers and said, when he had learnt of their departure for La Noiraude:

"I am very pleased to be able to bid you good-bye—I shall never see Véteuil again—"

Yet there was no tone of regret in his voice. Then there was a silence, that mournful silence which adds so much to the painful scene of a death-bed. William and Madeleine knew not how to withdraw, for Tiburce and Hélène sat mute and motionless, a prey to the anxiety which they did not even attempt to conceal. After a moment's pause, Monsieur de Rieu, who seemed to be delighting in the sight of the young fellow and his wife, suddenly continued, still addressing himself to his visitors:

"I was just arranging my little family affairs. Your presence will make no difference, and I am going to take the liberty of proceeding—I was telling our friend Tiburce the contents of my will, in which I have made him my sole legatee, on the condition that he marries my poor Hélène."

There was a chuckling sneer of tenderness in his voice as he uttered these words. He was dying as he had lived, ironical and implacable. In his last moments he was casting, with bitter pleasure, one parting shaft at this world of misery and shame. All his dying energies had been spent in inventing and maturing a scheme of torture to which he would condemn Hélène and Tiburce after his death. He had succeeded in so exasperating the latter, by preventing him from getting the smallest preferment, that the young fellow had at last broken with Hélène, after a scene, during which he had shamefully beaten her. This positive rupture drove Monsieur de Rieu to despair, as he saw his vengeance escaping. He had gone too far, and now he must reconcile the lovers, and unite them so closely to each other that they would be unable to break their bonds. It was then that the diabolical thought occurred to him of making young Rouillard marry his widow. The young fellow, he was sure, would never let the opportunity of becoming heir to a fortune slip, even at the price of continual disgust, and Hélène would never be possessed of enough sense to refuse her consent to the man to whom she was a trembling and submissive slave. They should get married, he said to himself, and live a life of ceaseless annoyance to each other. The dying man could see Tiburce chained to a woman twice his own age, whose shame and ugliness he would drag after him like a weight, and he could see Hélène, worn out with debauch, begging for kisses with the humility of a servant, and beaten morning and night by a husband who was avenging himself at home on his wife, for the scornful smiles that she brought on him out of doors. The life of such a couple would be a hell, a torture, an hourly punishment. And Monsieur de Rieu, as he pictured to himself this existence of degradation and beatings, could not refrain from jeering, though his body was racked with terrible pains.

He turned towards Tiburce, and continued, in a tone of the most bitter mockery:

"My dear fellow, I have been accustomed to regard you as my son, and I have your welfare at heart. I simply ask you, in return for my fortune, to be tender and affectionate towards my dear wife. She may be older than you are, but you will find in her a helpmate and support. Simply look on my determination as an earnest wish to leave behind me two happy souls. You shall thank me afterwards."

Then, turning towards Hélène, he proceeded:

"You will always be a mother to him, will you not? You have always been fond of young men. Enable this child to become a man, shield him from going astray in the shame of Paris, and incite him to noble actions."

Hélène listened with veritable terror. His voice had such an insulting ring, that she asked herself if he had not been aware all the time of her life of debauch. She remembered his smiles and his scornful serenity; and she told herself that her deaf husband had, no doubt, heard and understood everything, and that it was she herself who was turning out to be the dupe. The strangeness of his will explained his life of disdainful silence. Since he was throwing her into Tiburce's arms, he must know of their intimacy, and be seeking to punish her for it. This marriage terrified her now. The young fellow had shown himself so cruel, and he had ill-treated her with such fury on the day of their rupture, that the dread of fresh blows silenced her carnal appetites, and she thought with a shudder on this union, which would expose her to his brutality for a life-time. But her base and enervated body did not even dare to dream for a moment of escaping from the will of her lover. He should do what he liked with her. Passive and gloomy, she listened to the dying man, nodding her head in approval from time to time. To console herself, she thought: "No matter if Tiburce does beat me, there will always be a few hours when I shall have him in my arms." Then she reflected that the young fellow might run after girls with her first husband's money, and that he would doubtless refuse to bestow on her even the dregs of his affection. This thought quite overwhelmed her.

As for Tiburce, he was gradually recovering from the shock. He had succeeded in dismissing all thoughts of Hélène from his mind, and was making a mental calculation of the sum Monsieur de Rieu's fortune would produce when added to the income which his father, the cattle-dealer, had already bequeathed him. The total spoke with an eloquence that proved to him very clearly in a few seconds that he must marry the old woman, under any circumstances. But here was the rub. What was he to do with the hag? He could not tell, and his feeling of alarm came over him again, though his determination was not in the least shaken. If it were necessary, he would shut himself up with her in a cellar, in order to kill her by inches. The money he would have, even if he had to live in continual torture.

Monsieur de Rieu could read his resolution in his clear eyes, and in the cold, malignant expression of his lips. His head dropped again on to the pillow, and a last chuckle of delight passed over his face, now contracted in the agony of death.

"Now," he murmured, "I can die in peace."

William and Madeleine had stood by at this scene with increasing uneasiness. They felt that the final act of a terrible comedy had just been played in their presence, and they hastened to take leave of the dying man. Hélène, stupefied and huddled in her chair, did not even get up, and it was Tiburce who showed them to the entrance. As they were descending the steps he remembered the vile terms in which he had spoken to William of Madame de Rieu, and he thought he had better change his tone.

"I formed a wrong opinion of this poor woman," he said. "She is very much affected by the approaching end of her husband—It is a sacred charge that he is entrusting to me, and I will do all I can to make her happy."

Then, considering himself sufficiently exculpated and wishing to have done with the subject, he went on somewhat abruptly, addressing himself to William:

"By the way, I met one of our old school-fellows today." Madeleine turned quite pale.

"What school-fellow?" asked William, in a confused tone.

"James Berthier," replied Tiburce, "you know, that big fellow who used to stick up for you. You were inseparable—It seems that he is rich now. He has been back from the South some eight or ten days, it seems."

The young couple did not say a word. The entrance-hall, where this conversation had taken place, was rather dark, and the young man had failed to notice the alteration in their faces.

"Oh!" he went on, "he is a very good sort of fellow. I dare bet that he will go through what his uncle left him in a few years. He took me to his quarters, a delightful little suite of rooms in the Rue Taitbout, with an unmistakable odour of petticoats all about."

He gave a little laugh like a man who knew what life was and was incapable of committing any indiscretion. William held out his hand as if to take leave of him. But he continued:

"We talked about you. He did not know that you were in Paris and that you had a little place here. I gave him your address and he will come and see you tomorrow night."

William had opened the outer door.

"Good-bye," he said to Tiburce, excitedly shaking hands and stepping out on to the causeway.

Madeleine, left alone for a minute with the young fellow, asked him in a distinct and rapid voice the number of the house in the Rue Taitbout which Monsieur James Berthier was living in. He told her. When she had overtaken her husband, she took his arm, and they traversed in silence the short distance that separated them from the Rue de Boulogne. On reaching home they found a short, urgent letter from Geneviève informing them that little Lucy had a relapse, and summoning them in all haste. Everything urged them to leave Paris at once, and nothing in the world would have induced them to stay until the next evening. Madeleine did not sleep the whole night. Next morning, just when they were getting into the train, she pretended to discover that she had forgotten a package and seemed greatly annoyed at having left it behind. It was in vain William told her that the housekeeper in the Rue de Boulogne would forward it; she stood motionless and undecided. Then he offered to go back to the house himself, but this arrangement did not suit her. As the bell was ringing for the train to start she shoved her husband on to the platform, telling him she would be more comfortable if she knew that he was with their daughter, and promising to follow him in a few hours. When she was alone she went hurriedly out of the station. Instead of taking the Rue d'Amsterdam, she Walked in the direction of the Boulevards.

It was a clear April morning and everything was redolent with the breath of approaching spring. The air, in spite of the warm puffs and genial breezes, was still somewhat sharp. One side of the street still lay in bluish mist; the other side, lit up with a long patch of yellow sunlight, was bathed in a flood of purple and gold. Madeleine was walking on the causeway, in the full glare of the sun's rays. As soon as she had found herself out of the station, she had slackened her pace. Thus she walked on, slowly and absorbed in thought. Since the previous night her mind had been fully made up. All her energy had come back at the prospect of a visit from James. While she had been asking Tiburce for his address she had thought: "Tomorrow I will let William start off. Then when I am alone I will go and see James, tell him everything and implore him to spare us. If he solemnly promises never to try to see us again, it seems to me that I shall believe him to be dead again. My husband will never know of this step, for he is too agitated to see the necessity for it, but later on he will fancy that fate has protected us and he will grow calm like myself. Besides, I can represent to him that I have had some correspondence with James, or pretend that we have had some little tiff." All the night she had revolved this plan in her head; she modified its details, got ready the words she would say to her former lover, and toned down the terms of her confession. She was weary of dread, weary of suffering, and she wished to put an end to the situation. Danger was restoring to her the energetic and practical decision which she had inherited from Férat the workman.

Now, she had already put into execution the beginning of her plan. She was alone, and it was hardly eight o'clock. She did not intend to present herself at James's rooms till towards mid-day, which would compel her to wait yet for four whole hours. But this delay did not annoy her, for there was no hurry. There was not the slightest agitation in her resolution, which was the result of careful deliberation. She said to herself that it was pleasant in the sun and that she would walk about till mid-day. She intended to follow out her project scrupulously, without anticipating or retarding the details which she had so carefully arranged.

For years she had not been alone like this, afoot on a causeway. It carried her back to the time when she was in love with James. As she had time to spare, she began to look curiously at the displays in the shop windows, especially at the jewellers' and the milliners'. She felt a sort of pleasant sensation at finding herself lost in Paris in the April sunshine. When she came to the Madeleine she was delighted to see that it was the market-day for flowers. She went up, and walked slowly between the two rows of pots and bouquets, making a long stop before the bunches of full-blown roses. When she got to the end of the stalls, she turned back and stood absorbed in contemplation before each plant. Around her, in the yellow glare of sunlight, were spread patches of green, dotted with bright spots, red, violet, blue, and almost as soft as a velvet carpet. An all-pervading perfume filled the air at her feet, and played about her dress with almost inebriating strength; this perfume, as it rose to her lips, seemed to give a gentle, burning sensation to her face, like a kiss. For nearly two hours she stayed there, walking up and down in the fresh fragrance, rapt in her contemplation of the flowers. Gradually her cheeks had become rosy, and a vague smile played on her lips. The spring air was quickening the blood in her veins and mounting to her head. She was quite giddy, as if she had been leaning over a wine vat.

At first, she had only thought of the step she was going to take. Her brain was resuming its work of the night, and she could see herself going to James's rooms; she kept repeating the terms in which she would inform him that she was William's wife, and she mused on the consequences that were likely to follow from such an avowal. Then she began to be filled with hope. She would return to Véteuil, appeased and almost restored to happiness; she would resume with her husband their former peaceful life. Then, when these thoughts of hope had, as it were, lulled and soothed her heart, she gradually began to indulge in dreams. She forgot the painful scene that was to take place in a few moments, and felt quite unconcerned about the project. Half inebriated by the perfume of the flowers, and cheered by the warmth of the sun, she continued to walk about, giving herself up to a pleasing and transient reverie. The thought of the tranquil life that she would lead with William carried her back to the past. She was filled with the memories of days gone by, days of happiness and love. The image of her husband at last faded away, and she soon saw nothing but James. The thought of him was ceasing to torture her, for he was smiling at her as he used to do. Then she saw again the room in the Rue Soufflot, and she called to mind certain April mornings which she had spent with her first lover in Verrières wood. She was happy in the thought of being able to think on all this without suffering; she became more carried away by her dream, forgetful of the present and losing all thought of the coming interview. Thus she walked in the over-powering perfume of the roses, her whole being filled with an increasing sensation of tenderness.

As people were beginning to stare at her with curious eyes, she determined to continue her walk somewhere else, so she went towards the Champs-Elysées, carrying her dream with her. The paths under the trees were almost deserted, and she could remain there in the chilly silence. Besides, she saw nothing of what was going on around her. At the end of a long walk, she came back, almost unconsciously, to the Madeleine. There, she was becoming absorbed again in the genial and perfumed air, and giving way once more to the sensation of voluptuous inebriation, when she noticed it only wanted a quarter to twelve. She had just time to hasten to the Rue Taitbout. Then, with hurried steps, she rapidly traversed the Boulevards, still under the influence of the perfumes of the flowers, and with excited brain, almost forgetting the words which she had proposed to repeat. She walked as if impelled by some fatal force, and when she arrived she was quite red and uncomfortable.

Still she went up the stairs without the least hesitation. It was James himself who opened the door, and on seeing her he uttered a cry of joyful surprise.

"You, you!" he exclaimed "Well, my dear girl, I was hardly looking for you this morning."

He had shut the door, and was leading the way through several little rooms very elegantly furnished. She followed him in silence, until they came to the furthest room, which was his sleeping apartment, where he turned round and took her cheerily by the hands.

"We are not bad friends any longer then?" he said. "Do you know, you hardly behaved very kindly to me at Mantes?—You wish to make peace, don't you?"

She was looking at him, without opening her lips. He had just got up, and was still in his shirt sleeves smoking a clay pipe. In his new position as a rich young bachelor, he had not lost the free-and-easy ways of the student and the sailor. Madeleine fancied she had found him again just as she used to know him, just as he was represented by that photograph over which one night she had shed tears. His open shirt allowed her to catch a glimpse of his bare skin.

James sat on the edge of the tumbled bed, and the clothes were dragging on the floor. He still held her by the hands as she stood before him.

"How on earth did you get to know my address?" he went on. "Can it be that you love me still, that you have come across me in the street and followed me?—But first of all, let us sign our compact."

He drew her in a transport towards him and kissed her on the neck. She made no resistance or struggle, but dropped on to his knees and sat there in a sort of stupor. Although she had only come up a few stairs, she was quite out of breath. She felt half intoxicated as it were, everything seemed turning round, and she examined the room with a confused glance. Noticing on the chimney-piece a bouquet of flowers which were fading, she smiled and thought of the market by the Madeleine. Then she remembered that she had come to tell James of her marriage with William, and she turned towards him, with an unconscious smile still on her lips. The young fellow had slipped one arm round her waist.

"My dear," he said, with a broad grin, "you may believe me or not as you like, but since you refused to shake hands with me, I have been dreaming of you every night—I say do you remember our little room in the Rue Soufflot?"

His voice was becoming tender and earnest and his hands were burying themselves in the warm dress of his former mistress. He trembled in the excitement of awakening, and seized with burning desire. Had Madeleine come at any other hour of the day he would not have clasped her so closely to his breast. As for Madeleine, she had felt herself fainting away, since she had been on James's knees. A pungent perfume seemed to come from this man which troubled her senses. A flush of warmth passed over her limbs, her ears were filled with a vague hum, and she could not keep her eyes open in an unconquerable feeling of drowsiness. The words: "I came up to tell him everything, and I am going to tell him everything," revolved in her brain, but the sound gradually died away, like a retreating voice which becomes more and more feeble, and at last becomes inaudible.

By suddenly letting herself sink on the young man's shoulder she half pushed him over on to the bed. He seized her in a transport, and lifted her up from the floor which her feet were still touching. She became submissive to his embrace like a horse which knows the firm knees of its master. At the moment when she gave way, turning quite pale, closing her eyes and feeling carried away with an excitement that took away

ÉMILE ZOLA

her breath, it seemed as if she were falling from a great height, with long and steady oscillations full of cruel pleasure. She felt that she was going to be dashed to the ground, but the delightful sensation of being balanced in the air was none the less keen. Everything around her had disappeared. In the vagueness of her fall, in the temporary deadening of all her senses, she heard the clear tones of a clock striking twelve. These twelve light strokes seemed to her to last an age.

When she came to herself, she saw James walking up and down in the room. She got up, looking round her and trying to understand how it was she was lying on this man's bed. At last she remembered. Then she slowly put straight her disordered dress, and went up to a mirror to tie up her red hair which had fallen down on her shoulders. She was utterly prostrate and stupid.

"You will spend the day with me," said James; "we will have dinner together."

She shook her head in refusal and put on her hat.

"What! You are not going away, are you?" exclaimed the young fellow, in surprise.

"I am in a hurry," she replied, in a strange tone. "Somebody is waiting for me."

James began to laugh and did not insist. He showed her to the landing and said as he kissed her:

"Another time, when you can get away to come and see me, try to have the whole day free—We will go to Verrières."

She looked him in the face, as if these words had given her a box on the ears. Her lips opened for a moment, then she shook her head excitedly and hurried off, rapidly descending the staircase without saying a word. She had been with James not more than twenty minutes.

When she was in the street she began to walk feverishly, with her head down, hardly knowing where she was going. The rattle of the conveyances, the shoves from the passersby, all the bustle and movement with which she was surrounded, was lost for her in the whirl of thoughts and sensations with which she was carried away. She stopped two or three times before the shop-windows, as if absorbed in a sight which she did not even see, and each time she started off again with a more excited step. Her face had the besotted appearance of drunkenness, and people turned round as they heard her talking to herself. "What sort of a creature am I, then?" she muttered. "I went to this man's rooms to raise myself in his estimation, and I fell into his arms like a prostitute. He had only to touch me with the tip of his finger, and I felt no repugnance, nay, a vile sensation of pleasure came over me, as I felt myself giving way." Her lips were silent for a moment, and she hurried on. Then she continued, with secret violence: "Yet, I was strong this morning; I had calculated everything, and I knew what I was going to say. The fact is, I am accursed, as Geneviève says. My body is infamous. Oh! what disgrace!" And she gave a shrug of disgust, and passed along by the houses like a madwoman.

She had been walking like this for more than an hour when she suddenly stopped. The thought of tomorrow, of the days she was going to live in the future, had just presented itself to her mind. She raised her head and looked at the place to which she had found her way. She had walked mechanically to the Madeleine: she saw at her feet the boxes of flowers, and the bunches of blown roses whose fragrance had mounted to her brain in the morning. She walked through the market again, thinking: "I will kill myself, then all will be over and I shall suffer no more." Then she made towards the Rue de Boulogne. A few days before she had noticed a big hunting-knife in a drawer, and as she walked, she could see this knife; she could see it open before her, retreating as she advanced, fascinating her and drawing her towards their little house. And she thought: "I shall have it directly; I will get it out of the drawer, and plunge it to my heart." But as she was going up the Rue de Clichy, the thought of a death like this filled her with repugnance. She would like to see William before killing herself, and explain to him the reasons for her death. Her fever grew calm and the thought of a fatal thrust seemed odious.

She turned in the direction of the station and caught a train which was just starting for Mantes. During the two hours of the journey, one thought only revolved in her brain: "I shall kill myself at La Noiraude," she said, "when I have proved to William the necessity for my death." The regular and monotonous jerks of the carriage and the deafening noise of the moving train lulled her project of suicide in a strange fashion, for she fancied she could hear the rumbling of the wheels re-echo: "I will kill myself, I will kill myself." At Mantes she took the coach. Resting her elbows on the coach-door, she gazed on the country, and recognized, by the road side, certain houses which she had seen by night a few months before, when she had come this way in the gig with William. And the country, the houses and everything, seemed to repeat the only thought that filled her being: "I will kill myself, I will kill myself."

She got out of the coach a little way from Véteuil, in order to take a cross road which would lead her directly to La Noiraude. It was just growing dusk and the night was delightfully pleasant. The quivering horizon was disappearing in the gloom, and the fields were becoming black beneath the milky sky, peopled with the sound of expiring songs and prayers, which accompanied day's departing footsteps. As Madeleine was walking rapidily along a lane bordered with hawthorn hedges, she heard the footsteps of somebody coming towards her. A cracked voice rose in the air singing:

There was a rich pasha,
Whose name was Mustapha,
He bought for his harem
A certain Miss Wharem.

And tra la la, tra la la a,
Tra la la la, la la, la la.

It was Verdigris. The "tra la la's," at this hour of melancholy serenity, had on her lips a ring of painful irony. You might have thought it was the laughter of a madwoman who was becoming touched and melting into tears. Madeleine stopped, as if rooted to the spot. This voice, this song heard under such circumstances, in the midst of the thrills of the evening, brought a rapid and painful vision before her eyes. She called to mind their old walks at Verrières. At night-fall she used to descend from the wood with Verdigris on her arm, and both would be singing the ballad of the Pasha Mustapha. Far away in the lanes that were now filling with the shade, women's voices responded to theirs with other choruses, and they would see through the foliage white dresses flitting over the ground like mist, and gradually becoming confused with the shadows. Then everything became quite black. The distant voices sank into plaintive notes, and the smutty jokes and obscene couplets that had fallen gratingly on the ears from absinthe-scorched throats, floated gently on the air, filling the heart with a tender feeling of melancholy.

These memories filled Madeleine's soul with distress. She could still hear the footsteps of Verdigris, who was coming nearer, and she had begun to turn back to avoid finding herself face to face with this woman whose mournful features she could already make out. After a short silence the voice broke out again:

He bought for his harem
A certain Miss Wharem.
Her price was a sou,
And she was dear at that too.

And tra la la, tra la la la,
Tra la la la, la la, la la.

Then Madeleine, terrified by the maniacal laughter of the singer, and moved to tears by this hoarse and sad voice which sang of her youth in the freshness of the falling night, made a gap through the thorn hedge and fled across the fields. She arrived thus at La Noiraude. As she was opening the gate she saw the window of the laboratory quite red and casting a sinister light on the gloomy front of the house. She had never seen this window lit up, and its gleam in the indistinct light of the dusk caused her a singular feeling of dread.

XIII

A fresh blow awaited her at La Noiraude. Little Lucy had died during the day.

When William had arrived, he had found the child at the point of death. One of those sudden attacks of fever which not unfrequently return when a patient is perfectly convalescent was carrying her off. Her little body was quite hot, and she kept continually trying to bury her hands in the cool part of the clothes, and putting her poor trembling arms out of the bed. Then in the crisis of delirium she would writhe and struggle against some invisible object on which she appeared to be fixing an earnest yet vacant glance. You might have thought that her face consisted of nothing but eyes. Then their brightness would become dull, like springs of clear water made muddy by a sandy stream. When her father had come in she had not recognised him. As he leaned over the bed, gazing at her with tear-stricken eyes, he felt his heart breaking. By the anguish in his breast at each of her gasps, he knew that she was his entirely, and a deep regret at the thought of having been harsh towards her made him bend over her, and filled him with a desire to clasp her to his heart and wrest her from the hand of death. There was an unspeakable anguish in this awakening of his affection.

Yet Lucy was dying. For a moment she had an interval of consciousness and a pretty pouting smile passed over her lips. Then, looking round her, as if she were awaking from sleep, she seemed to remember herself and recognise everything. She held out her hands to her father, repeating, with affectionate endearment, her usual words:

"Take me, take me."

William kissed her, and became quite distracted with gratitude, as he thought her saved. But just as he was going to lift her up, he felt her little body crack with a sudden shock. She was dead. When he had laid her down, he fell on his knees in silence, unable to weep. Soon, he did not dare to look at her, for death was contracting her lips and James's serious expression was settling on her mouth. Terrified by this effect of the rigidity of death, which was gradually imparting to the face of his daughter a likeness to this man, he tried to pray again, looking now only at the little one's hands crossed on her breast. But, in spite of himself, he could not prevent his eyes from wandering to her face, and at last he left the room, leaving Geneviève alone with Lucy.

When Madeleine entered the hall, she felt a presentiment of something wrong. The dining-room was cold and dark, and the house seemed deserted. The mournful singing of a psalm guided the young mother to the first floor, till she came to the room where lay Lucy's body, with Geneviève chanting prayers at the bed-head. The terrible sight which awaited her, the child whose pale head gently indented the pillow, and the fanatic praying in the flickering light of a candle, held her rooted to the spot on the threshold. She saw everything at a glance. Then she stepped slowly forward. Since morning, the thought of her child had escaped her memory. She felt a sort of joy at finding her dead. It was one obstacle less in the way of her suicide; she could put an end to herself now, without a dread of leaving behind her a poor creature doomed to misery through its birth. When she came to the bed, she shed no tear, but said to herself, simply, that in a few hours she would be like that, dead and cold. If she had not had to die herself, she would no doubt have fallen on the corpse with heart-rending cries, but the certainty that she would soon be no more prevented her from feeling the loss of her child. She had one desire only, and that was to kiss her once more, for the last time. But, as she leaned over, she fancied she saw James before her, for it seemed to her that Lucy had James's lips, the lips that she had kissed with so much passion that very morning. She stepped back with a movement of terror.

Geneviève, who had just ceased her prayers for a while, saw this alarmed shudder. She was looking fixedly at Madeleine, with her implacable expression.

"Thus are punished the children of the guilty," she murmured, without removing her eyes from Madeleine; "God punishes sinners through their offspring, for ever."

Madeleine felt a sudden fit of wild fury at this woman, whom she found by her side at each fresh blow, ever casting her horrid beliefs in her face.

"Why do you stare at me like that?" she exclaimed. "I must be a curious object to look at. I had forgotten, you are going to insult me. I ought to have known that you would dog me to the very last hour, with uplifted arm, and as pitiless as fate. You are fate, you are punishment itself."

There was a gleam in the eyes of the fanatic, and she repeated with savage glee, in a sort of prophetic ecstacy:

"The hour is coming, the hour is coming."

ÉMILE ZOLA

"Oh! I have sorrow enough," replied Madeleine, bitterly. "I wish to be punished, and I will punish myself. But it is not you who condemn me. You have not gone astray, you have not seen life, and you cannot judge it. Can you comfort me?"

"No," replied the protestant, "your tears must flow, and you must kiss the hand that chastises you."

"Can you make William love me still, and find peace again? Can you promise me that I alone shall suffer, the day I humble myself?"

"No, if William suffers, it is because he is guilty. God knows where he is inflicting punishment."

Madeleine drew herself up in a sudden burst of pride.

"Well then!" she exclaimed, "if you can do none of these things, what are you doing now, and why do you torment me? I have no need of God. I judge and condemn myself."

She stopped through exhaustion. As she lowered her head, she saw the dead body looking as though it were listening to her with open mouth. She was ashamed of her anger, whose transports passed noisily over this poor sleeping corpse. She stood buried for a moment in the contemplation of this nothingness, as if attracted by the pleasant foretaste of death. Lucy's calm tranquillity, and the expression of settled repose on her face, promised her an eternity of sleep, and an endless, soothing dream in the arms of oblivion. Then the singular wish occurred to her to know how long it would take her to become stiff and rigid, like her daughter.

"At what hour did she die?" she asked Geneviève, who had resumed her prayers.

"At twelve o'clock," replied the protestant.

This short reply fell on Madeleine's head like a heavy blow. Could Geneviève be right? Was it really her fault that had killed her girl? At twelve o'clock she was in James's arms, and at twelve o'clock Lucy was dying. This coincidence seemed fatal and terrible. She could hear her moans of passion mingling with the death-rattle of her child, and she became mad as she compared that scene of pleasure with this scene of death. For a few minutes, she stood crushed and stupefied. Then she asked herself what she was doing there and what she had come to seek at La Noiraude. She failed to find an answer, for her head was empty. She said to herself, in her anguish: "Why did I hurry away so quickly from Paris? I had some object in view." And she ransacked her brain with painful efforts. At last her memory came suddenly back. "I know," she thought, "I want to kill myself, I want to kill myself! Where is William?" she asked Geneviève.

The old woman shook her head, never ceasing to mutter her indistinct words. Madeleine then remembered the red light that she had seen from the gate and which lit up so strangely the window of the laboratory. She guessed instinctively. She left the room, and ran up the steps.

In fact, William was in the laboratory. As he had escaped from the room in which Lucy had just died, he had fled into the park and walked about there till night, mad with grief. When the twilight fell, like a fine ash, giving to the country a uniform grey tinge of painful melancholy, he felt seized with dejection without bounds, and a bitter desire came over him to flee into some mournful corner where he might satisfy the wish for annihilation that filled him. Then, instinctively obeying the fatal force that led him on, he went and searched in a drawer where he remembered he had hidden the key of the room in which Monsieur de Viargue had poisoned himself. Since the time of the suicide he had never set foot in it. He could not have explained to him self the irresistible desire which impelled him to go in now: it was a sort of thirst after horror, or an uncontrollable impulse to fathom, at once, all fear and suffering. When he entered, the huge room, indistinctly lighted by the candle which he held in his hands, seemed dirtier and in greater confusion than before. In the corners lay piled heaps of nasty rubbish, and the stove and planks were still falling to pieces. Nothing had been touched; but the dust of five years had accumulated on the broken utensils; the spiders had spun webs from the ceiling which reached in dirty black masses down to the ground, and the close air of this forbidding place lay thick and offensive. William placed the candlestick on the table and stood up, looking round with a searching glance. He felt a sudden shiver as he saw at his feet the dark spot that his father's blood had left. Then he listened. A presentiment warned him that some final blow was going to fall on him here, in the midst of this filthy debris. This room, into which no one had entered and which he found calm and forbidding, seemed to have been waiting for him during the five years of his delusive dreams. And, now, it was opening its door and enticing him in, as a victim which had, doubtless, long been promised it.

As he stood waiting in dread, William called to mind his suffering, that continual weight of sorrow that had crushed his body and mind ever since his birth. Once more he saw his terrified childhood, his

ÉMILE ZOLA

sad school days, and the last few months of distraction and anguish through which he had just passed. In everything he saw the persistent persecution of fate which was now bringing him to some terrible final event that must be near. Now that the logical and implacable chain of facts, whose course he could follow so clearly, had brought him into this room that was stained with his father's blood, he could see himself ripe for the sickle of death, and he guessed that fate was going to have done with him in one final cruel catastrophe.

He had been listening like this for nearly half an hour, warned by a voice within him that some one would come to deal him the last blow, when he heard the noise of footsteps in the passage, and Madeleine appeared on the threshold of the door. She was still wrapped in her shawl, and she had not even stopped to take off her hat or her gloves. In a rapid glance, her eyes took in every detail of this laboratory into which she had never entered. From time to time mention had been made in her presence of this locked-up room, and she knew the mournful story connected with it. When she had noticed the horrible filth of the place, a curious smile passed over her lips. It was fitting that she should end her life among this decay and desolation. Like William, she could fancy that it had been waiting for her for years.

She walked straight up to her husband.

"I have come to have a talk with you, William," she said.

Her voice was clear and cool. All her feverishness had calmed down, and she stood with head erect and steady eyes; she seemed to have the inexorable attitude of a judge.

"A few months ago, as we were leaving the inn at Mantes, I asked this favour of you, to let me die the day when the life of torture we are leading should become unbearable. I have neither been able to calm my thoughts nor to appease my heart, and I have come to remind you of the promise which you then made me."

William did not answer. He guessed the reasons which his wife was going to give him, and he awaited them, ready to accept them, no longer thinking of defending her against herself.

"See what we have come to," pursued Madeleine. "We are both driven into a corner, and tracked into this room where fate has at last driven us. Every day we have lost a little ground and felt the iron circle which surrounds us contract and lessen our standing-room. One after another, every place has become uninhabitable for our poor disordered brains: our neighbouring retreat, the little house in Paris, even the dining-room at La Noiraude and the room in which our daughter has just died. Now, we are shut up here, in this gloomy laboratory, in this last asylum so fitting for our madness. If we both leave it, it will only be to sink deeper still, and to lead a more infamous and cowardly life—Is not that so?"

"That is so," replied William.

"We have reached this point now, that we cannot exchange a word or a look without distressing each other. I am yours no longer, for I am at the mercy of the memories which come at night to torment me with horrible dreams. You know all about it, for you woke me up once as I was falling into the embraces of a dream. Thus you do not dare now to clasp me to your breast, do you, William? I am too devoted to another man. I can see you jealous and desperate, and at your wits' end like myself—Is not that so?"

"That is so."

"Our love then would now be a degradation. In vain should we try to shut our eyes, for, at times, I should see your weariness and disgust, and you would read my thoughts and shameful pleasures. We cannot live together any longer—Is not that so?"

"That is so."

William replied like an echo, and each of his answers fell clear and sharp like a steel blade. The firm, calm attitude of his wife had aroused all the pride of his blood. His weakness had all passed away, and he wished to atone for all his want of moral courage by accepting bravely the fatal catastrophe which he fancied he could see coming.

"Unless," continued Madeleine, bitterly, "you are willing to live apart from me, you in one room, and myself in another, like certain couples who only acknowledge each other in public, for the sake of appearances. We have just seen arrangements of this sort in Paris; would you like to try a life like that?"

"No," exclaimed William, "I love you still, Madeleine. We love each other, and this is what is killing us, is it not? You have seen, in Paris, that we could not reconcile ourselves to this selfish existence. We must either live in each other's arms, or not at all."

"Very well, then! let us be consistent, for everything is over. You have said that it is our love which is killing us. If we did not love each other, we should live peacefully. But to love each other and yet defile our affection; to desire to embrace and yet not dare to touch with the tip of the finger; to spend the nights by your side, and yet in the embraces of another, when I would give my life-blood to be able to draw you to me, this would drive us mad—All is over."

"Yes, all is over," repeated William, slowly.

There was a short silence, and the young couple looked in each other's eyes with a feeling of assurance. Madeleine, still preserving her terrible, calm attitude, reflected whether she had not forgotten any of the causes which were urging her on to her suicide. She wished to proceed coolly, to prove clearly that all hope was dead, not to throw herself into the clutches of death in a fit of madness, but to meet her end, on the contrary, after having shown the impossibility of any escape from her troubles. She laid stress once more on the motives which were urging her to this step.

"Let us do nothing contrary to reason," she continued, "call to mind what has happened—I wanted to die in that inn. But though I did not say so to you, the thought of my daughter deterred me. Now Lucy is dead, and I can take my departure—I have your promise."

"Yes," replied William, "we will die together."

She looked at him with an air of astonishment and fright.

"What do you say?" she exclaimed in a rapid tone. "You must not die, William. That has never been a part of my plan. I won't let you die. It would be a useless crime."

William protested with a despairing shake of the head.

"Surely you have not thought," he said, "that I should remain alone to suffer."

"Who is speaking to you of suffering?" she answered, disdainfully. "Would you lose your courage again? would you be afraid of weeping?— If it were only a question of suffering, I would stay and struggle on. But it is myself who cause your suffering and keep your wounds always open. I am going because I distress you."

"You shall not die by yourself."

"I implore you, William, spare me, and do not increase my fault. If I were to involve you in my fall, I shall be more guilty still, and depart from life more desperate than before—My body is accursed, and it embitters everything around you. When I am dead you will become calm, and seek for happiness again."

William lost his cold tranquillity, for the thought of suffering by himself terrified him.

"And what would you have me do without you?" he exclaimed. "When you are dead nothing remains for me but to die too. Besides,

I want to punish myself—to punish myself for my weakness which has not been able to save you. You are not the only guilty one—You know, Madeleine, I am a timid child whom you ought to take with in your arms, if you do not wish to leave me to stay behind in cowardly nervousness and dejection."

Madeleine felt the truth of these words. But the thought of inflicting another blow on her husband, by inflicting a blow on herself, became unbearable. She did not reply, hoping that his excitement would pass away and that he would conform afterwards to her wishes.

But William had now lost his feeling of resignation, and he was fighting against the project of suicide.

"Let us try, let us try once more," he stammered. "Let us wait, I beseech you."

"Wait for what, and how long?" said Madeleine, bitterly. "Is not everything over? you said so just now. Do you think that I cannot read in your eyes? Do you dare to say that my death is not essential to your happiness?"

"Let us try, let us try some other means," he added, excitedly.

"Why do your lips utter those empty words? It is useless to try, for we should find no escape from our woes. And you know that, and you are only talking to deafen your thoughts, which are declaring to you the truth.

William wrung his hands.

"No, never!" he exclaimed. "You cannot die like that, I love you, and I will not let you commit suicide before my eyes."

"It is not suicide," replied his young wife, seriously; "it is an execution. I have judged myself and passed sentence. Let me execute justice on myself."

She saw that her husband was giving way, and she continued, in a stern tone of authority:

"I would have killed myself in the Rue de Boulogne, this morning, as I really felt inclined to for a moment, if I had thought I should find you so faint-hearted. But I came to the conclusion that I ought not to put myself away before explaining to you the reasons for my death. You see I know what I am doing."

William raised a terrible cry of despair.

"You ought to have killed yourself without saying anything to me, and I should have killed myself afterwards. You are cruel with your calculations."

ÉMILE ZOLA

He had sat down on the edge of the table, unable to hold up. Madeleine was determined to have it all over, for she felt weary and she was eager to repose in death. A secret feeling of selfishness was compelling her to leave her husband to his fate. Now that she had exerted every effort to save him, she would sleep in peace. She did not feel that she had the courage to live even to keep him alive.

"Do not oppose me like that, "she said, looking rapidly round her. "I must die, must I not? Do not say no. Let me do what I want to."

She had just noticed the little inlaid piece of furniture where M. de Viargue had put the new poisons that he had discovered. A few minutes before, she had said to herself, on coming up the steps: "I will throw myself out of the window. The room is three stories high, and I shall be dashed to pieces on the pavement." But the sight of the cupboard, with the word "Poisons" written in large letters by the fingers of the count on the glass-door, had made her choose another mode of death. She gave a spring of delight and rushed towards it.

"Madeleine! Madeleine!" exclaimed William, in terror But she had already broken a pane in the door with her fist. The glass made a deep gash in her fingers. She seized hold of the first bottle she found. Then her husband sprang towards her, and caught her by the wrists, thus completely preventing her from putting the bottle to her lips. He felt the warm blood from the cuts on her fingers trickling over his hands.

"I will break your wrists sooner than let you drink," he said. "I want you to live."

Madeleine looked at him straight in the face.

"You know very well that it is impossible for me to live," she replied.

She was struggling quietly all the time, and giving little sudden jerks to free her hands. But her husband kept them tightly clasped in his: he was panting and repeating:

"Give me this bottle, give me this bottle."

"Come now," replied Madeleine, in a hoarse voice. "Don't be a child. Let me go."

He gave no reply. He was trying to move her fingers one by one from the bottle so as to snatch it from her. His hands were quite red with the blood from her cuts. As Madeleine felt her strength failing, she seemed to make one last resolve.

"Has not all this that I have just told you," she went on, "convinced you that I must die, and that it is cruelty to prevent me from putting an end to myself?"

He kept silent.

"Don't you remember then," she continued more violently, "the room in the inn where I slept with my lover? and don't you remember that table where I had written, 'I love James,' and those blue bed-curtains that I drew aside during the stifling summer nights?"

At the mention of James's name, a shudder passed over him; but he strove with more fury to get hold of the bottle. Then his wife lost all control over herself.

"So much the worse for you!" she exclaimed. "I wanted to spare you one last pang: but you are compelling me to be brutal. This morning I told a lie—I had not forgotten anything at all, I only stayed in Paris to go and see James, I wanted to keep him away from us, and I fell into his arms like a prostitute. Do you understand, William, I come straight here from his embraces."

Under the sudden blow of this confession, William at last let go Madeleine's hands. His arms fell down lifeless and his eyes were fixed in a stupor on his wife. He fell slowly back. "Oh! you see very well," she said, with a strange smile of triumph, "that you consent to my death."

He was still stepping back. When he came to the wall, he leaned his back against it, without, taking his eyes from Madeleine. He stared at her aghast, and bent forwards so as the better to follow each of her movements. She raised the bottle and showed it to him.

"I am going to drink, William," she said. "You give me your permission, don't you?"

He stood mute, his eyes starting from their sockets and his teeth chattering noisily. He huddled himself together, and shrunk into little room at the frightful sight before him from which he could not take his eyes.

Then Madeleine slowly raised the phial and drank it at one draught, never losing sight of her husband, even when drinking. The effect of the poison, taken in this powerful dose, was terrible. She reeled, with open arms, and fell on her face. One convulsion shook her frame as she lay on the ground, and her huge chignon of red hair came undone and spread out on the floor like a pool of blood.

William had followed every detail of this rapid scene; as his wife was drinking he had doubled himself still more, and he was now crouching on the floor against the wall. When she fell with a dull thud, like a lump of lead, he felt the floor tremble beneath him, and it seemed to him that as Madeleine's fall resounded in his brain, his skull suddenly cracked.

For a few seconds he looked at the corpse under the table. Then he raised a burst of terrible laughter; he jumped up with one bound and began to dance about the laboratory, beating time by clapping together his bloodstained hands, and gazing at the red marks with hysterical glee. He went several times round the room like this, trampling on the broken crockery that lay scattered about, and kicking the rubbish into the middle of the floor. Then he stopped at last and jumped over his wife's body with his feet together, like a child at play. And he laughed more loudly, finding this amusement, no doubt, very funny.

Just at this moment Geneviève appeared at the door. Motionless and rigid, like fate itself, she cast a searching glance over this huge, gloomy room with its fetid exhalations, its corners filled with filth, and one solitary candle casting a faint gleam on its shadows. When she had distinguished the corpse lying flat on the floor, as if it had been stamped on by this madman who was dancing and laughing diabolically in the shadowy vagueness, she drew up her tall figure and exclaimed in her severe voice:

"God the Father has not pardoned."

THE END

A NOTE ABOUT THE AUTHOR

Émile Zola (1840–1902) was a French novelist, journalist, and playwright. Born in Paris to a French mother and Italian father, Zola was raised in Aix-en-Provence. At 18, Zola moved back to Paris, where he befriended Paul Cézanne and began his writing career. During this early period, Zola worked as a clerk for a publisher while writing literary and art reviews as well as political journalism for local newspapers. Following the success of his novel *Thérèse Raquin* (1867), Zola began a series of twenty novels known as *Les Rougon-Macquart*, a sprawling collection following the fates of a single family living under the Second Empire of Napoleon III. Zola's work earned him a reputation as a leading figure in literary naturalism, a style noted for its rejection of Romanticism in favor of detachment, rationalism, and social commentary. Following the infamous Dreyfus affair of 1894, in which a French-Jewish artillery officer was falsely convicted of spying for the German Embassy, Zola wrote a scathing open letter to French President Félix Faure accusing the government and military of antisemitism and obstruction of justice. Having sacrificed his reputation as a writer and intellectual, Zola helped reverse public opinion on the affair, placing pressure on the government that led to Dreyfus' full exoneration in 1906. Nominated for the Nobel Prize in Literature in 1901 and 1902, Zola is considered one of the most influential and talented writers in French history.

A NOTE FROM THE PUBLISHER

Spanning many genres, from non-fiction essays to literature classics to children's books and lyric poetry, Mint Edition books showcase the master works of our time in a modern new package. The text is freshly typeset, is clean and easy to read, and features a new note about the author in each volume. Many books also include exclusive new introductory material. Every book boasts a striking new cover, which makes it as appropriate for collecting as it is for gift giving. Mint Edition books are only printed when a reader orders them, so natural resources are not wasted. We're proud that our books are never manufactured in excess and exist only in the exact quantity they need to be read and enjoyed.

Discover more of your favorite classics with Bookfinity™.

- Track your reading with custom book lists.
- Get great book recommendations for your personalized Reader Type.
- Add reviews for your favorite books.
- AND MUCH MORE!

Visit **bookfinity.com** and take the fun Reader Type quiz to get started.

Enjoy our classic and modern companion pairings!

Printed in the USA
CPSIA information can be obtained
at www.ICGtesting.com
JSHW022220140824
68134JS00018B/1163

9 781513 282169